Alex String

Sword

TLW Savage

Books by TLW Savage
First Test Pentalogy (five books)
Alex Twice Abducted
Alex Terrified Hero
Alex Inner Voice
Alex String Sword
Alex and the Crystal of Jedh…coming soon

Alex String Sword
TLW Savage

This is a work of fiction. There are real cultures, real science, and real animals talked about. There are also quotes from some real people. All of the characters, organizations, and events portrayed in this book are either products of the author's imagination or are used fictitiously in this book.
Alex String Sword
Copyright © 2022 TLW Savage
Cover design created by William Melton/Xtreme Graphics

All rights reserved. Except as permitted under
The U.S. Copyright Act of 1976
No part of this publication may be reproduced, distributed, or transmitted in any form or by any means, or stored
First Edition: 2022
Printed in the United States of America

*For all of my fans and those who can be: those who are kids, young adults, and others still young at heart.
If you're reading this, that's you. Read on. Laugh, cry, gasp in terror and amazement, stay awake late into the night to find out what happens next, be fascinated, and enjoy.
Be warned. The first pages are captivating and the suspense builds the more you read.*

Pronunciations
And Definitions

- **A'idah** – Ī ē duh

    She is a twelve year old girl from Northwest Pakistan, one of Alex's best friends, a member of his flock, and maybe more

- **Amable** – Ă muh bull

    He is the leader of the aliens abducting and training the Earthlings

- **Anomalies** – Uh näm uh lēz

    Something wrong or different from normal

- **Cowl** – Pronounced just like the word, cow, with an l after it.

    A large loose hood.

- **Dark matter** – Easy to pronounce

    In our current world, dark matter is a purely theoretical substance. In this book world, it is real and has the unusual effect of making some living organisms able to play with the laws of physics.

- **Delli** – dĕl ē

    She is a Tasty and the daughter of Windelli.

- **Ekbal** – ĕhk bal

    He is a twelve year old boy from southern India and a member of Alex's flock

- **Enticing** – In tī sing

    Attractive, tempting, or alluring

- **Gaahr** – Gahr; simply ah with a hard g sound in front followed by the rrr sound

    A species of deem

- **Gragdreath** – Grag dreth

    A horrible monster

- **Gursha** – Ger shuh

    She is the nurse for Alex's flock

- **Haal** - Hăl

    A dwarf

- **Heyeze** – Hī ēz

    An evil philosopher of the dolphins

- **Hheilea** – Hhhī lē uh

    She is a Kimley sixteen year old girl

- **Hhy Soaley** – Hī sōl ē

    Hheilea in disguise as a boy

- **Hymeron** – Hī mer uhn

    Hheilea's brother

- **Kimley** – Kim lē

    An alien species

- **Lepercaul** – Lĕp er call

    An alien species, most are evil, but the new generation was changed by Alex and call themselves Alex's army.

- **Lillyputi** – lĭl ē poo tē

    A wonderful desert, which is dangerously addictive for humans

- **Maleky** – Muh lĕk ē

    He is the most evil person in the galaxy

- **Obfuscation** – äbfu skāSHun

    The effort to hide truth.

- **Osamu** – ō săm oo: the oo is the same sound in boo

    He is a Japanese man and a member of Alex's flock

- **Portal** – Pôrdl

    It is a shimmering circular hole connecting two different locations. It can be used to jump from one location to another. This is a scientific idea.

- **Riposte** – Ruh pōst

    This is a quick counter attack, generally made after a successful defense. It is usually a quick thrust, but can refer to any quick counter attack.

- **Sabu** – Să boo

    She is a snow leopard and a member of Alex's flock

- **Skyler** – skī ler

    He is a Blue Hyacinth Macaw and a member of Alex's flock

- **String Sword** – easy to pronounce

    A sword made of two substances which in our world are purely theoretical. The string material is theoretically what everything is made of. It is on the inside of the String Sword and is only visible at the cutting edge. The theoretical material, black matter, is the flat sides of the sword binding the string material on the inside. The black matter is extremely hard and the string material provides an edge which burns and cuts through other materials.

- **Titan** – Tī tăn

    A Lepercaul man, he's very evil and hates Earthlings.

- **Triage** – Trē äzh The z and h make a sound like sh, but with a vibrating z woven in.

    It is the emergency medical practice of deciding the order of treatment of large numbers of casualties. Those who might die even with treatment are given treatment after those who will survive if they receive treatment. Triage is often done in a hurry and emotional attachment has to be set aside.

- **Twarbie** – Twăr bē

    She is a Winkle female and looks like she might be close to Alex's age.

- **Twyla** – twī luh

    A young, teenage, Winkle female, she was Twarbie's cousin, a friend of Alex, and supposedly died in the last book.

- **Vapuc** – vă pook

    The result of dark matter affecting a living creature to allow it to alter the laws of the universe

- **Windelli** – wind děl ē

    She is an older Tasty female and is responsible for the use and protection of the Book of Prophesy.

- **Ytell** – yuh těl

    He is a raptor, the leader of Alex's flock, and the leader of the other raptors

- **Zeghes** –zāz

    He is a six month old dolphin, a member of Alex's flock, and one of his best friends

Dark Universe Series

Alex String Sword

TLW Savage

Preface

What we can do or not do is a recurring theme in my stories. This is balanced with another recurring theme of things which try to change or affect what we do. We have to decide what to do. Many things, fear, hunger, greed, desires, anger and many others can and do affect what we can do. The greatest of these, but one we can misplace or forget about is love.
Many people in our real world chose to use those things to gain real power from us. We ourselves chose to let those things affect who we are. We will also choose to turn our back on love.
    The first story I remember creating was at twelve to help calm my terrified sister. Now, I create stories to calm my frustration over my illness. I dare to dream that these stories calm your own storms and hopefully inspire you to sail through them to better days.

DEDICATION

This book is dedicated to those who dream of action, adventure, and romance, and to all those people who are uncertain about their futures and maybe even scared about their futures. I hope this encourages them to be heroes in their own ways.

Also, I want to thank my fans. They are my Muses. Their enjoyment of my stories is an elixir to my heart and a light to my vision.

I can't forget to mention all of my beta readers, editors, and family members. Thank you.

I must give a very special thankyou to my wonderful wife, Debbie.

Now, let us begin.

Chapter One
Attempted Murder

Alex and his teenage friend, Hheilea, popped out of the inter-spaceship portal.

As he landed, stumbling on the vast empty floor of the Bubble Bay, Hheilea yelled, "Alex run!"

In response, he sprinted after her, but the terrible sensation of danger yelled louder at him that they weren't headed into safety.

They both ran following what looked like a giant marmot with black fur.

The familiar odors of ozone and machinery had greeted him the moment he left the portal. Across the flat floor, a long horizontal opening, the length of the bay, gave a view of blue sky and scattered clouds.

Echoes of their running feet on the metal floor beat in time with a growing sense of danger.

The alien had said she was taking them to safety, and yet with every beat of Alex's heart he knew a growing sense of doom.

Alex yelled at the creature, "You've taken us into danger!"

Hheilea screamed, "Alex, you've got to go faster!" Following her own advice, she raced after the creature.

Alex tried to go faster. With his sense of the future, he desperately sought the source of the threat. The truth hit him, and he changed direction. "Stay away from me. I'm the one in danger." He dove to the side.

Buckew! Heat and fragments blasted him from the explosion of the blaster bolt hitting the metal deck next to him.

Hheilea screamed. "No!" Because she too could sense the future, she raced back toward him.

Alex landed hard on the metal deck, but already he'd started rolling back to his feet. Certain death screamed at him to move faster. He held his breath even as he pushed vainly off the floor in a futile effort to escape the next blast.

Hheilea screamed in concert with the second blaster bolt.

Time slowed for Alex as Hheilea crumbled to the floor and didn't move. Somehow, she'd gotten back just in time to take the shot meant to kill him.

Right behind her, the furry alien reached them, holding what looked similar to a large black umbrella in one hand/paw. "I can block the blaster shots with this. Pick up Hheilea and get over to the bubble platform. We've got to leave this spaceship."

Fighting back sobs, Alex scooped the injured girl off the ground and into his arms. What he saw gave him hope. Instead of the hole he'd expected from the blaster shot, there was just a circular area of her blouse smoking and in the middle blood seeped from a raw wound on her chest. Something about her clothing had blocked most of the weapon's energy, but did she still live? With an aching heart, Alex ran to the nearest green platform. He no longer felt the impending death. Had it been fulfilled?

He didn't hear any more blaster shots. Why had they stopped? Still, he ran as fast as he could.

Ahead of him, the steel gray of the deck was broken by the different material of a green bubble platform. It was a couple of inches thick and had five-foot wide yellow circles arranged in four neat rows across the large area.

Alex jumped onto the closest yellow circle hoping it didn't have any anomalies. While the familiar tingling signified a bubble encasing him and Hheilea, Alex looked down at Hheilea's delicate elven-like features framed by her white hair. Her pale eyelashes fluttered a message of hope, but they didn't open. Just minutes before, they'd

Attempted Murder

been laughing, celebrating a victory over evil. Unshed tears blurred his vision, and Alex looked away. He couldn't stand the thought of those eyelids stilling their movement and never opening again.

Why did they follow this strange furry creature? Anger, fear for Hheilea, and frustration warred within Alex. Why had he trusted this alien? His insecure trust of all the aliens shook, threatening to crumble. The alien in charge of his training and safety, Ytell, had said to go with this creature, but the giant alien bird had been wrong to entrust their safety to this other alien.

What else were the aliens who were trying to help Earth wrong about?

It wasn't that Alex was ungrateful. They had saved his life. Also, it was incredible that he could understand the languages of animals and the different aliens because of the miniature creature living by his ear.

Alex was grateful he had the one ability *dark matter's* presence gave him, the *vapuc* for sensing the future. Still, he wished he could do other vapucs the rest of his flock could do, such as lightning, illusions, or force. With them, he could've tried to fight back.

He remembered the last battle against evil and how with a *String Sword* he'd been able to block blaster bolts. If he still had it or if Hheilea had one, either of them would've been able to defend against the blaster attack. Unfortunately, that String Sword had exploded killing one of his friends and had almost killed everyone.

If only Hheilea and he could've stayed at the celebration, this amazing alien who'd just saved his life would still be safe and not in danger of dying. Why had the creature crashed the party? They'd been with friends and safe until they'd had to leave.

Intuition or just his normal peripheral vision pulled his gaze back down to Hheilea's face. Her eyelids had stopped their movement and Alex's heart clenched in agony.

Looking down at Hheilea's still face, Alex feared to try and sense her future. Would she live? Was she already—

Chapter Two
The Celebration

Amid the soothing, rushing water sounds, Alex looked down at the mysterious royal forms beneath the stream next to him. Why had the ship created them? The sunlight sparkling off the waves caused him to look up at the sky in wonder. Two suns, one yellow similar to Earth's, and the other blue hung above the peaceful sky.

Alex looked over at the celebration going on in the small meadow. His eyes sought out Hheilea. The young woman's white hair stood out from the others at the celebration, as other friends looked back at him and Alex looked away. His emotions were too raw to be with any of them.

He breathed deep hoping the forest scents would calm him, and yet he couldn't shake a growing cold creeping down his spine.

Frustrated by his memories, feelings, and this growing fear, he changed his thoughts back to Hheilea. If he'd given in to her strange ritual of the T'wasn't-to-be-is and not worried about others such as A'idah, he could've lived with the beautiful alien like royalty. Alex remembered what he'd been told about the ritual. The very name, T'wasn't-to-be-is, used a mix of past, future, and present tenses that Hheilea's people were familiar with. The ritual marked the passage of two Kimleys moving from being children to being adults. For them it happened by sixteen. The Kimleys said that the music the two heard in their heads was the future calling to the two individuals, helping them to love each other, and bringing them together into a perfect union. Alex still didn't really understand it, but with the additional ability they

The Celebration

would've gained to know the possible futures instead of just sensing the future, they would've finally been safe from all their enemies. He wouldn't have the cold feeling of fear anymore. Instead, danger stalked closer to him, Earth, his friends, and the beautiful alien.

Alex still didn't understand why Hheilea's people, the Kimley, with their ability to know the future were so weak and enslaved. What held them back? One foot slipped on the roaring river's edge, and he almost lost his balance. Alex knew what kept him from accepting the ritual. He'd only been fifteen and hadn't wanted to be forced into loving someone. It was wrong.

Laughter drew his attention back to his six fellow Earthlings and the aliens at the small celebration. Alex glanced across the meadow at them. His flock leader, the fierce, seven-foot tall bird, called Ytell, stood out in the group of shorter creatures.

Alex started in surprise. Slightly separate from the main group, Osamu, the older Japanese man, had his arm around their fiery illusions teacher. The last he'd known the teacher hated Osamu.

A'idah's pale face framed with red-gold hair banished that question. He understood her. He could feel her eyes on him, but as soon as he recognized her heart shaped face. She turned away from him. He'd started to wave, but in disappointment, he let his arm drop back to his side.

In his mind, he heard a message from A'idah relayed by the Artificial Intelligence on his scalp. |I need you.|

The raw emotion in the words made him think of the first weeks of their abduction, and how he'd almost failed to comfort his friend in the right way. Holding and being held by her pushed away their fear and helped both of them feel better. Unfortunately, Alex had almost let his emotions ruin their friendship. He wouldn't do it again. He needed her too. Carefully, he messaged A'idah back using his AI. |I need my best friend too.|

Her answer came back in a flash. |I'm sorry. I didn't realize my AI sent that message. It's been over a year since I got it. You'd think I'd have it figured out better. I'm sorry I bothered you.|

|It's okay. Remember, our AIs are still babies, and your message made me feel better. My emotions are a bit raw. We can talk later.| Alex understood AI trouble. His own AI gave him trouble at times even though because of his being in a time bubble for a year, he'd had his for over two years. Also, he knew A'idah needed him to spend time talking to her, holding her would be best, or at least standing near. Right now though, the idea of holding her frightened him. His emotions were too raw. At the very least, he'd probably break down in uncontrollable sobs.

The dark forest looming all around the happy party spoke to Alex of a dreadful danger ahead of them. The thought of more danger was too much to bear. This was supposed to be a celebration. They had won. Desperately, he forced himself to consider other aspects of the view, the sounds of the stream, and the pungent odor of the dark forest around the celebration. He shook his head at how hard it was, even with his experience, to remember he stood inside of a third-of-a-mile long space cruiser. Alex still couldn't believe the ship would be his. He didn't even know its name or how to use it.

This room altered reality with the same ease, as the Weird room on the gigantic spaceship, the Coratory. Instead of the confusion Alex used to feel about the strange alien technology, he now wished it could alter the memories in his mind and take away his pain. Alex held a hand out and spoke to the Artificial Intelligence which ran the room. "Room AI, give me a glass of water."

In his hand appeared the drink. Sipping it, Alex thought of good memories. The alien consciousness, Maleky, living in Alex's mind preferred them too. Alex thought of how he'd defeated the infatuation created by the bad Twyla, and how he'd helped and loved the sweet girl Twyla had become because of love. The strange creature called a tribble had freed the love in her. He remembered going to see her that last time before the evil Winkles had stolen her back and gotten rid of the tribble. Momentarily, Alex no longer saw his current surroundings. Instead, his mind was filled with the sweet past of that evening.

The Celebration

In the memory, Maleky had only weakly complained about Alex's plan. Emotion always quieted the alien. *This is crazy. Loving your enemies is stupid. Eventually, Twyla's inner voice will win. She won't be the same wonderful person.*

Alex hammered back. *Inner voices don't have to win. With help we can be who we would be.*

The clarity and intensity of the memory surprised him. Did it have something to do with the room he was in or something else?

That evening with Twyla had been wonderful. Learning how to defeat infatuation had been tough, but with revelations he'd done it. Love beat infatuation. Thinking on those good memories, Alex grinned as Zeghes, a dolphin and one of his best friends, swam through the air toward him. He didn't have any idea how the technology in Zeghes' fancy suit enabled the dolphin to swim through the air or how the tiny creatures living behind their ears translated the different languages.

Zeghes said, "Alex, come join the flock." He also sent him a message. |I think A'idah needs you. She's still shook-up by you almost dying.|

Alex loved his Earthling friends but didn't want to talk. "In a bit." He added in the much more personal AI messaging, |I'm sorry. Do what you can to comfort her. I need some time alone.| He had friends who still lived and needed him, but if he didn't take care of his own personal demons, he'd be of no help to them. The battle against the Gragdreath and the loss of another loved one weighed upon his heart and mind. Twyla had just beaten the hate and fear. She wasn't going to be evil anymore. Why did she have to die? Alex didn't have any answers. He'd almost sacrificed everyone's lives in his effort to save her, and she'd still died. Here, in this peaceful place, he just wanted to scream. Unfortunately, he didn't think his friends would understand. They might think he was going crazy and maybe he was.

A'idah sent another message. |Alex, are you okay?| The unspoken part he understood just as well. *Why aren't you over here?*

Even through the AI message, he could hear the concern of the twelve-year-old girl. Alex looked back at her to see A'idah looking at him again. Was she still that young? Something about how his pretty friend looked troubled him. He knew it wasn't just the expression in her face. He'd shared a lot with the Kalasha girl from northwestern Pakistan. A'idah and Zeghes composed his new family unit in this crazy life after the abduction. Their shared experiences had made them very close. He had said he'd be a good big brother, but even with them he didn't want to share the memories which troubled him. He couldn't go to her. Fear of saying or doing the wrong thing burned in him. His memories and emotions were still too raw. Something he didn't want to deal with gnawed at his mind and his heart. *A'idah could've died in that battle too.* He remembered how fierce she was in the few glimpses he'd seen of her during the battle. Within his mind, he asked his AI, which resided on his scalp, to send A'idah the response. |I'm doing better.| *Please understand.*

The battle. Alex shuddered. The idea of reliving that memory so vividly frightened him. He looked about for something, anything to distract him from the memory. Desperately, Alex looked down to the roaring stream, praying to forget, and begging for peace. Couldn't this raging water take the storm from him? He considered jumping into the cold fast flowing stream. Maybe the shock would help, but his friends wouldn't understand. They'd be worried because of his recent injuries. His imagination didn't have to work very hard to think of what A'idah would do. For a moment, Alex grinned at how fierce his friend fought for those she loved. An unwanted image of how she'd fought without concern for her own safety wiped away the grin.

Why did these memories plague him? His foot slipped again, but stopped short of the stream. Some of his drink sloshed out of the glass. At least all of the Earthlings were going to get the training to save Earth. If he could get a new non-defective String Sword, everything would be good. With the training everyone else was getting and a

The Celebration

new String Sword, Earth couldn't lose even if the next time he died. First he had to get the sword.

A touch startled him and almost sent him into the freezing water. His Deem friend stood by his side and asked, "What do you think?"

Alex looked up at Daren. He wasn't like any Deem known to anyone. He actually looked similar to a big human man. Alex didn't know what to say. He thought about the strangeness of the alien technology, which could take a room and make it for all intents and purposes the same as the surface of a planet or anywhere else. Alex quickly forgot the question. For a long moment, he stared thinking of how the abductions of him and the other Earthlings had led to a series of dangerous events. Yet, the training their teachers, the abductors, gave them could save Earth. Now, Alex knew they would rescue his home from the coming attack by monsters, the Deems. He just needed to get another String Sword.

"Alex, are you alright? Do you need to get back to your nurse's clinic?" His Deem friend looked at him in concern.

"What? Oh, I'm sorry. I didn't answer your question." It had been just two days since Alex fought in the life or death battle for himself and the whole Academy. He'd almost died. Everyone had almost died, but friends and the aliens' miraculous holo-fields saved him. "What was your question?"

Daren smiled. "That's okay. I saw you looking at the forms under the water and wondered what you thought of them."

"Not much, they're just statues."

"Actually, they're a mystery. At the real place, high up in regal mountains, when you touch the water, they disappear. The water itself is said to be rejuvenating."

Alex shook his head at yet another strange thing. The experiences just didn't stop. In curiosity, he asked, "Where's that place?"

"You wouldn't recognize it. It's a land above Narnia."

The name puzzled Alex. In some shadowy way, it seemed familiar to him. He gave up on it and thought of what he'd learned after the aliens abducted the Earthlings.

He'd found out Earth was in danger from the effects of something called *dark matter*. In less than nine years, it would arrive in Earth's solar system and enable many animals and plants to play with the laws of the universe. Chaos would win, and the terrible Deems would arrive to kill all life.

The aliens called the abilities caused by *dark matter* vapuc. They'd been looking for Earthlings able to do vapuc who they could train at the academy to return and save Earth in nine years.

An evil person named Maleky and the Kimleys had separately made sure Alex would be selected, even though Alex seemed able to only do one vapuc. He could sense the future, and his ability had gotten stronger. Yet, he had to work at sensing the future, and he couldn't do it all the time. This same alien, Maleky, had made a copy of his own mind, which he secretly had placed in Alex's head. No one knew what his plans were. Alex, lost in his own thoughts, stepped back toward the water missing the edge.

Chapter Three
The Warning

Just before Alex landed with a splash, the Deem caught him by the arm pulling him back, but the glass went spinning away and disappeared just before crashing into rocks.

"Thanks." And then Alex bitterly laughed, and said, "But maybe you should've let me fall. I think we all could use a good laugh after the battle we've been through. At least we won. Now, with your help, we'll get the training, and Earth will be saved. I'll go get my new sword, and Earth's going to be safe."

Daren jokingly said, "Well then." Playfully, He shoved on Alex pretending to push him into the mountain stream.

Alex laughed with his friend.

The Deem waved his arm at the celebration scene and continued talking. "This is wonderful. I'm so grateful you kept me from becoming a monster. I know the insane risk you took. Why did you do it?"

"It was the right thing to do."

"But you risked the whole academy and everyone you love. How did you know it was right?"

"I saw how much you loved living things. The monster you were becoming hated all non-Deem life. The honest truth is it would've hurt too much not to try and save you."

Daren spoke in subdued tones, full of emotion. "Wow, just wow. If we Deems had half or even a quarter of the compassion and care you have, none of us would've been lured into becoming monsters. I wish—" Daren interrupted himself to touch his face. "What is this water running down my face?"

"Daren, you're crying."

The Deem's mouth dropped open in shock. "My people don't cry."

Alex felt tears running down his own face. He reached out and hugged Daren. "Crying is a good thing."

For a long moment, the two aliens stood hugging each other.

Alex relaxed, letting his emotions free. Unfortunately for Alex, the moment of letting go also freed the memory he'd been working to repress.

The terrible memory took over his mind. They'd almost lost the opportunity to receive training to save Earth.

Yet again a scene replayed. In this memory, the old, terrible Twyla had resurfaced because the Tribble no longer forced her to love everyone, but the real love in her had won in the end. Twyla had been holding a vessel by two handles. It had contained the green-purple Gragdreath embryo coiling and twisting. Again, the past became all too real for him.

~**********~

Alex held his sword up. "No. You're not her. You're the monster the pet would protect her from."

"No!" Twyla screamed. A tear leaked and trickled down to her jaw. It hung there, small and insignificant, but it spoke volumes to Alex. He saluted it with his sword.

With another scream, Twyla twisted the two handles. "I'm not weak!"

With a screeching, ear piercing sound the vessel shattered. The Winkle girl dropped the handles, stumbled back, and her hands went over her ears. As the screeching sound rolled on longer than just for a shattered container, Twyla fell to the ground and curled into a fetal position. A cloud of thick green-purple smoke rose from the broken vessel. The screeching died away and with it the sounds of battle. Everyone waited.

A stench of sewage, dead decaying things, and undefined smells threatened to gag him. Stubbornly, Alex stood sword up and ready. He concentrated on his feelings looking for the future paths. The smoke writhed. As the horrible mass moved,

The Warning

Alex's thoughts of choices and fates burned in him. He could kill. He could die. Everyone would die.

~**********~

Alex gasped at the realism of the flashback. Heart pounding, he didn't want to re-experience those memories again. In Alex's mind, the alien Maleky objected to the memory too. *That was a terrible memory. Don't think about that battle. You need to see your nurse about these flashbacks. They aren't normal.*

In the desperate battle, there had been few opportunities for victory. Alex had needed to hurry, because his defective sword would at some point explode killing everyone. Earth would've been doomed. Against his will, his memories dragged him back to the battle.

~**********~

Alex dodged under a tentacle and looked for a path toward the Gragdreath's body. His heart froze. Two tentacles pulled Twyla closer to the beast. Her mouth moved and even over the chaos of the renewed battle he knew the plea from her love. "Save yourself."

Twyla's skin began to change color to a greenish-purple.

Maleky screamed a silent warning. *Alex, your sword.*

~**********~

Alex stood with Daren sobbing. He shuddered from the emotions wrapped in the memories. Why, how was he having these flashbacks? Back then, he'd waited too long. His defective sword exploded and except for the sacrifice of another friend it would've killed everyone.

~**********~

Maleky crowed. *Finish it.*

The monster continued to turn, and now Twyla stood clasped to it. Her defenseless body hung between Alex and the

Gragdreath. Even in her pain, she must've known. Somehow, she pounded the message out to him via her AI. |Kill it, Alex. Don't worry about me. Save everyone. I love you.|

Maleky screamed. *Love is for the weak. Don't let it stand between you and victory.*

~**********~

The memories ripped new wounds in his heart and mind. Alex hadn't been able to kill Twyla in order to kill the Gragdreath. His delay had cost another life and almost all of their lives. Through his tears and pain he decided to check with his nurse Gursha the first chance he had about these vivid flashbacks.

Finally Daren stepped back from their hug. "Thanks, I needed that." His face changed to more serious look. In a quieter voice he said, "Alex, the Earthlings' training is still in jeopardy. I know you care for both Kimleys, Hheilea and her brother Hymeron, but—"

The words were too much too soon after the vivid memories. Alex couldn't take in what his friend said.

The Deem paused obviously uncertain about the next thing he would say. In those seconds, Alex briefly thought of the idea of the training being in danger and rejected it. Everything was going to be fine.

Instead, he remembered how Hheilea and he'd been caught up in the alien ritual called T'wasn't-to-be-is. It had forced them to fall in love. The result had been wonderful and a problem at the same time. Hheilea had expected and really needed them to marry. Alex hadn't liked being forced into it.

The ritual, along with the genetic material contained in the alien creature within his mind, had also turned Alex into a human/Kimley hybrid. He thought about his hair and how it kept trying to look similar to a Kimley's becoming a man. He hoped Gursha, his nurse, would be able to keep hiding the shimmering multicolored hues for him. Alex wasn't ready to let everyone know about that secret. Only Hheilea's brother, Hymeron, and Gursha knew about it, and he trusted them completely.

The Warning

The Deem continued, "The money and resources I've given Amable to help you and the other Earthlings has bought you some time. Use it wisely. I think you should focus on getting a String Sword from the Gadget Lady."

He paused before finally saying. "Alex, you're not going to appreciate this information, but you need to know Hymeron is a growing danger to you Earthlings getting your training. You're—"

"What?" Shocked at the idea, Alex stepped backward. His foot caught the edge, but slipped. Arms windmilling, he struggled not to fall over into the fast moving stream.

This time, the Deem made no move to help him. Instead, he burst into laughter at Alex's efforts.

With a tremendous splash, Alex fell backwards into freezing cold water. Instantly, the strong current grabbed control of him. The roaring of the river filled his head, and everything spun. In the brief moments his head broke free, he gasped for air.

Alex fought to get his feet going first to protect his head. For just a second, he had a clear view. A huge boulder raced toward him. Sculling the water frantically with his arms, he got his legs up prepared to— and the current twirled him about. Panic gripped him. He tried to get an order out to the computer controlling this reality.

Head-first, he raced straight at the hard unyielding surface of the rock. "Room AI—" Bubbles escaped and with eyes wide in panic Alex shut his mouth.

Chapter Four
Party Pooper

Alex struggled to no avail. In the next moment, he slammed head first into the massive boulder. He cringed at the expected pain, but the rock gave way like a giant pillow. With a grin, Alex relaxed. The computer controlling this reality wouldn't let him get hurt. Under water again, he breathed in and didn't drown. Instead, he filled his lungs with air.

Alex calmly worked to gain control of the ride. Bouncing off a few more pillowy boulders, he gained a portion of control.

Ahead, Alex spotted a great black boulder with quieter water behind it. He shoved off from a different submerged boulder and succeeded on going to the right. Flipping over he swam as hard as he could for the opportunity. Alex broke the surface and grinned. He was there. Quickly, he flipped back feet first and caught the ebony rock absorbing his momentum with his legs.

Shoving off, he let the water slide him against the soft yielding rock. Rolling over, he caught the big rock with one hand. The current twirled him behind the rock and into the eddy. Alex let go and sculling the water with his hands stood to his feet easily balancing on the rocky bed of the stream. He shook his head and swiped his hands across his face to get rid of the majority of the water. Breathing more easily, Alex grinned. He definitely felt better. He should've jumped into the river on purpose.

Turning back to shore, he hoped none of his friends were upset by what had happened.

Party Pooper

Alex heard another message from A'idah and realized she'd sent identical ones during his wild ride through the rapids. It was actually more of a scream. |Alex!| He suspected she hadn't meant to actually message him. For someone not use to this type of computer generated reality, it would've been very frightening.

Another of A'idah's screams carried to him over the water. "Let go of me!"

Again he heard a message. |Alex!|

|A'idah, I'm okay. Remember, this is all just computer generated reality. There's no real danger, the reality around us can change in an instant. The computer actually made the boulders feel like giant pillows, and I could breathe underwater.| Alex didn't add that computer generated environments could be very real. Inside the weird room on the larger spaceship, he'd been hurt badly in its computer generated reality and at times could've died.

She messaged back, and he could feel her trauma. |You frightened me when you fell into the river. You aren't well yet. I remembered you lying on the ground after the battle. Gursha refused to give you aid. She said the rules of triage had to be followed. I was too injured to walk to you, but I could crawl. I watched as Twarbie kept you heart going, and Hheilea breathed for you. When I finally got to you and put my hands on you, I almost couldn't try to heal you. Your body was so cold.|

The message broke off. After a pause the message from A'idah resumed. |Hheilea asked if I knew how to heal. I said yes, but at first I was so frightened. I couldn't start. I couldn't try. I was too afraid. You looked and felt dead. I feared... we couldn't save you. Seeing you that way hurt worse than when my friend died back on Earth. I realized I.... I couldn't bear losing you. Together, the three of us fought for you and managed to bring you back.|

Her shared emotion choked Alex up. He couldn't think of what to say. He had his own trauma and memories, but he hadn't thought of others. |I'm sorry. I'm— Thanks again for saving my life, and I am sorry for your trauma. I didn't mean to bring it all back. The ride through the rapids actually helped me with my own memories and pain. We're going to be okay.| Even as he messaged that last bit, Alex didn't know if it was the truth.

A'idah sent him another message. This time, it had more spirit and felt more like the fierce girl he knew. The fragility of her earlier message bothered him. Alex didn't want to think of her that way.

|Maybe a jump in the river would help all of us.|

She had her troubles and fears, but he'd rather not think of them. A'idah's strength and fierce spirit always encouraged him. During the years of their abduction, Alex had come to rely on her.

He remembered how much she needed him. A thought crossed his mind of how the water could've been changed to anything he'd wanted. Chocolate pudding would've been interesting. That... gave him an idea. Alex spoke out loud. "Room AI, make a gooey three foot thick, five foot wide chocolate cake under A'idah and a large scoop of whipped cream on her head." Another scream, actually more of a squeal of shock, and then laughter swept over the water. He grinned and realized he was freezing.

Another of his alien friends, the young, Winkle woman, with blond-red-brunette locks flowing down either side of her face, waded out toward him. The water soaked her pantaloons going higher and higher the closer she got.

The distracting view took Alex back to when he'd first come to know her. He gasped at the intensity of yet another flashback. Fortunately, it only lasted for a few seconds.

Freed from the flashback, Alex smiled at his friend, through the water still dripping down his face. He really needed to find out what was going on with these flashbacks. At least that one was enjoyable.

She grinned back and offered her hand. "Want some help getting out of the river or are you going to stay out here? You're not going to pull me into the water again?"

Alex laughed and took her hand. "You're remembering our beginnings too."

Party Pooper

"Yes." Her grin disappeared. "Unfortunately, things haven't changed much. If my people, the other Winkles, knew we're friends, most of them would still force me to torture you to death, and then they'd kill me."

He squeezed her warm hand. "We'll find a way."

"Oh, Alex, back in my teens I might've agreed, but I've seen too much. Come on. Your hand's freezing. Let's get you out of this cold water. You still aren't well."

Back in her teens? How old was she? Shivering, Alex walked beside her. The warmth of the two suns felt good. He suddenly found the water gone, and he walked on dry ground. Someone, maybe the computer, must've gotten quite concerned about how cold he was getting. He'd thought Twarbie was still a teenager close to his age-of something over sixteen. Speaking to the Artificial Intelligence controlling the room he said, "Room AI, put dry clothes on us."

Immediately, the feeling of wet disappeared replaced by the warmth of dry clothing.

Alex heard more laughter and a few good natured yells. He looked over toward the celebration to see what was happening. He'd started a food fight with that chocolate cake. Out of the mess, A'idah ran to him.

Slowly she said, "Thanks for the chocolate cake. You look cold. I think you need some chocolate too. Room AI, pour gallons and gallons of warm chocolate syrup over Alex."

He grinned in appreciation as she ran to him. A'idah's clothing, hair, and face all still had remnants of the chocolate cake and whipped cream. Her exotic black dress with all of the Kalasha bead work swished about her long legs. Her braids danced about her face. Curlicues-not just curls lay plastered against her rosy cheeks. Her blue eyes danced merrily, accenting her laughing, full, red lips. This was his amazing, loving, and warm hearted friend, but when she started talking, Alex quickly held up an arm and rapidly interjected his own AI order. "Room AI, a ten foot wide, strong umbrella, open, over my head, and the handle in my hand."

A'idah had the misfortune of relishing the situation her words would create. In her spirit of enjoyment, she spoke slower drawing out the words painting her joke.

Alex finished talking before A'idah did.

She skidded to a stop six feet from him and looked up to see the warm chocolate syrup she'd asked for.

Alex laughed in anticipation of the result.

This all created a problem for A'idah. When she heard Alex laugh, she looked at him and didn't notice what was happening. The syrup hit the umbrella, and Alex had to lift his other hand up to keep the protection over his head. On purpose or just by coincidence, Alex tipped the umbrella. The warm, gooey, enticing, and deliciously fragrant confection poured in an undulating curtain down over the edge of the umbrella. It was rather a cool sight to behold.

When A'idah saw Alex using another hand to hold his umbrella stable, she looked back up. She was just in time to get the first of the syrup full in her face. It quickly coated her head and the front of her favorite black dress.

In reaction, Alex briefly laughed harder as the river of brown liquid splashed and undulated down over his friend's body. He quickly stopped laughing.

The syrup had stopped pouring over the girl, and she'd backed up sputtering and wiping it off her face. A'idah's beautiful dress stopped Alex's laughter and started the warmth of a flush traveling up his neck and exploding onto his face. He really couldn't see much of the dress any more. That was the problem for him. It was soaked in thick brown syrup. As a result, he did see the curves of A'idah's figure for the first time in a very, very, very clear way.

Chapter Five
Best Friends

A'idah must've realized what had happened, because she crossed her arms in front of her chest and turned her back to him.

For Alex, her backside with its curves didn't help. He tried to think of what to do as he stared.... Fortunately, someone was thinking clearly. He heard Twarbie's disgusted voice nearby.

She said, "Ugh, guy brains. Room AI, remove all of the chocolate syrup from A'idah and her dress. There, much better."

In shock from the unexpected view of his friend, Alex stood frozen. A'idah hadn't looked twelve years old. How old was she?

Without thinking, he pictured how her dress had clung to her. Frustrated at himself, he tossed the umbrella to the side. A'idah was his friend. He shouldn't react.... He shouldn't think of her.... He should apologize, but that would mean admitting how he'd reacted and mentioning how she'd looked. Desperately, Alex wished something, anything would save him from the terrible situation.

A voice Alex didn't recognize spoke in loud urgent tones. At the interruption, everyone else stopped talking.

"I need your attention. I'm very sorry, but Alex and Hheilea should come with me. Ytell, I know I told you to send them to us after the celebration, but things have changed. The dangers are growing and even now might be too late."

At first, Alex looked at the intruder in gratitude, but anxiety and worry soon pushed the other feelings away.

Light reflected off beautiful golden speckles in her or his glossy, black fur. Much of the alien's length was in the fluffy, three-foot-long tail. The alien looked like a giant marmot. Who was this? He wasn't certain, but the voice sounded female. Too late? Too late for what?

Hheilea asked, "How are we going to leave?"

"Via the Bubble Bay over on the Coratory."

Ytell, the seven-foot-tall, alien raptor, their flock leader and responsible for all of the other flock leaders, asked the intruder, "Do you need help keeping them safe?"

Alex turned back to the first speaker. The furry creature, about as long as Ytell was tall, stood on a section of the ship's real floor. A glowing circle of light surrounded and separated the creature from the virtual place everyone else occupied. Who and what was this creature? He'd seen one of them before.

Daren said, "Room AI, turn the simulation off."

The idyllic scene disappeared, leaving all of them standing in a large plain, white room. The warmth of the suns vanished. The furry creature bounded toward them with such grace that it almost flowed across the floor. "Thanks for the offer, Ytell, but I've arranged for safe transportation to meet us at the Bubble Bay."

"By Alex doing the right thing, even when dangerous people didn't like his actions, he has made many enemies. Now that Hheilea's secret is out, she could be kidnapped by one of a dozen different possibilities for the powerful knowledge an adult Kimley can share. They and only they must come with me. If we leave without delay, we should be okay. Everyone else should be at the main celebration."

At the words of danger for Hheilea, Alex's heart missed a beat. He looked over at the alien girl with her shoulder length, white hair and elven-like features. She was his age, but by her species a woman and should've been married.

He remembered how Hheilea used to pretend to be a younger boy in an effort to stay safe. To save him, she'd discarded the disguise. In return, he'd crushed her hope and expectation of getting married to him. Now, she was in more danger. Alex didn't have time to deal with his emotions about her and the other alien female in his life. He didn't dare to even think about A'idah.

The idea of action felt good to him. He understood that kind of danger. With relief, Alex stated, "Let's get going."

Before he could move, A'idah threw herself at him and hugged him fiercely.

Having her body against him so soon after having seen her coated in chocolate syrup sent a jolt through the teenage boy. For a long second, he didn't know what to do. He felt her curves and awkwardly brought his arms round her to hug her back. Yet, he held a bit back. Another flashback blasted into his awareness. He'd just had a terrible dream.

~**********~

The vision dropped him, and he fell out of bed, his last scream echoing in his ears.

Someone pounded on his door and then slammed it open. A'idah leaped into the room. Her night gown flapped about her. "What's wrong?"

For a moment, Alex just gasped. Finally, he managed to say, "Bad..., bad dream."

"Are you going to be okay?"

"Yeah. I'll be fine." He forced himself up onto his feet. Alex didn't think he was going to sleep anytime soon.

Right behind her, Zeghes swam into the room. "Were there sharks?"

"Yes, a bad one, but it was just a dream. I'll be fine."

Zeghes said, "Okay. I don't know why we sleep in separate rooms. We should be closer. A'idah, could you share his bed?"

She stepped back, face flaming. In a voice half laughing and half shocked A'idah said, "No, Zeghes. That's another of those inappropriate things."

"Oh, sorry. I... didn't mean to suggest something wrong. I could stay with you, Alex. I sleep floating."

~**********~

That flashback was bad enough, but another from the same night slammed into him.

Zeghes had stayed with him, but thinking of the vision and what it had meant had broken Alex and he'd been sobbing. Zeghes had messaged A'idah and she'd come back. Quickly, she had crossed the room and took him into her arms. Alex had collapsed against her, sobbing into her shoulder. A'idah had held him against her with surprising strength letting him sob. They had cried on each other's shoulders, two frightened kids in a strange situation, surrounded by terrible danger and tasked with saving their world.

Again, he remembered how he'd almost kissed her and her response.

She'd shoved him away, pleading with him not to make it hard for her. In the last of the flashback, he heard her words.

~**********~

"Thanks for holding me. I needed the comfort. Together, we'll make it through this terrible time. We're going to save Earth. I do like you. Later, when I'm older, much older, I'll think about letting you kiss me. For now, you are going to be my friend. Good night."

~**********~

That was what she wanted. Alex feared hugging her. Instead, he awkwardly patted her back. He wanted to deny the attraction he felt, but her hugging him made it impossible to ignore his feelings. Yet, this was his friend, his best friend, and she wanted, needed their relationship kept that way. Alex couldn't ignore how he felt, how she felt. Confused, somewhat ashamed of thinking of her that way and anxious to get away, Alex pushed away breaking her embrace. "Sorry, I've got to go. Take care of yourself."

He looked at her face as he backed-up and wished he hadn't. His friend's face looked desolate. It reminded him of his old girlfriend back on Earth. He'd been dying of an

Best Friends

unknown illness, and she'd come to see him, but he'd pushed her away. Her face had looked just the same. This wasn't the same. This wasn't the same. A'idah was his best friend.

His thoughts got more desperate. The other girl had been much older, thirteen or fourteen. He stopped trying to think.

Alex turned and ran. He ran away from— He didn't know and didn't want to think about it. He ran to this new, furry creature which had brought news of fresh danger. At that moment, the new danger didn't matter. Right then, anything seemed less dangerous than A'idah and his thoughts and feelings about her.

Zeghes and the rest of his flock hurried over. Their voices filled the air. With his back to his best friend, Alex escaped into the moment of leaving. His other friends' voices surrounded him, cocooning him from thoughts of A'idah. Even in this new moment of insecurity, Alex grinned at the familiar thoughts and ideas expressed by them, and yet he could hear the growth from their experiences. At the same time, he didn't feel good about the delay in leaving. His sense of the future urged him to move faster.

The blue hyacinth macaw, said, "The flock will be there when you need us."

The snow leopard, said, "If there are too many people, think of them as just snowflakes and focus past them."

The older Japanese man, said, "Practice your feeling vapuc ability."

The furry creature interrupted Alex's friends, "Let them through. We must go now, before it's too late."

Daren got to Hheilea just before Alex. "Hheilea, the offer still stands. I could help you restart the T'wasn't-to-be-is. It would draw someone to you again."

"No thanks. I'm going to try something new."

The Deem man hugged Alex. In a voice filled with meaning, he said, "Thanks again for saving me and giving me a new life." In a much less serious voice, he added, "Take care of my ship I'm giving you. Knowing you, you're going to have some interesting times with it."

Amable, the leader of the aliens, asked, "Can I say something?"

The furry creature said, "We're out of time. As soon as Amable has his say, we've got to go."

Amable stepped up to Alex and waggled his thick eyebrows. Alex couldn't help but grin at the alien leader's face and foot-long tufts of lime-green and violet hair gently waving back and forth over Amable's ears. The leaders large, golden eyes circled with black in the pale face looked back with the bushy eyebrows waggling over them. In a serious voice, the man said, "While you're gone, I'm going to figure out how to either get a new String Sword for you or to help you get to the Gadget Lady. I know she'll have one."

The furry creature said, "Ship, open an inter-ship portal to the coordinates I gave you earlier. Let's go. Don't pause for anything. We'll be landing in the Bubble Bay. We should be safe, but as soon as you hit the ground, run."

A swirling pattern opened a pulsating circle, and the creature jumped in. Hheilea followed. A premonition of danger prickled at Alex. This wasn't a good idea, but he followed anyway. The last words he heard were from Amable and the Deem.

"Don't trust Maleky. He's planning something."

"Remember my warning. You don't have much time."

A message from A'idah followed Alex into the portal. The fierceness of the first part widened his eyes. |Alex, you take care of yourself.| The ferocity of it died away and other emotions flavored the rest of the message. His own feelings he didn't want to examine were stirred in response. |Don't die. I... I need you.|

Chapter Six
Escape to the Tasties

Alex held Hheilea close as the bubble finished forming.

"Let's go. Move in tight."

He looked at the speaker. The furry creature's bubble had finished forming and it hovered beside them.

Obeying, Alex lifted off and bumped his bubble against the other one. Immediately, they both accelerated out of the bay's wide opening and into the sunshine. Staggering, Alex shifted his feet on the flat bottom to keep his balance. "We need to get Hheilea to a nurse."

Speaking quickly, the creature said, "We'll be somewhere safe in a moment, and I'll look at her wound then." In a more forceful tone, she commanded, "Don't try to control your bubble's movement. I'll get us to safety."

Not worrying about how he sounded, Alex pleaded, "I don't know if Hheilea can wait that long. I don't even know if she's still alive."

In a more compassionate tone, the creature said, "Trust me. If we have to, we'll stop at the Academy down below for help. Everything's going to be okay."

Trust? Trust? Alex wanted to scream. Trusting this creature who he didn't even know the name of had gotten Hheilea hurt and... and... He tried not to think of how still her body was or how cold she seemed.

Alex could see the Academy miles below them. It stood on top of its island surrounded by the sea. The pearlescent sphere rested on top of three gigantic arches. The size of the miles tall structure had never ceased to amaze him, but this time with his heart in his throat the miles wide sphere was only a thing. In desperation, Alex remembered how some creatures could use a vapuc to heal others. Concentrating, he focused on just the little body he held. Her heart had to keep beating. Alex whispered to her, "Hheilea don't die. Please don't die."

Misty white of a cloud surrounded them. It quickly grew dark. As they traveled through the concealing dark cloud, a brief question flittered past his mantra. Why had the killer stopped firing after hitting Hheilea?

Light from a break in the cloud illuminated Hheilea's face. At the brilliant light, her eyelids fluttered again, but this time they opened. Gazing down into her violet eyes, Alex sighed in relief. He asked Hheilea, "Are you okay?"

In a pain filled voice, she answered, "It hurts, but I'll be okay. Lucky for me, I took the blaster bolt on my chest. A head shot would've killed me. You need to get these type of clothes. You were the one someone tried to kill."

"She's right."

A metallic clanking sound assaulted his ears, interrupting his thoughts. Light blossomed around them. They were inside a large metal container. Alex's bubble dissipated, and he braced himself not wanting to joggle the injured Hheilea. He landed with barely a jolt on the metal floor. Different fragrances, mostly of plants tickled his nose. As Alex wondered where they were, the furry creature hurried over to him.

"Brave girl, let me help your pain." It sprayed a blue haze over Hheilea's wounded chest. The haze immediately turned pink over the injury.

"Thanks."

"You're welcome. This sprayable holo-field isn't as good as the real thing, but it'll take care of the pain and heal the surface wound. Once we get to my city we'll get you fixed up."

Looking at Alex, the creature added words just for him. "She's going to be okay."

Alex felt acceleration and asked, "Where are we?"

"We're inside a sky whale heading back to my home."

The name brought to his mind the image of a giant whale-like creature, but bigger with big rippling fins flying through the air and swallowing green clouds. He remembered it leaving long thin brownish clouds behind it. Alex recognized the faint underlying odor of sewage or a feedlot. His eyes grew wide.

In a stronger voice, Hheilea said, "Cool. I've never gotten to fly in one before."

Looking in confusion at the metal walls, Alex said, "I thought they're a living organism. It certainly doesn't' smell like a machine."

"They are living. We're inside a shipping container it holds in its mouth. They have proven very useful for moving supplies. This one had a shipment of vegetables." With a chuckle, the creature added, "They do have bad breath."

The creature pulled open a drawer and removed a pillow and a thick blanket. From another drawer, it retrieved a much smaller white blanket. It set down the pillow, and spread the first blanket out on the floor as it talked. "These whales are from a gas planet with a sun expanding toward its red giant stage. The Coratory was big enough to save some of the sky whales by moving them here and to a couple of other planets. In return, they do whatever they can to help. Bring Hheilea over here and lay her down."

Alex gently laid Hheilea down gazing into her eyes. He couldn't help but remember how shattered she'd been when he'd destroyed her plans and hopes.

She smiled back at him and in a weak voice said, "Don't look so worried. I'm going to be fine. The pain's mostly gone now."

Alex tried to smile back at her, but he couldn't quite manage. How could Hheilea be so cavalier about what had happened? She could've died.

The creature pushed Alex back and spread the second, small, white blanket over Hheilea's upper body. "It's warm enough in here that you really don't need this, but I know how your species reacts to nudity. I thought you'd appreciate having your chest covered."

At those words, Alex felt his face grow red. In his concern for Hheilea, he hadn't thought about... reflexively his gaze traveled to the curves the sheet revealed. At the sound of a door opening, Alex turned around, very happy for an interruption.

Another furry creature bounded into the room. A faint spicy fragrance came in with her. "Grandma, what happened?" Not waiting for a response, it kept talking. "You told me everything would be alright by going when you did instead of waiting for others to help. Are these Alex and Hheilea you told me about? Is a predator following us? I'll go check and warn Oulue." With a swish of its tail it departed.

Alex grinned to himself at the younger creature's behavior and at the relief it gave him from thinking about Hheilea. Maybe no one saw his embarrassment.

The voice of the Kimley, Maleky, in his head, whom he'd been ignoring, finally said something so outrageous he couldn't ignore it. *That's one Tasty you could take advantage of easily. She's so immature. Of course, Hheilea is incredibly open for you to take advantage of after you crushed her hopes so smoothly. I think you're finally learning from me.*

At those thoughts from Maleky, Alex remembered. Tasties, that's right. These creatures were Tasties. What a crazy name. At the same time, irritation flooded him at the suggestions. He responded back to his enemy. *I'm not going to learn from you, and you can't make me give into your plans or be like you at all.* He hated Maleky and didn't want to be like him. The problem was Alex couldn't stop the thoughts the man created in his mind.

Maleky grasped the opportunity to keep Alex's attention. *You have to admit the information I've given you about others has helped.*

I don't have to admit anything.

The evil man kept at him. *You forget. I know what you're thinking. I know you've thought about my advice. Just now, I helped you remember Tasties. They are an important species and very wise. Pay attention to them.*

Alex gritted his teeth. The alien was right. He had considered the advice. At times, it made such good sense, but then he'd be reminded of how evil the person in his head was. He had to stop listening to what Maleky told him. Back when his parents were still alive, his dad had told Alex how some powerful people used information to control how people acted and thought. The best lie has an element of truth. That was what Maleky was doing to him.

Yeah. Information is power, but I'm also not as evil as you and others make me out to be. There are many areas I agree with you and others on. I'm just not as weak.

Alex nodded his head. His dad had said wars like the Spanish-American war had been started by newspapers.

Maleky's thoughts lectured him. *Information changes everything and everyone. You'll find people controlling what others hear and believe everywhere you go. Beware and be one who controls it. Remember what I just told you about Tasties. They are wise.*

Alex didn't understand why an evil man would consider others to be wise.

Just because you think I'm evil doesn't mean I don't recognize wisdom. You really are naive. What you call evil is just a different perspective. I believe in putting self-first. If you don't take care of your own needs, how can you help others you want to help?

Alex had to admit Maleky's argument made sense. A quiet voice pulled him back from listening to the inner voice. "Alex, Alex, Alex."

"Huh?" In confusion, he looked around.

Hheilea spoke from her bed on the floor. "Is Maleky bothering you again?"

"Well." Alex hated admitting to the reality of what he'd been doing. "Yeah. Sorry. I know I shouldn't pay any attention to him." As he spoke, Alex realized that Maleky had him reconsidering a basic tenant of his Mother and Father. They'd always taught him to consider others first. Arrrg. He so hated Maleky and his ideas.

The Tasty said, "Alex, sit down by Hheilea and hold her hand. It'll comfort her while we cross over the sea to get to my home. By the way, my name is Windelli. Sorry I didn't introduce myself earlier, but there wasn't time. That youngster who flew in and out of here is my granddaughter, Delli."

Alex sat down by Hheilea and took her hand. He gazed down at her face. Her violet eyes gazed back with... humor?

"You're cute when you turn red."

His eyes started to shift to the source of his earlier embarrassment, but he resolutely kept them on her eyes. Alex didn't know what to say in response, and he could feel warmth traveling up into his face again.

"It's okay."

Hheilea's words helped, but the depth of her incredible violet eyes threatened his emotional stability. He wanted to comfort her, but... part of him wanted to be back at the party relaxing. At the very least not looking into her eyes and thinking of what her burned top had revealed.

Instead, Alex focused on his need to get back to climbing the Gadget lady's mountain. In his mind, he pictured a String Sword with its blade of black *dark matter* and a glowing white edge. With that weapon, Alex could help the other Earthlings defeat Earth's enemies, the Deem, or if he died, the sword would also be a great help to a number of other people he could think of. After his recent experiences, Alex understood all too well his own mortality. "Windelli? You said we're going to a city. Where is it and how long will we need to stay there? I need to climb a mountain."

"You know there's a wedge for each group of alien students at the inner edge of the crater where plants and animals from their home worlds live. Separating those areas are narrow farms producing food for all who live here. My city is in a farming wedge next to your planet's area." She turned her head toward Alex and paused.

Alex looked into her face surprised at the concern he saw there. How could a furry creature's face show emotion the way hers did?

"About how long you'll need to be there, I'm not sure. I agree that you need to climb the Gadget lady's mountain and get a String Sword. Meantime, you'll continue your training with us."

Escape to the Tasties

The furry creature reached back into the drawer, removed another pillow and blanket giving them to Alex. "You can let go of Hheilea's hand now. She's sleeping. You should get some rest too. I heard about your wounds."

Alex accepted the pillow and blanket. Getting comfortable, he thought of other questions, but weariness he hadn't noticed pushed all but one away. Who had shot at him, and how did they know about them leaving via the bubble bay? He realized something else. Whoever it was had only fired twice. They hadn't fired immediately after the three of them arrived. That would've been the best time. The delay had helped Alex to survive, and after they shot Hheilea by mistake they'd stopped firing.

If someone had wanted him dead, why hadn't they shot sooner? Were they troubled at the idea of really killing him? Maybe they were just getting there too. Who would've been bothered by shooting Hhcilea?

Alex gazed back at the sleeping teenager. Who would be bothered by you getting hurt? Alex couldn't help but think of how he'd hurt Hheilea even worse by shattering her plans and hopes. Stubbornly, his mind returned to his act of crushing Hheilea. He remembered how he'd chosen to risk letting the strange alien ritual, the T'wasn't-to-be-is finish in order to get the green crystal. Pretending to sleep, Alex felt the tears escaping his eyelids as his memories raged in his mind.

Alex forced himself to stop remembering. What he couldn't do was force himself to go to sleep. Another face kept coming to mind, one with braids and the thought of A'idah's face stirred feelings he didn't want to consider. Even in his exhausted state it took a very long time to go to sleep.

Chapter Seven
Revenge

A'idah had watched Alex and Hheilea leave. She hadn't wanted those two going off by themselves. They always seemed to get into trouble of one kind or another. Moments later, Ytell proved her worries to be correct.

Ytell said, "Flock, gather around. Someone attacked Hheilea and Alex. We're going to go and try to find the attacker. The attack took place at the Bubble Bay of the Coratory."

Heart in her throat, A'idah hurried over. She could feel her hair radiating out from her head. She'd have to control her lightning ability, but if she caught the one who'd tried to kill Hheilea and Alex...

Daren, the Deem, said, "Could you use my help?"

Ytell said, "The flock and I can take care of this. Go ahead and start getting the Coratory ready for the voyage to your repair yard."

Mel, the illusions teacher, stood holding Osamu's hand. "Can I help?"

"Fine. I'm going to open another of those inter-ship portals. We'll be jumping onto a balcony up above the Bubble Bay floor. Ship, open the inter-ship portal I asked you for."

A swirling pattern opened a pulsating circle. Ytell stepped over closer to it and said, "Some of you can do the time vapuc. Work with me to speed up time for our flock. It will give us a big advantage over whoever we find."

A'idah tried to speed up time, but she couldn't tell any difference. "Did it work?"

Revenge

Ytell pointed a scaly hand at Daren. A'idah laughed. The Deem seemed to be in the middle of a step. The man Alex had saved from becoming a monster seemed to be very slowly moving.

Ytell interrupted A'idah's thought of a joke she could play on Daren.

"Okay, I'll go first and everyone follow after me. Remember, we are hunting for someone who is armed and dangerous. Our time flow advantage will only last for a short time, so hurry." Ytell jumped through the portal.

Embarrassed at momentarily forgetting someone tried to kill Alex and Hheilea, A'idah crowded past Ekbal and jumped next. As she went, she called back, "Zeghes, come on. We'll make those who threatened our friends sorry."

Going through the portal disoriented A'idah, and she stumbled on a floor of a slightly different height from where she'd jumped. The white room was gone replaced by the huge, empty expanse of the Bubble Bay. Far down below were the small squares of bubble platforms and all along the far edge of the bay was the gap in the wall revealing the sky and clouds outside. She'd arrived high up on a balcony that ran off into the distance. All along the narrow platform, A'idah could spot doors at irregular distances.

Ytell said, "Hurry out of the way. Go over to the wall. Start scanning the area and watch for any movement. Everyone else should still be at the other celebration, the big one."

She moved just before Zeghes barreled through the portal.

Ytell repeated his instructions for each member of the flock. Osamu came through last, and he came through holding a small gadget. The Japanese man stood looking at the device as he turned back and forth. "There does not appear to be anyone out in the Bay, Ytell."

Ytell said, "I hoped you had that device with you. Osamu and Mel, take Ekbal and Skyler with you and go down to the lower balcony. Do you know where the secondary entrances are?"

Both of them answered, "Yes." Osamu continued, "We will also checkout some other possibilities. Ekbal, use an artificial gravity generator and Skyler, follow us." Osamu ran at the rail.

A'idah gapped in surprise as the Japanese man suddenly ran up into the air and dove over the rail. How had he done that? Using her AI she asked, |Osamu, how did you just run up into the air?|

Mel followed, vaulting the rail as Osamu answered.

|I have been practicing at using small burst of the force vapuc to create small platforms of kinetic force as stepping or running stones as I call them. I could help you learn how to do it.|

Ekbal levitated off the ground and followed the Japanese man. Skyler burst into flight. He circled once, trailing his long blue tail and dove after the others.

Ytell asked, "Sabu, do you remember how blaster fire smells?"

"Yes. It's nasty stuff."

"Check along this balcony for the smell. Our friends were attacked with a blaster. A'idah and Zeghes, checkout the rooms along this stretch of the balcony. I'll go to the main entrance."

Blaster fire? The words sent a shiver down her back. A'idah hoped neither of her friends had been hurt, but surely Ytell would've said something. She pushed those worries aside and started for a door on her left. She told Zeghes, "I'll check out the rooms this direction. You take the other." Remembering Ytell's instructions to hurry, she started jogging. The first few rooms were empty, but then she found something strange.

Hurrying into another room, she looked around. Seeing no one she started to leave, but something drew her farther into the room. A'idah stepped around some equipment or something. She couldn't tell what it was. Back in a corner, huddled against the wall, with his knees pulled up to his chest was Hymeron, Hheilea's little brother.

He must've heard something, because his head slowly started to come up. A'idah hadn't liked the boy much before, but this time he looked so sad and lonely, and he was Alex's friend. Something strange lay on the floor beside him.

A'idah asked, "Hymeron, are you okay?" Only after asking did she realize he probably couldn't make sense out of her sped up voice.

The little boy disappeared. A'idah gasped and hurried toward where Hymeron had been. There wasn't anything there. |Ytell, I just spotted Hymeron. He was huddled on the floor of one of the rooms I'm checking out, and then he just disappeared. I felt around for him, but he's gone.|

|Thanks. I'll contact some others to try and find him for questioning. Eventually, he'll probably head back to his home. Sabu has found where the attack occurred. Come on down the balcony. You'll see the rest of us where it extends out into a point over the bay below. It was the perfect spot for the ambush.|

Leaving the room and the unanswered question of what Hymeron was doing there, A'idah hurried back out onto the balcony. Way down the balcony, she spotted the distant figures of the flock. A voice behind her startled A'idah.

"Want a ride?" Zeghes zoomed up beside her.

Quickly, she swung up and held on as he accelerated. It didn't take him long at all to reach the rest of the flock.

Ytell said, "Now that we're all together, we are going to carefully search this area. Look for anything. If you see something, don't touch it. Just let me know what it is and where. We need to hurry up with our investigation. Daren has let me know he wants to get going as soon as possible. His temporary repairs will only last for so long, and he wants to get it to his shipyard before anything else fails. The good news is, he'll scan this whole area of the balcony for any possible clues, but I'm hoping we can spot something to give us a lead. Spread out and be careful."

The flock started the search for clues, slowly things were found.

"I found a white hair."

Skyler said, "I've found two statues, but I think they're moving."

The rest of the flock let out surprised yells and came running. Skyler had landed on the balcony's rail. "They are moving. What should we do with them?"

Running up, A'idah saw a foot tall Lepercaul adult dressed in their normal green clothes, big wide belt with a gold buckle and a curly reddish beard. He looked just like a Leprechaun from a book she'd read, but this wasn't any funny and cute little make-believe creature. The Lepercaul had a very mad expression and A'idah knew how mean he could be. With him, in a brown cloak with a cowl, a dangerous Winkle stood in a funny unbalanced pose. The Evil Winkle slowly moved to finish a step. A'idah laughed at the sight even as she felt her own hair radiating out from her head.

These enemies must be the ones who attempted to kill Alex and Hheilea. She'd make sure they never tried to hurt anyone again.

A'idah's thoughts were followed by action. Static electricity crackled around her. Someone hit the two intruders with a wave of force, and the two toppled over in slow motion with funny efforts at saving themselves. Lightning struck where they'd been standing.

Thunder boomed, followed by Ytell's voice amplified into a shout which hurt her ears more than the thunder. "No attacking! We don't want to trigger another battle!"

A ripple moved through her line of sight and suddenly everything speed up.

The voice of a Lepercaul starting at a very low pitch, slow, and threatening even as it made her chuckle at his slow mouth movements and drawn out words, said, "How dare—" sped up and rose in pitch to finish. "you."

An answering wave of force to the flock's attack tumbled her backwards. Painfully landing on her belly, A'idah pushed herself up and lifted an arm to fire off chain lightning at both of her enemies. She felt a compulsion from the Winkle to fall flat on her face. In response, she fought the demand to surrender and drop to the floor. She'd take out these enemies.

Skyler said, "Defend the flock."

Revenge

"Everyone, stop. This is Ytell, and I won't have another battle happen here. I have the ship's boarding protocols turned on, and anyone attempting to attack another will be frozen in place. I've been told it's very painful."

With a squawk, "Ahhh!" Skyler fell out of the air in the midst of flying at the intruders. His half formed gigantic beak disappeared.

Other, angry voices rose and a mob of other Winkles and Lepercauls poured out of an entrance behind the first two. Through the tumult and yells two phrases kept being repeated.

"Where is the foolish boy?"

"He'll pay."

Ytell landed with a thump in between his badly outnumbered flock and the angry people. "Alex is not here. Consider your own actions. The battle some of you were involved in where the Gragdreath monster appeared was your fault. If you refuse to accept the responsibility for your own actions and behaviors, you will be banished from the Academy."

The Lepercaul stepped forward on his short little legs and with a snarl said, "After what the Earthling Alex did to our people, we don't want to be here any longer than it takes to get our revenge. I think killing this flock of his would be a good start."

One of the Winkles stepped forward. In a hoarse, evil sounding voice she said, "Titan, I agree with you about your and our revenge, but there's a better day coming for it. The nasty human isn't here. Meanwhile, Amable and his foolish do-gooders have a problem."

Somehow her voice became even more evil and threatening. "Ytell, the Gragdreath is part of our religion. By killing our god, that nasty boy committed an unpardonable sacrilege. He also interfered in our associates' upbringing of a whole generation. By your own rules, he's committed crimes, and he must pay for them. If you don't allow us to make him pay, then you must hold him accountable. We'll look forward to the trial and punishment."

Shouts filled the air.

"Yes!"
"He must pay!"
"Make him suffer!"
"He's terrible!"
"Make him pay!"

The hatred boiled through the air, and A'idah involuntarily took a step back. Angry at her reaction, she stomped up to stand beside Ytell. She felt a very painful and focused force attack jab her in the stomach. The force teacher, Titan, grinned wickedly at her. How did he get away with doing that?

A'idah refused to give him the satisfaction of showing any pain. A small attack must get past the protocols. A'idah stood up straight and returned the favor with electrical sparks in his nostrils.

At his resulting expression of pain, she grinned.

Ytell must've realized things could still very easily get out of hand. "Amable has received your complaints, and you will be given an opportunity to express your legal complaints against Alex. Now go home." With a scaly arm, he reached out turned A'idah around and pushed her back toward the rest of the flock.

Behind her, she heard Titan say, "You're just protecting the little wimpy Earthlings."

A'idah growled. That little midget didn't just say wimpy. She turned around to fight, but both Osamu and Mel grabbed her by the arms. She leaned forward and with her hair radiating out from her head gave Titan an icy glare.

She drew in a breath to express her views about the ludicrousness of the complaints and her opinion of their intelligence, odor, looks, and behavior. How could these terrible people accuse Alex of crimes?

Mel whispered, "A'idah, I understand your anger. I'm angry too, but don't let it get the best of you. Titan is just baiting you. Don't give him the satisfaction of knowing he's hurt you."

A'idah knew the illusion teacher's temper very well and if she was encouraging temperance, then it must be a good idea. Zeghes and Skyler flashed past her.

Revenge

The horrible, little man, Titan, still stood waiting with a sneer on his face.

Zeghes and Skyler both dive bombed the angry group. They pulled out of their dives at the very last moment.

Mel's advice and a message from Ytell kept her bitter words choked up inside A'idah. They tasted terrible. She hated this final interruption.

|Flock, all of you get back here behind me. Do not say anything else. Let them leave.|

She couldn't help saying something. "You're all evil."

The old Winkle cackled in response and said, "You naïve little girl. I'd much rather be evil than so gullible. We'll give Amable some time to make things right, but we also will make our own preparations. With Titan's help, we're up to what it will take to make Alex pay." All of the Winkles tipped their heads back and laughed at A'idah. Incongruously, one of the brown robed Winkles had kept her head bowed. The teenage girl, surprised by that one, hardly heard the next words of the old crone.

"We have a surprise for Alex."

Chapter Eight
Tasties

Distant lightning flashed in the night. Air currents tossed Alex to and fro. Terror of falling threatened to wake him from the dream. Someone screamed, land us before we die. He wanted to wake from the dream, but couldn't. The turbulent terror faded away, and Alex breathed a sigh of relief in his sleep. Darkness surrounded him. Something moved out there. It felt so real. Someone boxed with him, but it wasn't training. They wanted him dead. The other person had dreadlocks, and Alex could tell they had the advantage over him. They were going to kill him, but there was a way out. When Alex thought of that, he held a knife. A mountain lion charged into the fight. The dream became more chaotic, and a terror grew. He tried to run from the unnamed horror, but his feet wouldn't move. The knife burned in his hand and he couldn't let go of it, and that was the source of the terror.

Against his will, Alex found his eyes pulled to the weapon. There on the bloody blade was a face. In agony, Alex recognized the face of the one he'd decided to marry. Agony at her death filled him.

The shock of that thought shook Alex free from his dream and woke him. Jerking up into a sitting position and blinking away the shadows of the dream and sleep, his heart raced. Even as he took in the details of a small sandy-tan colored room, his mind struggled with what he remembered. The dream was crystal clear in his mind. The clarity of it reminded him of a horrible dream, a T'wasn't-to-be-is vision. That time, Hheilea had messaged him to explain what a T'wasn't-to-be-is vision was. They warned

Tasties

about terrible dangers. As his T'wasn't-to-be-is partner she had experienced the dream too. After that dream, A'idah and Zeghes and come in response to his screams. This time, all Alex had was his emotions, loud heartbeat, and his thoughts.

He wished A'idah was with him. Alex thought of holding her and being held by her that other time, but other thoughts and emotions stirred up by that thought rattled him. Shaking his head against his desires, Alex firmly shoved away his need for A'idah's comfort.

Instead, he forced himself to consider the dream. Did it have any meaning? Could it be associated with his sense of the future? It could be a T'wasn't-to-be-is vision. Alex refused to accept that thought. He'd beaten the alien compulsion of the T'wasn't-to-be-is ritual. No longer could it force him to marry Hheilea. Alex remembered her injury. Where was she? Concern for her motivated him to get going. Quickly, he tried messaging her.

Instead, the babyish voice of Alex's own AI spoke in his head. *I can't message her. I think she must be sleeping. Why aren't you sleeping? I should still be sleeping. I'm tired. Why are we getting up?*

Alex didn't know how to reply to his AI. Gursha, his nurse had told him to be careful with it after the injuries the artificial intelligence on his head had suffered. Instead, he got out of the bed and looked around.

There were clean clothes set out on a large stool. Alex quickly dressed. At one point, he rested a hand against the wall, and its rough texture felt like sandstone. He also noticed a faint musky smell. The memory of Hheilea saving his life back in the bubble bay hurried him. Specifically, the fact he hadn't thanked her for risking her life to save his. Alex was unsure if it was Maleky or his own conscience making him feel bad. He was sure Hheilea must think he was ungrateful. He didn't need that added to the problems between them.

Leaving the room, Alex found himself in a pastel colored tunnel. The musky smell was more noticeable here. At his thought of which way to find Hheilea, a ripple of color ran over the wall surprising him. He gazed at it and consciously considered which way he should go to find her. Again a ripple of color ran over the wall from the right to the left. Alex turned to the left.

He met a few of the Tasties as he walked, but they didn't say anything to him. A couple of times, a wall seemed confused. At least once, he doubled back and another time he recognized a door. Some of the Tasties followed their own ripples of color. At one point, a tunnel opened onto a ledge in a big cavern. Alex saw more Tasties traveling about their business on other ledges and down on the floor of the chamber. A sense of something not good began to trouble him. Alex couldn't tell if the premonition concerned his future or a friend's. Walking along a narrow ledge led Alex to the entrance of another tunnel. A bigger Tasty than the others he'd seen bumped into him, staggering him. Alex turned about to say something to him.

He caught a few words from the Tasty that interrupted his own. "... shouldn't be here..."

Uncertain, Alex paused for a moment before continuing looking for Hheilea. The sense of trouble faded after the encounter. Not everyone wanted him to be in their city.

Alex had just about decided to stop following the bands of colors when a burst of brighter color outlined a door. After a knock, it swung open and a grizzled Tasty greeted him. "I've been expecting you. Hheilea's doing fine. Sit down by her, and I'll go get some food for both of you. She needs to get up."

The furry creature moved out of his way. In the middle of the room, Hheilea floated in a blue holo-field. At the sight of the blue surrounding her, he grinned. Blue instead of pink meant she was healed. Alex was also relieved to notice Hheilea's damaged clothing had been replaced.

As he moved closer, her eyelids fluttered, a sign the holo-field was waking her up. A section of the floor rose up morphing into a chair, and he sat down next to her as her eyes opened. "Good morning. How are you feeling?" Now that he had the opportunity to thank her, he was uncertain about how to start.

Tasties

"I feel better. I'm hungry. Where are we?"

"I'm not sure. I guess it's the city of the Tasties. We're underground. Outside this room are tunnels connecting other rooms and at least one big cavern."

The nurse, Alex presumed it was a nurse, carried two platters toward them. Steam rose up from the food, and Alex noticed some familiar and other not familiar odors.

The holo-field supporting Hheilea shifted to support her in a sitting position. A lump of the floor between them rose morphing into a table.

The nurse placed the two platters of food on the table. "If you need me, I'll be back in my office."

After she left, they concentrated on their food. Alex only played with his. The problem of needing to thank her for saving his life preoccupied him and soured his appetite. At the same time, a question gnawed at his mind. Who wanted him dead, and how had they known where to be? The first part made him bitterly chuckle. It was more a case of which one of many had tried to kill him. The Winkles hated him for interrupting the torturing they were doing and for converting some of them from their evil ways. Next on the list was the Lepercauls. They hated him for helping a whole generation learn to be different. He grinned to himself as he thought about what that generation called themselves, *Alex's army*, but he also remembered how one of them sacrificed himself to help Alex save everyone.

Hheilea's voice interrupted his thoughts. "Alex, what's wrong? You're not eating."

Alex stopped staring at his food to look up at her. "Uh.... Well, remember back on the Coratory?"

"I don't have a clue what you're talking about."

"You saved my life by jumping and taking the shot meant for me."

"Yeah, I'd do it again."

"Uh.... Well, I never thanked you for risking your life. Thanks. I didn't mean to seem ungrateful." At the same time, he wondered how she could still care for him after he'd crushed her hopes.

"You goofy guy, after all we've been through, I know you. You're not ungrateful. And you are welcome."

Her words about all they'd been through cut Alex. He didn't want to broach the hurt he'd caused her, but Maleky's agreement about it being a bad idea confirmed his thought to talk about it. Maleky couldn't be right. Alex sat up straighter, and said, "Hheilea, uh, I mean. After the uh— What are you— Uh..."

Hheilea slammed her spoon down. "Your use of *uh* so much has to be one of the most irritating things I know about you. Just spit it out."

In a desperate rush, Alex said, "The T'wasn't-to-be-is was destroyed for you and me. What are you going to do now? You told me that if it got permanently interrupted you'd never get to marry. Are you going to be okay?"

Her face turned white. Dropping her head, she held her face.

Alex continued much slower and with more emotion. "I'm sorry for you. I... u—" He choked off another *uh*. He remembered how terrible she'd looked and felt after he'd ruined her life. How could he say anything, and what would help?

Time seemed to stretch as Hheilea slowly straightened, removing her hands from her face. Slowly, quietly she said, "My dad told me not to worry. There is still a possible path. After destroying the T'wasn't-to-be-is, you showed me I could still feel. I've decided to... well... with the T'wasn't-to-be-is gone we're no longer getting pushed to love each other and to get married. Could we just be friends?"

Partial relief flooded Alex. He nodded his head. "We've always been friends. Now, it'll be easier." He didn't acknowledge the pain he felt at Hheilea's phrase of *could we just be friends*.

Alex shoveled in some food. Chewing he remembered his other question. "Who do you—" Coughing interrupted him trying to talk while eating.

"You okay? Take a drink first. I'm not sure what it is, but it tastes good."

Tasties

He tried the drink. Strange flavors amidst familiar hit his tongue. "Thanks. That helped. I was wondering. Who tried to kill us?"

"Alex, they were trying to kill you. It was one of the many enemies you've made. Figuring out which one isn't so important. I'm wondering how they found out where you would be. You can't be trusted to be out on your own. If I hadn't been there, you would've been killed."

"Who would've known ahead of time?" Briefly, he thought of the warning Daren gave him. Maleky shared a strange idea. Well more of a partial idea, but it had an odd feel to it. It seemed the Kimley man in his head was troubled by his own thought of who could've been responsible. Realizing his flock might be a help, Alex reached out to them via the AI on his scalp and the messaging system it had access to.

|A'idah, someone tried to kill me in the bubble bay as I left yesterday. We're both safe in the Tasties city, but ask around the flock if anyone mentioned me and Hheilea leaving to anyone else.|

The strength of her response almost made him choke again. |We heard. Zeghes and I should've gone with you. I've been worried about you. Zeghes and I talked to Ytell about you. It isn't right for us to be separated.|

After Alex recovered from his initial shock at the strength of her reply, he grinned at her obvious concern. Once again, he wished A'idah was the only girl he had to worry about. He knew she had confidence in him. She just wanted to face the dangers with him.

A'idah continued her message. |Ytell and our flock tried to find the person who tried to kill you. We didn't succeed, but we did find a suspicious group of Winkles and Lepercauls. Titan was there. I think one of them attacked you. We got into a fight with them.|

|What? Is everyone okay?|

|Ytell stopped the fight before we could get any satisfaction. He let those horrible people leave. I'm still mad about it. Why do Amable and his team let such horrible creatures be a part of the Academy?|

Alex responded. |I think he's taken help to defeat the deems wherever he could find it.|

|Yeah, that's obvious. I've got some good news. Today, our flock will do some training with you. I wish Zeghes and I could stay with you, but we have to keep going to our classes. Make sure you protect Hheilea, although from what I've heard about her actions in the Gragdreath battle, I think she's more likely to protect you. You tend to jump into dangerous situations without thinking. See you soon.|

"Hheilea, my flock is coming out today."

"You better finish eating then." She put her own spoon down and stood to her feet.

Hheilea's movement must've alerted the nurse. She bounded out of her interior room. "Good, you're done eating. Well, one of you is. Alex, hurry up and finish. You're going out to meet your flock. Hheilea, come with me."

The nurse headed for the door and Hheilea followed. "Have a good day, Alex. I'll ask my brother, Hymeron, if he has any ideas how someone would've known. He might've told someone."

"Thanks, you too." The door shut as he thought of her words about Hymeron. How would Hymeron have known? The answer came from himself and from a troubled Maleky. Hheilea must've told him. Alex didn't want to ask the Kimley in his head about why he was troubled. He also didn't want the thoughts his own mind surfaced. Hadn't Daren said something about Hymeron being a threat? How could he be a threat? Hheilea's brother was a friend and just a kid.

A'idah was probably right. It had been Titan or someone else of the horrible people they'd found at the Bubble Bay.

Chapter Nine
Hymeron and Suspicions

Alex didn't want the thoughts his mind gave him. How could Hymeron be a threat? Hheilea's brother was just a kid and a friend. When Alex first met Hymeron, he'd been a troublesome prankster, but just a kid with a bad attitude, except he'd known so much. He'd provided the snake-like Zorms with supplies. How did a kid do those things? He also knew a secret way of getting around on the spaceship, the Coratory. Alex remembered Hymeron's warning not to tell about it. In fact, the boy hadn't warned him, he'd threatened him.

Everything began to fit together in Alex's mind. He pushed his food away not wanting to eat anymore. His ideas roiled the food he'd already eaten. Hymeron was his friend. How could he be a danger to Earthlings?

A troubled thought from Maleky splattered into Alex's already unhappy thoughts. *Don't blame him. His life's been terrible. You forget what Amable told you. Teenagers are capable of all kinds of things. As a Kimley, Hymeron is a teenager. I started gathering my power at his age.* Maleky's thoughts and Alex's continued swirling about in a sickening dance. The door opening gave him a welcome interruption.

Windelli entered. "Are you done eating? We should get going. There are things I need to talk with you about."

Gratefully, Alex left his food and his own thoughts. "What's up?"

She replied as they left the room. "We're working with Amable to figure out how to get you back climbing the mountain. You're going to need another String Sword, but there's multiple dangers including one new one. Amable wants people guarding you all the time, but he doesn't have the extra people. Your flock can't do it because of their training."

"What's the new danger?"

"I'll get to that. In the short term, when the people of the academy learn about Daren supplying help because you saved him, they'll be happy with you. With the new ships temporarily replacing the damaged Coratory and the added funds taking care of the budget problems you're going to be a hero, but once some time passes, people will start to think of the risk you took and remembering who is in you. They'll go back to not trusting you. Some will think Maleky made a gamble to gain something which just didn't work out or you were responsible, but took an insane risk potentially ruining everyone's efforts here. When that time comes, you'll be in more danger.

"Speaking of danger, I've been trying to find out who tried to kill you, but no one knows. Ytell said they found a group of angry Lepercauls and Winkles. He didn't think any of them had been involved. They'd just arrived and were looking for you. You Earthlings have a very special enemy in Titan. He's a nasty bag of worms. Unfortunately, there's a new thing I've learned about your dangers. I think it's the worst thing you need to be concerned about."

"What's that?"

Windelli looked at Alex. "There's a bounty out on you. Unfortunately, it appears that a group of very dangerous assassins has taken the bounty on. They don't fail. They are known by their dreadlocks and are called Dreads. Tomorrow, we'll get you started on a training program designed to help you survive an attack by one of their assassins. In the meantime, you'll need to be watching out for another attempt on your life."

Alex quietly followed her through the maze of pastel tunnels. Curious about the musky smell, he asked, "What is that smell?"

"Smell? Describe it."

"It's kinda musky."

Hymeron and Suspicions

Windelli laughed. "All of us Tasties can't live in this city for as long as we have without imparting our odor to it. Of course, we don't smell it."

Alex laughed too, but cut it off at the worry it could be impolite to laugh about how others smelled. In the friendlier and more relaxed atmosphere, he went back to thinking quietly. Danger and threats to his life weren't new. He could deal with them.

She interrupted his thoughts. "Gursha, your nurse, is concerned about something else. After the battle, the injuries, and the loss of your friend you're going to have some problems. One result, you've probably already noticed is how your emotions, thoughts, or current situation will trigger very vivid memories, flashbacks. There's more to this, but I think I've given you enough to deal with for the moment."

Yeah, those memories were too vivid. Alex needed to know more about this problem. Maybe he could— Concentrating on what she'd said, he rounded a corner, and bright light assaulted his eyes. Stumbling, he almost fell, and he reached a hand out to the rough wall to catch himself. Ahead, sunlight poured in through large windows. The roof above arched sharply up. The ceiling came to a sharp peak high above. Squinting against the brightness, Alex could see two large doors fifty feet ahead and through the windows fields down below bathed in the bright sunshine.

Windelli stopped beside him. "Stupid isn't it?"

"Huh?"

She said, "You really need to speak with more eloquence. *Huh?* Really doesn't sound good. I know you're more intelligent. I'm talking about the design of this hallway. Walking around a turn into bright light is a perfect setup for predators."

"Huh? I'm, I'm sorry. I meant to ask. Do you have predators down here?" How could that work?

Windelli turned to look at him. "We don't have carnivores down here waiting to eat us, but there is what I call other kinds of predators in life. We've already talked about some who want to kill you."

51

Alex shuddered at her words. He knew all too well of others who wanted to kill him.

"Also, there are bullies everywhere including big ones who don't think about narrow ledges and bump into you or give you a shove. The result can be the same."

Alex remembered the bump from the big, muttering Tasty.

"You don't want to be afraid all of the time either."

At those words Alex grinned. After all his experiences, he knew he could handle danger. "I don't need to worry about fear."

"Oh, but you do. During your last battle you had someone you cared for who was in danger and could be killed when you killed the Gragdreath."

"How do you know about Twyla?" at the mention of her name his heart clenched in pain. The nightmare of that memory stirred in his heart and mind.

"It was your fear for her that caused another to die, and yet you didn't save Twyla either. In her last moments, Twyla celebrated life. You have to accept the past and move on, or it's going to affect your ability to use your vapuc to sense the future. Don't let emotions cloud your view, and I don't think it's wise to consider fear so easy to deal with. You're choosing to ignore something that did and will cause you problems."

Alex knew he hadn't said the right thing about fear, but he couldn't bring himself to acknowledge out loud how debilitating fear could be and had been for him. Before he could think of a way to respond to her statement, Windelli continued talking.

"Your eyes should've adjusted to the brighter light. Let's continue. Remember, in the future, whenever you move into a new and especially strange situation to give yourself time to adjust before moving farther into the new environment. You're going to continue having new experiences and need to learn how to deal with them better. You also need some help with how you're dealing with fear. Right now, you're at a character-changing point in dealing with your fear for others. The ability to love is amazing and wonderful, but it brings with it pain. You've let that pain control you. Our philosophy of *celebrating life* is the direction I hope and pray you go. Another, easier option is to harden your heart. That would be a disaster."

Her words and the associated ideas swirled in his mind as she led the way out into the fields. He hurried after her, gazing around at the new experience. Alex caught glimpses of an animal, black and white striped, moving in the field. Windelli made a turn onto a narrower path between rows of cabbages, mixed with summer squash and other vegetables. This path took them closer to the black and white animal. In his hurry, Alex almost stepped onto a long yellow squash.

A squirrel raced past almost tripping Alex. Another one came right behind it, and Alex stepped to the left to avoid it. He didn't want to go right. That would've brought him next to the black and white animal. He stepped onto something hard and stumbled trying not to fall. Almost stepping on another plant, he hopped over it instead.

A rabbit jumped out of the plants yelling, "Watch where you're going."

Something squealed, down where his foot landed in the plants. Alex hopped to the right, but a squishing sound showed he'd squashed one of the squashes. His arms windmilled, as he tried not to fall. With a crash into the plants, he lost the battle. A thumping sound by his head interrupted his groans. He opened his eyes to see the rear end of the black and white animal.

The skunk said, "You almost landed on me. I've got half a mind to blast you. It would teach you to be more careful."

"I'm sorry. I'm sorry. I'll be more careful."

"Okay, but next time there'll be no warnings. I'll blast you so good your mama won't even want you around."

Trying not to think about the pain of having no mother or father alive to want him around, Alex carefully got back to his feet. "Windelli, could you go slower for a bit. I'm not used to walking through a field with animals running around."

"Good idea. Remember, be careful with new experiences. This time, it'll mean we'll have to go faster later on, but that'll be fun. I enjoy flying fast. Come on."

Flying fast? Going slower and looking for movement in the plants, Alex followed. Something about her idea of fun bothered him, but he decided instead of asking about it to ask about all of the creatures in the field. "What are all these animals doing?"

"They've decided to try civilization. Their jobs are weeding, pest control, and harvesting. Not all of them adjust well to having work."

Alex wondered about the idea of animals trying civilization and how much of a change the squirts living behind ears and translating everything were going to make back on Earth. He also started to notice a feeling of unease. He worried it might be associated with her idea of fun. Flying fast? Occasionally, they passed other creatures. Some spoke briefly, and others obviously tried to act as if they were working hard when they realized Windelli walked through the fields. A fat rat lay on the ground resting. It looked up at them. "I've hurt my leg and can't work anymore today."

Windelli said, "Okay. I'll call a medic to come help you."

The rat flexed its leg. "You know. I think it's better. I'll try working again, at least for a while."

"Good."

Alex grinned at the conversation. He started to ask Windelli about it, but she turned off the narrow path onto a wider walkway going straight out toward a distant uneven edge and started to run. Alex shifted to a run, while trying to stay in the middle of the wider path.

In the distance, trees rose up over the edge of the field. Soon, the running revealed bushes, trees, and grasses growing on the other side of a straight edge. Where were they going? When would he be meeting his flock for training? Alex looked around in concern. He felt more than just unease. In fact, something in the future frightened him. "Where are we going?"

Hymeron and Suspicions

Windelli stopped running and sat up on her haunches. She turned her head back to look at Alex. "Out into the Wild Lands. Take my paw."

Alex hesitated to obey. His sense of the future warned of something very scary about to happen. Not wanting to appear frightened, he went ahead and grasped the hand/paw. Windelli grasped his hand back with a very strong grip. Gladly, accepting a distraction from the fear, Alex wondered about the strange feeling of the unusual appendage. With a tug on his arm, she pulled him up into the air.

An involuntary yell burst from him. "Ahhh!"

After the initial jerk off the ground, some kind of force lifted his body up level to Windelli's. Overcoming his initial surprise, Alex calmed down. They were moving slowly. It would be okay. Actually, he felt like a superman soaring through the air.

Feeling a sudden acceleration, Alex squinted against the increasing wind. He tried to see what was ahead of them and hollered. "What? How are you—?"

Her answer interrupted the question. "I don't really like using bubbles. I prefer the wind in my fur. It's better. Don't you agree?"

He choked on an unspoken warning. The trees, the trees at the edge of the field, they were going to hit the trees ahead of them. Alex tried to speak, but with another burst of acceleration, the two of them soared higher. How was Windelli lifting them? It didn't feel like an artificial gravity machine. Instead, it felt as if both of them were just... flying through the air. Then, they were higher and just below them the tree tops whipped past. Not being in control, he didn't want to consider his sense of the future. Blinking tears and trying to see where they were going, while desperately hanging onto her paw, Alex tried to answer with confidence. "Yeah, better." The squeak as he yelled probably gave away his real state of mind.

His AI must've sensed his terror. *What's going on? I'm not going to get hurt again? Please, don't let me get hurt. Not again. No. No. No. No.*

Alex didn't want them to get hurt either. He also didn't want to come across as a coward. His AI's thoughts weren't helping. Alex tried to ignore them even as he tried to ignore and control his own terror.

The first part of the trip seemed to take forever. By squinting his eyes and looking away from the wind Alex found he could see. With a gulp, he saw the ground was a long way below. His grip on her paw seemed way too weak. The wind was too strong to talk to the crazy Tasty. Alex swallowed, trying to keep from losing the small breakfast he'd had. |Windelli, couldn't we go down closer to the ground.|

She answered. |I could take us down, but is that really a good idea. I it's nice up here.|

In desperation and realizing it would make its fear greater, Alex begged his AI if it could use a gravity generator to save them if they fell. Briefly, he considered what he could sense of the future. Lack of control, fear, and danger screamed at him. Another feeling lurked just past those, but he didn't consider it.

He got an even more frightened reply from his AI. *No. There aren't any in range. What are we going to do? I'm too young to die. It's your fault. You're always getting us hurt.* The AI didn't stop.

Alex often forgot his AI was just a baby and got frightened easily. He didn't believe it himself, but he tried to calm and encourage his AI. *We'll be okay.* Alex tried to control his own feelings. He hadn't sensed injury or death. He could deal with this fear. He breathed slower and deeper trying to calm himself.

Hheilea's message ruined his efforts. |Alex, are you okay. I'm sensing terrible fear and danger. What are you doing?|

Unwisely, he answered very honestly. |I'm flying through the air without a bubble, and going as fast as I've ever gone in one of them.|

|That sounds crazy. Can't you stop? Where are you?|

The fear roared back. |It's crazy. I'm being towed over a forest by Windelli. I think she's nuts.|

Hymeron and Suspicions

Hheilea's tone changed in her responding message. |Oh, I trust her. You'll be okay. You're just frightened of a new experience. I'm surprised at you.|

What? Just frightened? He'd like to see her trying this. He didn't respond to his friend. Instead, Alex decided to beg Windelli to go lower and maybe slow down.

Before he could, she messaged him. |I'll take us lower.|

Alex gave a sigh of relief as the tree tops racing by drew nearer. Now, they would have a chance to survive this crazy trip.

Noticing the wind wasn't quite as hard and the tree tops weren't racing by quite as fast, Alex gave another sigh of relief. Starting to feel better, he tried again to control his fear. Everything was going to be okay.

Windelli dropped even lower. She zigzagged under and over branches, back and forth between bushes. Alex's stomach dropped. He screamed when they went around another bush. Directly ahead, a massive tree trunk waited with deadly doom. Alex's eyes popped wide in terror.

Chapter Ten
Dangerous Mice

Windelli tugged on his wrist. In his terror, Alex hadn't noticed when she'd switched to holding onto him. With her tug, the trunk, bark, and a bush spun past all too close to his face. Way too late, he shut his eyes. The terror kept him from throwing up and breathing.

The world stopped spinning, deceleration hit, and he fell face down on the ground. Alex didn't want to get-up from the soft grass. He wanted to kiss the ground or thank God for the miracle of still being alive. He didn't need enemies trying to kill him. He had this crazy Tasty. What a wild name. Why were they called that? It couldn't be because of— His thoughts didn't want to go there. As he hugged the ground, Alex suddenly realized members of his flock spoke around him.

"Zeghes, do you think our friend is going to say hi to us, or is he going to scream again?"

"... like more fun than surfing in a wave behind a boat or using bubbles. I don't know why he screamed."

"... scream? He was just flying."

"Alex, are you okay?"

Embarrassment washed the terror away. Breathing deep, Alex forced himself to slowly stand to his feet. He started to thank Windelli for the ride, but he spotted her rapidly leaving through the air. "I'm okay."

He took a step toward his friends and stumbled. Standing still until the world stopped moving felt like a better idea.

A'idah hurried to Alex and grasped his arm to steady him. "Are you sure you're okay?"

Dangerous Mice

"Uh, yeah. I just need to stand still for a bit."

Ytell, the seven-foot tall alien raptor, their flock leader, ruffled his feathers and said, "Now that we're all together, I'll go over what we're doing today." He paused, stretched his wings and turned around.

Alex noticed they stood at the edge of the grassy safe area surrounding the Earthling dorms. Other flocks of Earthlings with their flock leaders stood spread out around the edge too. Looking back at his flock, Alex noticed Osamu carried something on his back.

Ytell said, "Remember my first lesson. Always be aware of your surroundings. Have you noticed the other flocks? Today, all of the Earthlings begin their study of what your home planet will become when the interstellar cloud of *dark matter* enters your solar system. You're going out into the Wild Lands. Remember, Alex doesn't have the extra vapuc abilities you have. Watch out for him. Take your time exploring and be cautious."

Taking a deep breath, Alex studied the area. Sunlight darted brilliantly from between low wispy clouds. The bushes and trees beyond the edge of the grass silently waited. No leaves moved, and no sounds came from them. Out there in the wild, he and his fellow flock members would finally learn about what Earth would have to deal with when *dark matter* entered the solar system.

Stumbling forward, Alex turned to see who had bumped him. Behind him, Zeghes nodded his head up and down.

Zeghes said. "I've just realized you were embarrassed. I'm sorry. I should've watched what I said. I know you're brave. That must've been a very scary ride."

"Thanks, Zeghes. I was embarrassed, and it was terribly frightening. We weren't in a bubble, and she went so fast and changed directions so quickly. I was getting sick, and then just before you saw me we were headed at a very fast speed directly at a massive tree. I thought she was going to kill me."

"I'm glad she didn't."

A'idah said, "Are you going to be okay?"

"Yeah, and I'm really excited about today's lesson."

Before anyone could say more, Ekbal, the boy from India, spoke. "We had an amazing class yesterday on how to make rocks erode faster, and that wasn't the coolest part. We learned how to make sand and clay turn back into rocks."

Alex looked at him in shock.

A'idah grimaced. "Yeah, rocks. He and Osamu really got into it."

Ekbal asked, "Alex, do you want to know how we can do it?"

Behind the small dark boy, A'idah frantically shook her head no.

"Uhm, I'd love to later, but right now I think we should pay attention to this lesson. I'm excited about it too."

A'idah asked, "How come?"

"This is what it's really about," Alex said. "We've been distracted by the Winkle's evilness and their almost destroying this in their search for power and glory. The lessons we've had at the Academy are important, but there's so much to learn. We've barely started to study and prepare for this—"

At a loud roar, Alex stopped talking. With heart pounding, he looked around trying to see where it came from. Some of the other flocks had already started out into the Wild Land. "That, that's what I'm talking about. Remember what Ytell said about the exact same type of roar. That was a mouse."

"Forget the shark patrols," Zeghes said. "I should go on a mouse patrol."

A'idah standing nearby snorted.

"What's so funny," Zeghes said, going higher. "I don't see the mouse beast. How big is it? Do they have bigger teeth than a shark?"

Alex laughed at his friend's misunderstanding. Ekbal must have overheard, he laughed too. Osamu turned red from suppressed laughter. A'idah had gained control over the humor until a guffaw escaped her, and then she held her sides shaking with laughter.

Dangerous Mice

Zeghes said, "What is it. What's so funny? Is a mouse so big and dangerous that I would look ludicrous trying to fight it?"

Alex managed to say, "No, not so big," before he laughed even harder.

Skyler said, "They can be dangerous. Sometimes they eat eggs or babies."

Sabu said, "This is stupid. Mice are prey. They are little, much smaller than any of us. They are not dangerous. I would never be frightened by a mouse."

A confused Zeghes dipped up, down, and around the group.

"They are too dangerous," Skyler said, flapping over to Sabu. "I've heard of parents returning to the nest to find a mouse eating their babies."

"Small, prey," Zeghes said, and then he laughed. "I get it. It is funny."

Just then, another loud roar similar to a lion's came from the taller grass and bushes. Members of one of the flocks came running and flying out of the woods. Their yells carried to Alex.

"Is it after us?"

"Hurry."

"I think it caught..."

The laughing stopped.

Sabu said, in a quiet, annoyed, and complaining tone, "but, it's just a mouse. No one should be frightened by a mouse."

"Come on," Osamu said. "We need to help. Alex, take the lead."

Alex was used to the oldest member of the flock encouraging him to be the leader. He hadn't always enjoyed it or understood why Osamu did it, but after his experiences in the last year he was more than ready to accept that role. Before he said anything, Alex checked for Ytell, and saw him watching them from up on a hill. "Okay, we'll form three groups. Osamu, Skyler, and Ekbal will be the first. Levitate with your AIs using the local gravity generators. Get over there and stay high. Skyler, you can just fly. Try and see what's happening. Be careful.

We don't know what type of vapuc these mice are using. Remember the giant earthworms. There could be something strange and actually dangerous about these mice. Zeghes and A'idah follow them at a lower height, but stay back and prepare to help either them or my group. Sabu, stay close to me. Let's go."

Sabu said, "I still can't think of mice as being dangerous."

Ahead of them, a cat bolted onto the short grass and raced up the hill covering one of the dormitory buildings. A wide eyed teenager was next. Alex grabbed him.

The boy tried to tear himself lose, but Alex refused to let go. "Can someone do the calming vapuc on this guy?"

Alex continued talking just to the boy. "It's okay. You're safe. This is the edge of the short grass. Remember, Amable told us it would be safe here."

The boy relaxed even as Alex heard Osamu message via his AI. |Alex, you can let go of him.|

Alex released his grip. "What did you see?"

"It was terrible. A mouse as big as an elephant," the teen age boy said. "I think it was going to catch—"

"You should've stayed to help your flockmate," Sabu said, ears back and tail lashing. "A mouse, you were frightened by a mouse?"

Taking a deep breathe, the boy said, "Your right. I was just so scared. You don't understand."

A loud voice called, "Flock members come to me."

"I've got to go, thanks," the boy said.

In his mind, Alex heard Ekbal. |Alex, we don't see anything.|

|Okay| Alex responded to Ekbal and then to both groups in the air he messaged. |Sabu and I will head in on foot. Keep watch from overhead. The boy told us they saw a mouse the size of an elephant. You should be able to spot that from above. I suspect it has to be some kind of a temporary thing similar to the giant earthworm.

Sabu still quite annoyed couldn't stay quiet. "A mouse as big as an elephant? What's an elephant? I can't believe a mouse can be that frightening. I refuse to be frightened of a mouse."

Dangerous Mice

Alex started to go first but motioned for Sabu to go ahead of him. He couldn't get any real sense of danger right ahead of them.

Still, there was something fearful, but not particularly dangerous. It didn't make sense to him. Alex trusted Sabu's reactions to keep her safe, and he doubted she'd be easily frightened. Grass rustled on either side as they carefully moved forward. Somehow, Sabu went through the grass with hardly any sound at all. A twig snapped under Alex's foot.

Sabu turned her head back to silently snarl at him.

Responding to Sabu via AI, Alex said, |Sorry.|

Turning around, Sabu froze. One paw in the air and ears focused on a large clump of grass waving gently a little ways in front of her. The end of her long fluffy tail slowly twitched.

|There are mice in front of us.| Sabu slowly gathered herself together like a large spring, her tail twitched back and forth. She was going to pounce—

"Roar!"

In front of them, a huge mouse appeared. Sabu sprang to the side disappearing into the tall grass. Fear flooded Alex's mind. The screams of Skyler sounded above him.

|A huge mouse just appeared out of nowhere in front of Sabu| Osamu, A'idah, and Ekbal reported at once.

Their voices echoed in his mind. Those voices in his head took away the worst of the fear. Alex didn't think the mouse was moving. He decided to try talking to it. "Hey, we're not here to try and kill you or eat you. We just want to talk."

Another roar, just not as loud filled the air. A quiet voice said, "Knock it off, he's just standing there."

The giant mouse said, "But that big cat was going to pounce on us."

Alex said to the flock, |Stay back everyone. I think I'm getting a conversation going here.| To the mice, he said, "I'm going to sit down here. Okay? No one is going to attack you."

"Do you want a civilized moment?" came the first of the voices.

"Yes," Alex said, sitting down slowly, as the huge mouse disappeared.

"No tricks," said the second more aggressive voice, "or we'll find where you sleep and chew your ears off."

"We couldn't do that. Stop being so stupid." Then a fat mouse and a skinny mouse jumped out of the grass.

"We chewed the ropes off that—"

"Hello, that was a very impressive mouse you created," Alex said.

"We can also make you want to run away," the bigger mouse said.

A wave of fear struck Alex. Breathing deep he fought it. |Flock members calm me please. One of them is trying to scare me.| A sense of calm washed away the fear.

"You're not scared," the smaller mouse said. "He's an idiot. I told him to stop scaring other animals all the time. It's going to stop working with predators."

"I scared the cat," the big one said, puffing his small chest out.

A growl came from the direction Sabu had gone. The two mice disappeared back into the grass.

|Hello, everyone, this is Ytell. There's a small hill a ways past where the mice are. Everyone join me there.|

Using his AI's ability to use a local artificial gravity generator, Alex levitated out of the tall grass. That allowed him to see the hill. The occasional rock stuck out of the ground, and a few trees grew on it. Soon all of the flock had arrived.

Ytell landed on a large flat rock atop the hill. "Get comfortable everyone. We're going to talk. You all saw how the mice have learned to use *Illusion* and *State of Mind* vapucs."

"I shouldn't have gotten scared," Sabu said, interrupting, with her tail lashing back and forth, and ears flat against her head.

"Alex, why did you let Sabu take the lead?" Ytell asked.

"Because she has incredible senses," Alex said. "I knew she's tough enough and reacts fast enough to stay safe."

"Sabu, you reacted just the way Alex expected you would," Ytell said. "It gave him time to consider the situation. The threat was focused on you, not him. If it was a threat focused on Alex, I'm sure you would've protected him."

"The fear was incredible," Alex said. "It was only the team talking in my head that helped me to stay and deal with it."

"This has been a great lesson for all of you," Ytell said. "*Dark matter* is affecting plants and animals around you just as it does the flock. Many of those things will be much more dangerous than normal. Alex isn't affected by *dark matter* except for his feelings about the future. That has been accented by his unique experiences with the Kimleys. Everyone else in the flock can do multiple types of vapuc, some different and others the same. The mice can probably do only two forms of vapuc. We're going to run into some other situations. Let's go."

For a while, the flock moved slowly through the vegetation not finding anything stranger than a bush waving its berries at them. The most prominent object was another big, flat rock on another hill. It was cracked in half, and the two halves rested on other stones underneath. Something about it and the red stain on it made Alex think of a story he'd read.

Sabu interrupted his thoughts. |Be quiet. Something large is grazing up ahead. It's past that tall tree in front of us.|

|Flock, all of you need to observe this carefully.| Ytell messaged all of them. |I'll have Sabu stalk this animal after everyone is ready, but she needs to be very careful. Sabu, you'll need to leap to safety at some point. It uses lightning.|

|Ekbal, use vapuc to make the rest of the flock small. Everyone work together to perch in that tree over there.|

After everyone was perched, Sabu started forward, ears perked and tail gently twitching. From above, the flock could see glimpses of a bull elk browsing. It looked peaceful even with its many forked antlers. Below, they could barely see Sabu slinking through the woods. Her dabbled black and white coat seemed to blend in with the shadows. The bull jerked his head up looking around. Sabu froze.

"What's out there?" the bull asked.

A bird spoke up, "Oh majestic one, there is something creeping under my tree toward you."

A snarl came from Sabu, and then a flash of light followed by a boom.

|Everyone, retreat back to that big flat rock.|

Again the flock gathered. Sabu arrived shaking her paws. "That was as close as I want to get to its lightning strike."

"Back on Earth, a hunter would be in for a rude surprise," Osamu said, shaking his head.

"All predators will have to adapt," Ytell said. "Animals that respond to the influence of vapuc will over time become more prevalent, and all animals will become smarter to deal with the increased dangers."

"How do you know all of this?" Ekbal asked.

"It's happened before," Ytell said.

"How did the elk understand the birds," Ekbal asked.

"Most animals of your planet understood each other to a very limited degree. That has been changed by the squirts you and everyone else has. Once squirts arrive at a planet, they rapidly spread throughout the biospheres. This results in almost all species of any size having a real understanding of each other's communication."

"That bird sounded smart," A'idah said. "Are all animals going to be like Zeghes, Skyler, and Sabu?"

"All creatures are smart in their own ways," Ytell answered. "It's just that some are going to get smarter, because they will have new learning experiences from the squirt helping with communication. Remember, Earth's going to have chaos and confusion during this time. These changes in understanding, intelligence, and vapuc abilities from *dark matter* will make life more dangerous on Earth. This is a big part of what your training is for. Osamu, can you roll out the bubble generator pad you have. We'll use bubbles to travel toward the crater wall."

Dangerous Mice

Pulling the tube off his back Osamu unrolled a green rectangular pad with a yellow circle on it. Everyone took turns standing in the circle as a bubble encased them.

Before Alex stepped onto the platform, Ytell stopped him. "Wait, Alex." A thin scaly arm reached out of the bird's feathers. In its long fingered hand rested a small black disc. "Take this and put it into a pocket."

Automatically, Alex obeyed even as a sharp feeling of frustration swept through him. He hesitantly stepped onto the platform. What was that feeling about? Ytell wouldn't set him up for a problem or danger except... All too quickly he felt the familiar tingle as the bubble encased him. Without thinking, he lifted the bubble into the air to join the others.

Even as Ytell talked, Maleky whispered in Alex's mind. *Remember when he set you up to almost get killed by Titan?*

Alex only partially listened to Ytell's talk as they began to move together through the air. The feeling of frustration grew stronger, but now he felt an undercurrent of danger. Not again.

Chapter Eleven
Forgetting or Remembering What's Important

Ytell's lecture continued, "We're using the bubbles because we are going much farther than you can levitate using your AI or vapuc. Remember, your AI gets tired using artificial gravity generators. Also, doing things with vapuc will wear you out. The first sign of over doing vapuc will be a headache. In extreme cases, people have died from overusing vapuc. Always try to keep a reserve of energy in case of a need. I'm using a bubble and not flying for a similar reason. We are traveling to the north side of Earth's wedge. Each of the seven wedges averages about two hundred and sixty-five miles wide. Today, we'll be traveling one hundred and twenty-two miles to the nearest edge. Alex should recognize it. First, we're going to make one more side trip."

At those words, Ytell shifted direction toward the towering crater wall. In the foreground, foothills rose, climbing up to rows of rugged mountains above the forest. Behind them, loomed the incredible crater walls.

The view took Alex's mind from the danger he sensed. He craned his neck trying to see the crater rim high above the clouds.

A contrite message from Hheilea reminded him of his terrifying rollercoaster ride through the air. |Alex, I'm sorry for how I must've sounded to you. I meant it to be encouraging. The Tasties really are wise, and I don't think Windelli would risk your life. From what I know of Tasties, she probably had an ulterior motive for scaring you.|

Forgetting or Remembering What's Important

Grudgingly, Alex reconsidered what had happened during his morning with Windelli. She had been giving him lessons as they walked, and he'd told her that fear didn't bother him. |You're right. I set myself up for that lesson. I told her fear didn't bother me. Sometimes, I'm pretty stupid.|

Hheilea's laughter bubbled in her next message. |Sometimes?| The laughter died away, and she continued. |The truth is when it comes right down to needing to take action you don't have any trouble with fear. I think you're amazing.|

|Thanks, and don't worry about it.| Hheilea was a great friend. He thought again of what she'd just said. Hheilea didn't know about how he'd let fear stop him from taking action and how that had led to the loss of another friend. Alex couldn't bring himself to let her know.

Sabu interrupted his thoughts. "Hey, Alex, watch this." She jumped out of her bubble and fell through the air. Her tail whipped around behind her.

A yell tore Alex's eyes from her. At the next sight, his mouth fell open. Ekbal jumped out of his own bubble and fell with Sabu.

Alex thrust his hands against the wall of his own bubble moving it toward them. He would be too late. They were going to die. "What are you doing?!" This must be the danger he'd been sensing, but he hadn't reacted in time to save them.

Ekbal fell next to Sabu and swatted hand against paw. They separated, and then their two bubbles arced back to them. Each of them fell back into a bubble.

Alex slowed, and his heart rate started to return to normal. There wasn't any danger. What was wrong with his sense of the future, or was it something else he needed to be watching for?

Sabu and Ekbal's bubbles turned the falls into two graceful arcs rising back up to the rest of the flock.

Alex said, "You guys scared me to death."

Ekbal laughed and said, "We learned we can control the bubbles motions after we jump out. Going over the sea to classes and back we've been playing with it."

"How did you ever think of it?"

Ekbal said, "Sabu discovered it by accident. She and Skyler were playing around, and Sabu jumped out of her bubble. She started tumbling through the air toward the sea down below and let out a roar for her bubble. It arched down and gracefully caught her."

"Once we all stopped laughing, I had to try it. It's fun. You should try it. Just don't forget your bubble."

Alex nodded his head. "I've done this before, but not for fun. This should be easy after that experience."

Going up above the rest of the flock, he jumped out. At first Alex tumbled, but he quickly remembered his freefall experience on the cloudberry planet. Relaxing, with his arms and legs out, he let the wind stabilize his fall.

He gave his flockmates thumbs up as he blasted past them and their bubbles. The air whistled past, and the ground rushed up toward him. Alex hadn't noticed how enjoyable it was to freefall on the cloudberry planet. They'd been involved in a life and death struggle. On that planet, the combination of higher air density and strong thermals meant a skydiver could actually go up.

Busy in his recollections and playing with the wind rushing past him, Alex hadn't thought about the obvious fact he was falling and falling a long way. Suddenly, he noticed how quickly the ground was approaching. He'd forgotten the all-important part of having his bubble arc around to catch him. "Ah!"

"Hello. Want a ride?"

Stopping his scream at the voice he recognized, Alex looked to the left at A'idah in her bubble just before the bubble gobbled him up. The wall immediately changed to hold him inside even as the g-forces of the bubble cancelling his fall pressed him and A'idah together against the flat floor. It took him a minute to be able to breathe easily again.

Meanwhile, A'idah said in a very matter-of-fact voice, "Zeghes and I discussed who should save you. He conceded it was my turn. Seriously, how do you survive without him or me around?"

Forgetting or Remembering What's Important

Alex remembered too many times of not just A'idah saving him, but also Hheilea and Twarbie. He decided it would be wisest to just not answer her question.

The next time he dove, Alex played with the wind whistling past him. He remembered his skydiving experience with Daren and using his body as an airfoil mimicked Ekbal's moves. They all ended with a rousing game of tag. Diving back into his bubble just tens of feet above the tree tops, Alex sat down on the floor gasping from the excitement and exercise. He barely noticed his bubble arcing in-between two tall trees and presumed his sense of fear was just from the exciting time he'd just shared.

Ytell messaged, |Okay, everyone, come closer so I can talk to you without shouting.| He waited until the flock closed in tighter to continue. "We brought from Earth samples of different viruses, bacteria, prions, and many different kinds of protozoans. This was done to learn what changes *dark matter* might cause in their behavior. This knowledge will be part of your study during the next eight years. It's also very important for keeping you alive. You'll also learn about the complicated process we had to go through to make this arrangement. We had to get permission from the higher order creatures for experiments which was very time consuming and expensive, but PETA, the people for the ethical treatment of aliens, and some other alien's rights organizations follow what we do and how we do it very carefully. Some of them are very against this experimenting and want to shut it down. Because of how important it is we must be very careful. We'll also share what we've learned with your medical staff back on Earth. To show you how strange and deadly some of the pathogens become we have an example for you to see today. Be careful not to land anywhere near where I'm taking you."

The view distracted Alex from the words of Ytell. Below them, the solid forest transitioned into a mix of grass lands, isolated clumps of bushes, and a few scattered trees. Past the grass lands were hills, rugged mountains and then the miles high crater wall reared up into the sky. He had to look almost straight up see the crater's rim.

A'idah messaged him. |Alex, I can't wait until we're done with this training exercise. I'm going to use a bush. Keep the rest of the flock away, but don't tell them what I'm doing. Just say I'm hovering over some flowers. Okay?| Her bubble slowed and angled down to a thick clump of bushes.

Alex slowed his movement. What was she talking about using a bush? Again his sense of danger bothered him. Was she going to be in danger? Alex turned his bubble to follow her. |A'idah, I don't understand. What are you doing?| Alex didn't like the danger he felt. Maybe it hadn't been about the skydiving. He should warn her. What she's doing could be dangerous.

|Alex!|

Her mental tone of frustration halted his movement toward her and his thoughts of warning her.

|I've got to pee.|

|What? Ohhh.| Embarrassed, Alex flipped his bubble around, stopped thinking of A'idah, and made sure to keep from looking toward her. He slowly moved toward the rest of the flock.

Ytell's annoyed message cut through his embarrassment. |Alex and A'idah, what are you two doing? Get back over here with the rest.|

She'd kill him if he told. |We're just looking at something. We'll join the rest of the flock right now.|

Maleky again whispered in his mind. *Aren't these feelings just like when your friend sacrificed herself to save you? Which of your friends will it be this time? Maybe A'idah is in danger. You should tell Ytell what she did.*

A'idah's bubble blew past him. She rubbed at an arm. |Come on, Alex, we better catch up. Thanks.|

At their words, Alex's feelings grew much worse. Not sure of what to do he sped up to fly beside her. Together they rejoined the rest just in time to hear Ytell starting another lecture.

Forgetting or Remembering What's Important

"Down below you'll see a gathering of different creatures of Earth. They're having a civilized moment where very basic rules of civilization are followed. The ability for better communication from the squirts living at everyone's ears allows for this change to animals in your world. This gathering has one very dangerous part to it. There are some creatures in this group who are infected with one of the rabies viruses. It is making them very friendly. Like many effects of *dark matter*, we don't know what causes this neurological symptom. After a period of time the virus causes a dramatic change in behavior. Those infected become very violent, scratching and biting everyone they can. This is when the virus is transmitted to new hosts."

A'idah bumped her bubble against his. Her voice radiated concern. "What's wrong?"

Alex said, "I don't know. Something—"

Ytell continuing his lecture overrode their conversation. Alex just shrugged at A'idah and focused on listening to the flock leader.

"On Earth, your medical science can't cure rabies once neurological symptoms develop. We can cure it, but it is very painful and can leave some lasting effects, which are expensive and time consuming to remediate."

Ekbal asked, "What about these animals?"

A'idah said, "You're turning pale. Somethings wrong."

Alex started to answer, but his bubble abruptly changed course. He lost his balance falling against the wall of the bubble. Pushing off the wall to stand back up, Alex looked around in concern, readying a message to send to Ytell about his bubbles behavior.

Ytell said, "Ekbal, we've finished with the research on rabies and after the different flocks see how it's spread we're going to eradicate it and none too soon. I hate this disease. It's terrible to see its affects."

Before Alex could send the flock leader the message, he realized Ytell's bubble was right next to him and the leader messaged him.

|Alex, don't talk about the feelings you're having. Your sense of the future would ruin what your flock members will observe.|

"You—"

|Yes, I moved your bubble to prevent you from talking to A'idah. Now, be quiet and observe what happens. Try and control yourself. Only use messaging and only to me.|

Also, A'idah messaged him. |Alex, what happened with your bubble? What's going on? Are you okay?|

He answered just to her. |Something. I can't talk. Ytell's orders. Be on the lookout.|

Below, The grasslands and streams passed quickly by. Again they flew over a forest. Alex struggled to accept Ytell's leadership even as Maleky continued to torment him with thoughts of the other time.

From over the horizon, a strange feature came into view. All of the trees came to a stop in a line. Behind it, Alex could make out a patchwork of rectangular fields. It was the Tasties' fields. From their height, he could see the fields stretched from the sea up into the foothills of the mountains. Instead of studying the view, Alex remembered almost dying and his friend whom he hadn't been able to save. The time Maleky kept reminding him about. The time he didn't want to remember.

Alex tried to look at the view, but he saw the interior of the Academy. The Academy itself was a spherical structure with a diameter of almost two miles. It had structures for classes and other things on the inside of the sphere. In the middle was a vast open area over a mile across with creatures moving through the air on the air-paths in between those structures. The feelings he had now and then were too similar. Would this trigger one of those flashbacks Windelli had warned him of?

Back then, he'd known something bad was going to happen. A'idah had been concerned about him. She'd missed the real danger until too late, and his other friend paid the price. A'idah had thought his Winkle friend was the source of danger. They were standing on a platform attached to one of the structures when it all started. They were going to their first class in the use of *force*, another

Forgetting or Remembering What's Important

vapuc involving kinetic energy. The alien girl, his winkle friend, had been involved. She never should've used the red disk, the terribly dangerous enhancer. If only he could've saved her, instead she'd saved him from Titan.

Alex didn't want to remember. He didn't want the pain. He didn't want this flashback.

A'idah messaged him. |Alex, are you okay? Your face is white.|

She'd said the same thing in the past. In terror, he fell back into the past. Remembering what he'd told her and what had followed.

Chapter Twelve
Obeying or Giving in to Maleky

In that past, Alex again struggled to stay alive, and watched his friend's lifeless body fall.

"What's that?" Ekbal asked.

The voice brought Alex back to the present. His feelings of danger had grown stronger. He didn't want the past to repeat itself. He'd do anything to prevent it. Back then, his fellow flock members had been confused, thinking his Winkle friend was a danger to him.

The danger had always been Titan. The horrible little Lepercaul hated all of the Earthlings and Alex in particular.

"That's one of the wedge borders," Ytell said. "Inside the border are fields. Outside the borders are the Wild Lands. We shall land in that open area near the edge."

Coming closer to the border, the bubbles slowed and descended. Below, small figures could be seen moving about some of the fields.

"Who are those figures in the fields?" Ekbal asked, pointing down and hollering his question across the gap between his bubble and Ytell's bubble.

|Those are Tasties and other creatures working with them.| Ytell messaged. He added. |Be quiet. Only use messaging. They raise much of our food in the border fields, and they maintain the separation of the flora and fauna of each planet's wedge. The technology that keeps the wedges separated is of their design.|

At the mention of the Tasties name, Alex looked from the creatures below to Ytell, and the raptor's massive beak with its sharp hook caught his eyes. Tasties? What a name. Could this be another predator/prey relationship similar

Obeying or Giving in to Maleky

to the spider-like egers and the fly-like creatures? He remembered them all too well. Those memories didn't help his feelings at all. In growing desperation, he messaged Ytell. |Ytell, something's wrong. There's danger and it's getting stronger. You're not setting us up for another deadly training exercise?|

|Stay calm, Alex. I understand. It's going to be okay. I'll explain later.|

Growing terror from the past and present tore at him. He couldn't hear Maleky's thoughts and didn't notice A'idah trying to message him. His own thoughts kept growing louder. Patient! Calm! Ytell almost got Alex killed. He doesn't care if some of us die, just so long as the rest get the training to try and save Earth. But the budget problem is fixed. He doesn't have the same reason to take those risks.

Alex struggled between trying to control himself and considering what he could do to foil Ytell's plans. Together, the flock drifted over the trees and other vegetation just outside the fields. Ytell stopped, and everyone gathered around his bubble.

Sabu messaged with evident excitement. |There's a hunt going on just a little ways farther.|

Ytell messaged. |Everyone, stay high and be quiet. Follow me and look at that large tree. There's a Tasty under it.|

Slowly, quietly they maneuvered.

A'idah messaged him. |Are you better now? Ytell said not to bother you. Is this what you're sensing? It's just nature. Life can be harsh.|

A hunt? At that thought, Alex knew the source of the danger. Maybe Windelli was right, and I've let the past affect me. This isn't a danger to me or the flock. He spotted the hunt, and soon everyone stared at the scene. Below, the Tasty gathered something from low hanging branches of a pine tree. A tawny lithe form, similar in shape to Sabu, moved forward a paw at a time. Slowly, it moved closer. Its long tail, but not as bushy as Sabu's, twitched. In the bubbles, everyone quietly drifted lower. They were mesmerized by the scene below. Even Alex found himself staring. His feelings kept pounding at him and forced him to send a message. |Ytell! Something terrible's going to happen.|

Ekbal messaged his concern and fear of the developments below them. |What's going to happen? It isn't right to just watch. The Tasty is going to get hurt.|

The deadly looking stalk continued.

Osamu asked, |Should we warn the Tasty?|

A'idah, Sabu, and then Ytell all answered telling everyone not to interfere.

Alex couldn't help but think of some of the Tasties he'd met, the older one, Windelli, who'd saved him and the younger, cute, impulsive one.

Ekbal's comments and the answers made Alex glance away from the creeping feline predator to see the other's reactions. Poor Skyler opened and shut his beak. He would look to the left toward Sabu and then shuffle to the right in his own bubble. Alex himself looked back at the predator which slunk through the vegetation moving slower. At times, it would freeze staring at the Tasty. Alex glanced up at Sabu and caught both her and A'idah staring at the hunt with open mouths. Sabu panted with lips slightly pulled back revealing her sharp teeth.

Alex looked back down just in time to see the stalking cat pause. It was close to the Tasty. With a barely restrained gasp, Alex recognized the Tasty. It was Windelli. |Ytell, that's the one who came to get me and Hheilea. She saved our lives. I'm not going to—| His thoughts froze. He couldn't finish the message. He could feel the disc burning in his pocket. He wanted his bubble to go down and interrupt the hunt. Instead it drifted up against Ytell's.

Maleky's thoughts gave him a way out. *Ytell is using the disc to keep you from saving the Tasty. Surrender your will and body to me, and I'll get our bubble down there and save Windelli.*

The feline predator tensed. Alex saw it gathering its strength to pounce.

Obeying or Giving in to Maleky

Alex tried to surrender to Maleky. He'd do anything to save the Tasty even if she was crazy. He didn't think about the consequences.

Chapter Thirteen
Tested and Tried

Alex tried to surrender to his enemy, but nothing happened.

A scream rent the air.

The feline sprang at the Tasty. In a fraction of a second, its brown body arched through the air, front legs reaching out, paws ready to grasp the prey, and jaws wide open revealing wicked looking canines.

The scene played out just like a slow motion video. The Tasty started to turn its head. It held a pine cone in a hand-like paw.

The paws of the cat reached for the Tasty. The long sharp claws curved out of the paws to greet the Tasty. The cat pulled up its hind paws as it descended, preparing to land on the Tasty.

A branch brushed past Windelli. With a *whomp* the branch hit the cat. The cat flew backward, landing on some bushes. Snarling and spitting it struggled free of the bushes and sprinted away.

The Tasty turned back from watching the cat run away, to gaze at the tree. It stood calmly, one paw cupping its chin. Fingers from the paw stroked the fur of its chin.

"We can land in the clearing now," Ytell said.

Everyone's bubble landed in a small clearing next to the border area with its fields.

Alex's bubble dissipated with the others dropping him a few inches to the ground. He staggered. The release from his emotions and from his battle against the disc left him limp and exhausted. He looked at the calm Tasty. Had it

Tested and Tried

been in danger? What about his feelings? Wasn't he feeling the future right?

A'idah hurried toward Alex. "What was wrong? Are you alright?"

"Oh, you're here," the Tasty said, turning from its contemplation of the tree to run to them. The Tasty's black fur with golden speckles rippled as it ran, its movements were so graceful it seemed to flow across the ground toward them.

Squatting on its hind quarters, its head reached four feet into the air, the fur underneath its body was a creamy white, "Hello Ytell. This is the civilized moment you asked for."

In the middle of the conversation, Alex didn't want to talk aloud. Instead, he messaged A'idah. |I'm fine, just confused. I sensed something dangerous about to happen. This Tasty, Windelli, is the one which saved me and Hheilea yesterday.| Alex didn't say how he had tried to give Maleky control over his body. What would have happened? Instead of thinking about it, he listened to Ytell.

"I am honored to see you again." Ytell bowed his head low. "Flock, this is Windelli. Windelli let me introduce my flock. You already know Alex."

While Ytell introduced the rest of the flock, Alex wondered about what was going on and what had happened. Why did Ytell bow so low? He doesn't treat anyone that way. What happened to that cat? What is a civilized moment? The mice said the same thing.

From the flock came two of the questions.

"Windelli, what is a civilized moment?"

"What happened to the cat?"

Windelli answered, "Outside the area of your dorms is the wild or Wild Lands. When you live in the Wild Lands you're under the rules of the wild. You don't use technology from civilization against other creatures. Predators will kill and eat prey. Any person can ask for a civilized moment. A civilized moment means the rules of the wild no longer apply and rudimentary rules of civilization do apply.

"As for the cat, well you see that tree over there. It's a Chilgoza Pine. I study how Earth plants and animals respond to *dark matter*. The fascinating thing is they respond very strongly to it. In the past, Earth must've had vapuc in its atmosphere for a long time. Plants respond to it by instinctual behavior. Their instincts are just waiting for vapuc to be present. With this pine, the tree somehow responds to a creature picking its pine cones, by treating it as an ally. The tree naturally wants its seeds spread far away from it. When another creature tries to attack the first creature, the tree will defend it by using force. We just don't understand how it's doing these things. In this case, no one understands how the branch can move as it does without breaking or cracking. Like many things involving vapuc, it's a mystery and some refer to it as magic. In reality, we just don't understand the physics involved."

While Windelli spoke, Ytell messaged Alex. |If I hadn't kept you from reacting, what would've happened?|

|I don't know, but why were my feelings about the future overreacting?|

|Alex, one of the things I love about humans is the strength of your feelings. Unfortunately, it is the very thing which causes you great problems. It appears that both you and Hheilea have become better at sensing the future. In your case, this is going to combine with your recent experiences and stress to magnify your emotional reaction to your sense of the future. Gursha warned me about it and giving you opportunity to be aware of the problem is the best answer we have for now. From Windelli, I knew about the cougar stalking her. Gursha also said your memories are going to be very vivid and maybe quite uncomfortable. Sorry. For now, you'll have to try and sort it out on your own.|

Briefly, Alex thought of his feelings during the recent battle with the horrible Gragdreath. Those feelings about the future had helped him survive, and at the same time his feelings for Twyla had kept him from killing the monster at his best opportunity. Twyla would've died by his hand, but his friend, Giyf, would still be alive and Twyla still died. The past opened like a whirlpool drawing

Tested and Tried

him down. He hadn't been willing to kill the sweet girl he loved to save everyone else. The monster would've won except for the sacrifice of his friend Giyf. Thinking back brought up all the anguish of the battle and the cost of victory. How could he deal with the feelings? Did he need to become like the sci-fi character Spock who tried to always be logical and not let emotions affect his choices? Alex knew his feelings about the future were real and important. Yet, he also knew he had let his feelings for Twyla keep him from doing what he had to do. He knew love for Earth and life fueled his fight to save everyone back there from the oncoming disaster. Yet, he'd let love almost cause a disaster. He shied away from the truth. He hadn't been willing for his own pain.

Windelli finished with a short phrase. "Follow me into the fields."

The flock all turned to go with her, except for one. Alex stood still gazing at nothing, caught up in his thoughts.

"Alex, are you willing to join us?" Windelli said.

"Huh. What? Oh, yeah. I'm willing. I just don't know if I can." He spoke partly about her request and partly about his own thoughts. The whirlpool started to take him back down, the Tasty's expression saved him. One eye widened and its bushy eyebrow lifted.

Windelli must've known she'd caught his attention. She turned and ran toward the fields, her three foot long tail waved back and forth behind her. Alex automatically followed toward the fields. His own thoughts about his emotions still occupied his mind. At first, he was unaware he'd stopped following Windelli or turned around to run back into the Wild Lands. What was he doing? Looking around, Alex could see the rest of the flock at the edge of the forest.

"That cat is watching us," Sabu said, head up and ears twitching.

"Where is it?" Ekbal asked. "Will it try to attack one of us?"

"It's over in that tall tree. He's just watching us," Sabu said. "There are too many of us, he's nervous."

"What are we doing over here at the edge of the woods?" Alex asked. "Aren't we ... I mean, we were going..." He couldn't remember where."

"Flock, come back over here," Ytell said, standing in the clearing by the fields. "Just a moment ago, all of you were following Windelli out into that field. This is the answer to Ekbal's question about the barrier. All animals will find themselves not able to go into the fields. They will even forget wanting to.

"This time the barrier has been modified to allow all of us to follow Windelli into the fields."

Hesitantly at first, the flock followed Windelli into the field. Windelli left behind the clearing and scampered in-between two fields. On each side of the path grew lettuce, beans, corn, squash, and other plants.

"How do you harvest these vegetables?" Alex asked. "They're all mixed up."

"The harvesters work in the fields to gather the crops at peak ripeness," Windelli said. "They also control weeds and insects. The polyculture and companion crops you see help the plants to be healthy."

"Where are the har—"

Just then, Sabu jumped onto a spot in the grass. A scream split the air.

"Help, save me. Someone has gone wild."

"Let it go," Windelli said, rushing back.

Sabu lifted her paws off of the ground and jumped to the side. She started to snarl, and then crouched with her mouth open.

"Haven't you learned how to be civilized," Windelli said, poking her muzzle right into Sabu's face. "You're going to have to go before the council."

Out of the grass, a rat limped over to Windelli, "My leg. Oh my leg. My leg. I think she almost tore it from my body. Oh woe is me. I think I'm dying."

Alex couldn't see any blood on the small animal.

The rat continued moaning and said, "One more second and this brute would've swallowed me. I could smell her fetid breath as saliva dripped out of her mouth onto my face."

Tested and Tried

Choking back a laugh at the creature's theatrics, Alex heard A'idah's laugh. This rat was ridiculous, but then it continued with. "This uncivilized brute is a threat to any prey around her. She should be kicked out of civilized company."

That statement shocked and worried Alex. What? Could Sabu really be forced out of the flock?

"We're outside," Sabu said. "No one told me I can't hunt when I'm outside."

The voices of the flock crowded together adding to the confusion.

"No one told us about not hunting."

"What is this council?"

"Sabu can't be kicked out of civilized company. She's part of our flock."

"We were told about not hunting."

"No one told us there is no hunting in the border fields."

Other rats and mice scurried out of the field and raised their voices.

"Why is this flock thing special?"

"You got something against rats?"

"Because of wild behavior the council kicked my poor brother out into the Wild Lands for just a minor problem."

"You hated your brother."

"I loved him."

"You were the one who told about him getting ready to—"

Ytell flapped his wings. The resulting wind knocked over some of the mice and quieted all of the harvesters. "Sabu's behavior is my fault. I'll go with her to the next council meeting. She will not have any more wild behavior during our visit to the border. If there is any more wild behavior by any of my flock, we will all leave the border."

"That is sufficient," Windelli said. "Everyone get back to your work."

"I think the council should kick her out," one fat mouse said, as it slowly nosed its way through the grass. Reaching the edge of the grass it stopped to look at a seed on the ground. "Can't have that growing here," it said, picking it up in its paws to eat it.

"I can't work," the first rat said. "I'm dying."

A'idah laughed again and said, "Stop it. You aren't dying."

The rat stared at her, and then walked toward Windelli dragging a leg. Alex thought it was a different leg than it was limping with before.

The rat said, "I think the big brute broke something."

"Can you use your AI to call for help, or do you need me to do it for you?" Windelli asked.

"Call them, please and ask them to hurry." the rat said.

"A medibot will be here soon," Windelli said to the rat and turning to the flock added, "Follow me, and do try to keep from causing more trouble. It has been a pain working with many of Earth's species."

"You don't like us. You don't like us," Skyler said.

"That did come across bad. It isn't that I don't like Earthlings. You're different. It seems that in general, Earthlings are more sensitive to *dark matter* than any other planetary group of species. I don't know why that is. It's a scab wanting to be scratched. I need to find out what's going on. I've asked for some samples of species from some of the moons of Jupiter and Saturn, and I think the other planet's name is Mars. The Mars species aren't so important to me, but if you could collect some of the higher organisms from some of the moons, that would be wonderful."

She added a surprising statement. "When you get to Earth, I'm afraid you are in for a surprise."

"What kind of surprise?" Ekbal asked.

"When are we going?" Osamu asked.

"There are going to be many organisms that are still reacting to the small residue of vapuc left over from the last time our spaceship the Coratory was there," Windelli said.

Ytell said, "We won't be returning for at least a year and then just for a visit."

Windelli turned around and with her effortless flowing gait led them down the grass path. Far across the fields, a

Tested and Tried

machine started coming into view over a hill. No supports were visible under the machine. The bottom of the machine just barely cleared the tops of the tallest plants. It moved steadily across the field drawing closer all the time. A rustling sound rolled across the field from it. Something about it bothered Alex.

His eyes kept turning toward the machine as he followed Windelli. What was that machine doing? He couldn't see anything about it that made him think of danger, but his sense of the future again had started to bother him. Machine and flock drew nearer to each other. What's going on under that machine? Things were rising up out of the field into the machine.

"What is that machine?" Alex asked Windelli.

"It's an autonomous harvester," Windelli said. "It's collecting seeds, vegetables and fruits. We just finished harvesting the field on the right. Now everyone is in this field."

"Who's running it?"

"No one's running it. We use artificial intelligence to control all of our machines."

"How does it get all of those things out of the field?"

A plump rabbit jumped out of the field onto the path. "We help. See this thingy here. I point it and it cuts," the rabbit said, hopping around. "We pick the vegetables. With this, I cut it free and up it goes. I get to eat all kinds of good stuff and no predators, but I'm not supposed to eat any of goes up into the sky. Bye."

The rabbit jumped back into the field.

"That rabbit sounds crazy," Skyler said. "It sounds crazy."

"I can think of someone else who sounds that way," Sabu said poking at Skyler with her paw.

Alex laughed, but again something bothered him. His sense of trouble and again a mix of emotions troubled him. Quickly, he became certain something dangerous headed his way.

The rest of the flock laughed too.

Alex struggled with his feelings of the future trying to figure out what the danger was and how real it was.

Filtering slowly into the laughter of the flock came another sound, a low hum, over the horizon came another machine, smaller. It rapidly came closer.

A message from Hheilea exploded with a warning in his mind. |Alex! You're in danger.| She'd sensed it too.

"What's that machine?" Ekbal asked.

"That's the medibot for the rat," Windelli said, and then paused, looking at it closer. "Its engines shouldn't be that loud. It's headed... right for us."

"I've got a bad feeling about that machine," Alex said, glancing at the others. He caught Ytell looking at him. Once again, Alex guessed the flock leader already knew the danger and had a plan, but waited to give the flock or the one he looked at a chance to take charge.

"All of you creatures out in the field, run back toward the city." Windelli said.

She too wasn't worried about herself or trying to help the flock. How could Windelli and Ytell be so calm in such a deadly serious moment? Again Alex remembered the deadly seriousness of their training and the willingness of Ytell to take risks if it meant the flock learned better and faster. Already, there had been deaths. He didn't need Maleky's incessant warnings about Ytell's past actions. This time he was certain about the danger.

Hheilea confirmed it with another message. |Alex, someone is trying to kill you. Save yourself.|

Chapter Fourteen
Great Danger

Meanwhile, Alex had slapped a plan together. He didn't know if it would work, but he wasn't willing to wait and see what Ytell or Windelli would do. He said in a loud voice. "Everyone," followed in a rush by, "Use force on the count of three, try and push it toward the edge of the border fields and over the field to the right." Quickly, Alex sought the help of the artificial intelligence that lived on his scalp. *AI, if you have a gravity generator available, on my count of three pull this machine coming at us toward the field to the right and out toward the edge of the border fields.*

As Alex spoke the machine continued to speed through the air, the humming growing louder. They had just seconds before impact. "One."

Yells came from the field as frightened creatures crashed through the plants seeking safety. Where could they go?

"Two."

The machine, its stressed engines screeching, slashed down at them. Impact was eminent.

"Three."

It was the last possible moment before a deadly impact.

The front of the machine crumbled from their giant invisible fist of force hitting it. With the machine's inertia redirected, it tumbled through the air, gouging into plants and soil of the field to the right. With a last flip and flinging soil, plants and parts of itself the machine slammed down into the clearing the flock had landed in.

New noise replaced the noise of the crash, voices raised in yelling from all around competed to be heard. Animals jostled the flock, as they ran for the woods.

"Civilization is terrible."

"Machines are terrible, machines are terrible."

"They're trying to kill us."

"We're safe it's okay."

"This is crazy. This is crazy."

"Work together to calm everyone."

"I'll look for survivors from above," Ytell said, beating his twelve-foot wings he leaped into the air. The wind stunned some of the smaller creatures and left them huddling in fear.

Through it all, Alex tried to think. Was this another case of sabotage or a case of equipment failing due to lack of maintenance/corners cut to save money. Darker thoughts lurked, Ytell didn't do anything to save us. Was this disaster another of his tests of us or one of Alex's enemies trying to kill him, and Ytell just used it as a training opportunity?

Hheilea distracted him with her message. |Are you okay? What happened? Whoever attacked you understands how our sense of the future works and is trying to confuse us by how they chose what to do.|

|I'm okay. We can talk later. It's kinda chaotic right now. Everyone else is okay too.|

What shook Alex more than the attack was that he'd almost added to the message, *I love you*. He did care for her, but he still worried about the T'wasn't-to-be-is. He'd hated the loss of control over his life represented by his past illness. Then, he'd been abducted by these aliens and for months always following someone else's directions and under their control. Finally, to top all of that off the T'wasn't-to-be-is had almost stolen his control over who he could love. Alex knew he was sensitive about it, but didn't know what to do.

The other voices distracted him from his thoughts.

"What happened?"

Chests heaving, some animals stopped surging past to stand with wide eyes staring at Windelli.

Great Danger

"It's okay now," Windelli said. "That machine isn't going to hurt you. It's dead. Everything's going to be fine."

"It is, it is," a rabbit said, nose twitching, it took a few hops toward the forest.

"Maybe it is," a rat said. "It sure looks dead, but I don't trust these machines. How do I know the harvester won't crash onto us?"

"You're right," Windelli said. "No one should work with the harvest unless they are comfortable with it." Turning to the rabbit and others that were still leaving the field for the forest, she added, "You all need to remember that outside of the fields the law of the wild rules."

"Predators," a rabbit said. "Predators, I understand predators. I understand the wild. Bye."

Yet, a different rabbit stopped and stood shuddering. "I've seen how being prey works out. I watched as a predator ate my brother." The poor creature continued talking but its voice rose into almost a scream. "And my brother was still alive and screaming, while getting eaten. It's terrible out there, but I'm frightened. Please help me. I want to stay, but I'm terrified."

Windelli said, "Come here little one. It's okay to be afraid. Do you think this flock wasn't afraid? They just did what they had to do."

"I couldn't spot anyone in the wreckage," Ytell said, flying back, "or in the damaged field."

Windelli patted, petted, and comforted the shuddering rabbit calming it down. "Thanks for looking and for your patience in not taking charge of the danger. That was amazing. Your flock rewarded your confidence. I've just received word that the robot left before the medic could board it. Your flock responded great to that danger. Alex's and the rest of your flock's quick actions saved our lives and many others. A team is going to come and investigate the crash. We need to continue to the city."

That said, Windelli patted the rabbit one last time, and turned resuming her flowing gait down the grass pathway.

Alex nodded at her words about Ytell not taking action against the danger. He'd used it as another test and another learning experience. The teenage boy shuddered at how Ytell willingly exposed the Earthlings to deadly danger. What would the raptor have done if Alex hadn't taken control of the situation? Would he really have let some of them die?

The flock followed Windelli, quietly discussing what had just happened.

In time, Alex's heart rate returned to normal, but his thoughts had a harder time calming. Of course, Maleky didn't help his thoughts at all, but Alex did his best to ignore him.

A rustling passed through the foliage of the fields. The gust causing the rustling passed through the flock as they followed Windelli. Overhead, cumulous clouds swelled, their undersides started turning dark with the promise of another evening storm.

Alex gazed up at the changing weather relishing the idea of a lightning and thunderstorm. Watching them was a favorite activity of his, especially when he had a storm raging on the inside. Watching the weather usually calmed him.

Ahead on the path, a form appeared, foreshadowed by a faint call. The form grew larger with each passing moment. It was another Tasty just smaller and golden brown. This one looked familiar.

Running up to them, the Tasty said, "Grandma, you're okay. I was so worried after I heard the report of a strange accident over here, and I knew you were over here, and I left as soon as I could. What could've caused the problem? Our machines don't fail."

"Slow down," Windelli said. "You don't need to say everything in one breath. I'm surprised as fast as you were running that you can talk."

"Oh Grandma, don't be so silly. You know I was the fastest of my school. This was just a short run, and you didn't answer my question. What happened and did anyone get hurt?"

"We avoided deaths and injuries because of this flock. Specifically, the quick thinking of Alex," Windelli said, pointing Alex out, "He saved everyone, including myself."

Great Danger

"Oh..." Alex started to say, but the wind was knocked out of him by the young Tasty fiercely giving him a four legged hug. The weight and momentum of the Tasty leaping at him, knocked Alex down and a warm furry face, smelling of enticing spices pressed close against his.

"Thank you. Thank you. Thank you for saving my grandma."

"It... I... The..." Alex stammered. His arms were around a warm furry body just a little smaller than A'idah. His hands felt the softest of fur, and the scents were making him light headed. Finally, he managed to say, "The flock I'm part of saved her. I really did very little."

"Okay dear, you need to let him up. Humans aren't used to getting knocked to the ground by a hug. Where are your manners?"

"I'm sorry," the female Tasty said, letting go of Alex and wriggling to get free. "Uhmm, you need to let go of me so we can get up."

"What? Oh yes, I'm sorry," Alex said, face getting warm.

Others reached down and helped Alex up. One face in particular caught Alex's attention. A'idah looked at him with a raised eyebrow, shaking her head.

Brushing himself off, Alex sighed. How embarrassing.

Zeghes said via AI, |Alex, what is it about you and females? First, there was Hheilea and the Winkle girl, and I think you and A'idah—|

|Zeghes,| Alex responded interrupting, |this isn't anything like Hheilea, and don't talk to A'idah about this. A'idah and I are just friends.|

To himself, Alex added, Just friends and something else, but I don't know what, plus she's so young. I just don't want to mess with our friendship. In this crazy new life, we both need our friendship.

Zeghes responded. |Yes. I remember you telling me she's too young and human males are not supposed to press the issue of what's embarrassing for you to talk about. You're supposed to just be friends. I promised if you started getting interested in her, as more than a friend

I'd swat your head and stop you. When will she not be too young? She's looking like an older human female.|

Unconsciously, Alex responded to what Zeghes said by taking a quick look at A'idah. She was— ummm... Embarrassed even more at where his thoughts were going he felt his cheeks getting warmer yet. Desperately, he tried to think about something, anything else. Delli spoke about machines not failing. The Tasties must keep up on maintenance.

Ytell contacted Alex via AI, |Alex, you handled yourself very well with that young Tasty woman. It would be very hard for me to be hugged by a Tasty. You need to bow to the Tasty and tell her you're welcome. Tasties need to be treated with honor.|

Turning to look at the young Tasty woman, Alex bowed, "I'm honored by your thankfulness."

"Silly," she said. "You don't need to bow like a Thrip. Grandma, use your AI to contact my sister, and tell her about how Alex saved you. She would enjoy seeing how his face turns red."

At the word Thrip, Alex felt momentary confusion. He almost said, *huh*, until he remembered Thrips were Ytell's species. At the same time, her talking about his face being red just added to his embarrassment. Alex wished he could go invisible.

Windelli said, "You're heading by yourself into the Wild Lands for your fledgling ceremony?"

"Yes, Grandma." The younger Tasty spoke as she bounded over to Windelli and gave her a gentler hug.

"I love you, dear."

"I love you too, Grandma."

Somewhat awkwardly, Windelli asked, "Do you have somewhere picked out for shelter from the coming storm?"

"Of course, Grandma. There's a dead fall with a great cave under its root-ball."

Windelli pointed off toward the trees. "Oh, the one over there?" For some reason the older Tasty looked at Alex while she spoke.

Great Danger

He had the distinct feeling she wanted him to see where her granddaughter was headed.

The younger Tasty stepped back. "Yes, Grandma."

Windelli turned back to her granddaughter and placed a hand-like paw against her granddaughter's. "*Celebrate life,*"

"Celebrate life," Delli said, turning, she gracefully started toward the forest her golden fur rippling on her back. Her voice carried back to them. "Good bye, everyone, celebrate life."

"What's she doing?" A'idah asked.

"She's going into the wild to live," Ytell said. "It is the fledgling ceremony."

"Isn't that dangerous? That large cat's out there. I don't understand." Ekbal said.

"I understand," Sabu said. Walking up to Windelli, she lowered her head. "I don't understand many things of this new life in civilization, but your species understands the wild."

"Thank you, Sabu. When you and your flock were watching that poor cat trying to attack me, did you happen to spot the deadfall my granddaughter is going to?"

Sabu lifted her head. "Yes, I think there was only one in that area."

"What do you think of her choice?"

"It looked good to me."

"Thanks, Sabu," Windelli said, and then added. "Come on, everyone. Look at those clouds. We need to hurry. We don't want to get caught outside in the evening thunderstorm." She looked directly at Alex and added, "Like my granddaughter."

Alex looked back after the young Tasty for a long moment and even took a step toward the Wild Lands before he went after the flock. She was going into danger, and naturally, Alex didn't like it. Something else, a new threat lurked in the woods, and she didn't know about it. Could he trust his sense of her future?

A message from Hheilea confirmed his worries. |Alex, I'm glad you're okay, but I'm sensing a greater danger.|

At that message, his footsteps slowed even as the sky continued to darken. Soon the rain would be starting. He didn't consider the tumultuous day he'd already had or the fact he was wore out. Alex was worried about the young Tasty out in the woods. He didn't know the danger's source, but he felt pretty sure young Delli didn't know about it.

|Thanks, Hheilea. I'm feeling something too. Did you know about the young Tasty, Delli, going out into the woods by herself for her fledgling ceremony?|

|No, that isn't good. I don't think this is a normal type of danger. She wouldn't be expecting it. We should warn someone.|

|I know her grandmother. I'll talk to her.|

|Great. Just talk to her. Alex, don't do anything stupid.|

Chapter Fifteen
Disobeying and Tested Again

The first splats of rain hit the big leaves of a tall plant next to the path. Its big yellow flower head hung upside down. Alex ducked under the flower head for the shelter it gave as he waited for a crowd of smaller creatures entering the path ahead of him.

He wanted to catch up with Windelli, but found the mice and other smaller creatures made it difficult to walk very fast. Alex kept worrying about stepping on them. The deepening gloom made it increasingly difficult for him to walk without stepping on anyone. Just ahead, he could make out the low hill with the city's entrance. The grass path, filled with other creatures hurrying the same direction, led to the stone walkway he'd come down earlier in the day with Windelli.

Alex started to ask his AI to use a local gravity generator for a lift through the air when lightning lit up the sky followed by the boom of thunder. That choice didn't seem too wise. Finally, he resorted to calling out. "I can't see the ground very good. If there are any mice or other small creatures in front of me, please stay out from under my feet. I don't want to step on you."

From the ground, he heard responses.

"Thank you."

"Thank you."

"We little folks will stay to the right and you can stay to the left. Okay?"

Gratefully, Alex said, "Sounds good."

With less worry, Alex picked up his pace. Again, he though he thought of using his AI. This time he tried to send a message to Windelli.

His AI answered after a brief pause. I can't get her.

From down below him, Alex could hear the little creatures passing on the message about staying to the right because of a big clumsy human who was half blind. He grinned at it and looked for the older Tasty.

Ahead of him, Alex recognized the opening into the city with its high peaked roof. In the light pouring out of the windows, he could see a crowd of creatures escaping the oncoming thunderstorm. Another bright flash lit up the sky over the hill followed by the boom of thunder. In that brief flash, Alex thought he noticed a figure moving away from the entrance.

The first wave of rain had subsided, but from out in the fields came the drumming sound of an approaching deluge. From down by his feet came the sound of voices expressing urgency.

"We're going to get drenched."

"I hate getting wet."

Alex recognized the voice of the skunk. "Jump on my back I can carry some of you mice."

"Jump on the human's feet he can carry many of us."

Alex stopped to let the hitchhikers jump on. He felt tugging on the bottom of his pantaloons and more than once a scratch from an over eager hitchhiker. "Hey, be careful with your claws down there."

"Sorry."

The skunk said, "Follow me and you can go faster. I'm warning you. Don't step on my tail."

Alex could see the white stripes standing out from the dark, moving in front of him. In response, he picked up his pace. The wind carried the familiar smell of rain mixed with the smell of the damp creatures all around him.

The skunk added, "When we reach the area of light up ahead, stand still to let your passengers off."

Gladly, Alex stood still when he entered the area of light. Passengers gone, he moved farther under the

Disobeying and Tested Again

protection granted by the high peaked, caul-like roof. He arrived just in time to hear Ytell.

"Flock, this Tasty will show you around the Tasty's city."

Alex hurried forward, and he heard his friends' voices.

"That made me think of the charge class," A'idah said. "I still get shivers thinking of our teacher, Spark, with his gold hair sticking out in all directions making that chain lightning hit us without hurting us."

"I wish I was his barber," Ekbal said. "I wonder how he grows real gold as hair. Exploring this city sounds fun."

One of the flock members, Sabu, didn't follow after the others. Instead, she stood with Ytell looking back at Alex.

"Where's Windelli," Alex asked, looking around in the bright light spilling out of the cave-like entrance.

Ytell answered, "Come with me."

He led Alex back to the entrance and pointed off to the left. "She's out there. You can go to her."

Almost total darkness had descended outside. "I want to, but I can't see in this storm to find her," Alex said.

Sabu had followed them, and she said, "She's right over there. She's under that ledge."

"Where? I can't see anything. It's too dark out there."

"You know, your senses are rather useless. Stay close and follow me."

Alex followed his friend out into the gloom. Stumbling in his effort to keep up in the darkness, Alex remembered he needed to warn Windelli about the danger in the woods. He called out to Sabu. "Wait up. I can hardly see you."

Sabu answered. "You're quite helpless in the dark. I'll wait for you. Walk right beside me, and put your hand on my back. Out here, you're as helpless as a kitten. If you were smaller, I could just pick you up by your neck and carry you.

For a while they walked together. Alex felt frustrated and more than a little upset about her condescending words. Gradually, he relaxed and actually enjoyed walking with the big cat. Lightning flashed across part of the sky. Ahead of them a figure stood under an overhang.

"I see her."

Rumbling thunder filled the air.

"Windelli," Alex called, "Why are you standing out here in the storm?"

"I'm thinking of my granddaughter, and this overhang provides a great place to watch the storm. She's out there in the wild. The fury and rain should help protect her from predators. The rain will wash away her scent trail and most predators will seek shelter."

Windelli turned to look at Alex. "But, she's all alone. I hope she found a good safe place for the night."

"I still don't understand," Alex said. "Why is she out there? And there's—"

Thunder interrupted him telling about the danger, and before he could continue Windelli answered his question. "She's celebrating life."

"Alex doesn't understand," Sabu said. "He has never lived in the wild. There's a thrill to living in the wild. Civilization can't compare."

"We've had many times of danger," Alex said. "Just today we could've died, and—"

"True, but it's different. There's more freedom, and it isn't so confusing," Sabu said.

"Sabu you're right about the thrill of the wild and the freedom," Windelli said. "I miss living in the wild. My work gives me some of that. But the reason she's out there, and why I'll return to the wild in a few more years is to celebrate life."

"What does, *celebrate life* mean?" Alex asked.

"It is the act of being prey and maybe being preyed upon and yet more," Windelli said. "Many hundreds of centuries ago my people worked at living longer and longer. Life became all about being careful. Our culture stagnated. There was no joy. We no longer were happy being as we were created. Come on inside. This is not the topic for a thunderstorm. Even with this protection we'll get drenched before you can hope to understand."

"But...," Alex said. The idea of anyone wanting to be prey went against everything he felt about life and confused him. It felt so alien. What could he do? What could he say about these alien ideas? Flashes of light and wind driven rain buffeted Alex. The thunder deafened him.

Stumbling in the driving rain, Alex followed Windelli back inside. Echoes of thunder followed them. Attendants worked at one side of the entrance handing out rough towels for people to dry off with. Alex accepted one and started drying off.

Windelli pointed at the attendants and pegs with capes, "When I went out, I should've taken a cape with me. They do a good job of keeping one dry in a storm. Too bad Delli didn't take one with her."

In the bright light, a few creatures followed a winding trail deeper into the hill. A pleasant hum of activity came from a cavern below. Tasties and other creatures stood in small groups talking, while others walked around the groups, intent on their own purposes.

"I need to hurry down and help your flock get settled in to our city." Windelli said. "If you want a snack, there are bags of food back by the capes. They are labeled for predators, omnivores, and herbivores like my Delli. Too bad she didn't take some with her into the Wild Lands."

Alex felt her eyes on him for what seemed like a long moment. "Okay," Alex said, not sure what he was saying okay to. He thought of Delli out in the storm. Windelli didn't seem too happy her granddaughter was all alone out there. Alex didn't feel happy about it either. The sense of danger he felt hadn't gotten better. Instead, he felt increasingly sure about it and the danger felt worse. He remembered about not being able to reach the older Tasty with the messaging. "Windelli, earlier I couldn't reach you with my AI. Is yours having a problem?"

Windelli seemed to grin, but Alex wasn't at all sure how to interpret her furry face's expressions. "Sorry, I had my AI disable our message ability. I love storms and don't appreciate having my AI interrupt the experience."

The older Tasty turned around, but before she left, she said, "Remember the food."

Alex looked back at the bags of food again. *Remember the food?* Why had she said that? It was too bad Delli didn't have food with her.

At the same time, Maleky kept giving him advice about his feelings for the future. After Alex's recent experience with the cat attacking Windelli, he wasn't sure about his sense of the future. He knew danger existed for Delli out there, and something else lurked out there, but Alex couldn't tell who it threatened. He wished it was a simple fight. In a fight, he knew how his sense of the future worked for him.

Rubbing the rough towel in his hair felt good. Already he felt drier and warmer. If only, Alex could figure out what to do. He should've told Windelli about the danger both he and Hheilea sensed. What could he do? The growing sense of danger drove him to decide.

Sounding confused, Sabu interrupted his thoughts, "Did it sound to you as if Windelli was encouraging us to try and find her granddaughter? And Ytell..."

Alex tried to sort out his thoughts. There was one easy way out of making a decision. "Sabu, I think you're right, but we couldn't find Delli."

"I watched which way she went, and didn't you notice Windelli made sure I knew where her granddaughter would be? I could tell you how to find her."

Tossing caution to the wind, Alex said, "I've got to go out there and help Delli." Should he tell his friend about the presence lurking in the woods?

"Personally, I think that's a bad idea, but—"

"Please wait before you let the others know," Alex said. "I'm going to grab a cape from over there and get going. Once the storm is past, I should get some light from the nebula which is out in the sky at this time."

"Get one for me. If the Tasties can use a cape to keep dry, I can use one. I hate getting wet."

Alex stopped in the act of going to the attendants. "You're coming too?"

"Of course, you know nothing about living in the wild, and it'll be easier to show you where she went than to tell you."

Happy for the help, Alex hurried toward the attendants. Now that the decision had been made, he couldn't wait to get out there and face the growing threat.

Disobeying and Tested Again

Uncomfortably, he remembered someone else he should talk to, but he didn't want to. She wouldn't be happy. Instead of sending her a message he talked to the attendants about the food and capes.

It took just a moment to get the capes. An attendant had one handy that would work for Sabu and showed them how to use it for her. Another attendant handed Alex three bags of food. Upon leaving the shelter of the entrance, the rain and wind beat at them. At least the lightning seemed to be over.

"I'll use my AI to lift us over to the forest," Alex said over the noise of the storm. He looked at Sabu and chuckled to himself. It looked funny to see Sabu with that cape. Something else puzzled him. He hadn't said anything about a third person, and yet the attendant had given them a third bag of food.

Sabu turned her head to glare at Alex.

"What?" Alex asked, as his AI lifted them into the air using an artificial gravity generator at the Tasty city.

"You're laughing at me," Sabu said.

"No. Well, yeah. It's just that it looks funny to see you in that cape."

"It feels strange," Sabu said. "I think living in civilization is making me soft." A strong gust of wind shoved them through the air. "Right now, I just want to get back down to the ground."

"It is a bit turbulent, but I can get us to the clearing where we first set down."

"Alex, you're just like I was as a kitten."

"What do you— Ah" Getting dropped ten feet interrupted him. "Sabu, what do you mean?" *AI, what's going on?*

His AI responded. *I'm afraid of this storm. The winds are too unpredictable. If we fall, will I get hurt again?*

Alex didn't like his AI's problem with the storm, but he didn't want to give up on getting there through the air. His feelings of danger pushed him to hurry. *AI, can you hurry?*

Hurry? I'm afraid of going faster.

After the turbulent start, the winds calmed down a bit, and Alex gave a sigh of relief.

Sabu answered him. "As a kitten, I didn't know what I could do or not do, but I learned. You continue to act like a kitten. You ignore the possibility of failure."

"The storm's almost over, and it won't be long until we get there. It's much calmer. We'll be okay." Alex had a hard time keeping his tone civil. What was it about the females in his life? None of them thought he was smart. Thinking of females made him remember again that he should talk to her, that different female. There were others who wouldn't be happy not to hear from him, but this one was problem enough. With a heavy sigh Alex committed to sending the message.

His AI responded with a surprising message. *I can't send Hheilea a message.*

That surprised him. Alex considered sending A'idah a message, but that would start a conversation he knew wouldn't be good. Instead, he asked Sabu, "I'm having trouble with messaging. Can you message Hheilea for me about what we're doing?"

After a moment, Sabu answered. "My AI can't send her a message. I tried Skyler too without any luck. I was going to try A'idah, but I think she wouldn't be happy with us. I'm not happy with— Ahh!" The turbulence resumed and shoved her, interrupting. "This is idiocy. I think we should quit and walk back."

"No." Alex refused to give up or set them down, even though walking wouldn't be much slower. The danger, whatever it was, was increasing.

A strobe of light flashed across the sky followed all too soon by rolling thunder.

"I dare you to message A'idah. I bet she calls you an idiot."

Alex bit off saying he wasn't an idiot. Sabu would just start telling him all of the examples when he'd proved just how stupid he was. The closeness of that lightning bothered him, but he felt driven by the increasing sense of danger to keep them in the air.

"Have you messaged A'idah?"

Disobeying and Tested Again

Why did she keep asking about A'idah? Just thinking about messaging her or Zeghes bothered him. "I don't want to trouble her." He also didn't want to get her involved in this danger he sensed. A'idah was so young and brave. She never thought of herself. He worried about her safety. Somehow, part of that slipped out and in the very worst way. "A'idah's too young, and she wouldn't think about the dangers to herself. She'd be out here in a flash."

Immediately, Sabu responded even with the wind tossing her about. "Too young? What do you mean by that? She's much older than I am, and I could have kittens of my own soon. I've smelled A'idah. She could have her own kittens. She fought against the Winkles in the first battle you caused, and she help save you from that pint sized terror, Titan. Then, she fought in the bigger battle to help save everything. A'idah's an amazing female. You should take a more careful look at her. As I said, I've smelled her. She isn't a little girl. A'idah is a woman. I don't understand male and female relationships between you humans, but she obviously cares for you. If you're not letting her know, I will."

Alex didn't know what to say. The turbulence tossing them about reflected how he felt inside. Recently, he'd taken much too careful of a look at A'idah. Things were going from bad to worse, and what did Sabu mean by she'd smelled her? He just wanted this conversation over. Alex tried to think of a response, but just then a gust of wind flipped him first horizontally one way and then back the opposite way.

He gasped out to Sabu forestalling her complaint. "I don't want to set us down too soon. I know I can get us to the clearing." Alex hoped that Sabu would give up on the conversation about A'idah. He didn't enjoy the turbulent ride either, and he was starting to get worried. Maybe he should have his AI set them down sooner. Alex's AI really did have lots of trouble dealing with the strong gusts of wind. Another lightning strike illuminated hills and the sky. The thunder followed, but not quite so soon.

Sabu said, "The Tasty girl is somewhere near those tall trees ahead. We're close enough. Set us down already." She added. "I just tried to contact A'idah, and I couldn't get a message through."

The second part of the Sabu's comment brought relief and concern to Alex. What was going on with the messaging system?

|Alex this is Ytell. Where are you?|

He'd halfway been expecting to hear from Ytell. The flock leader always seemed to know what was going on. Alex decided he'd refuse any order to return. Responding via AI, he said, |I decided to find Delli and help her. How come our attempts to message others has failed?|

|If you continue, your AI will be disabled. I've disabled your messaging to some people.|

AI, land us near the clearing. |Ytell, thanks for the warning.| The fact that part of their messaging system had been disabled shocked Alex. What was the flock leader up to this time?

Finally, his AI responded in evident relief.

Ytell sent one more message. |Good luck.|

Good luck? Did he want Alex to do this? "Sabu, I just had a strange conversation with Ytell. I think he might want us doing this."

"Yes. You finally figured it out. He asked me to offer my help, but told me not to tell you his plan. He's always trying to train—" A particularly strong gust tumbled Sabu head-over-tail at that moment.

Alex's AI had also been talking in his mind with a very nervous message. *I don't know if I'm going to get us to that clearing. These gusts are terrible, and I'm feeling real—*

The same turbulence silenced the AI and tumbled Alex through the air. Through the spinning, he could see the ground rushing up at him and then falling away.

Sabu said, "What are you trying to do, kill us? Set us down already."

"I'm trying to get us down, but—"

Chapter Sixteen
Diversion

Back in the city, Windelli and Ytell had been looking out into the dark. She asked, "Has he gone to try and help my granddaughter?"

"Yes," Ytell said. "We succeeded with making this future happen. Does the Kimley's *Book of Prophesy* explain why this event needed to happen?"

"You still don't understand. You really should come and look into the book. It doesn't talk about events. It tells events, but that's too simple. First, it isn't one book but a whole library containing an incredible recording of history. Many of the past books have been lost. Some of them were stolen by people trying to learn about its secrets.

If I was looking at now in the current Prophesy Book, I could find this conversation. Yesterday, when I looked at the book, I saw we would talk here, but the conversation had a number of possibilities. Those differences were based on what events would lead up to Alex going or not going out to my granddaughter. The book shows possible futures. We Tasties call them future threads. The farther into the future we try to read the more unraveled and random those possible futures become. We have to be very careful about reading too many pages ahead of now. Just our reading them changes what will happen. In recent decades, we've come to recognize the Book of Prophesy is recording certain events happening that will affect Earth.

Ytell shook his feathers at her words. "It all sounds very complex and confusing. Why couldn't the Kimleys make better plans? If I was in charge, I would have written specific instructions and when necessary, I would've explained for the reader."

Windelli patted the agitated raptor on the back. "Now, Ytell, calm yourself. You keep forgetting the book is being written in the past as we read about the future events."

Ytell opened his beak to respond, but the Tasty held up her other hand/paw to silence him.

"Those Kimleys are seeing our future possibilities and are recording the threads which affect the distant future cataclysm they are trying to deal with. If Alex survives, he will have a major role to play in that future. I don't know what it is, but if he dies then the Kimleys will find other possible future threads which can correct what his being dead causes. They will record those possibilities, and we will find a way to safe guard them. One thread we're having great difficulty with is the String Sword. It's very necessary."

The raptor partially opened his wings pushing the calming hand/paw off of his back. In an even more agitated voice he said, "Every time you've tried to explain this it comes back to possible death. Why can't we read about them in time to save them?"

Now Windelli sounded exasperated. "Remember, remember, when I or anyone reads too far into the future it causes changes, and those changes quickly become chaotic in nature. The value of the book in the face of chaos becomes very little, and we both know what happens to Kimleys exploring future possibilities when their actions create chaos. When we cause chaos from reading their work, some of the Kimleys themselves die. Sometimes, I can look farther into the future. This is one of those times I couldn't. I've learned to notice when I need to stop reading. We just need to patiently, carefully read about the near future, and do what is necessary to keep events going along the best path. For now, it was setting up this lesson for Alex."

Ytell hung his head. "I understand. I'm glad for your help in setting up this lesson for Alex."

"It was easy. One doesn't live as long as I have without learning something about other people," Windelli responded. "He already wanted to do it. We just had to encourage his desire to help. He's an impulsive youngster, and so much is riding on him. People like Alex and you, Ytell, have so much potential, but too many of you die before they can fulfill the promise of their abilities. Now, we'll need to turn off his AI. My granddaughter is going to be furious with him. Too bad we couldn't warn him about that danger."

Ytell said, "I just warned him about his AI going offline. I hope he wasn't trying to use it to fly in the storm out there, but he didn't ask me to delay turning it off. So, he should be okay. This should be a simple lesson for him, right?"

Windelli answered, "After all I've told you, you're still placing too much confidence in me, and you didn't reply to my comment about you. My studying of the *Book of Prophesy* doesn't mean I'm a Kimley in my knowledge of the future. The book keeps changing, and it's just a tool created by the Kimley. I am still surprised by events. This afternoon's attack is a good example. I didn't know about it."

"You're right. I'm like most Thrips, and I tend to place you Tasties on a pedestal. Maybe I should go out and check on him. I'd never forgive myself if he died. About myself, I understand the risks I take, and I'm okay with them. Accepting a certain amount of danger is important for success."

She said, "You're right about risks, but not about going to check on Alex. You can't. One thing is clear in the book about tonight, if you or any of the flock goes out there, it'll be a disaster. Your flock has to be dealt with, A'idah and Zeghes in particular. It's a good thing we made those changes to the messaging system. We wouldn't want any of them contacting Alex. I'll go and look at the pages in the book for tonight. If Alex is in more danger than we think, it should be very evident. Remember, even if Alex dies, it isn't the end. I've seen the Book of Prophesy do some pretty strange things. The Kimleys have many different possibilities in play."

The feathers around Ytell's head raised a clear sign to anyone who really knew the Thrips that he was upset. "I understand, but I care for each and every one of my flock. All of us Thrips suffered when we lost those other Earthlings last year. One of Alex's greatest strengths also puts him in the greatest danger. He doesn't know when to quit."

"Yes. He's like you in that regard. Remember Ytell, giving up isn't a sin. It gives you the opportunity to try again," Windelli answered.

The big bird ruffled his feathers at her comments about giving up. "Now for the difficult part, I have to let his flock know what he's doing."

"Are you going to message them?"

"Yes, but I'll be careful. I won't tell them what Alex is doing until I'm with them. Some would immediately leave to help him. A'idah and Zeghes are not going to be happy. They're particularly close to him, but he's had many adventures where they couldn't help him. This might be one-too-many."

Windelli said, "When Hheilea finds out about this, she'll need to be locked up too. You know what's going on with her?"

"Yes. Much of the future rides on her and the others you mentioned."

|Flock, I need all of you to meet with me outside the rooms we've been assigned by the Tasties.|

Immediately the replies came back. They weren't at all what Ytell expected or what he wanted.

|Zeghes and I are going outside. Alex is in trouble again.|

|The flock needs to stay together. Why does Alex always go off by himself? I can't remember how to get out of here. Can someone help me? I found some great nuts.|

|Ytell, this is Osamu. I am with Ekbal. We think we know where Skyler is. We are going to get him. What do you want us to do? If Alex is in danger, should we all go help him?|

~**********~

Earlier, A'idah had gone with the other flock members on a tour of the Tasty's city. She'd left Alex and Sabu behind, but hadn't been worried about them. After all, the flock had been given instructions to explore, and she expected Sabu and Alex would be coming along too. They followed the Tasty guide through many twists and turns, stopping here and there for descriptions of the new area.

The Tasty lead them into a bigger tunnel. Together they all went through another door. This one led them into a vast room, with a high vaulted ceiling. "Good. We're just in time."

Zeghes leapt through the air in exuberance. "Finally, we've gotten out of those tight spaces."

Ekbal asked, "What is this room?"

"This is where we process our excrement."

A'idah couldn't believe what she thought the word *excrement* meant. It couldn't be right. There wasn't any terrible odor. "What is excrement?"

Ekbal answered before the Tasty could. "It's their poop."

"Yes, he's right."

The Kalasha girl's eyes grew big at the idea and again she wondered about the lack of a smell. "Why doesn't it stink in here?"

"Follow me," The Tasty said.

Together the group walked across the floor toward an immense brown pile. An intense odor burned A'idah's nose. Before she thought better of it she gasped and then almost retched at the taste in her mouth.

The Tasty said, "Back up, everyone."

A'idah stumbled backward. Fresh air rewarded her efforts, and she coughed, trying to clear her lungs of the horrid smell.

Osamu said, "That was not pleasant."

Not pleasant? A'idah thought. It was terrible. She'd never willingly smell that again.

Her fellow flock member, the dark skinned boy from India asked, "Why don't we still smell the revolting odor?"

"Do any of you notice the blue shimmer?"

A'idah looked back toward the horrid pile of—. She didn't want to think about what it was... and for the first time noticed a faint violet shimmering in the air between her and the revolting brown pile. "What is it? How does it keep that terrible stink under control?" She wasn't going anywhere near that smell again.

"This is a semipermeable force-field. It does keep the stink under control, but that isn't its main purpose."

"Really," Osamu said.

Ekbal asked, "What's the main purpose? Does it keep flies from the pile?"

"Watch. It's going to start."

A'idah started to ask, what's going to start, but just then the whole pile shifted and started floating up into the air. With a whirling sound, four sled-like craft she hadn't noticed off to the side, took off. They darted into the floating mass and proceeded to slice through it, breaking it up and mixing it.

Osamu said, "Wow. Some more of your incredible technology. Are you using a null-gravity field to cancel gravity in that area?"

"Yes, we are. When did you learn about null-gravity fields?"

With a loud mix of squishing, thudding, and splatting the horrid mix collapsed back onto the floor. The four sleds hovered off to the side, and A'idah saw showers start up, rinsing off the vehicles. After a moment, the showers stopped, and the sleds flew back into their cubicles.

Osamu answered, "We saw our first one with a floating bubble of water containing fish. It stirred my curiosity, and I've looked into how it was done."

A'idah listened to Osamu's response in surprise. How did he manage to find the time to learn about the alien's technology? Just keeping up with the regular lessons and practicing different types of vapuc kept her very busy. She asked, "Why were those sled things being washed? They're just going to get dirty again."

"Sometimes we use them for transportation. Also, we play with them just for fun."

Ekbal said, "They look fun to ride. Do they work like the bubbles?"

"Yes. You just have to hold on to keep from falling off."

Osamu looked around the room. "Where does the... result of the processing go after it is done in here? Are the controls for all of this technology in here, or is it all done remotely, or do computers control it?"

"That far wall has monitors and controls for making changes to the automatic routines. That's where the control is for opening the door to dump this batch. The door is over there." The Tasty pointed to a large door set high up on the wall and looked at them.

A'idah looked at it in confusion. How could you dump the pile up through a door?

Ekbal answered her unspoken question. "I presume it's dumped up through the use of an artificial gravity generator pulling it up, but why do you refer to it as being a dump?"

"Sorry, I used to work in sanitation at one time and it was a common joke among us about who wanted to take a dump to get rid of the finished pile. It isn't a very good joke."

Zeghes said, "I don't get it."

Osamu grinned. It was one of the first times A'idah had seen him grin. He said, "It is okay, Zeghes. You do not have to understand everything about different cultures."

Ekbal said, "I'll explain later, Zeghes." Turning back to the Tasty he asked, "Where does the door lead to?"

"To the backside of the city's hill. Fertilizer bots gather it and spread it over the fields as it is needed. Now..." For a moment he paused and then added. "I need to go help a friend. Will you be okay without me?"

Osamu answered for the flock. "No problem. I've got a map of the city uploaded to my AI. We'll be fine."

Again, the Japanese man surprised A'idah with his knowledge. Next, he startled her with a suggestion. "A'idah, why don't you lead us?"

"Me? I don't have your map, and I don't have a clue where we are in the city."

"Yes, you. With Alex often busy doing other things and not attending our classes with us, we need more leaders in our flock. I've noticed you have the makings of a great leader. You are always willing to take charge when there is danger. Why not now?"

"Does it matter which way we go?"

"No, just so long as the way leads up."

Ekbal laughed and when everyone looked at him he pointed at the big door set above the big pile. We could go up through that door."

A'idah wrinkled her nose at the suggestion and said, "No way. I couldn't be forced to go that way. Come on."

Together, the flock followed her out of the big room and back into the many tunnels. Occasionally, they'd see Tasties going the other direction.

Coming to another random fork in the light yellow-brown tunnels, A'idah stopped before choosing the left tunnel. "These tunnels are all the same. I'm tired of just wandering around. Having the tour and this walking is a waste of time."

Osamu nodded in agreement. "Yes, this is not Ytell's normal policy. He always has some reason behind our activities."

Ahead of her, A'idah noticed something different. Their tunnel opened into a much larger area than anything they'd seen to this point of the exploration other than the effluent room. Skyler flew past startling her.

Right behind the big, blue bird, Zeghes surfed past her too. "I see another big room."

Ekbal pointed out a recent example. "I agree. He waited during the danger we just had for us to do something. Alex jumped right in and took control. Speaking of Alex, where is he?"

The flock all poured out of the tunnel onto a ledge overlooking a large cavern. The sides of it had other ledges with Tasties hurrying about their business. A'idah looked around in concern. "Both him and Sabu didn't come down. I think something's going on."

Skyler flew out into the open space. "I say we go to the other side."

Diversion

The bird flew surprisingly fast and disappeared into the opening of another tunnel on the other side.

Osamu said, "I tried to get him to come back, but Skyler says the tunnel over there has colors rippling down the wall. He is terribly excited about them and wants to explore."

Zeghes soared out into the open area. "I'll go after him."

A'idah tried to message Alex, but her AI responded with bad news.

I can't send a message to him.

"Wait!" A'idah yelled. "I can't get ahold of Alex. I just tried messaging him."

Zeghes executed a maneuver in the air he never could've done in the water. He did an inverted flip to look back at her. Annoyance bubbled in what he said. "Has Ytell tricked us into letting Alex go off on another dangerous adventure without us?"

Even as she thought of what to say a message from Hheilea confirmed her worse fears.

|A'idah and Zeghes, Alex is in danger. Stay with him. Don't let him go back outside.|

Zeghes said. "No! Ytell sent all of us down into the Tasty's city, but Alex isn't with us. I think he was worried about that Tasty going out into the storm."

A'idah said, "Zeghes, I think you're right. We've got to get out of here."

What would've been a funny message from Skyler under normal conditions instead frustrated her. |Hey, guess what I've found. Nuts. Lots and lots of nuts.|

A'idah fired back a response. |Forget about the nuts, you stupid bird. Alex is in danger.| She didn't wait for a response from Skyler. Instead, she sent out a message to the whole flock. |Hheilea just sent me a message. Alex is in danger. We need to leave the city and find him.|

Zeghes asked, "What about Skyler? Should we just leave him?"

A'idah ground her teeth.

Osamu responded to the flock conversation with a comment preventing her from saying what she thought of Skyler. |I think I know where Skyler is.|

Then she got Ytell's message. | Flock, I need all of you to meet with me outside the rooms we've been assigned by the Tasties.|

Everyone started responding. As she added her message, A'idah remembered her father telling her not to help her friend who'd been raped. He'd tried and failed to distract her from helping, but she always wondered what would have been the outcome if he had tried to help, instead of trying to distract her. Could they have saved her friend?

Ytell's response confirmed her suspicions. He didn't want them going to help Alex. He messaged. |Flock, I need all of you to meet me outside the rooms we've been assigned by the Tasties. I'll talk to you about Alex when I get there.|

He wasn't going to let them help. |Ytell, Hheilea knows about the future. She sent us a message saying Alex is in danger. Please, help us save him. If anything happens to him, I'll never forgive you. It'll be your fault.|

|I'm sorry, A'idah. I want to go check on Alex too, but we can't. Obey me and meet with the flock outside our rooms.|

Chapter Seventeen
Rescue Attempt

A'idah wasn't going to let another friend die. |Hheilea, Ytell is trying to keep us from going to save Alex. How can we help him?|

|There's some kind of danger outside in the wild land. I think that's where Alex must've gone. I've got a terrible sense of danger for him. We have to get to him. When I think of going out the main entrance, all I feel is frustration. Do you know of any other way out?|

|Osamu has a map of the city. He might have an idea.|

|Thanks. I'll talk to him.|

A'idah took her own advice and turned around to talk to him. By his expression, she figured Hheilea had already started communicating with him. Impatiently, she waited. It felt like hours, but finally he looked at her.

"Osamu, I—"

He held a hand up and said, "I will tell you what I just told Hheilea. I think we should listen to Ytell, but if you think you have to try and help Alex, I will help." Then, he gave her one of his infrequent grins. "I know you. You are already set to help Alex. I will send your AI a copy of the map I have."

A'idah made a grimace. "I have trouble with my AI. It does simple things for me, but I don't know if it will be able to work with your map."

"Okay, we'll do this then. You heard Skyler talk about the colors he saw on the walls?"

"Yes."

Again Osamu surprised her with his knowledge. "The way it works in this city is if you think about trying to find something, the city responds to your mind by using color flowing over the tunnel walls to show you how to get there. We will have Skyler stay where he is and you can find him. When you get there contact me. There is a way out of that nut storage room. It is how the Tasties dump nuts from the outside. Get going and good luck."

"What are you going to do?"

"I will try and help by distracting Ytell. If he thinks we are trying to help Alex, he will work to stop us. I am going to meet him. I will make it sound as if all of us are coming."

A'idah didn't realize Osamu could be deceitful. "There's more to you than meets the eye."

The older Japanese man nodded in agreement and said, "Get going. Ytell will not be fooled for long."

At those words she fired off a message to her dolphin friend. |Zeghes, we need to get to Skyler. Can you give me a ride?|

A nudge on her back startled her. "I'm ahead of you. I listened in on what Osamu told you. Did you know when you sleep at night, he's out having adventures?"

The shock of this information distracted her from the driving need to rescue Alex. "What?"

"Yes, I've followed him."

"What?" But aren't you sleeping?"

"You forget that I only need to sleep with half of my brain at a time. It's true that I rest better if I don't do much, but I'm surprised by how much you humans sleep. Osamu doesn't seem to need much sleep. One time, someone attacked him, and we both got involved in the fight. Afterwards, Osamu thanked me for my help and asked me to not follow him as it would make his activities easier to spot by his enemy. Shouldn't we get going to Skyler? Hop on me and I'll give you a ride over to the tunnel he went into."

Stunned into silence by the information, A'idah just nodded her head and swung a leg up and over Zeghes. Pulling herself on up, A'idah wrapped her arms around him.

Rescue Attempt

It was a good thing she held on tight, because Zeghes wasted no time in whipping through the air. Approaching the tunnel entrance, A'idah concentrated on needing to get to the big blue bird. She didn't think of Skyler by name, not knowing if the city would understand. She looked at the opening rapidly approaching and hoped Zeghes remembered to take into consideration his rider. It wouldn't feel good to get smashed against the hard walls or ceiling. She breathed a sigh of relief as Zeghes slowed down.

Her dolphin friend speeded up and darted into the tunnel, and it seemed to A'idah that they only had inches to spare. At least Zeghes wasn't moving too fast. A beautiful blue color showed up on the wall, and Zeghes hung in the air waiting. The city must've gotten her need figured out because the color started moving on down the wall.

They followed it past the first junction of another tunnel and down a tunnel angling off to the right from theirs. A'idah bit her lip to keep herself from asking Zeghes to slow down. The walls zipped past.

Zeghes broke the silence. He sounded angrier than she'd ever heard him. "I hope Alex isn't hurt before we get to him. After we rescue him, I'm going to pound some sense into him. It isn't right for him to go off without us."

Zeghes anger frightened her. He was quite strong, and he really could hurt Alex. She wasn't happy with the older boy either, but A'idah felt much more concerned for him than angry. She needed Alex to be with her in this dangerous training and, and... There was much more to her feelings about him, but she didn't want to admit anything to herself other than needing him as a friend. Troubled by the conflict between her friends, she remembered what Zeghes had just talked about and decided to try and help. "It's a terrible thing for our friend to face danger without us."

"Yes, it is, and after we help him he's going to find out just how terrible he's been."

Not used to taking action with words, A'idah wished she had a physical threat instead of this problem between her friends to deal with. "I'm surprised at you having adventures at night without me."

Zeghes wasn't any dummy, and it was evident by his tone he knew what she was getting at. "That isn't the same thing."

Disappointed at her attempt, A'idah closed her eyes with the side of her face against her friend's back. In frustration she thought about her paralysis after having been shot and not being able to talk. She didn't feel much better at communicating now. Again, she wished Alex was with them. He always knew what to say. He was so gentle, kind, and understanding. Tears of frustration, sadness, and concern wet the cheeks of the teenager. She didn't notice Zeghes stopped swimming through the air.

"The moving color is gone. Are you still thinking about Skyler?"

A'idah opened her eyes to look at the nearby wall. "I'm sorry." Again she focused on finding the big blue bird. Beautiful shades of blue rippled across the wall, and she felt Zeghes moving again.

Her dolphin friend said, "I'm sorry too. I'm not sorry about getting to know you and Alex. I love both of you, but I'm still confused by a lot of what goes on. You try and understand me, but I feel Alex is often off in his own world. I'll try not to be too angry with him. I don't want to kill him, and after we save him I'll try not to hurt him too bad. Okay?"

"Okay. Thanks, Zeghes." She followed this with a scream. "Lookout!"

Zeghes had rocketed through a doorway. Blue feathers and another yell echoed her words. A'idah tried to dodge to the left. With a lurch, her dolphin friend swerved left and dipped. Like acid, the rough wall tore at her skin. She felt herself ripped from her perch on Zeghes and tumbling, twisting, she hit the floor. A'idah fought against her pain and struggled up.

At the same time she heard Skyler. "I'm so happy to see you. Thanks for finding me. This was terrible. I've been trying to leave, but the color on the tunnel walls keeps bringing me back here. I'm so upset. I haven't even eaten any of the nuts."

Quickly, A'idah said, "That's okay. We'll be fine." She messaged Osamu. |We're in the nut room. Now what?|

|Get out of there. I just saw Hheilea. She is caught up in a net. Ytell knows you are trying to get to Alex. They are using our messages. I think they will know you are in that room. You cannot escape via that room. Hurry and leave. Meet me where you would hate to go.|

"Zeghes, Skyler we have to leave." A'idah said. She no longer thought of her pain. It took her just seconds to vault back onto her dolphin friend.

Zeghes flipped around to leave and Skyler burst through the air past them and entered the tunnel first. A pulse of brown color flowed up the tunnel wall. At an intersection they followed it to the right. A Tasty blocked the way.

"Stop. I know you want to help your friend, but you must come with me."

Desperately, she hammered out a message. |Zeghes, turn around and go the other way.|

Even as the dolphin turned to obey, A'idah felt some force restricting their movement.

Skyler ordered. "Let them go."

A'idah turned around to see the big blue bird attack the Tasty with his big, powerful beak. The restriction stopped and Zeghes zoomed away. From behind her, she heard Skyler's voice. "Go. Save our flock member."

"Thanks, Skyler! We will!"

Together, A'idah and Zeghes barreled down the tunnels following a pulse of color. She clung to him. A'idah squeezed her arms and legs as tight against his smooth skin as she could get.

Zeghes said, "A'idah, I'm going to slow down. I'm afraid of knocking you into a wall again."

"I'll be okay. Don't slow down. Go faster."

"You're already injured. I saw the blood. You're going to attract sharks." Confusion colored his voice as he continued. "I mean... I don't know. Does blood affect... creatures on land in the same way as it does a shark?"

Humor colored her response. "No, Zeghes. Keep going fast and go faster if you can."

They whipped around a bend in the tunnel and A'idah saw Zeghes scrape against the wall before he got straightened back out. The pulse of brown color on the wall sped up to match their speed. A'idah called out his name before she could stop herself. "Zeghes."

"It's okay. I heal quickly."

Together they accelerated down another straight section of tunnel before the dolphin flipped to take another bend. Again, A'idah felt her friend hit the wall with his body protecting her as they rounded the turn.

In dismay, A'idah looked down the tunnel. Their way ahead was blocked by two large Tasties holding something in their hands and pointing the devices at them. A third Tasty ran from behind them.

"Stop. We have you surrounded. There are others behind you."

Zeghes slowed. |A'idah, what should we do?|

The brown wave of color on the wall slowed to a stop.

The third Tasty didn't look right. In fact, his image seemed to flicker.

|Zeghes, A'idah. It's me, Ekbal. Keep going. The way is clear. Osamu says to use the red button.|

The third Tasty slammed into the two Tasties knocking them down. The illusion shattered. Zeghes rocketed over them, and A'idah saw Ekbal struggling with the two Tasties. She remembered how he used to be a quiet, easily frightened boy who was just curious about everything. She couldn't believe how much he'd changed. They bounced around another corner. The brown wave of color pulsed down the tunnel wall and disappeared as if someone had flipped a switch. A'idah thought maybe they had.

Zeghes said, "The color is gone from the wall."

"Keep going."

He rocketed down the tunnel. "Yes. I've been making a map in my head as we explored. It's similar to exploring a coral reef. I think we're getting close."

Rescue Attempt

They passed an intersection with an unconscious Tasty lying on the floor. Slamming around another corner, they discovered the tunnel came to an intersection.

A'idah said, "It branches. Which way do we go?"

Zeghes slowed, even though A'idah wanted to be going faster. She couldn't sense the future but knew in her heart that Alex faced mortal danger. They had to get to him. At the end of the tunnel, the dolphin turned first one direction and then the other direction. "I'm not sure. I think the direction we want is straight through, but I don't know which will get us there."

"Turn back to the left again."

There ahead was another intersection. That tunnel looked bigger. "This way."

Without questioning, Zeghes rocketed down and turned right. The large tunnel continued far ahead of them. He said, "You chose right. The door should be just down here."

From the distant other end of the tunnel they heard the sounds of running feet.

"Quickly, Zeghes." Expecting a surge of acceleration A'idah hugged him tight with her arms, pressing the side of her face against his dorsal fin. Her legs wrapped around his lower torso with her feet hooked under the flukes of his tail.

His acceleration still ripped her arms free. She whipped back. A'idah's feet hooked around Zeghes tail flukes were the only thing keeping her from falling. She struggled to pull herself back on. A'idah tucked her upper body up just in time to see the approaching doorway. Realizing what would happen she pulled her arms up to protect her head. When they slew to a stop in front of the door, A'idah slammed into the wall falling off Zeghes. Through the pain she recognized the door opening.

Lurching to her feet, A'idah spoke, not realizing how slurred her voice was. "Go, go hith the reth buthon. I'll geth on a sleth and geth outh."

"A'idah, are you okay?"

She screamed. "Go!" Following her own command, A'idah lurched, stumbled, and finally somehow managed to run to the sleds. Reaching one she grabbed the handle and stood trying to remember what she was going to do. A'idah had to save her friend. A dripping sound caught her attention. Looking down, she saw blood dripping on the floor. Another sound lifted her head. Above her came a whirring. A huge door high above was opening. Other sounds, footsteps, spoken orders, and her heartbeat.

What was she doing? Alex. Alex, he needed her. A'idah threw a leg over the sled and willed it up and toward the door. It lifted up and started to go. Something held it back. Confusion, why wasn't she going? What friend was she going to save?

Twisting her head back A'idah saw a Tasty holding on to the back end of her sled. She considered kicking, but that would take too much effort. Hair radiating out from her head she pointed a finger. "Leth go or thie. I musth go save my frienth. She's been rapeth."

The Tasty let go, and the sled soared up accelerating toward the opening. Confusion shook her mind. No, not my friend who'd been raped, A'idah was saving Alex. For some reason it was important to correct the earlier statement. Turning her head back, A'idah looked for the Tasty, but only saw brown goo lifting obscuring the room. Ewwww.

Nausea gripped her. Only by force of will did she hang on as she threw up. Cool air greeted her sweaty brow. She couldn't see. Was she going blind? And then A'idah realized. She'd made it outside.

Lifting her eyes, she saw a few stars. Now, she could go save Alex. She just wanted to get back on the unmoving ground for a moment to rest for only a second. Something blocked the sparkling lights above her. Puzzled, she cocked her head to consider this mystery. What had followed her?

Realization and terror hit moments before the brown goo. A'idah and sled finished slamming onto the ground buried by a giant stinking brown pile.

A'idah only had time for one quick breath before getting buried. She willed the sled to move and felt it sliding up. The goo forced its way up into her nostrils burning. Instinctively, A'idah desperately wanted to gasp

Rescue Attempt

and scream, but kept her mouth clinched shut. The sled lurched at her command to move faster. One hand slipped free of the handle.

The goo seeped into her ears. Her eyelids burned. A'idah couldn't keep them shut tight enough. Her lungs screamed for air. She wouldn't give up. Her other hand slipped off. The sled slid out from under her. She couldn't fail Alex.

Chapter Eighteen
Danger in the Night

"Ah!" Alex gasped. *AI, what happened? Why did we drop?*

A message has been piggybacked on my use of the artificial gravity generator. I have been informed that you are interfering in a fledgling ceremony. All technology will be blocked. I'll try and land you in the clearing before I'm turned off.

Sabu said, "Why did we fall?"

"We're losing access to our AIs and the local gravity generators." Something else distracted Alex. He knew something irritating and embarrassing would happen, but something else, someone dangerous and with a very deadly intent distracted him. He desperately tried to sort it out and to be sure of his feelings.

"The ground's coming up fast," Sabu said.

With an explosion of breath, Alex fell hard rolling forward to land in a bush.

"You need to work on your landings," Sabu said, bounding up to where Alex rested feet up in the bush and head down on the ground. She reached out a paw and gently patted the side of his head.

"Hey, knock that off." He wiggled trying to get free. How much time did he have?

She patted his head again. "I'm trying, but it's on too tight."

Even with the rain pouring inside his upside down pant legs, shirt, and down his nose Alex had to grin. "Make yourself useful and look around for Delli." If he knew the

Danger in the Night

danger, he could warn her. Alex could feel he would be free in time, but urgency drove him to get free sooner.

After one last pat, Sabu said, "Okay."

Alex struggled some more, but only managed to get a branch up his pants. Something, he could sense something, but not sure what. Anger and—

"Get yourself untangled from that bush and come toward my voice. The Tasty is near. I can smell it. This is funny. You came to help the Tasty, but you are much more helpless than it is."

"I'm not helpless." Alex said, upside down. For a moment, the clouds opened to reveal the bright green-blue nebula shining with the stars above them. Again darkness enveloped him.

"Who's out there?"

Even in the storm, Alex recognized Delli's voice, except this time, it was very annoyed. If only he knew who else lurked, and where they would come from.

"It's me, Alex, and one of my flock members, Sabu. I thought in this storm you might need help. I don't have much to help with, except for an extra cape and food, I brought with me. My AI is turned off."

"You're stupid. You shouldn't have come."

"But, you're out here all alone in a storm, with predators all around." Something else approached. Danger came closer. He needed to focus on his sense of the future.

Delli said, "That's kind of the idea of the fledgling ceremony. I could have done it with a friend. Two of us thought about it, but yesterday, Grandma suggested I go alone. Also, didn't you notice the storm is over?"

"The big cat's watching us from a tree," Sabu said. "Do you have a place of safety?"

"Yes, come over here," Delli said. "I've a hollow under this tree trunk up against its roots."

Sabu said, "You might need to help Alex. He's stuck in a bush."

"What?"

With a last effort, Alex tore himself free from the bush. "I'm coming." He pulled a branch out of his pants and stumbled toward where he thought Delli was. He could smell the wonderful odor she exuded, and yet his sense of the future supplied a very strong feeling which overrode his thought of that scent. Someone came, and he could feel their intent to murder him. The cat above, Delli, and Sabu were distractions.

"Not that way," Delli said. "There are vines in that area which will give you hives. Stand still, I'll come to you. You really are quite blind in the dark."

"The cat's jumping," Sabu said.

Instinctually, Alex started to dodge, but a paw grabbed his arm. Startled, he jerked back.

"It's me," Delli said. "Come."

A thud and a yowl of complaint from above Alex pulled his attention to the darkness above. Frantically, his eyes scanned the dark for the real danger. He yielded to the tug of Deli's paw. "What's going on?" Where was the threat of murder coming from? There was no danger for Delli and Sabu. He'd been a fool to come. Alex could tell warning them wouldn't help. In fact, if he warned them, they would be in danger.

"Your friend has quite the Vapu created paw. She swatted the cougar out of the air in mid leap. That was a very good thing. We would've been injured in the fight. You really are defenseless in the dark without any technology."

"Hey, I can fight," Alex said, trying not to stumble as he allowed Delli to lead him through the dark. At the same time, he tried to locate what direction the threat came from. It couldn't be the cat. He could feel the eminent threat of death if he didn't have more room to maneuver. Alex considered his options.

"Your skin feels rather soft and tender. You have no fur and no hair to speak of to help protect that skin. You don't have any claws and your teeth are puny."

"She's right, you're puny," Sabu said, bumping against his other side.

Alex stumbled from the bump and went with it, falling and using the momentum to pull free of the Tasty's grasp. He tried to block out Sabu's voice and focus on his feelings of the future.

Danger in the Night

"The cat or cougar has left. I'm too much for it to handle. As defenseless as you are, you need to stay close to us, Alex. We're in the wild now, under the rules of the—"

Turning the fall into a tumble Alex dimly heard "What?" from Delli and then a muffled "Lookout."

Sabu snarled and a muffled "No, I won't be held captive."

Alex sprang up from the tumble to launch himself over what he felt had to be another bush. He landed balanced, waiting and tense. The first attack would come soon.

A chuckle came out of the dark. "Not bad. At first, I thought your fighting ability must've been overrated and hyped by the stories going around. How did you avoid that bush? I thought you were almost blind in the dark."

From Delli came a warning. "We've been caught in some kind of netted traps. Watch out for what he throws."

"No, he doesn't want to capture me. He's planning on killing me."

"Ooh, you do have the ability to sense futures. What are you?" The attacker said.

"I'm a human." He didn't add, and somehow I've become a bit of a Kimley. Alex shifted, staying ready. A little nebula light started to break through the overcast. At the same time, he focused with all his might on future paths he could take. One tantalized him, but he couldn't quite.... He'd been avoiding listening to Maleky's thoughts, but this one sounded helpful.

I think I know what type of person is attacking you. They're deadly.

Alex jumped over a leg sweep. Kicking out he barely caught a thigh his shin. *Really?*

I've hired them. Get me sometime to remember.

Alex could barely see. He struggled to keep his balance.

The attacker switched styles. Fists jabbed at Alex.

If I can remember it, I have a code.

Some blows, Alex shifted to avoid. Others he redirected. He jabbed back, only connecting once.

Shift the battle from where Sabu and Delli are.

Only with the combination of improving sight and his sense of the future did Alex hold his own. A right hook jolted him.

It would be bad if too many know I can communicate with you.

Alex managed to land a stiff jab. A grunt rewarded him. He was very grateful for all the boxing and other fighting training he'd already gotten.

Some would try and question me through you.

The attacker had a longer reach, and when Alex tried to close in to gain an advantage he caught two jabs himself.

They might not use very gentle methods.

Two paths for the fight flashed in his mind. It was going to get darker. Alex quickly back pedaled and then shifted his own style. Instead of using his lead hand to block and redirect the next blow, he caught the wrist. With a twist, Alex used the attacker's momentum to pull him forward. Thrusting his other fist into the opponent's solar plexus, Alex used the power of a fulcrum to throw the bigger man through the air.

Alex jumped back and dodged behind a bush. A cloud blocked the nebula's light. Total darkness fell. Alex froze, listening, and desperately searching for an edge in the future paths. He knew the watcher above.

Sabu still sounded muffled as if she had something between her teeth. "Watch out. He's moving around to get behind you."

In Alex's mind, his feelings gave him an open path. He pushed through the bush. The wind of an attack just missing him spoke of urgency.

Yes. This would work. If he could— He sprinted forward dodging to the left to avoid something sharp being thrown at him. If Alex could just, jump high enough. The other person was faster. He couldn't only run.

With all Alex's strength he sprang up reaching, reaching, and praying. The sense of the future he'd been relying on went blank. His hands slapped onto a branch. Swinging up, he tucked his legs in. His hands slipped.

"You can't get away by climbing."

Danger in the Night

Alex's feet whipped up, and he let go.

"I'll just shoot you when the cloud moves. I'd rather test myself against you. Fighting hand to hand will give you a chance, although you're going to lose either way." A nasty laugh followed.

Even as the attacker below spoke, Alex roared as loud as he could at the watcher. "Yaaaaaah!!"

Startled from its perch, by feet coming at it and the yell following, the cougar leapt down. Immediately, cursing and snarling broke out.

Alex landed upside down, painfully on other branches. Now the blank wall in his sense of the future evaporated. Again, he could sense possibilities. What had happened? Alex wanted to yell *surprise* down at the combatants but scrambled for a hold. He didn't want to fall on the battle. That very possible future wouldn't be good. The senses of what could come spun. Branches scratched at him. Handholds broke free.

He grasped a small branch desperately trying not to fall. It broke. He fell. The snarling, cursing stopped. The clouds shifted. For just a moment he saw the nebula. He twisted to see below.

Dreadlocks flipped through the air, as the attacker turned.

Controlling his mid-air roll, Alex tucked his feet up. Into the right leg he focused all his energy.

Below, a bearded face rotated toward him. Black eyes widened.

With all his focus, Alex jammed his right heel down in to the visage. Bones cracked. He pushed off from the devastated face. With a back flip, Alex landed on his feet. Still, more futures pushed at him. In one, death seemed very probable. Again, his sense of the future met a blank wall. Was his very possible death erasing any possible future?

His assailant held one hand against his face. Fierce eyes glared over the bloody mess. The other hand clawed at a holster. The bloody hand flung out, flinging blood at Alex's eyes, but Alex ducked closing his eyes for just a fraction of a second.

In that time, he shoved in against the bigger man. With a grunt, Alex lifted his knee, hard and high into the taller man's crotch. With his hands, he grappled with his enemy's hand, which now held a blaster.

Maleky screamed in his head. *Don't let him shoot us! Don't shoot him! Don't let him shoot us!*

The assailant's other hand clubbed against the side of Alex's head. The gasps gave evidence of the damage Alex had done to him. The jarring slams of the blows told him of danger. His sense of the future told him he had to gain control of the blaster.

With his right foot, Alex stomped down missing the instep. He spun, twisting the small blaster out of the other man's grasp.

Don't kill him.

Finishing the turn, Alex leveled the stubby gun as it molded itself to his palm and wrist.

The man froze in the act of lurching after him. "Go ahead. Kill me."

Don't, don't, they always have an out. Just in case they're beat. Tell him 42J.

"Go ahead or is your fancy sense of the future telling you what will happen. You can see futures, but I know your past. You're not tough. You wouldn't kill the Winkle girl."

Alex said, "What? 42J." Even as he said it, Alex knew it wouldn't work as Maleky wanted. Desperately, he looked for future paths. When he thought of killing the assassin, Hheilea came to mind. All he could sense about Hheilea was a blank wall. If that blank wall was a possible death, he couldn't kill the assassin.

The assailant laughed. "Maleky, you are in there. Sorry, but someone is paying more than you to get Alex killed."

"Who?"

"You wouldn't believe me if I told you, but it's someone you know."

Alex couldn't believe his best option, but he shot there anyway.

The assailant screamed. "What are you doing? Stop!"

Danger in the Night

"Vow to leave and I won't shoot the other dreadlocks off the other side of your head."

With deadly words, the dread vowed, "Next time, you'll die slowly and with lots of pain."

"Maybe," Alex said. "Hurry up. My friends are uncomfortable."

"Okay. I vow to leave, but you can count on another coming soon." The assailant turned his back on Alex and started running away, dreadlocks flopping down his back.

Alex carefully aimed and shot as he said, "I didn't say anything about the dreadlocks on top of your head."

The blue-green light of the nebula gave enough illumination to show the person stumble and then fall.

Maleky screamed in Alex's head. *You've killed him! You've killed Hheilea!*

Alex raced forward to find the alien man lying face down with smoke rising from his burnt scalp. He hadn't believed his sense of the future, but it worked. With a nervous voice that grew more confident, he said. "Ha. I got lucky. I've got a prisoner." Alex went back to ignoring Maleky. With a couple of breaks, he dragged the guy over to Delli and Sabu.

"You two want some help? Delli, is it okay to use technology to free you?"

Delli stuttered, "How, how, how did you defeat him?"

"I guess I'm not totally defenseless. Now, about freeing you two?"

Delli used her paws to hold the net away from her body. "Come close and don't miss."

Carefully, Alex stepped close and angled the shot.

He left her to work her way free while he freed Sabu. With Delli's help they searched the captive and found a surprisingly large assortment of knives and strange gizmos. In a few minutes, they securely tied the assailant up using his own nets. Alex looked at Delli and pointed to their captive. "What do we do with him? I'm not sure why the wound he got knocked him out. Also, I can tell with my sense of the future that he'll recover."

Delli waited to respond until Alex finished and then said, "The border is closed to all of us. We'll have to keep him here until morning."

Sabu asked, "This creature attacked us and tried to kill you, Alex. Why don't we just kill it and get rid of the danger?"

Alex shook his head, both at the idea of just killing a captive and because of what would happen. "We can't. I can see what happens if we kill him. If he dies, Hheilea will die. I don't know how. Also, someone wants me dead, and he knows who. Hopefully, we can get that information from him."

Delli rolled the man's head over and looked at his bearded visage. "Back in the city, there are individuals who can help solve those problems." She rolled the head back over. "Too bad we can't use Sabu's solution. Alex, you'll need to drag him over to where my hollow is. Follow me."

Alex's eyes had gone wide at the surprising news that Delli thought Sabu's solution was good. Once again, an alien's perspective surprised him. Picking up the captive's feet, Alex started dragging him after her.

Sabu paced along beside him. "I could help you drag him, but the result of my bite might not be good."

"Thanks for the offer." Alex gasped out and stopped to catch his breath. The alien must've outweighed him by at least double. He wished his AI could help with a gravity generator.

Shadows deepened as the clouds began blocking the nebula and stars. Dimly, Alex could make out a narrowing path between bushes, and Sabu moved ahead.

"Sabu, stay behind Alex and don't enter my hollow," Delli said.

"Why not?" Sabu asked.

"Why can't he come in?" Alex asked.

"Sabu, I think you know why," Delli said.

"What are you talking about?" Alex asked.

"We are in the wild," Sabu said. "I'm a predator, and she's prey."

"What? That's crazy talk. Sabu wouldn't kill you."

"I don't know or trust Sabu."

Danger in the Night

"That's crazy, Sabu's my friend."

"She's right. Why shouldn't I eat her? I do want to. She smells so good, and I'm hungry."

"What?" Alex knew the smell Sabu spoke about. All of a sudden, his stomach growled. "You won't kill her, because that isn't civilized."

"This isn't civilization, and I'm not very civilized. I'm a wild animal."

Not civilized? "Sabu won't kill me. I trust her. She's my friend."

"I'm your friend, as I understand the idea, but she's not my friend, and this is the wild."

Alex couldn't accept the statement. "She's someone we know."

"If I don't know my prey, I would starve."

"Argh," Alex said, He'd finally gotten the alien sliding again, and now he banged his head on a thick branch.

"Just let it go," Delli said.

"No, I don't let things go," Alex tugged again on the captive, but now branches jammed into the captive preventing Alex from dragging him deeper into the thicket. "Why do you come out here?"

"Sabu, I don't think Alex can get our captive much farther into the thicket. Would you consider him prey?"

"No, he doesn't smell good, and Hheilea would die if I ate him. Besides, we brought some bags of food. I'll eat mine."

"Good. Can you watch over him and still get a good rest?"

"Yes. Delli, is your hollow warm enough for Alex? He won't be able to stand the cold of the night."

Alex let go of the alien's feet. In spite of himself, he shivered. "I'm not that weak."

She said, "With me in there he'll be warm enough."

Chapter Nineteen
Life for Life

Delli called back to Alex. "Alex, can you see good enough to come on in?"

He nodded his head. "Yes." Taking the last two bags of food, he moved into the thicket. The darkness deepened, and he stumbled, holding his hands out in front to protect himself from unseen branches. His sense of the future hinted at minor problems. Alex didn't take the effort to probe more deeply into the possibilities. One searching hand felt fur. Alex gasped in surprise.

"Here let me lead you."

A warm hand/paw grasped his. He stumbled some more. With a surprising strength, Delli supported and guided him. "Is this too fast?"

A branch swatted Alex, and he ducked his head. "No." With extra care, he lifted his feet higher trying to avoid the unseen branches. Suddenly, the dim shape of a huge log appeared in front of Alex. Beside him was an indistinct form, Delli. Looking up he could see part of the nebula, in between some fast moving remnants of the storm.

"Is this log where your hollow is?" Alex asked.

"You can see it?" Delli asked.

"The nebulalight is helping, now that the storm clouds are dissipating again."

"Follow me," Delli said, letting go of Alex's arm.

The indistinct form next to Alex moved toward the log and disappeared. Clouds thickened and the darkness deepened. Stretching hands out in front, Alex carefully stepped forward.

"Watch out for the hole," Delli said.

Life for Life

"Huh," Alex said, setting his foot down into nothing. "Ah!"

Tumbling forward, he landed face down on soft warm fur that slipped out from under him, leaving him face down in dirt. In the enclosed space, the smell coming from Delli almost overwhelmed him.

Her voice held laughter. "I'm sorry. I should've warned you about the hole," Delli said. "Crawl forward and under the tree. Use your hands to pull yourself through."

Not being hurt and chuckling himself at the humor of his fall, Alex crawled forward under a gap beneath the trunk. He had to lie down and pull his head and shoulders under. Roots sticking out of the ground caught at his clothing, but he wriggled and grunted his way under the log. On the other side, he couldn't see anything. Alex's hands groped about seeking anything to grab ahold of and pull the rest of his body through. Delli's warm hand/paws clasped his and pulled. With a grunt, Alex wriggled out from under the log. He could feel dry leaves and hear their crackly noises under him.

Out of the darkness came Delli's voice. "Let's get comfortable."

What did she mean by that? He found out a moment later as her warm furry body cuddled up to him. Quickly, he shifted back away from her. A bubbling laughter surprised him. It must've been Delli's

"If you come over here, you'll be more comfortable."

"I'm fine." Alex said trying to control his embarrassment.

Out of the darkness, Delli said, "Suit yourself." Changing the subject, she added. "Earlier you asked why I came out here, but I didn't answer. Do you want the answer now?"

Alex wiggled to get more comfortable and tried not to think of how comfortable and warm Delli had felt. "Yeah. I don't know if I'll understand, but I'll try."

From above the hole came Sabu's voice. "I want to hear this too."

Delli said, "Don't fall asleep. It's a long answer. My species, the Tasties, long ago made a choice."

137

"How long ago?"

"Two hundred thousand years ago."

"Wow. That's a long time." Alex decided to snack on his food while she talked.

"No more questions until I finish. Within a couple of thousand years, our civilization developed some problems. First, our population expanded. One of the ways we dealt with that was birth control, but then our population began to get older with fewer and fewer children. There were a number of habitable planets in the solar system we lived in. We spread out to those other planets.

"The colonists on one planet found themselves in a battle just to survive. There existed an intelligent, apex predator on that planet which gladly greeted the colonists as very tasty prey. In the colonists' battle for survival, they killed off many of the native predators. The apex predator proved to be a problem even with our advanced technology. Our religious beliefs didn't help. They were contrary to exterminating other species. The struggle went on for a thousand years.

"Back on the home planet the population kept getting older with fewer and fewer children. They and the colonists couldn't relate to each other and they grew to dislike each other. There was an athletic competition held every three years. Over the years, the colonists' athletes began dominating in that competition and in all sports. What surprised everyone was when the colonists began to surpass the home planet in intelligence. The one thing the home planet people continued to be best at was politics. This created great friction within our society.

"Next, the colonists made a breakthrough in understanding the nasty predator's language. We could talk to them. They were no longer just beasts. Back then, we didn't have squirts to translate everything. Some Tasties, we didn't call ourselves by that name back then, wanted to leave the planet to the predator species. Others wanted to try and live in some kind of joint society with them. It was a time of great social upheaval. Everything changed, when one Tasty, David, saved a starving predator.

Life for Life

His story of saving Johnathan is an incredible epic of courage. David had gone out into a wilderness area to study the Thrips, the same species as your flock leader, Ytell. David had a disaster at his camp and lost all of his equipment. Without any tools, he started working his way out of the wilderness. Next, he stumbled onto Johnathan, a badly injured and starving thrip. David treated Johnathan's injuries and dragged the predator for many miles, while fighting off dangers. At one point, David decided Johnathan would die without better food than David was finding for him. David offered his own life and body. For some reason, Johnathan, a wild predator, with just the faintest ideas about civilization refused. They worked together and made it out of the wilderness. It resulted in a revolution of thought for my people. It recreated our society and saved countless other species from extinction. David was the same age I am now, and my coming out here is to celebrate life as he did in that event and in a later more important event."

"What happened to David and Johnathan?" Alex asked.

"They became great friends and traveled about talking to the flocks of thrips, trying to convince them to embrace change and civilization. In their latter days, an event happened that sealed their legacy and started the Thrips on their two hundred thousand year journey to civilization."

"It took them that long," Alex said.

"That's actually a long running joke between us and the Thrips, but it did take many years. In fact, it was just in recent years the last wild flocks embraced civilization. Your flock leader during his fledgling ceremony helped make it happen."

"Ytell?"

"Yes, but this isn't his story. It's about the event with David and Johnathan."

"What was the event?" Alex asked.

"They were making a journey across the Great Western Desert. A large number of Thrip tribes challenged them to the journey. The Thrips said civilization had turned Johnathan soft. They said if Johnathan and David would make the journey, they would make the journey of becoming civilized. Their friends tried to talk them out of it. They told David and Johnathan they should enjoy their last years in retirement. The two friends insisted on making the journey, saying this was the goal they had been striving toward for most of their lives, and it was more important to be able to live in the wild when you were old than to be able to keep living in civilization. Another accident happened. Johnathan was unable to fly. Together they struggled not to escape from the desert, but to finish the journey. They both were starving, but David had been able to find more food he could eat. Eventually Johnathan healed and could fly again, except he was too weak from hunger. They'd reached the last stretch of the desert. It was a part of the desert David couldn't cross alone, and Johnathan was too weak with hunger to fly.

"They made the decision that was incredible. Johnathan killed and ate David. With the added strength, he made it out.

"We have a saying based on that.

"In the morning, I am like grass which sprouts. In the afternoon, I flourish and grow up. In the evening, I am cut down. I would not just wither away but give life to another.

Alex couldn't believe what he had heard. He just stared into the dark with mouth open. How could they?

"Because of David's victory they succeeded, and the Thrips began their journey to civilization."

"That's incredible," Sabu said. "Life has become so much more complex for me. Now, I too feel the need not to just wither away, but to give my life to a higher calling."

"Thanks for the story," Alex said. He still couldn't believe what had happened to David and Johnathan. To give your life and to willingly accept the life of your friend so you could live. He remembered Twyla's willingness to die so he and others would live. "I... understand better what you are doing. Sorry for interfering. We'll leave in the morning."

If Alex had been Johnathan, he couldn't have killed David. It troubled him to think that then both of them would've died, and the thrips would've remained wild. That event had been a huge turning point making a whole new future path available. Thinking of that made him think of the efforts Hheilea was involved in with her people to make something very unlikely to happen, happen. That must be a bigger turning point.

"Thank you," Delli said, "and thanks for trying to help. That's a wonderful way to be."

"I thought you said it was stupid?"

"Sorry, I was upset."

Alex started thinking about the Winkles. They had started a mutiny at the academy which had almost destroyed everything. Now, because of A'idah stumbling upon a burrow created by the Winkles using a giant earthworm, they knew the Winkles were planning something here in the Earth's quadrant. They'd already told Ytell what they knew about the Winkles, but the flock leader was too busy to help. Alex needed to figure out what they were up to. Growing weary, Alex couldn't follow his line of thought about future potential paths. Just as he was drifting off, a scream pierced the air. "What was that?"

"The cougar. Go to sleep."

Before he knew it, Alex heard Delli speaking again.

"I thought you were leaving in the morning?"

"Huh, What's...," Alex said. His mouth felt full of cotton. "Is it morning?" He could hear birds. Cranking his eyes open, light poured in. Above, the mass of a bush filtered the sunlight. Sticks poked him as he struggled to his knees.

Delli turned her furry face to Alex, "Now that you're finally awake, I'm going back out to talk with Sabu some more. I think we're going to be friends if she can keep her instincts under control." With a laugh she added, "I'm just so irresistible to her stomach."

Following her, Alex crawled on his hands and knees to the log. He slid onto his belly and wriggled himself back under it. He got halfway, and in the hole in front of him Alex could see the tails of Sabu and Delli swishing back and forth. Faint sounds of conversation reached him.

Wriggling and squirming Alex pulled on roots trying to squeeze out, "I could use a hand here."

"Just dig your claws in. Oh wait, you just have fake claws," Delli said with a laugh.

Alex tipped his head back to better glare at his tormentor, "I'll...," Was Sabu laughing? He didn't know Sabu could laugh.

"Sorry for the hard time. Let me help," Delli said. She jumped down into the hole and offered a hand/paw to pull Alex on out. "My friends say, if a predator was eating me, I'd show him how to do it better, or else it's you're too ornery to get eaten."

Climbing up out of the hole after her, Alex tried to find the right words to say. "I guess it's time for us to go. This wasn't what I expected. I..."

"It's okay. Sabu told me about your battle to be what you would be and not what some mind worm would have you be. Thanks again for being who you are. I can see now why the elders have been talking about you."

Turning to Sabu, he wondered. She did? Sabu doesn't talk that much. Looking back at Delli, and her bright shining eyes, he felt the ground giving under his feet. Alex said, "Celebrate life."

He moved, worried about the ground giving way and falling back into the hole when she rushed to him and gave him a big warm hug almost knocking him back into the hole.

Delli's warm breath tickled his ear as she spoke, "I always hug my special friends whenever we part." With a chuckle she added, "Usually, I knock them down with the force of my hug."

Feeling the ground shifting again under one foot, Alex was very glad she hadn't knocked him down. The result would've been both of them falling into the hole and getting hurt. "I'm—

She said, "I'll have to tell my sister to give you a hug. I should warn you about her. She'll probably complain about you having clothing on. It does feel odd to hug someone with clothing on. One thing for sure, she'll love seeing you turn red."

Life for Life

Overwhelmed by her fragrance, the warm hug, and talk about getting hugs without clothing, Alex stepped back quickly when she released him. The ground under his feet gave even more. Alex moved farther from the hole as he tried to deal with his embarrassment and the thoughts he had from her. Between his confusion and her words about the elders, he didn't know what to say. He didn't want her sister to hug him, even though it had been pleasant just very embarrassing. "I—"

Delli interrupted him. "Someone is coming."

Alex looked up just in time to see Hheilea, in a bubble, crashing through the branches above them.

"Alex!" Her bubble dissipated, and she barreled into him knocking him over and into the hole.

Alex landed on his back with a grunt. His breath exploded out of him.

Hheilea landed on top of him knocking the last of the air out of his lungs. "Alex, I couldn't message you. I could sense a terrible danger. No one would listen to me. I couldn't get your AI to answer. They wouldn't let me leave last night. You're alive. I— What happened to you?"

She gasped a quick breathe. Alex wanted to answer, but he couldn't get a breath. Between getting the air knocked out and her hugging him, he couldn't breathe and felt dizzy. Hheilea continued with barely a pause for her own breath. "I tried to sneak out and almost succeeded. Ytell caught me right at the exit. Then they posted a guard on me. Are you okay? I knocked my guard out and found a different way out of the city, but it took me all night. What happened to you? I couldn't get your AI to answer. Why aren't you talking? Are you okay?"

Finally in the dim light of the hole, Hheilea must've noticed he couldn't get his breath. Maybe, she could tell he was turning blue or the fact he was trying to push her off. Alex didn't know.

Hheilea said, "Oh, no." She rolled off him. "I'm sorry. Breathe deep, it'll go away."

Relieved of her weight, he finally managed a couple of painful breaths. "I was... alright."

Hheilea said a very repentant, "Sorry."

The dizziness passed and he started to breathe easier. Her actions and words worried him. Could it be the T'wasn't-to-be-is was going again? But he didn't hear its music in his mind. In the dim light, Hheilea's distraught face reminded him of another time and again a flashback roared into his mind.

~**********~

"Alex!" Hheilea raced into him, throwing her arms about him. Through her sobs, she said, "I couldn't get your... AI to answer. I watched Titan... try to kill you... as I rode an airpath... to get here. I couldn't do anything.... I almost lost you. My father, he should've told me about your danger."

~**********~

Back from the memory, Alex didn't know what to say. That time, they'd been in love because of the T'wasn't-to-be-is. Now, they were supposed to be just friends, but.... Did she still love him, but didn't think he did? He hated another possibility. Maybe the T'wasn't-to-be-is really hadn't gone away. What was going on? Alex didn't know what to say. He tried not to think about how she felt in his arms or how he really felt. Surprisingly, Maleky didn't bother him.

Fortunately for him, Sabu stuck her head down into the hole and said, "What's going on down here? I think we're supposed to be going back to the Tasties' city."

Not looking at Hheilea, Alex said, "We better get going."

Together, they clambered out of the hole, and Alex showed Hheilea the bound assassin. She hurriedly tested his bounds. "What happened?"

When she heard the events of the night, Hheilea's eyes looked watery, and she told Alex. "You can't be without some kind of guard. Who knows when another attempt will be made on your life?"

Hheilea looked around as if expecting another assassin to appear at any moment. "I just sent a message to Ytell about the assassin. He's going to meet us in the fields. We better get going."

Delli said, "She's right. You should hurry back into the fields and to the city. I'll take care of the boundary for you, get going."

Alex and Sabu's AIs still couldn't use any gravity generators so Hheilea used one to lift the captive, and they started back toward the city.

A message from Hheilea alerted him to the fact his AI was back on. |I'm sorry I overreacted. Last night, when I was trying to get to you my sense of your future kept running into a blank wall. That meant you were going to die.|

Alex could feel a mental choked off sob before the message continued.

|Actually, it meant there was one very possible line of actions just happening which would result in your death. I've been a bit frantic to get to you.|

Alex forced himself to ignore his worries about the T'wasn't-to-be-is. Instead, he focused on trying to find the right response to her feelings. He considered trying to make light of her concern, but fortunately Alex remembered a painful experience of how that wouldn't result in helping his friend at all. He had to validate her feelings. Hesitantly, Alex tried to say the right things. |I understand. I ran into the same kind of blank wall too and it was concerning you. In fact, you should know that this assassin needs to live. Somehow, he's tied his life to yours. If he dies, you die too. It wasn't much fun fighting him and knowing you would die if he died.|

|Oh, no.| A long pause followed that message before Hheilea explained. |Last night, after I knocked out my guard. I started using my sense of the future to find which way to go. I... I... I sensed the danger for you growing worse. My coming to you then would've made it worse. What really surprised me was when I reluctantly considered not getting to you as soon as I could. I felt a danger to my life. I couldn't figure it out. I didn't want the Tasties catching me. So I hid. During that time, I kept considering my danger. I found the source. It was a

necklace my dear little brother gave me the last time I saw him. I left it in the city. He… he…| The message died away with great sadness.

The emotions in this message were worse than the first. Now, Alex wanted to stop and take her into his arms. It was Hymeron, and Hheilea knew her brother willingly tied her life to this assassin's. Alex said the first thought that came to him. |I'm sorry.| He thought he should say more, but he didn't know what to say. Hymeron was her brother and his friend, how could he?

Together, they had crossed the boundary and started on a path toward the city. Through the other emotions, Alex started to feel nervous. It wasn't quite a feeling of danger but almost. He checked on the assassin and looked at Hheilea out of the corner of his eyes. It didn't seem to be either of them.

Hheilea messaged him again. |I expected to find A'idah with you.|

|What?|

|You Earthlings are amazing. Ytell and all of the Tasties were focused on keeping me and your flock from getting out to you. Somehow, Osamu shutdown the whole city. They're still working on getting everything running. I heard A'idah managed to escape. They've been searching outside the city all through the night.|

Alex immediately searched his sense of the future for A'idah.

Chapter Twenty
Trouble with Friends

A'idah screamed. Gasping and panting, she tried to understand. She hadn't died from being buried in poop.

She was out.

A'idah rolled over onto her hands and knees. Her nostrils and eyelids burned. She gagged at a horrible taste in her mouth. A'idah's stomach roiled. Pain pounded in her temples. Fighting against the nausea, she struggled up. The muscles of her stomach clenched forcing the contents out, but she held it back. A'idah slipped and fell with a splat back into the poop on her face. She couldn't breathe. Refusing to give up, she got up onto one knee. Her whole body trembled. The battle took all her strength.

A'idah surrendered to the nausea. The vomit burned up her esophagus and out her mouth. A new taste filled her mouth and nose, disgusting, but not as bad as the other taste. The retching went on and on until finally her stomach quit out of exhaustion. For a long moment, her head just hung as she gasped. Wearily, she wiped a hand across her mouth and nose getting rid of the strands of mucus hanging from them. The action replaced the vomit with another layer of poop across her face.

Moving slowly, she pushed up and got to the second knee. A'idah waited trying to catch her breath. Part of her wanted to give up and just collapse back into the poop.

She wouldn't give up. Somewhere, out there, her Alex was in danger. She clung to that thought. She had to go help him. A'idah force herself to her feet. She stumbled to the sled and slid back onto the seat.

Lifting up, she headed out into the fields. Where to? She couldn't think. Her heartbeat lanced her head. A'idah had to stop the pain so she could think. A crazy thought came to her. Stop your heartbeat and the pain will go away.

A'idah laughed, and to her it sounded like a crazed person's cackling.

Leaning out, she looked down at the passing fields below her. All she could see were plants. Even those were just indistinct forms. Where was Alex? This was crazy.

She leaned farther out, hoping that by trying harder she could make a difference in the futile search. One hand slipped off its hold on the sled, and she almost fell. Only by a combination of rolling the sled under her trajectory and desperately holding on with her other hand did she prevent a disaster.

A'idah slowed the craft's forward momentum and slumped forehead down on the handlebars. Bitter tears fell and with her left hand she pounded on the handlebar in frustration. The vibration didn't help the pain in her head. She had to... A'idah couldn't think past the pain. Lowering the sled onto some plants, she tried again. She had to...

IDIOT

She knew how to heal.

Placing her mucky hands onto her equally mucky face, A'idah breathed out and slowly breathed in again. The often practiced healing pulled her efforts along. The mantras of healing followed a path. At the end of the path was always the order of getting some rest. Curling up on the ground A'idah closed her eyes and ignored a part of her trying to scream.

Hours later, shivering woke her up. Bewilderment greeted her. Where was she? What was she doing? Bright light burned her sore eyes. The answers hit at the same time. Morning. It was morning. Where was Alex? Was he okay? Heart in her mouth, she dreaded the answer even as she had to know.

A'idah stood up and looked around. She couldn't see the city. In the far distance, the morning light glinted off something up in the air. Shaking off the cold, ignoring the stench, and her hunger, A'idah hurried onto her sled. It responded to her command and up she flew. Over the horizon A'idah made out other glints in the air and finally the hill of the city. Wow, she'd gone a long ways before giving up and healing. Where would Alex be?

A'idah turned over to the edge of the fields and forest. Scanning the ground, she moved along the border. Far ahead of her a small group of people crossed the border into the fields. She knew it was Alex. Down she shot her sled. He was okay.

~**********~

The sound of a distressed engine caught Alex's attention and memory. He'd just found the future thread of A'idah. She was alive, but he hadn't been able to get more from it. The noise reminded him of the medibot disaster. In panic, he looked for the danger. Looking away from Hheilea, Alex saw something he didn't recognize screaming down at them. *AI can you use a gravity generator.*

Yes. Is there danger?

We're under another attack.

Quickly, use the generator to grab the incoming device—

Hheilea's voice interrupted his half formed order. "There's A'idah."

Alex's eyes opened wide in realization of what he'd almost done. His AI answered. *I've got it. I'll throw it out into the woods before it can hurt us.*

"No!" Alex screamed. *AI don't. It's a friend.*

The incoming device lurched as if an invisible giants hand had grabbed it. The sled slammed bouncing down in the field. A mucky figure wearily climbed off. In a very tired voice, A'idah said, "Wow, that was a rough landing."

She shook herself and goops of guck dripped off her.

Her words of concern got to him first, followed by a terrible stench.

"Are you alright? They tried to stop me from leaving in the night. I'm sorry I didn't get to you sooner. I got hurt and had to heal and rest before I could continue my search. Who's tied up and floating along with you."

As A'idah stopped to breathe, Alex stood staring with wide eyes. As she moved closer her stink started to make his eyes burn, but he didn't notice. She was covered in dripping, stinking muck, but he didn't notice the muck. It was her dress that captured his attention or rather how her dress was stuck to her body. After getting the fierce hug from Hheilea, he felt nervous about the girls, and he wasn't sure in Hheilea's present emotional state how she would react to another girl hugging him. It was very obvious to him that Hheilea still loved him and obviously wanted what the T'wasn't-to-be-is would've given her. At least that's what he thought. A'idah's appearance and his reaction to it made him more nervous and he didn't know what to do. This was his best friend, his first friend after getting abducted. She was younger than him. She wasn't the woman he was seeing.

A'idah kept coming at him and her slender arms began to lift. His eyes kept going places he didn't think was right. *She's going to hug me.* Alex took a quick step back trying to get himself under control and needing time to do the right thing.

Desperately, he tried to talk. "I... I... I'm okay. That's someone I captured last night." After Hheilea's reaction he didn't specify the man had been trying to kill him.

Hheilea messaged him. |You idiot. It's obvious you just avoided meeting her. Didn't you hear what A'idah said? She almost killed herself trying to get to you. You should've given her a hug. What's holding you back? Is it her stench or the muck covering her?|

He couldn't process everything Hheilea said. One thing stuck in his head. *She wants me to hug A'idah. What's going on?* In shock, he just managed one word. |Huh.|

A'idah stopped moving toward them. "I'm sorry. I forgot about this excrement covering me."

Why? Why? Why would Hheilea encourage him to hug a different girl? He found in A'idah's words something he could respond to. "Excrement? What happened?"

|You idiot, you've just hurt her feelings.|

"The way out of the city was with a big pile of poop. I got buried, and it interfered with me getting to you."

|How? I didn't do anything.|

|Arggg. Exactly. Listen to her. Really listen. She almost died under a pile of—. Well, you heard her. Poop.|

"I... I... I should go get cleaned up. I'm a mess."

The volume of Hheilea's next message hurt. |Don't let her leave without at least hugging her and thanking her.|

Ow. She's loud. She must think you're too dumb to hear quieter messages.

This was too much. Now his AI was getting into this mess. "Arggg."

Hheilea barked, "What? And what was that?"

Alex looked at her and got hit by a laser-like glare.

A'idah stepped forward, stumbling as she did. She repeated her earlier question. "Alex, are you okay?"

"I'm okay, but what about you? You look terrible."

Hheilea messaged again, not screaming, but the words made him wish it was the earlier message with the screaming. |You just insulted her appearance. Of course she's all covered in poop, but the guy I thought you were wouldn't be concerned about that. I'm disgusted. What's wrong with you?|

"You won't be okay when Zeghes gets here."

Alex jumped onto the chance to change the conversation. "What? Why?"

"He's pretty upset that you left without him. You promised him you wouldn't have adventures without him."

"It was a spur of the moment thing." Alex saw Zeghes rocketing through the air toward them. In an effort to interrupt his three way discussion, he quickly said, "Speaking of Zeghes, I think I see him coming now. Wow! His suit can really get him moving."

Zeghes seemed to be almost rocketing through the air. He still looked as if he was swimming, just very fast. Standing, waiting for his friend, Alex realized at the last moment that Zeghes wasn't stopping.

Alex threw himself down and to the side as Zeghes just missed ramming him. "Hey!"

"You talk about us being a pod, and then you go off without me. There are sharks about. Maybe not sharks like I understand, but they are the same. It's not safe to be alone." Zeghes' permanent smile didn't fit the feelings he displayed at all.

"I had Sabu with me," Alex said, scrambling back onto his feet just to dive back for the ground as Zeghes aimed for him again. A slap from Zeghes' tail left his head spinning.

Alex said, "You know, with you trying to kill me why do I need to worry about any sharks?"

Arching around for another dive at Alex, Zeghes paused. One eye glared at Alex, incongruous next to the grin. "Has A'idah told you, she almost killed herself trying to get to you last night?"

Dismay added itself to the turmoil in Alex. His mouth dropped open in shock. Glancing at A'idah, he noticed for the first time dried blood mixed with the poop.

Without another word, Zeghes turned and leapt through the air quickly disappearing into the distance.

Standing up and brushing himself off, Alex saw A'idah looking at him. She almost killed herself? What happened? Why hadn't she told him? Was she upset with him too? Then, he realized Hheilea had been trying to make him see that. His heart clenched in his chest and Alex forgot to breath. If Hheilea and Sabu weren't there, he would've eagerly, tenderly, willingly swept his amazing A'idah up in his arms. At that thought he gasped. What was going on?

Hheilea closed the distance to A'idah and hugged her. A'idah returned the hug.

Hheilea said, "Trust me. I know how boys can get quite messed up with emotions." Choking up she added, "They... they do stupid things."

Alex badly wished he could be fighting against the assassin again. It had been terrible and dangerous, but he'd understood the situation. "What can I do?"

|You should hug her and apologize.|

"You could treat us as family. Remember the first time we talked in Gursha's clinic. I explained how Zeghes thought of you and me as family because of what

Trouble with Friends

happened right after the abduction. You said you would try to be a good big brother. We thought you cared for us, but all too often you don't seem to show it by your actions. You don't turn to us first. It hurts."

Hheilea messaged again. |See. You've hurt her.|

Alex finally noticed A'idah's watery eyes. The trouble was he was having feelings that had nothing to do with being a big brother to her. "U— I'm sorry. This time I could've and should've reached out to you and Zeghes, but the other times it hasn't been my choice. You either weren't available or it was something I was forced into." Alex didn't say he thought Ytell had planned for him to go with just Sabu. At that thought, he tried to send Ytell a message.

Alex's AI responded to the effort. *Sorry. I still can't send messages far away, but it's coming back.*

Hheilea gave A'idah one last squeeze and stepped back. "I care about you and so does Alex. He's just a clueless guy." She coughed. When Alex glanced at her she nodded her head at A'idah.

Huh? What was she trying to tell him? At least she'd stopped messaging him.

|Hurry up. Can't you see how much she cares for you?|

|| Alex cut off his reply message before he said huh again. A'idah needed him to just be a friend, and she was way too young for him.

A tear cut a path through the muck on A'idah's cheek. "We need you to do better. Even with the new funding from Daren and not having to worry about the first year test, we're having a hard time. I don't have any other real friend. Zeghes is having trouble understanding the new things, and new experiences don't stop coming just because we don't understand. Zeghes tried talking to fish the other day, and then he couldn't eat."

Alex noticed Hheilea's expression changing. Oh, no, she was getting madder.

He really didn't appreciate getting forced to hug his friend.

With dangerous tones her next message hammered at him. |I'm waiting.|

A'idah shook her head. "Zeghes is having a harder time than Sabu and Skyler, because he understands more than they do. Well, our bird friend's having a tough time too, but I worry about Zeghes."

|You've got to hug her.|

The Kalasha girl continued talking in a stronger voice more like her normal tone, but she didn't look at Alex. "It isn't all bad. We no longer have training in the evening, and we get whole days off to just relax and practice. Surely, we can spend more time together." A'idah looked up at him and finished. "I need to be with you. I..."

Alex nodded his head. "Yes." Had he interrupted her? He recognized he needed their friendship too, and he wanted to be with her, but what did she almost say? It hurt to see her so vulnerable. She was his best friend. A year ago, she'd told him she needed him to just be a friend, and that she was too young. She was and he tried hard to think of her as just a friend. Not someone he—

Sabu messaged him. |What's going on between you and A'idah? From what I can smell... Are you—|

Alex interrupted her message. |Sabu, stop it.| Embarrassed at her message, he was sure he was turning red, and he was tempted to smell under his arm, Alex tried to think of something else less dangerous and embarrassing.

|Alex.| This time Hheilea's message had a much different tone. |I know you're better than this. A'idah loves you. She risked her life to try and get to you. She was afraid you were going to die. Both of us were afraid.|

Ouch that hurt. Alex thought, really thought of what the two girls had gone through. Hheilea cared for him more than she was willing to admit, but she was still willing for him to comfort another girl who loved him. He was still confused and uncertain, but Alex no longer felt forced. Instead, it was his own desire to make things right.

He looked A'idah in the eyes. "A'idah."

"Yes?" Surprisingly, she looked nervous.

Alex stepped closer. You know this poop all over you doesn't matter to me."

A'idah took a half-step back. "It doesn't?"

Trouble with Friends

He stepped closer and put his hands against her back and rubbed them up her back. The dress had started to dry and felt very stiff, but he pressed them against her and shuddered at the touch. He hoped no one noticed. As his hands worked their way up he gathered clumps of still wet poop. Pulling his hands back he smeared the poop down the sides of his face. "See, it doesn't bother me at all."

A'idah took another half-step back. "Oh."

He put his hands back behind her and slowly pulled her closer. "What really bothers me is trying to be the best friend I can be for you. You're my best friend, and I still remember you want and need me to be just a friend, but you're becoming more beautiful every day."

He'd pulled her into an embrace, and he heard her softly speaking near his ear. "I am?"

"Yes." He squeezed her tight. "Sometimes, it makes me forget how young you are. You're amazing. I—"

Hheilea messaged him. |Okay, now you're overwhelming her, and others are almost here.|

Alex pulled back from the embrace to look into A'idah's face. His breath caught in his chest at the way she looked at him. Did she want a kiss? In desperation, he searched for something else to say.

Quietly A'idah said, "I'm older now."

He quickly tried to change the conversation. "A'idah, find out when your next free day is and let me know. We can use the time to check up on the worm tunnels." As he finished talking to A'idah, Alex saw more bubbles approaching. What would the reaction be to the assassin he'd fought and captured?

He glanced back at A'idah and hoped they'd have more time together to figure things out between them. Behind her, he saw Hheilea looking at him. He knew her very well, and yet he didn't have a clue why she had encouraged him to—

Chapter Twenty-One
New Training

In the moment of silence, Hheilea said, "A'idah, I've let Ytell and the Tasties know where you are. Ytell was very happy to hear you're okay."

Still looking at Hheilea, Alex realized that she was amazing at taking care of things and taking care of people. That second part was why she'd wanted him to hug A'idah. She cared for others without thinking about herself.

"Thanks. I guess I should've done that myself. I hope my flock isn't in too much trouble. The worst of it is we didn't accomplish anything."

Alex looked at her considering what had happened that morning. He was tempted to tell A'idah that she had accomplished something. Alex just wasn't sure if either of them was willing to acknowledge what was being accomplished. Again, he thought of the future path Johnathan and David made happen. Had A'idah and he both opened up a new future path?

Quickly, the bubbles grew closer. Alex recognized Ytell in one just before the flock leader's bubble dissipated and the raptor dove at them. The other bubbles behind him carried Tasties.

With flaring wings and tail Ytell landed. "A dread attacked you last night, and you've captured him. Great news, these Tasties will take him back to the city. They'll learn what they can from him. Good job on surviving. The Dreads underestimated you, but next time, you'll have a more dangerous foe or maybe two. They're very dangerous. We need to track down who is paying the

New Training

bounty to have you killed. If we don't, eventually the Dreads will kill you."

At those words, Alex turned to the girls to see how they reacted. Hheilea just looked determined, but she'd already processed this new danger to him. A'idah's face on the other hand, Alex could see it go pale even through the coating of muck. He wanted to comfort her again. That first hug had been good. He knew he should say something to her, but new feelings confused his thoughts. He didn't want to say the wrong thing.

Alex turned back to Ytell and said, "Our flock tried to help me last night. I've heard just a little bit of what happened. I hope they're not in trouble with you or the Tasties."

Ytell's ruff partially raised around his head. "They aren't in trouble with me. I'm impressed with how they worked together. I am upset with how I handled the situation. If any of them had gotten to you, it could've resulted in disaster."

Resulted in disaster? Why? Alex tried to take that in. How would Ytell have known? He remembered Osamu shutting down the city. "What about the Tasties? I hope they're not to mad. Was the flock's behavior considered uncivilized? I heard about Osamu shutting down the city. How did he do that?"

Ytell squatted down to Alex's eye level. "Alex, the Tasties are impressed by your flock. They think A'idah is amazing. This morning, I heard from at least five people about how she single handedly escaped from first two, then three, and then five Tasties. The last story I heard going around said she escaped from twenty Tasties, all while bleeding from her ears from a bad head wound. The Tasties think trying to help another is the highest of aspirations. Unfortunately, the other side of the stories is how badly you needed help and are in general lovable, but inept."

Listening to Ytell, Alex grinned, but when he heard about how he was considered his grinned dropped. He considered asking another question, but instead of asking out loud Alex messaged Ytell. |Ytell, the dread had a blaster. Why didn't he just kill me instead of fighting?|

Ytell messaged back |If he'd just shot you, his own people would've killed him. It's a matter of honor and reputation for them. Also, I think your sense of the future would've warned you. You're not the same teenager we abducted. You've had almost two years of intense combat training of different kinds. That in combination with your sense of the future has made you very capable and dangerous in your own right.|

Those words of praise perked up his spirits. Even if the Tasties had a low opinion of him, at least Ytell thought better of him.

Ytell continued. |The Dreads have a reputation and work at keeping it. First, their assassins will try to kill you with a physical attack before resorting to weapons. There is some good news because of the Dreads. No one else will take on the bounty because of them. If we can somehow help you defeat all of the Dreads efforts, you'll be safe from the bounty.|

Alex said, "I'll go with the Tasties. I need to learn more about these assassins. Can my AI use the local artificial gravity generators again? A'idah, do you want to come with me?" Maybe he'd find an opportunity to get her alone and talk to her.

Ytell answered first. "Alex, Windelli has some training setup for you, and you going with the captive would be unnecessary. The Tasties have a technology for asking questions directly to the brain. You'll find out if they learn anything useful."

In an unusually subdued voice, A'idah said, "I need to get cleaned up, and I better go talk to Zeghes. We're going to have to go soon anyway. I'm sorry. I would love to be with you longer. Speaking of my cleaning up, you might want to get that poop off your face."

A forceful message stopped Alex from responding to her. It came from Hheilea. |You idiot, give A'idah another hug and a more heartfelt apology. She's becoming a woman, and I know from my own experience with you how difficult and emotional that is.|

New Training

A'idah must've decided to use a local gravity generator. She'd started to slowly levitate off the ground.

She's becoming a woman? In shock at those words, Alex noticed again how much curvier A'idah was. He thought she was just twelve. He managed to blurt out. "Wait, A'idah."

She dropped back to the ground and turned toward him. Alex suddenly felt awkward and uncomfortable. He didn't want to overwhelm her, but if he hadn't apologized enough... He felt a force blow shove on his back, and he stumbled forward. Hheilea messaged. |Now! What's your problem? I know you care for her. Just don't overwhelm her.|

Hurriedly, he closed the distance to his best friend before another force blow knocked him down.

Another voice, one he couldn't get to stop and couldn't always ignore mocked him. *I know what's going on. I know how you feel.*

Leave me alone. Carefully, he gave A'idah a one armed hug. "You're my best friend. I'm sorry for how I acted when you got to me." For a dangerous second, he looked into her eyes framed by long lashes and quickly averted his gaze.

Maleky wouldn't stop. *You love her. That's too bad. When someone loves you, you can always find a way to use that for your benefit.*

Hheilea messaged. |Give her a real hug. Just not as long as last time.|

Alex shouted. "Shut-up."

Embarrassment struck hard as he realized he'd shouted out-loud. In the sudden silence Alex could feel the stares of those around him. What he saw in front of him confirmed the feeling. They all stared at him, except for one. She looked at him with concern.

A'idah said, "Maleky's bothering you again."

He didn't think of the others around them anymore. Instead, he returned her look of concern and care. Slowly, he enveloped her in a hug lifting her up. "I'm sorry."

Alex was sorry for the situation they were in. He was sorry he hadn't been there for her and for all of her pain.

He was sorry for all the danger. He was sorry they got so little time together. He was sorry he didn't treat her better. He was sorry A'idah was so young. Holding her helped. The reality around them seemed less demanding even immaterial. In that moment, she was all that mattered. Speaking quietly, his words just made it into her hair and just for A'idah. "I've missed you. I need being with you too. I love… being your friend."

A loud cough interrupted their world. Alex realized he'd heard other coughs.

"A'idah whispered to him. "Thanks, I needed that and the other hug, but you should let me go."

Alex realized he held her tight against him. He should've been embarrassed, but instead, he felt disappointed at releasing her. Slowly he let her slip from his arms. "Take care."

Lifting off the ground, A'idah's last words carried back to them. "Good bye, everyone."

At her words, Alex's sense of the future provided a stark sense of danger. He tried to focus, but it disappeared replaced by a blank wall. What? Shaken, he paused uncertain about what to do. He tried again to feel the future of A'idah. This time he didn't notice anything unusual. He looked at Hheilea and Sabu. "Do any of you want to come with me?"

"I was up most of the night watching over our prisoner and doing a little hunting. I just want a place to take a good nap before we leave to get back to our own training."

Hheilea said, "I could use something to eat, clean clothes, and a nap too. I'll see you later. Good luck with your training."

At Hheilea's answer, Alex remembered her danger. "Ytell, somehow the dread had a link to Hheilea. If he's killed, she'll die. She thinks it might be a necklace she had." Now, he didn't feel danger for A'idah. What had that been about? Was it his emotions messing with him again?

Ytell responded. "I'll let the Tasties know. They wouldn't have killed the dread, but now they'll check out the necklace and remove the danger to Hheilea."

New Training

"Good." Alex messaged Windelli. |Where am I supposed to go for this training?|

|Just go to the city, and think about the training you're supposed to be getting. Our city responds to brains. Yours was a bit of a problem. You might've noticed it had some trouble guiding you, but it's got you now. Just follow the colors. That's how you found Hheilea. Use your journey to look at how the lightest of breezes moves leaves. Before your training, you might want to get something to eat.|

Using a local gravity generator, Alex lifted off and soared through the air. Still thinking of his best friend, he messaged her. |A'idah?|

|Yes?|

|Be careful.|

|I will. You too, I'm afraid of those assassins.|

Alex didn't know what he could say to encourage A'idah. The truth was thoughts of the assassins bothered him much less than thoughts of her. Taking a risk, he messaged her again. |I'm not as frightened of the assassins as I am about you. I care for you, and I want to be with you and to take care of you.|

For a long time he didn't hear a reply. Had he said too much?

A'idah responded and her message made him grin. |You better be frightened of me. I'm much more dangerous. I...|

Once again though, she left something unfinished. What had she almost said? With a heavy sigh filled with all of their unfinished business and another separation, Alex started paying attention to things below him in the fields. He watched the gentle movement of the air evident by the rippling of leaves in the fields. At first, he thought of how gentle breezes would stir the curls framing A'idah's face. With another sigh of longing, he pushed the thoughts of her out of his mind and considered his upcoming training. Why did Windelli want him to pay attention to light breezes? Strange and he couldn't think of any answer. Another question bothered him. How had Osamu shutdown the whole city? Ytell hadn't said anything about that. There was more to Osamu than Alex knew, but he didn't know if it was important to know or not. At least, the older Japanese man was on his side. Soon, Alex arrived at the Tasties' city entrance.

Landing, he followed the path toward the entrance. Before he got to the door, a big leaf drifting on the wind dropped on his face. It took a second to swipe it away. Alex stumbled and would've fallen, but a little Tasty put a hand/paw against his side, and it steadied him. "Thanks."

The little one said, "Your welcome. You need a bath. You stink."

Alex entered through the big double doors. Tasties bustled about just the same as the previous day. Briefly, he considered getting one of the snack bags. One look at his filthy hands banished the idea. He left his dirty, smelly cloak in the hand of a disgusted Tasty and descended out of the bright light. First, he'd find out about the training and then consider what to eat after getting cleaned up.

A pulsing green color began moving in waves along the wall. Alex followed it winding down through tunnels, halls, across a vast chamber, and along narrow ledges above the chamber. Walking along the ledges, he couldn't restrain a shiver up his spine at the memory of the big Tasty, which had bumped into him. This time he would be on the lookout for trouble.

A small Tasty with gray streaking his brown coat limped toward him. The old one stumbled and with an, "Excuse me," barely touched Alex in passing.

Alex started to say no problem but instead he gasped at a sudden loss of balance. Before he could cry out, Alex found himself falling toward the edge. Another gentle touch on his other side and he found himself back in control of his balance. Alex turned to thank the one who had saved him from the fall to see the large Tasty who had bumped into him so severely the day before.

The Tasty nodded at the speechless Alex. "Your second lesson has begun. Follow me."

The pathway was suddenly crowded with Tasties. Alex found himself struggling to keep up. The bigger creature somehow dodged and turned to smoothly move counter to the flow of traffic. Ahead of Alex, the large Tasty entered a

New Training

tunnel to the right of the ledge. The sudden pulse of Tasties using the ledge dissipated, and Alex hurried down the tunnel to find the Tasty waiting at an open door.

"Avoid getting wet, and tell me what you see. Enter. Be aware of the little things."

"What?" Alex stepped into the shadowy room and found himself stumbling at the sudden step down into the room. Two sagging bags swung back and forth across the room. They hung from thin strings. Not recovering from the stumbling in time, Alex knocked into one of the bags, and it burst showering Alex with water.

"What do you see?"

Alex turned to answer, but on the suddenly slippery floor his feet slipped out from under him. Even in the confusion of the moment, Alex remembered how to go with the fall and slap his arms down at the last minute to change his momentum and avoid getting hurt.

"Nice fall, your previous training shows."

Alex let himself smile at the complement.

"But you still haven't told me what you see, and you're wet."

With a rueful grin, Alex said, "Water."

"Where is the water? Is it on the ceiling?"

From his back, Alex gazed up at the dry ceiling as the other bag swung above him and past. "The other bag."

"Is there water on the outside of the second bag?"

The bag sagged just like the other bag, and so Alex said, "Its inside."

The Tasty flung something at the bag and it burst just above Alex showering him with a fine powder. "You might want to pay attention more to the little things. Think more before entering a room or guessing answers. In the corner is a door to a shower. You stink and have something disgusting smeared on your face. Get cleaned up. You'll find clean clothing waiting for you on hooks."

Alex wiped at the sticky paste on his face and gratefully, carefully moved to get the shower. In the room hung two sets of pants and shirts, one a cream white and the other much fancier blue clothing with gold stripes. Later, he opened the door back into the training room wearing the loose cream white clothes. In the middle of the room floated a small ball the size of a lemon. It glowed orange.

The Tasty walked casually across the still wet, slippery, but now clean floor. He carried a long thin stick. "You chose the right clothing. Now, to finish your lesson for today poke the orange ball with this stick. You might want to take another shower when you're done, because there's going to be a party in five hours. I hope your hunger isn't too big a problem. Try not to be late."

Alex grinned in amusement. "You've got to be kidding?" He'd finish this before hunger could bother him.

"Nope. Are you going take the stick?"

Alex took it. He started to say this is going to be easy, but thought better of the idea.

The Tasty walked toward the door. "Pay attention to your feelings of the future and learn to work smoothly with them."

"That's it. This is my lesson for today?" Alex jabbed the stick at the ball and it slid to the right just enough that he missed.

In his mind, Maleky spoke for the first time in a long time. *You should've eaten before starting. This could be similar to a training routine I do. It teaches focus, control of your attacks, and how to get into a place where your actions flow without interference from your thoughts. I won't bother you with my thoughts. This isn't going to be fun. I hope you don't get us hurt too badly.*

For a second, Alex considered the thoughts from the alien passenger in his mind. Hurt? Was there more to this than he understood?

"Try not to be late." The Tasty left the room closing the door behind him.

Late? How could a simple training exercise take one hour let alone five? With all of the training he'd already had this should be easy.

Chapter Twenty-Two
Lesson One

Alex stabbed at the orange ball again. This time it slid left, and he missed again, but as he tried to poke the pin into the ball he noticed with his sense of the future where it would go.

He paused before trying again. He could sense it would bob up, but something else was going to happen. As he stood considering future possibilities, another little ball, a black one appeared. Alex jabbed with the stick, but this time at where the orange ball would be. What should he do after he'd finished this? The new black ball knocked into the end of his stick just enough that he missed again.

With his next attempt, he paused longer trying to see what would happen. A red ball and a white one would appear. After that, the future possibilities began to get crowded. If he hit the red one, he could sense pain. With the white one, he wasn't sure what would happen. Alex stepped to the side trying to see a clear path to stab the orange one. The red and white ones appeared. The red stayed close to the orange, but the white one started bobbing in front of his face. He could sense two blues would be appearing unless he jabbed quickly.

In growing desperation, Alex started jabbing. He kept away from the red one, but couldn't make contact with the orange let alone stab close to it. At least, no more balls appeared. From his sense of the future, he suspected jabbing at the orange ball kept more from appearing. Dancing carefully to the side, trying not to slip, and bobbing his head to avoid the white one Alex kept stabbing at the orange. A part of him confirmed the blues hadn't appeared. If he paused too long between jabs, more balls would appear.

Dancing about and jabbing, he started breathing harder. Alex saw a chance and lunged. His stick grazed the red one and pain lanced through his hand, arm, and shoulder. Alex didn't follow through with his attack, and the orange ball moved just fast enough to avoid the stick.

Instead of stabbing it, Alex jerked back to avoid the red ball, and his feet slipped on the floor. He rolled as he went down and tumbled across the floor.

Alex bounced back up pausing just for a moment to try and sense how to continue. Two blue balls appeared. One of them started pummeling his stick arm. Alex danced away stabbing and trying to get away from the blue ball. As he took a step the other one hit his moving foot, and he stumbled almost falling again. Another red one appeared.

Alex forced himself to concentrate harder and stepped with more care taking the hits and stabbing knowing he would miss. He sought a rhythm. Eventually, his stick arm started to dance smoothly around the attacking blue ball. Alex almost closed his eyes trying harder to sense the movements of the balls. He began moving with more assurance avoiding the attacks. Time passed and sweat started to roll down his face. Hunger gnawed at his stomach, and he wished he'd had something to eat. Alex blinked and swiped his hand across his eyes to free them from the burning sweat.

His jabs kept getting closer. Then, he saw an opportunity, but just as soon he saw one of the reds would get stabbed too. Alex could almost feel the pain. He let the opportunity pass, but now he noticed fatigue slowing his efforts. His breath came harder, and he jabbed without trying to hit the orange. For a while, he only avoided the reds and kept the black from hitting his stick. Alex marshaled his energy even as he looked for another opportunity. Again he could stab it, but the other red would fry him with pain.

At that moment, Alex remembered the other fight. During the struggle against the Gragdreath he'd faced similar choices of trying to find the killing opportunity. At

Lesson One

that time, he had held off because of the pain at the idea of killing Twyla. Gritting his teeth, Alex slammed the attack home. Briefly, pain lanced up from his hand to his shoulder and then it quit.

Alex stood there panting. Instead of the orange ball skewered on his stick, he saw the hall of flight after his battle with the terrible Gragdreath. People lay scattered about. Others limped about trying to help. That pain still tormented him. He tossed the stick with impaled orange ball to the side and walked across the floor to the shower.

The hot water felt wonderful. After a bit, Alex began to consider the training. It had been about choices and the resulting paths. Again, he thought of Johnathan and David. How had they made that terrible choice which opened up such a wonderful path for the future?

Somehow, Alex needed to make the right choices. He didn't know what future path he was responsible for. At the very least the survival of life on Earth could be affected by his choices. The weight of that thought took away from his enjoyment of the shower. Alex vowed to get better at dealing with choices. Later, still damp from his quick shower and dressed in the fine clothes, He opened the door and stepped out into the tunnel.

The big Tasty, his trainer, stepped into view from around the nearest corner and said, "You finished. What did you learn?"

"To... I don't know...." Guessing at what the Tasty wanted, Alex continued with a sour face. "Ignore pain to win the battle?"

"You need to learn about celebrating life."

Alex shook his head at those words. They were the same Delli and Windelli had used, but that was giving your life. He didn't want to finish the thought, and how did it apply to himself?

The Tasty continued talking. "That is a difficult lesson for many to learn. The other lesson I want you to learn is easier. You have an advantage with your sense of the future. You need to learn to work with it smoother and faster without much thinking. Walk with me, and we'll talk as we go to the party."

Walking with the big Tasty, Alex considered his words. He'd been forced to go with his sense of the future with less thinking. He recognized the use of pain to overcome what Windelli told him was his fear of pain, but the problem he'd had was different. Wasn't it?

"There's something else about your sense of the future you should know. I don't know if you've noticed, but when the future seems to be shifting there is a way for others to try and give you trouble with your sense of the future. If they set up a plan based on luck, such as rolling dice, which is still aimed at a certain goal, it will cause your sense of the future to shift and waver. You'll feel uncertain. Be very careful if you notice that problem. On a totally different note, Alex, what do you think celebrating life means?"

"It means… to u— to offer your life to another." Alex thought of the story about David and Johnathan. Yet, what Delli was doing differed. "It's also to go out in the wild to prove you can do it?"

"Your answer is close. There is an underlying meaning between the two. It encompasses more. We Tasties have been studying you humans for a number of years. Your berserkers of old knew in part the meaning of celebrating life. They would joyfully go into battle without fear of death, but it isn't about having a brutality of action. You humans as you've gotten civilized have lost this celebrate life, except in certain situations and times. Then, heroes will selflessly sacrifice all to save others. In your Bible, a man named Jonathan celebrated life in defending David, even though it would mean giving David the kingdom Jonathan could've had. Also in the same book, another is recorded giving everything including his life for all to have opportunity for life."

Ahead of them, Alex could hear the noise of a large group. He asked, "Why do you Tasties research so much about humans?"

"Because of a prophesy, you are going to marry Hheilea."

At those words, Alex stumbled. "What?" He had beaten the T'wasn't-to-be-is hadn't he? His old frustration with the alien ritual forcing him and Hheilea together

Lesson One

boiled stronger than ever at the idea. This prophesy sounded too much like getting forced to do something.

The idea of a prophesy saying he would marry Hheilea shook him. Would the T'wasn't-to-be-is music start again?

A thought from Maleky almost stopped Alex in his tracks. *I hadn't heard that part of the prophesy.*

Alex fired his own thought back at the evil man. *What is this prophesy?* At that, he knew he needed to learn more about this prophesy. He didn't want to be forced into any future path.

I agree. I don't want to get forced into anything either.

Maleky's thoughts, specifically his agreement troubled Alex. The noise of many voices had been growing louder, and as he turned a corner, the mouth of the tunnel revealed the cavern Alex had seen a number of times. Thousands of Tasties and other creatures crowded the area. The few tables held bowls and platters of food.

Also, a few servers carried large, precariously balanced trays laden with bowls and platters of more food. Wow, those would be hard to carry. What a mess they'd make if a server dumped a tray.

While Alex paused to take in everything, his trainer entered, weaving his way through the crowd.

Alex took his first step to follow and paused second foot up in the air. One of the Tasties tails had moved under his foot. He stretched his step to avoid it and found to the right a small vacant spot. Alex had to push off his back foot to shift his weight forward, but a Tasty in front of him leaned back. Trying to avoid falling against that one he took a quick step just on his toes to the left, but another Tasty's tail swished under his heel. Losing his balance, Alex almost bumped into one of the servers. Moving a foot, he caught himself just in time.

He shifted his direction to take advantage of a good gap in the crowd. How did his trainer move so effortlessly? He remembered the melody of the T'wasn't-to-be-is, and in his mind he almost heard again the tinkling notes rising and falling similarly to waves on a tropical shore. A chill ran down his back.

When he saw Hheilea, would the ritual of her people force them together? In growing terror, Alex remembered how it could control him forcing him to be one with Hheilea. What could he do? He remembered again how it had been the first time he'd known of its power and how it had almost finished.

The memory of that time and the power of the T'wasn't-to-be-is shook him. What could he do against it? That time, Hymeron had stopped it by stunning Alex and Hheilea.

Ahead of his trainer, some young human men stood around a raised area. He almost recognized a voice coming from that crowd. He had no clue how the ritual had made him hear music or drew him and Hheilea into falling in love, but it frightened him. This prophesy shook him to his core. What could he do?

Alex remembered back to when he thought he'd beaten the T'wasn't-to-be-is. Daren was changing into a monster, and Alex had seen beating the T'wasn't-to-be-is as the only chance to stop it from happening. He'd guessed he could beat the alien ritual in a similar way he'd defeated the infatuation caused by the Winkle's poison. Even though he knew it would hurt Hheilea, he'd done it.

Briefly, Hheilea had entered with him into the beginning of the adult Kimleys' experience. Their consciousness lived in some strange experience of time and the possibilities of future times. Alex still didn't understand what he'd briefly seen and experienced.

He had beaten the alien ritual before. Alex shook himself and squared his shoulders. He'd beat it again. From the raised area ahead, Alex again heard a melodic voice he knew well, but refused to remember.

The big Tasty turned back toward Alex and waved at him to close the gap. The crowd between them thinned.

With a sigh of relief, Alex walked more easily in the less crowded area toward the rendezvous he feared. What would happen?

The trainer said something, "Look—"

The crowd shifted and he saw Hheilea smiling at a young man. Alex stopped in shock. She looked so beautiful

Lesson One

in the dress she had on. In terror at her beauty, he held his breath. Would the T'wasn't-to-be-is music start again? Desperately, he looked for something, anything to distract him.

Chapter Twenty-Three
A'idah

A'idah fidgeted, looking around the large cavern filled with Tasties and a few other people waiting for the celebration. She wanted to go find Alex, but Ytell told her he would be coming once his training for the day finished. Would Alex be happy if she did go find him? What would he do if she found him all by herself? What would he say?

A'idah wondered where and what his training was. She could leave and surprise him all be herself. A big grin followed her thoughts of how that would be, could be. But in frustration, A'idah accepted the fact she didn't know where to find him. She was forgetting something, but couldn't think of it. Absently she rubbed at the side of her head. It still ached. She didn't want to wait to see him. For the thirteenth time, she considered messaging him.

How would he respond to her being at the celebration? A'idah bit her lip at that question. Alex always seemed happy to see her in the past.

Maybe, he was just being nice to her. She worried about what to say to him. He'd given her two wonderful hugs the last time they were together, but A'idah had noticed what was going on with Hheilea. Had she really forced Alex to hug her? That last time he'd hugged her she'd notice him stumble toward her. A'idah knew what that meant. Someone, and she suspected Hheilea, had pushed him using force. Why? Did A'idah look that emotionally fragile that she needed comforting and extra care? If Hheilea had forced him, had what he'd said been real?

A'idah

She bit her lip again at those solid possibilities. A'idah's AI didn't work very well for her and a couple of times it had sent out a message when it hadn't been what A'idah had wanted to say. She shifted her weight from foot to foot and back. Maybe, she could tease him. A'idah could say something about how badly she was missing him this evening. She considered other things she could say. At the same time A'idah was careful not to think about her AI. She didn't want to accidently send him a message. *Words bubbled up in her mind. I love— What? No. AI, send a message to no one.*

Who's no one?

No. No. No. No. Send no messages.

Silence in her mind caused her to let out a big sigh of relief. That was terrible. A'idah loved being with Alex, but those words in her thoughts weren't the right way to say that. He might've gotten the wrong idea. Maybe she could say—

Zeghes' message interrupted her thoughts. |A'idah, I'm getting tired of waiting. You asked the flock and Ytell not to message Alex about our still being here. I know you wanted to surprise him, but....|

In a rush, the rest of the message poured into A'idah's mind. |I left our friend in a terrible way. I'm still upset at not being with Alex when he's been in danger so many times, but I want him to know I love him, and I'm still his friend. Do you think he's upset with me?|

A'idah didn't immediately answer. Her thoughts raced. Of course she and Zeghes loved Alex. They loved each other too. That was how family felt toward each other. Oh, yes, she did want to surprise him. |Zeghes, I want to message him too, but please be patient. You know Alex. Remember, I talked to him after you thwacked him with your tail. He's sorry he didn't reach out to us this time. He wants to be with m— us too. When we surprise him, he'll be happy and excited. He'll probably hurry right over to us.|

He would. He would be happy to see them. He has too. A'idah bit her lip again. This time she tasted blood.

|Okay, I'll try and be patient. How about you? Are you okay? I still don't understand your moods. I'm guessing here, but you seem unsettled, disturbed, or distraught. Are any of those right? You don't seem okay.|

A'idah took a deep breath and smiled at her friend. |I'm okay, Zeghes. Well... Alright, maybe I'm a little of all those things. It's just this waiting. You know I hate just waiting.| She rocked up on to her toes and back down. A'idah held a hand out and caused sparks to dance about her fingers. Just working on one of her control lessons from the Charge class calmed her. When Alex found them there he'd be happy and come to her first. Everything would be fine.

She held a hand up with its sparks dancing about it. |Zeghes, find something to do. Maybe you could work on control lessons too.|

|Good idea.|

Once again, A'idah wondered what the celebration was all about. No one had told the flock what it was for.

She looked around at the rest of her flock waiting with her in a group at the edge of the expansive underground cavern. Poor Sabu, the snow leopard stood with her mouth open and long fluffy tail down. Crowds stressed her. Ekbal, the dark skinned boy, from India stood close to her. She could see Osamu, the Japanese astronaut talking to Sabu and probably trying to encourage her. He had a very mixed relationship with the non-humans in the flock. The animals were now considered to be people. Osamu originally had a hard time understanding that idea. For a long time, he kept reverting to calling them animals. The non-humans didn't appreciate him forgetting. At the same time, he had great ideas for helping them to adjust and really did care for them.

Skyler, the blue hyacinth macaw sat on Osamu's shoulder. He preferred to stand on the highest point available and thought the ground or floor to be inherently dangerous.

Others, mostly Tasties filled the space around them. Some of them had stripes, spots, or other patterns and others had solid colored fur. A'idah started playing at making sparks dance across their fur. She noticed some of the fur lifted and fell as if stirred by an errant breeze. Smirking, she thought those looked like force touches, a very deft practice form of using force.

A'idah messaged Zeghes. |Are you using force to play with the fur of these Tasties?|

|Yeah. I noticed your sparks. It is you, right?|

She chuckled. |Yeah.|

Just then, someone said ow. One of her sparks had gotten a little too big.

A rather smug message from Zeghes alerted her that he'd notice her shocking someone. |My control is better than your control.|

A'idah grinned as she thought of what else she could do, but a message from Osamu changed her mind. |A'idah, Zeghes, are you two playing with vapucs? Don't get in trouble.|

She let out a sigh and resumed trying to wait. When would Alex show up? Maybe she could send him a message, but not let him know they were waiting. When he arrived he would come over to them first. Alex would. A shifting in the crowd around A'idah alerted her to a change.

Turning around and following their gaze, she saw Hheilea crossing the cavern floor moving toward an elevated area where fewer people stood. A'idah's eyes opened wide at the change in Hheilea. The young woman wore a strapless, red and blue dress. She looked amazing. The ceremony must have something to do with Hheilea. A'idah messaged her. |Hheilea, do you see me and the rest of my flock? We're on the far side of the cavern.|

|A'idah, I'm glad you got to be here. Alex will be happy to see you.|

At Hheilea's words, A'idah pumped a fist in the air. Alex would be happy, and he'd hurry over to her. Talking to Hheilea brought back a memory and with it a question. |Hheilea, your dress is beautiful, but how come you've stopped pretending to be a boy. Doesn't this put you in more danger?|

|I gave up hiding to help save Alex. It seems pointless to go back to hiding. Plus, I'm enjoying finally getting treated as an adult. The Tasties have been showing me the Book of Prophesy given to them long ago by my people. I've just started looking at it, and what's written in it is complicated, but I think it's helping me to chart my course for the next while. Could you help Alex for me?|

|Of course, but remember if you're in need of help, call for me and Zeghes.| She's getting treated as an adult? Amongst her own people, the Kalasha, A'idah was old enough to be treated as an adult. Just thinking about them brought back a wave of homesickness. She missed her dad, grandmother, and friends. A'idah started to think of one friend, but Hheilea's response interrupted her.

|Okay. Thanks. I'm glad he has you. Just hearing you and thinking about your offer gives me a real sense of need for your help at a future time. I think there's going to come a time when I'll need your help more than anyone else's.|

Hheilea continued moving toward the raised area of the floor. Meanwhile, A'idah remembered the first time she'd promised to help Hheilea. Her own experience with a young woman in danger had made the memory crystal clear. Many a day she'd thought of it. Zeghes had called the mysterious boy Hhy by another name, Hheilea. It had surprised both her and Alex.

A'idah stood shaking not realizing tears ran down her face. Something touched her head and she looked up.

Above her, Zeghes rolled over on his side to look at her with one eye. "You're leaking water. Are you okay?"

With one hand she reached up to her friend and laid it on the side of his head. A'idah nodded, wiped the tears from her face and said, "I was just remembering finding out about Hheilea's danger and our promise to protect her." Firmly she stated. "Remember, Zeghes, she's our friend, and we're not going to let anything hurt her." Whatever the cost she would save this friend.

Zeghes lifted his head and moved it from side to side. "Are there sharks about? I mean, do you think there's danger here? I could do a patrol."

A'idah

A'idah grinned at her friend. She remembered how Zeghes used to always do what he called shark patrols. He was learning and changing. "I think this is a safe place, but she's going to need our help. We'll need to be ready."

Her dolphin friend nodded his head at those words. "We'll be ready. The vapuc classes and practice sessions are helping. You're not so dangerous with your use of lightning, and I'm getting better with force."

The young Kalasha woman-child stopped listening to Zeghes. Her friend, Hheilea was getting treated as an adult. Again A'idah remembered one of her Kalasha friends, a girl. She'd gotten married back on Earth at the same age A'idah was now. It seemed so long ago and yet not much over a year in the past. A'idah lifted her chin. She was old enough to be treated as an adult too. She refused to think about the Muslims and the danger associated with the idea of being an adult.

Zeghes touched her head with his beak as he continued to talk and drew her attention back. "The rest of the flock is making progress, but I'm afraid Skyler can't do much better."

Their fellow flock-mate and friend didn't look good. A'idah could see where he'd been pulling out some of his feathers. "Gursha's trying to help him cope with the stress, and Osamu has asked Skyler to help him work with the flock better by biting him on the ear when he calls anyone an animal."

To herself, she admitted her own stress at being abducted and surrounded by strange events and people. She'd be just like Skyler if she didn't have Alex and Zeghes. A'idah laughed at the mental image of her hair partly yanked out, but sobered up thinking of how hard it had been for her not having Alex around more. Having him around made it easier not to miss her family and friends.

Thinking of Alex made her wonder if he was okay. A'idah wished she had his sense of the future. Then, she could check on him. Maybe she should message him. What should she say? She wished he stood beside her. In the crowded conditions he'd have to stand very close.

Her mind and heart thought of the two long hugs Alex had given her. Emphatically, she decided from now on they would be together more. He was her best friend, and even though she hated to admit it, she needed him to survive this experience. Nothing and no one would take him away from her. A'idah gave a long sigh.

Zeghes messaged her. |How long are we going to have to wait. I'm bored.|

She nodded her head in sympathy. A'idah wanted something to do too. Automatically she messaged him back suspicioning he had an idea which might not be approved by everyone. |What's your idea?| If nothing else, it would take her mind off Alex.

In an excited and yet drawn out slow message, Zeghes had a proposal. |We... could... practice control... of our... force vapuc.|

|Come on, Zeghes. Spit it out. What are you thinking of?|

|See the trays being held up in the air? We could take turns using force touching to bump the bowls and platters on them.|

|We wouldn't want to hit them too hard. If any get dumped that wouldn't be good.|

Zeghes message sounded very mischievous. |We'll be careful and if one gets dumped by accident, no one will know it's us.|

A'idah looked around. |Let's start next to the big entrance on the opposite side.|

Zeghes messaged back. |Okay, I'll go first. The black and white Tasty with the tray.|

She saw a big bowl on the tray slide just a bit. A'idah nudged it back. The server had to swing the tray out to regain his or her balance.

Soon a pattern of wobbling trays moved across the waiting assemblage. Once, A'idah almost pushed a bowl over the edge of a tray, but Zeghes pushed it back. She giggled in relief.

Together, they played enjoying the excitement. A'idah noticed a particularly big Tasty come in. Zeghes had nudged a platter and she'd nudged a bowl. Ignoring a growing head ache, she went to nudge his platter back, but Zeghes interrupted her concentration.

The dolphin's voice had more excitement in it when he said, "Look, here comes Alex."

"What? Where?" Immediately, A'idah started breathing faster. She couldn't wait for him to get to her. She tried to see him, but couldn't tell which direction Zeghes was looking. She looked back at the bowl she'd nudged. She'd hit it too hard. It was getting harder to keep the force touches under control and a headache pounded in her temples. Alex was there. It was going to be okay.

"He's right behind the big Tasty by the server whose stuff we just moved. I think we should stop with the practice exercises."

Finally, A'idah spotted Alex walking behind the particularly big Tasty. |Alex, we got to stay for the celebration. We're over near the far wall from where you are.|

A'idah gasped as the server tipped his tray toward Alex. She tried to help, but it moved farther than she expected. She felt a hand on her arm.

Osamu yanked her focus away from trying to save the situation. "Are you and Zeghes playing around with force?"

~**********~

From next to Alex a Tasty said, "Excuse me."

A message from A'idah distracted him. |Alex, we got to stay for the celebration. We're over near the far wall from where you are.|

What? She was here? Alex started to look for her. Too late he saw the young Tasty carrying a tray of food. Alex bumped into the server. The Tasty stumbled back fighting with his unbalanced tray. It started tipping, threating to spill all of the food on top of a Tasty. Quickly, Alex stepped forward, stretched, and caught the tray with one hand, but he lost his balance. Moving quickly, he tried to keep from falling or dumping the tray.

Chapter Twenty-Four
Embarrassment

In a voice full of concern, Hheilea called, "Alex."

Dimly, he registered her voice. Alex almost stomped on another Tasty's tail. He hopped over it landing on his toes, but the tray shifted. Alex countered by moving to his left and bumped into a different Tasty offering a bowl of something in water to someone else.

The Tasty stumbled backward. The bowl fell, but Alex had seen the danger and had already stepped forward. He caught it with his free hand turning in a circle to slow his momentum without spilling the liquid. The platter just missed that Tasty's head.

He finished the turn lifting the bowl over another Tasty. Alex grinned. He'd survived.

At that moment, he backed into a table. It caught him behind his legs. Alex lost his balance, but went with it pushing off to sit on the edge of the table. In victory, he smiled up at Hheilea's face. He could handle anything. The table tipped.

Hheilea gasped aloud, "Alex."

Fortunately, he caught himself with his feet and the table didn't tip farther. Others must've grabbed it.

Again A'idah messaged him. |Alex, are you okay. I'm so sorry.|

Alex answered. |I'm okay. Any idea what the ceremony is about?|

Her message sounded quite worried. |No. Hheilea is here too.|

|Yeah. I know. I'm going to talk to her. I'll find you later.| Maybe A'idah thought her message startled him and

Embarrassment

caused the problem. Alex wanted to go to her, but first he needed to talk to Hheilea.

The Tasty on Alex's left grabbed the bowl from him. Another on his right took the serving tray with two hand/paws and said, "That was a close call. I hope you can navigate your future paths with as much luck."

Alex slid off the table onto his feet. Not hearing a crash behind him, he presumed others had caught the table as it fell back. Alex firmly walked up to Hheilea. Resolutely, he ignored everything. He had gotten used to ignoring Maleky. He used that ability to ignore everyone else.

Her beauty frazzled him, and he tried to find a safe place to look while trying not to think of how pretty she looked. Taking her hand, Alex said, "Hheilea, I need to talk to you. Can we move over to the edge?"

"Okay. That was quite the entrance. Good job catching the tray and the bowl. The server seemed to be having trouble holding it steady." She turned back to the others and said, "Nice meeting all of you guys. Thanks for telling me your stories about how you and your families helped get things setup for the abductees from your world. I look forward to spending more time with you."

Alex pulled her out of the press toward the wall behind the raised area. Grimly, he led her to that quieter spot. He'd keep the T'wasn't-to-be-is beaten. All he had to do was to love someone else. Alex thought of someone he cared for and wanted to be with. This would work. He wouldn't be forced to love someone.

Hheilea looked at him with a worried expression. "Alex, what's going on? Are you all right?"

He remembered how she charged into him and just about killed him with her hug. She was still in love with him and wanted to get married. Alex thought her face looked a bit pale. Hheilea senses what's coming. He, himself could feel turmoil, but didn't try to sort out his feelings. This friend thing was just some game.

"Alex, I thought you wanted to talk to me?"

They'd reached the quieter spot and Alex had turned to talk, but he couldn't say anything. Her question loosened his tongue, and he finally started talking. "Do you hear the T'wasn't-to-be-is music? I don't."

Hheilea's face turned white. She didn't speak and Alex continued talking. "It isn't going to force us to get married. I won't let it. I beat it, and its staying broken."

"A tear leaked, rolling down her cheek and more threatened. With firm lips and a straight mouth. Hheilea spoke in determined tones, but Alex knew her, and he could hear the deep hurt. "I know. I don't hear it. It's gone. Could you let go of my hand. You're hurting me."

Alex looked down at her hand. It was white around where he held it. Releasing it, he could see his hand print. He'd been considering telling her who he did love, but instead said, "I'm sorry. I didn't mean to hurt you."

"I know. Your flockmates are here. Go spend time with them. Just leave me alone, so I can meet others as a woman for the first time instead of pretending to be a boy." She turned and walked away not waiting for his reply.

Alex didn't know what to say and didn't know what to think about her telling him to leave her alone. He was tempted to say gladly, and that the one he did love was over there. He heard the hurt in Maleky's thoughts and they echoed his own mixed-up feelings.

Maleky complained. *She doesn't want us around. This is your fault.*

I didn't do anything. Alex thought of what he'd said. He knew the depths of Hheilea's feelings from past conversations. He'd hurt her. His own heart hurt. The memory of one conversation in particular came to mind. He still remembered the embarrassment, the love he'd felt, and every detail even how it felt to fall on the damp ground.

Alex reminded himself, the love hadn't been real. The T'wasn't-to-be-is had forced him to feel that way. Alex wished he knew how long before the last traces of it disappeared especially right now. These memories weren't helping. In them, the love he felt for her pounded at him, and now he'd crushed her again.

Embarrassment

Alex didn't want to go back into that memory. Trying to distract himself, he tried to think of time. But he still didn't understand how time could have its own dimensions. There hadn't been anymore visions since he'd beaten the T'wasn't-to-be-is so maybe it really had stopped, but what did that mean for Hheilea. What did it mean for her love and for—

Neither he nor Maleky wanted to think about it. Alex remembered the end of that conversation with Hheilea. He remembered what he'd almost done. Hheilea had been talking and he'd felt—

~**********~

|Is 'Oh' all you can say? Young Kimley women get married at this time of their lives. Only a disaster keeps them from getting married. If they don't, then they never get married. I want to marry—I love what my folks have. I want that too. More importantly, my species is dying out, because of how we've been mistreated. I should have children. I'm sorry. My dad told me not to dump all that on you.|

Alex made a decision. |It sounds as if you need to get married. I—|

Hheilea interrupted him.

~**********~

It had been fortunate she'd interrupted him. At least Alex thought it had been good, but knowing what had followed he wasn't sure. Confusion, embarrassment, and a wistful longing for what could've been twirled his emotions and thoughts. Maybe it would've been better if he had told her he'd finish the T'wasn't-to-be-is, and they'd gotten married.

Alex could've helped to save Twyla, but would he have been able to help her know real love? Would Twyla have lived full of hate and fear and never had the victory of being a person who loved and would make sacrifices for others? He couldn't handle the thought that maybe the events which lead to Twyla's death were better for her.

That she'd become a better person, and she'd had joy and love because of the events.

For some reason, Maleky stayed quiet and didn't berate him for the obvious pain he'd caused Hheilea. Alex weakly protested to himself that he loved— He thought of how the Tasty had mentioned his hope Alex could navigate his future paths with as much luck. Luck? Alex didn't need luck. He needed many miracles to navigate his future paths right. What would be right? He felt very clueless.

Someone thumped him on the shoulder. "Hey." A young man stood glaring at him. "What did you say to Hheilea? She's been great, but now somethings changed. She's just pretending to smile."

Alex weakly held up his hands. He wanted to defend himself, but growing embarrassment held him back. "Just something from our past. She'll be okay."

He looked after the slight figure of the young woman he knew so well. He hoped she'd be okay.

Someone spoke over the noise and the crowd quieted. Grateful for the interruption, Alex turned away from the human and listened. At the same time he ignored a growing warning. His sense of the future rang loudly clamoring for attention. The feeling of embarrassment getting worse, much worse warned him to hide.

How could it get worse? Alex just tried to shrug it off. It's only feelings. He swallowed. He'd manage.

"If I could get your attention please, let me introduce our two guests. Over here is Hheilea."

The crowd on the raised area backed away from the pretty, elven featured, young woman with white hair. She raised a hand and waved. "Hello, Everyone."

The introducer said, "Until she's married, Hheilea is facing great peril. We'll help. Give her a big Tasty welcome."

Alex heard the married word and reacted by gritting his teeth. What was going on? He still hated the idea of being forced into— ,but after having had more of his flashbacks he had very, very mixed feelings.

The crowd responded with different things.

Embarrassment

The human's clapped, and Alex forced himself to join in. She was a good *friend* of his.

Many of the Tasties shouted.

"Hello, Hheilea!"

"We'll help!"

"We love you!"

"Enjoy the evening!"

"We'll keep you safe!"

The crowd said other things and eventually the person introducing Hheilea got them to be quiet. "Quiet down please. And over there near her is Alex." There was a pause and the crowd all looked toward the raised area. "Alex, show yourself to everyone. Don't be shy."

Alex really didn't want everyone looking at him. He usually didn't mind, but this time nausea gripped him at the idea. At the very least, Alex wanted to run away to a very dark and quiet room. Shrugging off his queasiness, he decided to do what he had to. Getting introduced would be fun. Adamantly, Alex reminded himself introductions weren't embarrassing. He needed some encouragement. Alex worked his way over to a table. He climbed up on it. Fortunately, this one didn't have much food just a few glasses of some drinks. Alex stood up and waved. "I'm over here."

The introducer said, "Once again, he's in the wrong place. We'll have to be patient with him. There's so much he doesn't understand, and his paths are fraught with peril. Some of you have already been involved in helping with his lessons."

Alex waved trying not to think of the disconcerting words of the introducer. He waited for him to make the same request that everyone should give him a big Tasty welcome, but the introducer didn't. Alex uncomfortably looked around, and the crowd looked quietly back. The young men standing around Hheilea didn't look very friendly. That hurt the worst. They were humans too. He did hear someone up close to him.

"He doesn't look very tall."

Hheilea messaged him. |Alex, the Tasties are worried about you. They aren't meaning to be so rude.|

Her words meant well, but coming so soon after Alex knew he'd hurt her... They didn't help. Instead, he just wanted to disappear.

A welcome sight made him feel a bit better. A weak grin crept over his face. A'idah forged through the crowd, shoving Tasties out of her way. Tasties that looked at her were hastily moving out of her way. It must be a great help to have her kind of reputation.

Right behind her, Zeghes swam through the air. The rest of the flock followed moving more gently through the crowd. A'idah, raised a hand and shouted, "Alex, that table doesn't look stable."

She'd just about reached him, and Alex stepped back toward the edge of the table. A group of very young Tasties waved at him from below. "Hi."

He leaned down to better hear them. Part of him felt the table shift under him, but these Tasties... the only Tasties he'd seen in the crowd of faces who looked friendly had captured his attention. Their waves and greeting helped him feel better.

"Are you the one our parents talk about?"

They talked about him? He said. "I don't—"

Another with white and brown fur asked, "Have you seen the *Book of Prophesy?*"

One of two with all black fur, very seriously said, "Be brave. I think you'll be the one."

The other black furred Tasty said very seriously, "I know it's hard to navigate life's choices, but look for guidance and be willing for it."

Guidance? Alex knew Maleky was willing to guide him.

The little guy added. "Be sure you're following the right guidance."

Alex nodded his head. Yeah, not Maleky. His friends would help and his parents had worked to point him to the right guidance. That all made sense, but what about the Book of Prophesy? Was that what his trainer had referred to? Alex shook his head to the questions and again the table wobbled with his movement.

The announcer said, "Okay, everyone, that's enough staring at Alex. We do welcome you, Alex. You'll—"

Embarrassment

Alex didn't hear the rest of what he said. At that moment, his table collapsed. Not wanting to land on the youngsters, Alex pushed off against the falling table. He hoped to avoid landing on someone's tail, but with the room and crowd spinning about him he didn't have any control. Some in the crowd who could use the vapuc force buffeted him with force blows and he went higher. He heard the raised voices of many around him, but couldn't make out what they said. In relief, Alex glimpsed the crowd thinning in front of him. He only had time to be grateful no one would be hurt except maybe himself and his own feelings. Things couldn't get much worse.

A'idah yelled, "I've got you."

Chapter Twenty-Five
Pain and Joy

A'idah couldn't believe she and Zeghes had almost made a tray dump. What did Alex think? Upset and concerned she messaged him. |Alex, are you okay. I'm so sorry.|

He answered. |I'm okay. Any idea on what the ceremony is about?|

She couldn't decide if she should apologize again or not. Did Alex realize what she'd done? Worried, A'idah just answered his question. |No. Hheilea is here too.|

|I know. I'll talk to you later.|

Later? He wasn't coming to her now? She watched Alex walking farther away. Indignantly, she saw him find Hheilea and started leading her away. What was he doing? She was an alien and not as close a friend. Why did Alex go to Hheilea first? He was her friend.

She didn't feel good. She rubbed at her temples. The headache had started to fade. She probably should've stopped practicing force sooner. Something else hurt not just her head, but she didn't want to figure it out. She'd tried healing her head injury using vapuc, but it still bothered her. Maybe she should go see Gursha about it.

A'idah snorted. Her nurse would help, but she'd also probably tell her to take it easy. That wasn't an option. She looked at Alex and Hheilea again, for some reason she felt worse.

Zeghes spoke up, "What are they doing?"

Pain and Joy

A'idah looked up at him as he swam above her. Petulantly, she answered. "I don't know. Alex should be with us."

Nodding his head up and down, Zeghes said, "I expected him to hurry to you. I thought he was... well... interested in you as his best friend and more."

She nodded her head trying not to cry at her disappointment. "Me too."

"I know what I'll do. I'll go see what their up to. They've already had too many adventures without us. Alex might be getting into more trouble with Hheilea, and we've got to keep an eye on her too. I think the two of them could get into shallow water again. They won't even know I'm there. This time, Alex won't leave us behind. I'll stop him."

A'idah forced a smile and said, "Great idea." She remembered Zeghes almost ramming Alex earlier. |Zeghes, be careful not to hurt Alex. He doesn't mean to do these things without us. He does care about us.|

She watched as Zeghes swam away. Inside her own private thoughts A'idah wasn't as sure about how Alex cared.

|Okay, but it would make me feel better to have a good excuse to ram him.|

Impatiently, A'idah waited watching her dolphin friend arch up high over Alex and Hheilea. A stray thought brought a grin to her face. Maybe she needed a good excuse to ram Alex too.

In sudden worry, she messaged her dolphin friend. |Zeghes, what will you do if Hheilea or Alex catches you spying on them?|

Zeghes slowly descended tipping over on one side to keep an eye on them. |No problem. If they look up, I'll just drop down and talk to them as if that was my intent all along. This is fun.| Slowly, he moved in circles above them. Some of the Tasties looked up at Zeghes and then ignored him.

Even with his confident answer, A'idah chewed on her lip. She didn't want Alex getting upset with them. At the same time, something in A'idah hurt at the idea of him and

Hheilea going off on another adventure without her. It was probably her stomach churning. A'idah's fists clenched without her knowing it as she thought of Hheilea and Alex taking off without her. Alex was her best friend not Hheilea's. Why did he go to the Kimley girl first instead of coming to her? Without thinking about it, she started forcing her way through the crowd. Tasties quickly yanked their tails out of her way after the first couple of yells of pain and loud complaints. When they recognized who it was pushing her way through the crowd the Tasties hurried to move out of her way.

A'idah didn't pay any attention to them. She forged her way forward, not thinking of what she was doing or what she would do when she got to them. Instead, she started grinding her teeth. Would Zeghes be able to play it cool and not just say she'd agreed to him spying on them?

Hheilea and Alex stood still for a while. What are they talking about? Hheilea turned her back on him and walked away. What happened? A'idah slowed her pace.

In earlier days, she'd seen Hheilea pretending to be Hhy, a boy. At times, Hhy had acted strange and very emotional. One time, the Kimley girl had clung to Alex sobbing. A'idah had wondered what was going on between them. Thinking back and knowing it wasn't a boy behaving strange but a girl, A'idah gave a gasp. Hheilea behaved as if Alex was her boyfriend. A'idah came to a jarring stop. Hheilea loved him. But... but... but... They were different species. Alex cared for her. She—

Zeghes messaged her. |I'm not sure if I understand what I overheard, but Alex spoke of being forced to get married.|

At those words, A'idah stopped hearing the rest of the message or even the crowd around her. Alex getting married? But she was his best friend. We're waiting to grow older and get further with our training before we— She just stood still not able to think.

A bump on her nose, suddenly she saw Zeghes in front of her. His beak just inches from her, and he gazed at her with one eye. "A'idah, you didn't answer my messages is your AI working?"

Pain and Joy

Someone spoke over the noise. A'idah turned to see who it was. At the same time she messaged Zeghes. |Sorry. It is working. Let's talk after this is over.|

The crowd quieted. "If I could get your attention please, let me introduce our two guests. Over here is Hheilea."

The crowd on the raised area backed away from the pretty, elven featured, young woman with white hair. She raised a hand and waved. "Hello, Everyone."

Seeing how mature and beautiful Hheilea appeared in her beautiful dress, made A'idah feel ordinary, plain, and way too young. She stifled an involuntary cry of pain.

The introducer said, "She is facing great danger as a young Kimley woman. Until she's married, Hheilea will be in great danger. We'll help. Give her a big Tasty welcome."

With grim determination, A'idah nodded her head. That was the reason Alex had to marry her. A small voice in her wondered if he wanted to and louder if it was fair. Even as her own heart hurt, A'idah decided they should do it as soon as possible.

She heard Zeghes' message in her mind and did her best to ignore it.

|Married? What does that mean? Maybe that's what Alex... This isn't making you happy. Who else would she? Would that affect how you and Alex are to each other?|

The crowd responded with different things.

"Hello, Hheilea!"

"We'll help!"

"We love you."

"Enjoy the evening."

Adamantly, A'idah shouted, "We'll keep you safe!"

The crowd said other things and eventually the person introducing Hheilea got them to be quiet. "Quiet down please. And also, over there is Alex." There was a pause and the crowd all looked toward the raised area. "Come on, Alex. Don't be shy."

A'idah looked back at Alex to see him climb onto a table. It wobbled as he stepped around the food on it. She started shoving her way toward him again. A'idah could tell the table wasn't stable.

Alex said, "Hi, everyone. I'm over here."

The quiet of the crowd bothered her. Why didn't they cheer for Alex and offer him support? He was worth two of Hheilea. He'd already done many amazing things.

The introducer said, "Once again, he's in the wrong place. We'll have to be patient with him. There's so much he doesn't understand, and his paths are fraught with peril. Some of you have already been involved in helping with his lessons."

Annoyed and worried, A'idah, raised a hand and shouted, "Alex, that table doesn't look stable."

She'd just about reached him, and Alex stepped back toward the edge of the table. A'idah heard a few young Tasty voices. "Hi." And something else she didn't catch.

The announcer said, "Okay, everyone, that's enough staring at Alex. We do welcome you, Alex. You'll—"

The table Alex stood on collapsed. With quick jabs of force, A'idah tried to protect the youngsters in front of her. Using force, she shoved at the table. Others must've too, because it flew backward and Tasties behind it tumbled to the ground. With another jab of force she pushed Alex higher so he wouldn't land on the children. In evidence of others doing the same thing he flew too high. A'idah backed up to catch him.

She yelled, "I've got you."|

Alex fell, and A'idah braced herself for the impact. Someone must've helped him slow with a gentle blow of force. Still, he slammed into her.

A'idah staggered at his weight. She refused to drop him or fall. With a grunt, she forced her smaller body to exceed its ability. He started slipping and she squeezed him. A'idah held Alex tight against her. He stopped with his blue eyes inches from hers.

A'idah remembered back in the dorms after his nightmare. She and Zeghes had come in response to Alex's screams. She'd held him close. They'd both been frightened and lonely. At that time, she'd known he wanted to kiss her. He'd been holding her and rubbing her back, but she'd pushed him away telling him they needed to just be friends. She really had wanted him to comfort her and kiss her. She smiled at the memory, but then the idea of him getting married to Hheilea hit again. Alex could never know how much that hurt her. Valiantly, she kept on smiling.

A'idah said, "I guess I'm not as big and strong as I think I am. Sorry for almost dropping you."

Alex gave her a big hug. "I like you just the way you are. You've got the biggest and strongest heart I know of. Thanks, A'idah." And then he grinned about something and added, "I like falling for you."

Falling for her? What did that mean? She hugged him back. "We're family. We take care of each other." She would take care of Hheilea too. She would not let her get hurt.

Alex said, "Let's go outside and look at the stars. Do you think Zeghes has forgiven me and would want to come with us?"

Zeghes bumped Alex on the head. "Yes. I still want to ram you, but I'm trying to understand. Let's go outside."

In a private message, Alex added to her, |I would rather go out there with just you, but I've got something to talk with both of you about.|

Alex took A'idah's hand and slowly led her out of the cavern. Not able to think, she just went along with his leading. His words swirled about inside her and made her feel... She wasn't sure. He would like to go out there with just her. And he liked falling for her. Both of those statements sounded romantic. Still what about Hheilea?

A'idah wanted to know more, but hesitated unsure of herself. They'd left the cavern behind, and her natural tendency to jump right into things won out. "What about Hheilea. Wouldn't she like to come with us?"

"What?" Annoyance or a sense of ridiculousness filled that one word.

That first response thrilled her.

Alex continued. "She wouldn't want to be with me, and I don't want to go for a walk with her right now."

Those words thrilled her even more. Still, Hheilea needed to be getting married. This time, a fear of what a conversation about the Kimley woman would reveal held her back, and Alex stopped it all.

"I don't want to talk about Hheilea."

A'idah didn't know what to say. Without thinking about it she said, "Remember the night you had the terrible nightmare, and Zeghes and I came to your room in the dorm?"

Alex slowed his walking. "Yeah."

Now that she'd started talking about it she didn't know what to say. A'idah felt her cheeks growing warm.

Again, she remembered that night. Afterwards, she'd been embarrassed by how little clothing she'd had on. Her nightgown wouldn't have been considered appropriate clothing by her grandmother. She'd also been frightened by how lonely and needy she'd felt. Alex and Zeghes were going to share the same dorm room from then on, but she had to be by herself. She'd wanted to be with them, but that wouldn't be right. A'idah had known Alex wanted to kiss her. She'd told him she needed him to just be a friend. Now though... What should she say? Her grandmother had told her to be careful with men, but Alex would respect her.

The problem about Hheilea nibbled at the back of her mind. A'idah's concern about her and Alex ebbed. Maybe, she'd been wrong about them. The cold, night wind greeted A'idah as she stepped outside with Zeghes and Alex. Involuntarily, she shivered. She rubbed her upper arms trying to fight off the chill.

Alex put his arm around her. "You're cold. We could go back inside. There isn't anyone in the entrance. We could stand in the shelter and watch the—"

"No." A'idah interrupted and sighed with satisfaction as she leaned against him. "No, it's beautiful out here. Thanks for suggesting the idea."

"At least, let me go back in and get a cloak for you." Alex didn't take his arm away or make any other moves toward leaving her.

A'idah looked up at the stars and the big beautiful nebulae dominating the night sky. It was beautiful. "I don't need a cloak. You're warmth enough." She turned her head

Pain and Joy

and caught him looking at her. For a long moment they just looked at each other. She could stay that way all night, forgetting for the time being the deadly seriousness of their training. A'idah wanted, no needed the comfort of knowing he cared for her. An earlier thought tried to interrupt the moment, but A'idah chose not to think of it. She remembered again the first time he'd held her close. They'd both been terrified kids. Back then, he'd wanted to kiss her, but she'd said no. Would he try and kiss her again? She was older and—

Zeghes interrupted the moment with a message to A'idah and then spoke out loud. |A'idah, what are you two doing? I don't understand the forbidden subject between humans, but this seems very much what Alex told me not to let him do. I thought you were both just supposed to be friends.| "Alex, what did you want to come out here for?"

A'idah had forgotten their dolphin friend. At his message she felt her cheeks growing warm.

As usual, Zeghes was right. She wished he wasn't with them. Even more, she didn't want to reply. Getting Zeghes involved in that discussion would be embarrassing. The dolphin didn't have any filter about what he'd say. A'idah took the safest option of just not answering him.

At Zeghes voice, Alex turned his eyes away from A'idah. At first, he spoke with a disappointed tone. "Oh yeah."

Alex cleared his throat and continued on speaking quieter. "Come closer, Zeghes. I've got an idea. You'll need to keep it a secret. Only you two can know. I need to get back to climbing the mountain, but I've got these assassins trying to kill me. Would you help me?"

A'idah forgot the cold and stopped leaning on him. With a strong and determined voice she stated as much as asked, "How?"

Zeghes whispered from up close. "Great, do you want me to do an assassin patrol while you climb?"

Alex whispered back. "No, Zeghes." In the quietest of whispers he continued. "I'll get setup for having some free time, and when you two can get away from your training. The three of us go into the worm tunnels hunting for what's going on. I think solving that mystery is very important, and it will give us time together." Alex squeezed A'idah at the last words.

He continued speaking. "Ytell told me to let him know if we learn anything else about the tunnels. You'll get me a disguise cloak to use. Only you two come out of the tunnels. I'll sneak out either before you or a different way. We'll have to explore first before we put our plan into action. You'll inform Ytell that I died. I'll hide out until the search is over. Then, I'll go back to climbing the mountain, and you can bring me food each day."

Zeghes nodded his head up and down in excitement. "That's a good plan. Our family will succeed."

At the words of Alex pretending to die in the tunnels, A'idah remembered the darkness of the tunnels, the dirt, the rocks, and most of all Alex and Zeghes almost dying in rescuing her.

She pushed away from his arm holding her and with both hands grabbed his shirt high on his chest. Shaking him and with heart beating hard, she said, "That's a terrible idea. It's too dangerous. You really could die. What about the Dreads? When you leave here to go exploring with us they could attack you again."

Alex pulled back from her hold. Off balance, A'idah fell with her forearms pinned against his chest and looking up at his smile.

Zeghes messaged her. |That was a nice move of Alex's, but are you two doing the things I'm supposed to slap Alex upside of his head to stop. I'm under the impression you're supposed to be just friends.|

Cupping A'idah's face with his hands, Alex said, "A'idah, this is what I love most about you. How you don't care about yourself and are so fierce in defense of everyone else. You're the most wonderful girl I know, but you have to realize we can't just float along the river of time letting events happen by chance or by others plans. I don't want the Tasties controlling my life or anyone else. I want..."

Alex paused and A'idah felt her heart up in her throat. She desperately wished Zeghes hadn't come outside with them.

Swallowing, Alex continued. "If we're going to save Earth, we have to learn how to take control of events and make things work out right. We've got to do this."

A'idah nodded her head. Somehow, she managed a short message to Zeghes. |No. This is okay.| Slowly, a big smile spread over her face at Alex's words of love. And they wouldn't just float along, but make things work out right for both of them. They'd be together in the end. Everything would be great, but his words of how fierce she was in the defense of others slowly brought a thought she'd shoved to the back of her mind wiggling forward.

A'idah had to bite her tongue to keep from crying out. She really thought Alex and Hheilea needed to get married. He couldn't love her, not the way she wanted or needed not in any right future. Ignoring her own distress, A'idah said, "Okay, but get ahold of Osamu. He might have some ideas. Just don't ask him about making rocks. Osamu and Ekbal are crazy about those lessons. I don't see the use. Did you know he has his own adventures at night?"

In response, Alex's eyes opened wide in surprise.

Chapter Twenty-Six
Awesome

A foreboding dream rolled Alex first one way and then another. In the nightmare, the big Tasty, his trainer stood in front of him with a stick. He kept swinging the stick at Alex saying you've got to do better with your sense of the future or you're going to die. Your possible death has been foreseen, but we're doing all we can to help you survive.

The dream shifted and Alex had the floating balls attacking him. Different colored ones danced around him. The blue ones pounded on his body. They didn't really hurt badly until they hit a bony spot. Pink ones zapped him when they touched and above it all an orange one floated. It had the face of Hheilea on its surface, and tears rolled down her face. Alex could hear her saying I tried to warn you, but I couldn't the results would be worse. It's tearing me up to know this danger to you and not to be able to tell you. Don't you dare die. I'll never forgive you or myself.

The balls morphed into multiple assassins attacking him at once. He thrashed about trying to defend himself. Part of him knew it was just a dream and tried to stop it or change it. Another part of him knew it was almost real.

The assassins drew back into the shadows of the nightmare, and Alex breathed deep trying to calm himself and to gain control. In front of him, a large individual Tasty moved. He picked up a large round object. It seemed to be a basket. Terror of what it held began to grow in Alex eclipsing the entire nightmare he'd already had.

A clarion warning sounded in his head. He had to wake-up. The pain would be terrible, but he couldn't shake the dregs of sleep.

Awesome

The Tasty heaved the contents at him. Small round little creatures with lots of small sharp teeth flew through the air at him. Alex tried to scream, but nothing came out. Desperately, he swatted at the beasts. Some he knocked away, but others latched onto his arm and the pain jolted him. His efforts slowed. Two were coming at his face. The little piranha-like creatures were going to eat him alive. The terrible little beasts hit him and began biting at him. Screaming he sat bolt upright in bed.

In the gloom, he could see his trainer standing at the foot of his bed. The Tasty held a large basket in his hand/paws. It couldn't be... Alex rolled backwards off the bed and landed on his feet hands out in a defensive posture.

"Ah, you're finally awake. I'll save these little beasties for another morning. Your sense of the future doesn't seem to do much good at waking you up, but it did help you avoid the worst of the punishment. Get up and get dressed. I'll wait out in the tunnel."

Heart pounding crazily, Alex stared at the trainer. At the Tasty's words, Alex realized he had many new aches and pains scattered over his body. After the Tasty turned around and left, Alex slowly gathered his wits, trying to remember, and make sense of what had just happened. The thought of his possible death hung in his mind. Tentatively, he started getting dressed.

Almost done, he stopped in shock at the sight of one of the little round terrors from his dream gnawing on the front edge of his bed frame. What had that crazy Tasty been doing? He hadn't really been getting ready dump a whole basket of those little monsters on him? Was he trying to kill Alex? Hurrying out to the tunnel, Alex exclaimed to the waiting Tasty. "One of those little beasts you have in the basket is gnawing on my bed."

The Tasty shrugged. "I'll let someone know about it. They'll come by and get it. Start running and try to keep up. Remember, to always be aware of your sense of the future. It must become just like walking. It has to be there without your having to think about it."

The Tasty took off down the tunnel holding the basket balanced on one hand as he ran. Soon they came to busier tunnels and Alex had to dodge around other Tasties. He could only sense something frustrating about the future and hunger. The last thing could just have been his stomach talking.

Still carrying the basket of beasts balanced on one hand, the big Tasty dodged through the crowded situation, and he started to pull away from Alex. Stubbornly, the teenager refused to call out to the trainer to slow down. Instead, he just worked harder at dodging, moving faster, and ignoring a growing feeling of hunger gnawing in the empty pit of his stomach.

The big Tasty stopped at a door and Alex tried not to show his relief at getting to stop running.

"Are you ready for some breakfast?"

"That'd be great."

The Tasty lead Alex inside a room with a chair set at a table. On the table sat a big platter with small, round, golden-brown balls on it. A wonderful fragrance made Alex lick his lips in anticipation. To the side of the platter lay two small slender sticks.

"Enjoy your breakfast, but be sure to use the sticks to eat." Just before he left, he added, "Don't take too long. I'll be back in a little bit and breakfast will be over."

Even as Alex went to sit down his sense of the future warned him about this meal and something awe inspiring later. Tentatively, he reached for the sticks. He considered using them as chopsticks, but when he moved them out to pinch a ball. The ball skittered away.

In shock, the boy stopped. Different possibilities ran through his mind. When he considered using his hand he realized from his sense of the future the platter would shock his hand. Before long, Alex resorted to stabbing with one stick at the little round morsels. The awareness of not having much time and his growing hunger made him hurry. Frustration made him jab too hard, and the stick snapped.

Picking up the last stick, Alex considered the problem. Now, he had a lesson to work through even while he ate. Frustration tried to control him. Knowledge of his limited time to eat tried to hurry him. Tempted to just stab, Alex set the stick down beside his plate. He took a deep breath and let it out slowly. He could do this, but it certainly wasn't awesome. What would be awe inspiring?

Taking the stick in his hand again, Alex looked at one of the morsels considering where it would be when he stabbed. Quickly, but with care he poked at his plate. His stick caught the morsel. Lifting it up, he popped it into his mouth. Savory warmth rewarded him. Chewing and swallowing, Alex continued carefully and methodically spearing and quickly eating the morsels. Even as his sense of the future helped him, it also gave him the feeling that something very awesome was going to happen.

All too soon, the door opened and his trainer said, "Come."

Regretfully, Alex left the remains of his breakfast. Again, he followed the big Tasty through a crowded tunnel. A feeling of surprise mixed with awe made him curious. What would he find awesome and surprising?

His instructor talked as they walked. The trainer said, "You've thought the training I've been giving you is frustrating and hard? We've just gotten started. You've got an amazing ability to sense the future, but you're not using it to its full potential. I don't know how to get you to where I know you need to get with this ability. Hheilea says Kimleys have training routines to develop their sense of the future, but they would take too long. Tasties don't have a similar trait of being able to sense the future, but we use variations on this type of training to develop our own skills. Hheilea thinks this might work. If you die, it won't be because I didn't give you the best training I could. We just need to help you improve faster."

The large Tasty stopped at a door and gestured for Alex to enter.

Alex thought it was the training room he'd been using, but there were two little, black Tasties waiting in it. They bowed to him. Their pale faces with black bars under their eyes made him grin. They were just so cute. Something about them was familiar, and he remembered the two black furred youngsters at the celebration.

Maleky's thoughts were excited. *This could be fun.*

What?

Just wait and see. Unfortunately, it won't take them very long.

Alex had stopped ignoring Maleky during training, as the Kimley residing in Alex's mind had fighting ideas which worked. This puzzled him. When they'd fought before, Alex hadn't thought Maleky really knew how to fight, but now he wasn't so sure. The guy knew what he was talking about. Had the Kimley let him win before?

The two little Tasties bowed to him again. "Hello, Alex. We hope our demonstration helps you."

These twins are going to demonstrate for you."

The room seemed to be bigger than when they entered. Normally it was about twenty-feet across, but now Alex thought it had changed to at least forty. What was going on?

One of the twins said, "We understand you've trained in the Weird room on the Coratory spaceship. So, you should be used to this, but we wanted to be sure you understood. We prefer training in a more natural setting."

Alex and the Tasties no longer stood in a room. Overhead, the crescent of a large planet filled a big part of the sky. From the other direction, he felt the warmth of a sun. A cool breeze blew on his skin. The grasses and flowers moved in response to the changing wind. A few trees and bushes grew around them. Burbling and splashing drifted from a small stream. In the distance, hills rose against the blue sky.

His trainer said, "The demonstration is starting."

The words pulled Alex's attention back from the beauty surrounding them. He looked around in time to see each of the twins grab a long pointed stick exactly like the ones he'd been using. An orange ball appeared, bobbing gently in the air.

Surprising Alex, the twins squatted holding the sticks against their bellies. They calmly waited as black balls, white balls, red balls, and blue ones appeared circling the orange one. He didn't understand why the white balls didn't go after the twins. The only times he'd dealt with those they'd bobbed in front of his eyes blocking his view.

As Alex considered this one of the twins jumped up and ran back toward some bushes. Turning back, the little Tasty raced back on all fours, carrying the stick in its mouth. Its twin crouched, with one hand/paw held back towards its sibling. The other hand/paw held its stick pointed toward the balls. What were they doing?

Awesome

Maleky commented in Alex's head. *One is watching the balls and prepared for what they might do. The other one is going to attack. This is going to be so awesome.*

The excited enthusiasm of the Kimley surprised Alex. He almost sounded giddy. The evil Kimley still managed to surprise him. The demonstration which followed made Alex think of a crazy mix between the wonderful book series *Redwall* and the fantasy heroes *Teenage Mutant Ninja Turtles*.

The running twin leapt. This in itself looked awesome, but Alex didn't understand what it hoped to accomplish. Instead of leaping high into the air, its hindquarters rotated up and its front paws were reaching down. The other twin dropped his stick. Three white balls moved down spiraling together between the Tasties and the other balls. Now with both hand/paws free the standing twin caught the hand/paws of the leaping twin and threw him high into the air at the balls.

Alex's eyes bulged in surprise. The thrown twin spun with the throw. He could see its stick slashing and twirling through the air. Alex heard the smacks as it hit the various balls. They flew off on different tangents leaving the orange unprotected. The spinning Tasty lashed out with a foot and kicked the orange ball. Finishing the arch of its spinning journey it nailed its landing. The other twin with its stick now in its mouth had calmly walked across the grass and caught the orange ball calmly tossing it back and forth before tossing it over its shoulder.

Wow. They could've finished this training so easily if they'd wanted to. They'd beaten the training room in incredible style. Alex grinned. Now, he understood Maleky's excitement. This was cool.

Maleky responded to Alex. *I don't think they're done yet. The Tasties aren't just wise, but they're incredible fighters. A Kimley would beat one of them with their sense of the future, but the Tasty would still go down with incredible style. They're just awesome.*

That was interesting and reinforced Alex's idea that Maleky had let him win their earlier fight. Why? What was his plan? For just a second, Alex almost considered that Maleky was evil and any plan he had must be evil.

The trainer said, "The training room still has to keep the balls within a certain area, and it can't have the orange one too far away for the twins to attack it."

Four blue balls moving fast sped towards the twins. What would they do? Alex remembered even as the balls tried to attack the twins.

They only tried, because the twins beat them off with their sticks. It became obvious that the twins were not just on the defense, but aiming where they hit the blue balls. They all were knocked at the orange ball. One of them hit it. That must've counted as an attack on the orange one, because Alex didn't think any new balls were appearing. They were so many he couldn't be sure.

It seemed to Alex that the training room was going with a different more aggressive plan this time.

A sound behind Alex startled him. What he saw shocked him. Some kind of a big cat, Alex thought it looked similar to a mountain lion, just bigger. What was it doing here? Was it part of the training demonstration? Would he have to fight them in his own training sessions? Alex didn't like the idea of having to fight it. He didn't think it would end well for him.

The big cat moved slowly, one paw at a time. It focused totally on the twins who were continuing to battle the balls and seemed ignorant of the approaching danger.

Maleky knew Alex's thought. *Don't try and warn them. Just watch. This is going to be even better.*

The twins danced, spun, and flipped through the air around the orange ball. Their laughter filled the air. One of them threw a stick and speared a red ball before it hit the other twin. The stick landed in the stream. With a big splash the Tasty dove into the water after it.

A shadow moving over the ground drew Alex's eyes up. He gasped at a large raptor circling above them. It looked bigger than an eagle, but smaller than Ytell. Still, it would be big enough to take one of these tasties. He glanced around for the cat. It still stalked the two little tasties. He wanted to warn the tasties.

Maleky instantly reminded him. *Don't do it.*

Awesome

Quickly, Alex used his sense of the future. Danger? No. Instead, humor. At that foreshadowing of what was to come, he grinned. Maleky was right. This was pretty cool.

Of course, I'm right about most things. You should listen more carefully to me.

Alex nodded in agreement, and that should've scared him, but he didn't notice.

A scream, from above, startled Alex. Before he looked up, he spotted the big cat leaping and heard its yell.

"Die!"

From above the raptor plummeted. Alex cringed back from the scene unfolding in front of him.

As if in slow motion, one of the Tasties exploded up out of the water. Spray flew into the air and for a brief moment a rainbow appeared. That twin whipped the stick it held at the big cat. The other leapt into the air and flicked a foot out at one of the balls.

Alex gasped at what they did. How could it be an effective defense?

From where it had been speared on the stick, a red ball flew off. The big cat, flying through the air with paws and claws out to catch its Tasty prey, looked almost cross-eyed at the red ball flying at it. The ball flew into its mouth and must've gone part way down its throat. Instantly, it went from yelling dire threats to choking and its hair standing on end.

Alex knew how painful the red balls were. He could sympathize with the poor cat. Alex wondered if his own hair stood on end when he got hit by a red ball. The cat landed tumbling through the grass. With one last roll, its head slammed down onto the ground. It started to cough up the ball, but the little Tasty got to the cat first.

Alex knew the Tasties looked thickset and strong, but he didn't know how strong they actually were. With one paw/hand it grabbed the cat by one ear and yanked its head off the ground.

Alex winced. That must be really painful on top of the pain from the red ball stuck in its throat.

The Tasty used its other paw/hand to buffet the cat's head back and forth. At first, the cat moaned in pain and complaint.

Until finally, its eyes rolled back in its head and the cat went limp.

The eagle-like raptor had been plummeting, beak wide open, screaming its own dire imprecations. The other twin had kicked with incredible precision another red ball. The raptor saw it way too late. It had been plummeting like a lightning bolt down onto its Tasty prey. There was no time to change course or shut its beak. Its head slammed backward from the force of the ball ramming into its beak. From the predator's expression, Alex knew it wanted to scream in rage, but all that escaped was a squeak. Its feathers all stood on end changing its appearance from a mighty carnivore to be feared to a hilarious visage of pain.

Alex laughed out loud at the funny sound coming from the huge eagle-like raptor and how it looked. What happened next was even funnier and at the same time awesome. The bird slammed into the ground tumbling head over tail. At some point it managed to cough out the red ball.

Moving fast, the Tasty had scampered after it. With its stick it speared the ball before it could hit the ground.

What was the little guy going to do? The pain gone, the big bird lifted its wings. Alex could tell it was going to take off. It slightly squatted.

The young Tasty leapt.

The big bird pushed off with its feet and down with its wings. Alex felt the wind from the down-stroke.

The Tasty smacked down onto the raptor's massive back.

The weight of the passenger didn't stop the bird from launching into the air, but it screamed. "You dare!" Wings lifted for another powerful thrust even as it twisted its head back with beak open to savage the little Tasty.

The little passenger ran up the bird's back. With one hand it held the stick and swung the red ball on it toward the bird's eye. "Chase the orange ball or I'll slam this against your head."

Instinctively, the bird yanked its head back.

Alex knew that Tasties had claws, but now he learned how effective they could be. The bird obeyed and flipped through a series of maneuvers getting its head closer to the orange ball. All the time, the young Tasty clung to its back with what appeared to be ease.

At that moment, it flung its stick at the orange ball. From the ground below the aerialist the other stick arched up from the ground.

Both sticks speared the orange ball. The raptor disappeared, the Tasty flipped through the air and landed beside its twin smack in front of Alex. They bowed and swept one hand/paw out. "That's how it's done."

Alex said, "Wow."

His trainer told them, "Thank you."

One of the little guys held a hand out and a stick with a pain inducing red ball on it appeared. The tasty grabbed the stick. "Remember, pain is temporary, but death is forever.

His trainer said, "Pain is your greatest weakness. Yes, I know you have faced and fought through great pain, but we both know you're afraid of pain of the heart. I know of your friend you loved and how the pain you feared of taking her life cost the life of a hero. Great leaders have to send people out to get hurt and die. They can't let the pain of their feelings affect how they make their choices."

At those words, Alex reached up and grabbed the red ball on the stick, and yanked it off. Shuddering from the pain, Alex remembered the lesson with the chrinkey. Still shuddering, he shoved it into a pocket.

The little Tasties said, "Wow."

His instructor nodded his head. "The story about you hugging a chrinkey must be true. There is hope for you."

Stuttering at the effort to talk with the pain, Alex asked, "Who... who... are you? I've... I've... never learned... learned your name."

"My name is not important. I'm the leader of this city you are the guest of."

The leader? Time passed as Alex looked at him. Finally, he asked the question, "Why... Why give me so much of your time?"

"You're already doing better with the physical pain, but we both know the emotional pain is worse. You helped that girl, Twyla, have a great victory. To die with love is much better than living forever with hate. As to why I'm your instructor? Amongst all of my people in this crater, I'm the best instructor. I don't know about that, but I accept the opinion of others. You get the best of our efforts because of what the Book of Prophesy shows about you. You have already proven your worth by many things you've already accomplished. You found Lepercauls had an unknown ability to be healers, and you helped a whole generation of them to become good. You've helped more Winkles than just Twyla and Twarbie to leave hate. You chose to help a Deem, and somehow helped him become something no one would've expected. You don't just ignore the existing rules and ideas. You shatter them. We don't know what the future holds for you to do and be, but we expect it to be great."

In a quieter voice and with compassion the Tasty continued. "You do realize what you do might be a great victory involving your death? I know that. That is why I'm pushing you so hard. You and I don't have enough time, and I know the limitations of what I can do. I've thought of adding music to your training, but I haven't been able to figure out how."

Death. Alex was accepting pain, and he could accept dying if it meant victory. Yet, he thought of Hheilea and the pain his death would cause her. For a moment, he considered A'idah, but the pain he knew she would suffer was too much for him to dwell on. "Why... Why music?"

"Pain is a great clarifier. It is making it hard for you to focus on my words, but you'll remember them so much better because of it. I should've had you holding a red ball sooner. My apologies. I wish I was a better instructor. Music is better and much different than pain. Pain over too long becomes debilitating, but music makes you whole. It makes you accept feelings. It makes you one with them and one with what is around you. You are not one enough with your feelings of the future. I think music could help you solve that. It would give you the focus you need. I've been looking for a musician to help with your instruction, but there wasn't enough time. Speaking of time, you need to climb the Gadget Lady's mountain and get another String Sword. I've been trying to find a safe way for you to get back to that quest."

Alex asked, "What... What makes the String Sword so special?"

"It's a special weapon in many ways. From the descriptions I've heard about how you used the defective Sword, I'd say you know part of what is special about it. The large quantity of String material in the sword makes you able to see and respond to other vapuc attacks."

"What makes it so sharp?"

His instructor nodded his head. "Good question. The dark matter constrains the string material and only exposes it in a one string gap. That is smaller than an atom or a quark. It never needs sharpening. Now, you need to start your next training. Please, get as far as you can."

Chapter Twenty-Seven
Preparing

Each of the following mornings started the same way, except without the exhibition. Alex's instructor led him to the training room. The Tasty would set Alex up for the day's lesson and leave.

Each day, Alex had immediately pushed himself to finish the lesson as soon as possible. He needed to make time to prepare for setting his plan into action. Thinking of his plan made him feel like a spy, but just thinking about it wasn't enough. It would be terrible if A'idah and Zeghes were available, but he wasn't ready. He could never finish the lessons quickly enough and, those first days left him exhausted. Alex wanted to talk to her, but not having any good news kept him from making the contact.

Somehow, he had to find the time and energy to get his equipment. After completing another long brutal training session, Alex stood in the shower letting the hot water massage his sore muscles. Maybe he should go visit the nurse. The thought of his plans with A'idah and Zeghes blossomed in his mind. With a grin, he shrugged off the idea about the nurse and instead considered how to start preparing to explore the worm tunnels. Today, he would make some progress on getting ready. What would he need? Who could he talk to for help?

A'idah's strange comment about Osamu came to mind. Alex didn't know too much about the older Japanese man. He'd been an astronaut, but that was about all Alex knew of the man. The man hadn't reacted well to working with animals as people. He also hadn't at first thought of vapuc as terribly important.

Preparing

Both of those things had changed, and Osamu had always tried hard to help everyone. Alex couldn't imagine the guy had been having adventures at night. How could he do that and still have his training during the day?

It was if the man was some kind of secret, super spy. That was a crazy thought, but not much crazier than the Japanese man having secret adventures at night and his training during the day. Yet, there was Osamu's shutting down the Tasty's city. How had he done that? Alex decided to reach out to him. |Osamu, do you have time to answer some questions?|

The reply came instantly. |Yes, Alex. What is up?|

Even as Alex recognized the formal, measured way of speaking Osamu had, uncertainty slowed his own thoughts. |Uhm, well, I'm looking at exploring some of the worm tunnels with A'idah and Zeghes. Do you have any ideas?|

|You are still in the Tasty's city?| Osamu didn't wait for a response. |Every Tasty will know who you are. Ask anyone in the tunnels where you can get supplies. Even faster, just think I need special tools and supplies, and the tunnel you are in will have a wave of color moving in the direction you need to go. Asking the individuals first might give you more specific information. The tunnels only work off your thoughts. If you are uncertain, the tunnel might send you where there are shovels or some other type of tools totally unrelated to what you need.|

Overwhelmed, Alex just replied, |Thanks.|

Osamu wasn't done. |There is someone I know. I will talk with them about what type of devices you might need and send you another message. Also, I have been thinking about you and those assassins. I have an idea for how to help.|

|Really? That would be great.|

|I think it would be a good idea to help the captured assassin escape.|

|What? Why? How?| That was a crazy idea.

|I have come up with a plan. Trust me. There is more to the city than meets the eye. If we do nothing, the Dreads will keep throwing assassins at you. The solution is to take control of what will happen. By humiliating their first assassin, you have set up a great opportunity for resolving this.|

Taking control appealed to Alex. |When could we do this?| As he messaged, he still had uncertainties. Maleky tried to get him to listen to some contrary thoughts. Alex thought of what Hheilea might say about this plan. He doubted if she would be happy. A'idah would hate it too. Was this the right choice? |But... The Tasties are supposed to be very wise. We should—|

Osamu's message cut Alex's off. |Do not tell the Tasties about this idea. Wisdom applies only to what you know. They do not know about what I am doing.| After a pause, he continued. |I will arrange to free him in the next couple of days. Don't talk to anyone else about this via messaging. The system isn't secure.|

Alex's mouth gapped open in surprise. He didn't know what to think. How could Osamu free a prisoner from the Tasties? Was this really a good idea? |If the messaging system isn't secure, why is it okay for us to be talking about this?|

|You remember Flit, the Feelings teacher, Hheilea's uncle? It turns out, he is really good at computers. I have worked with him on some things. He has got a special security routine setup on all of my messages. We are safe. Speaking of the Kimleys, Hymeron is hip deep in trouble. Be very careful about any dealings you have with him. On second thought, avoid him at all cost. I have reason to believe he is behind both the attack in the bubble bay and this bounty.|

Alex wasn't sure about what to say. He already knew about Hymeron, but the fact that Osamu knew surprised him. He finally settled with. |Okay.| Another thought shed the unwanted concerns. Taking control of his own future instead of just reacting to events was what he wanted. This would work. Finishing his shower, he got dressed and left the room. On the tunnel walls, a green wave of color traveled off to his left, and a blue wave of color traveled off to his right. Alex wondered what kinds of equipment were at the two different locations.

Osamu sent him another message. |Look for a strong force disabler. That will get you to the right location. There will be other gadgets where it is at and someone to help you. The disabler is very dangerous, and I would not want you to use it, but that will get you to the right place. Good

Preparing

luck and listen to what the Tasties tell you about the devices.|

Even as Alex considered the message, the colors on the walls changed. Now just a purple wave traveled off to his left. Following the color down the tunnel, Alex wondered what a strong force disabler was. There was another question bothering him. What would he tell the Tasties he needed the equipment for? He remembered how the best lie contained an element of truth. He would tell them about exploring the tunnels. Ytell had agreed to that. He would keep the real goal of the plan a secret. With a grin at the idea, Alex considered trying to act like the made-up British spy. He'd be another Blond, James Blond, double-oh-seven and always calm, debonair, in control, and of course the consummate lady's man. Alex almost laughed at that last thought.

From around the turn ahead of him, a golden brown Tasty bounded into view crashing into his thoughts with her exuberance. "Alex!"

"Delli! You're back."

He just had time to brace himself as she grabbed him in a fierce hug. Again, he felt his senses overwhelmed with her special warm scent. "I thought you were going to live in the wild?"

"I was and I did. The fledgling ceremony doesn't have to last for weeks. I quit mine early. I wanted to check on you and to help you prepare for your own fledgling ceremony in any way I can."

"Fledgling ceremony? What do you mean?"

The adult Tasty let go of him and stepped back. Her voice grew more intense as she spoke. "I spent my childhood preparing and growing to become an adult. That effort culminated in my ceremony. You are part of a plan, a path, and a hope. All of that is coming to a test, basically your own fledgling ceremony. You'll become what you could be... or—" For a moment she paused, until with each word a declaration Delli said, "And that's not an option."

The words weren't terribly different from what Alex had already heard, but what they expressed resonated with recent and much earlier memories. He desperately wanted to be who he could be, but what would that be?

Maleky kept pushing at him. Hheilea pushed at him. A'idah wanted him to be something that he wanted too. Most importantly, Alex wanted to save Earth. What choices would help him take that path? Anger and frustration gnawed at him from not knowing for sure what to do, and a terrible suspicion that even if he did know, would he be willing for what he needed to do or needed to become?

Alex only just held in a scream of frustration. With the scream blocked, turmoil burned in him. Desperately, he sought some idea or memory to help. His parents had talked about willingness. Desperately, Alex thought back to his dead parents. They had talked to him in the past about choices and paths those choices lead to. What else had they tried to teach him? Everyone needs unmerited help even with willingness to do the right things. Quietly, Alex choked out the words, "I could use some help."

Delli continued speaking with hardly a pause. Obviously, she hadn't heard his emotional words. "First, I need to find out what your current plans are and make sure you've made good preparations." After a pause for a breath, she continued. "So, what are your current plans?"

Plans? Could he tell her his plans? He trusted Delli, but right now, he just wanted to get away from her before he broke down. Alex needed to get her off this subject and get away. He needed to be the suave and debonair British spy. If only he could control his emotions.

Leaning a hand against the wall, Alex tried. "Plans? Right now, I have a date." The image of A'idah in his arms under the beautiful night sky came to mind. He might've pulled off his acting effort if his emotions hadn't betrayed him. The words came out a bit tortured and mutinous tears started down his cheeks.

"Alex, are you okay? What's wrong?"

At those incongruous words, laughter bubbled up into the crying and out.

Delli said, "City, give us a room, please."

Preparing

The tunnel wall on the left side dissolved or shifted and suddenly there was a door where there hadn't been one before. Alex felt himself lifted and carried into the room.

Delli asked, "Are you okay?"

Alex didn't know the tunnels could be changed by the city. The shock calmed him, but also slowed his answer. Delli must've been busy as large cushions appeared, and she settled down onto them with him. She didn't say anything just looked at him.

Where did he start? He wanted to ask about what had just happened. Was the whole Tasty city a type of huge weird room? He knew the training room was a weird room, but the whole city?

He shook his head at that incredible idea. How big could they make a weird room? The thought was beyond his comprehension.

Alex decided to answer one of her questions first. "I'm sorry. It just struck me as funny how we tend to ask people if they're okay, when we know they aren't okay." Alex knew he really hadn't answered her question, but instead just rattled. He said words just to fill the empty space trying to prevent having to talk of the deep issues. "The laughter helped me feel better." He didn't know what to say in answer to the words which had resonated so strongly. They had touched deep, important, emotional memories and thoughts. "I hope my laughing didn't bother you. I say the same kinda thing. Are you okay? Ha, it's si—"

She interrupted the meaningless words filling the quiet. "Alex?"

He sighed. He was still tempted to talk about meaningless things, but Alex knew she wasn't fooled. Taking a deep breath, he tried to order his thoughts. "It's been very evident that my life is part of some bigger plan. This evil guy, Maleky is in my head. Hheilea's mom helped to make sure I was abducted. There's this prophesy about me. I've thought a lot about it. I'm frustrated about having my life controlled and yet… if it is necessary, I want to be willing for anything to save others."

"Much of this plan you spoke of just plainly scares me, but what you said made me think of it all in a different way. Before my mom and dad died they always said there is a plan for me. It was in place before everything started."

"My path's end isn't preordained, but all along the way I'm given help to get to the right end."

Delli asked, "What is this other plan you speak of?"

"According to my parents the entire universe was created for one goal. That any of us would come to know and serve the Creator, but that we all have free choice. Our choices either make it more or less likely we will serve God."

Delli answered, "We have the same belief. It is part of why we chose to be who and what we were created as."

Alex could only say, "Wow."

Delli asked, "But why did this make you cry?"

"Sorry. I probably seem pretty ridiculous to you. Thinking of this made me miss my folks."

"Ridiculous? No. That's one of the things I appreciate about you. Alex you don't hide behind pretense. You show your true feelings and go for what's right. I know you. I want to help you."

Her words of hiding behind pretense embarrassed Alex. He trusted Delli. He shouldn't have tried to act like the debonair spy. Alex said, "I have a plan to explore one of the worm tunnels. The Winkles are up to something with them. I told Ytell we would look into it and he's approved the idea." For a second, he paused and then continued with the rest of the truth. "But there's more to it. I'm planning on faking my death to be able to get back to climbing the Gadget Lady's mountain. A'idah and Zeghes are going to help me. I think getting another String Sword is very important. I—"

Delli interrupted him. "Great. You'll need some equipment. I know just the person to talk to. Let's go." Suiting actions to words, the Tasty shoved Alex up and jumped to her own feet. The cushions disappeared.

In a blur of motion, a new opening appeared in one wall. Instead of the tunnel, Alex looked into another chamber. Stacks of stuff obscured his view of it. "What did

Preparing

you just do? This makes me think of the Weird room on the Coratory, but your whole city can't be another Weird room."

Delli chuckled before answering him. "Actually it is. Grandma told me about the training you've been getting. Haven't you wondered about how that room works?"

Alex hesitantly stepped forward into the new room, looking at the piles of stuff. He remembered how the training room created stuff and changed for each new lesson. He'd thought that room was comparable to the Weird, but a whole city? The enormity of the idea shocked the human boy. Alex thought about the Strong Force Disabler. No responding wave of color showed on any of the walls. He was where he'd been going.

"How did you get us here?"

"I had the City move our small room here after I knew you needed gadgets. Don't tell my grandma what I did. We aren't supposed to needlessly use energy."

At that, an idea slammed into Alex. "With all of the energy it takes for a whole city to be a functioning weird room how could Amable ever have been short of money? You guys are overflowing in wealth." He was kind of surprised Delli didn't interrupt him and even took a second or two to answer.

The Tasty woman waved her arms at the room of equipment. "All of this, the Coratory, the Academy, and the City Under the Sea must be an incredible amount of wealth to you. Compared to Earth it is. Our city is run very efficiently. Energy isn't wasted. I'll probably get talked to about this little escapade, but I'll use you as an excuse. You're very important to all of us Tasties."

This surprised Alex. He remembered how the Tasties had treated him at the celebration. "I'm important to the Tasties?

"Yes. Grandma told me about how you were treated at the celebration. Many of our fellow Tasties are nervous about you. At first, I didn't find you very inspiring. Others still feel that way, because they haven't seen you in action or gotten to know who you are. If they had, they'd believe the stories about you. I do. You're awesome."

Embarrassed by her praise, Alex wanted to ask about the stories, but he remembered his question about the wealth. "Waving a hand at what surrounded them. What about this wealth? You still didn't answer my question about how Amable could've ever been short of money. In fact, your answer just increased my doubt. You spoke of how efficient you are with your energy. The Academy and everything around the crater supporting it doesn't look to be very efficient. If the training for the different species at the academy is necessary for them to save their home worlds from the Deems, why hasn't the training been done more efficiently with something much cheaper? Just having us living in tents or on the Coratory should work for our training." Even as Alex spoke about the Coratory, he remembered how empty it was. The spaceship was huge. It could easily contain the Academy and all of the students.

For the first time since he'd met Delli, Alex noticed she was hesitant.

"You're right... The money problem didn't have to exist. Still, the wedges containing each world's plants and animals are very important for their training, but the money problem is also important."

Now that she'd answered what he suspected was true, Alex didn't know what to say. The aliens were playing with Earth's safety. Anger at that thought grew. In his mind, Maleky laughed and said. *I told you so. You're being manipulated. Just like many others, except for me. I live by my own rules. I've told you, but you don't want to listen. You should be like me.*

Here he was in the room where all kinds of equipment waited for him, but instead of looking at it he stood uncertain of what to do. Alex knew Maleky wanted him to react in anger to the manipulation, but that actually made him reconsider his own initial reaction. "Why?"

His short simple question seemed to galvanize Delli. "Because, strength and true purpose doesn't come from ease and wealth. I've told you about the choice my people made generations ago. We don't use our power or wealth to live easy lives. The result is our peace, strength, beauty,

Preparing

and our reputation for wisdom. You know the Kimleys better than most. Have you considered how such a powerful species has become enslaved and persecuted?"

Alex remembered the T'wasn't-to-be-is legend and how Hheilea's dad worked at making the right things happen. "So the financial problems were important?"

"Yes, Stick is so good at his job that it's been just about impossible to make the trouble real."

"How do you know so much? You aren't that old."

"My grandma is Windelli. From a young age, I've been helping her. Tasties are expected to start learning how to be wise at a young age. Our elders trust us with important work."

At her words, Alex remembered what one of the young Tasties said to him at the celebration. It hadn't sounded like a youngster. He nodded his head as he considered the words and what he'd noticed. Another question hit him, and Alex wasn't certain he wanted it answered. He looked into his friends eyes, and she looked patiently back. "Did my saving Daren and his solving the money shortage cause a bigger problem?"

"I'm pretty sure it was unexpected. You're not the only Earthling who's done unexpected things, which just proves that Earth is an important part of the future."

That wasn't an answer. Alex raised an eyebrow or tried to. He wasn't certain if he'd learned how to do that. Something in his expression must've worked.

"Sorry, I don't think I should answer that. Also, even though I have my own suspicions, I don't know nearly as much as my grandma. Why don't we get started on getting you the equipment you need?"

Alex nodded his head in agreement. He wasn't at all certain about what was being done by others to affect him, but he was positive that getting ready for the exploration was the next right thing to do.

Chapter Twenty-Eight
Tested to Failure

After getting his equipment, Alex messaged A'idah to let her know he was ready. Then, he just focused on his training, trying not to think about anything else. One day, training started very differently. If he'd known what it would lead to, Alex might've rebelled.

The big Tasty stopped Alex before he entered the training room. "I've reviewed your progress and talked to Windelli." His instructor uncharacteristically paused. "We're concerned about your survivability."

Alex asked, "What? What do you mean?" It couldn't be what he thought the creature meant.

It was.

"We're concerned about the progress you've made. In a future combat with the assassins or some of your other enemies, you will die. I'm not willing to just give up. I'm going to push you harder. I think you have the potential to be the one. Today will be different. Once you enter the room, you won't be able to leave until you've failed."

The one? Failed!? What did that mean? "Can I give up if it gets too hard?"

"No. I considered not telling you this was a test to failure, but Windelli insisted that I tell you. She said you need to be able to trust us. I agree. If you can't trust us, that would hamper your training. It's up to you. Do you want to enter the room?"

"Why?" What Alex thought, but didn't ask was what would failure mean? He had an uncomfortable feeling about it and wasn't sure if he wanted to know the answer.

Tested to Failure

"We need to establish the extent of your endurance, balance, reactions, connection to your sense of the future and much more. With those things established, I can improve the training to maximize your progress."

Afraid of the answer, he still asked. "How will I know I've failed?"

"You won't, but the system will know you're beaten."

For a second, Alex paused. He'd just have to work and try until the room decided he was beaten. Something about that didn't quite sound good, but Alex nodded his head accepting the challenge. "Okay." Even as he said okay, part of him rebelled at the idea of failure.

He entered the room. "I'm ready." A stick with a sharp pointed end appeared in the air. Alex grabbed it."

"You will have what you've already experienced with the different balls and the need to stab the orange one to finish a level. The next level will start after a five second break. There will also be rocks falling from the ceiling. They're going to be brittle. They'll shatter on impact, and you'll have no shoes. The room will keep the cuts from being too deep into your feet. Your feet have to remain useable, but the injuries will better establish your pain tolerance. I'll see you in the nurse's clinic when you come too."

Come too? Pain tolerance? No shoes? None of that sounded good at all, but it fit what Alex had already suspected.

The door shut. The orange ball appeared. Alex reflexively stabbed at it and glanced up at the ceiling. It was much higher than before. A big rock fell. Alex only just dodged in time as it fell to the floor with a crash. An involuntary scream burst from him. "Ahhhh!"

This was crazy! Sweat beaded on Alex's forehead. That rock would've knocked him out and maybe killed him. His heart beat fast as he considered what the last words might've meant.

Frantically, he sought his sense of the future. Ducking to the side he dodged another rock. The floor now had chunks of broken rocks scattered across it. Alex tried the door, but it wouldn't open. He'd neglected stabbing at the orange ball and other balls had appeared. Inadvertently, he stepped on a sharp rock. The resulting pain and lurch as he threw himself to the side left him momentarily distracted. A red ball hit his arm and pain lanced at him. The words, tolerance of pain pounded in his mind.

His sense of the future only gave him one out. Alex had to do the next right thing.

Time and beaten levels passed. He stumbled on the growing layer of broken rocks. Sweaty and in pain from injuries, Alex desperately maneuvered to the shower door and tried it. The door refused to open.

Maleky in agony from the pain had long ago suggested Alex should just give up. The pain had silenced him sometime after.

Alex refused the option of giving up. What? Just stand still until rocks pounded him down onto the floor? At what point would the pain stop? He wouldn't give up. Alex knew without a shadow of doubt, a very painful, disabling injury would happen at almost any moment. He refused to accept failure. His injuries slowed his responses and each level grew harder. Gritting his teeth, Alex dove head first at the floor. A rock crashed behind him. Rolling before impact, he found the clear path and again stabbed the orange ball. Painfully, he slammed into the jagged chunks of broken rocks. New wounds ripped into his skin.

Five second break.

One. Alex rolled back to his knees. If he won, when it beat him…

Two. He breathed deep seeking clarity from the pain to keep his sense of the future.

Three. Back on his feet, he swung his arms trying to loosen tight muscles.

Four. Alex closed his eyes. He would continue. Failure wasn't an option.

Five. With eyes closed, Alex dodged the first rock and jabbed through the red ball accepting the pain to have a chance with one step to stab the orange one. With all of his other pain, Alex hardly noticed the pain from the red ball. He couldn't make that step. He would twist his ankle and fall with two rocks smashing into him.

Instead, Alex hopped. He grinned at a path. Failure? If he ended victoriously, it couldn't be failure. The other paths led to

Tested to Failure

more injuries slowing him down until pounded to the ground he'd be unable to move. There was something about this path that blocked his sense of the future, but he knew this choice would let him end victorious.

Alex took the path. All this time, he'd been stabbing and dodging. He danced on the broken rocks never letting his full weight rest on either of his injured feet. He took one last breath and made the next right choice. Smoothly, he dodged into the path of a falling rock and stabbed the orange.

Pain exploded and didn't go away. The agony dragged on and on. Time itself seemed to have stopped. No thoughts interfered with the pain. His entire existence was agony. It wouldn't stop. If only, it would stop.

Blearily, he blinked. Something was missing. What had happened? What was gone? He couldn't feel pain. Alex sighed in relief. In the background, he could hear voices. One of them was very angry. It made him think of Gursha.

"As a nurse, I cannot consent to what you are doing. I can only imagine how Alex felt as the training room kept him stable until I could save him. He would've been conscious the whole time. You are torturing him."

"This has to be done. You have no choice. We have no choice. I just need you to keep him alive and healed."

Alex blinked again trying to bring the room into focus. The voices continued.

"You are pushing him too hard. My holo-field is having trouble keeping him under to get the healing and rest he—"

The voices faded, and then he could hear them better.

"Let him come to. He needs to eat. After, I talk to him you can do whatever you need to get him healed and rested." Alex could barely make out the words as his instructor lowered his voice. "I need him to be ready for tomorrow. It's going to be a tougher day. Could you be sure he gets good dreams. Hopefully, those will help him get through this. You'll have another patient tomorrow. I agree. It's wrong for Alex and anyone to undergo this type of training."

Tomorrow? What would happen? A tougher day? Hadn't today been tough? Another patient? Finally, he could see. Through the pink haze of a holo-field, Alex could make out his instructor walking toward him. From that, Alex figured he still needed more healing.

"Alex, you did great today. Your biggest asset isn't your sense of the future, but your unwillingness to quit. I should've done this type of training sooner. There was one problem. You cheated. I didn't get all of the data I hoped for. With some help, you'll only have one more day of training to failure. You have an incredible ability to focus on just doing the next right thing. Now, I just need you to get focused better on that next right thing being staying alive."

Staying alive? Alex puzzled over the words. His instructor left, not leaving any more words for him to consider. Instead, he thought of the terrible pain which had never stopped.

The nurse bustled over to Alex.

His holo-field lifted him into a sitting position. "Nurse, I remember feeling pain that never seemed to stop. What happened to me? It was horrible."

A small table rose up from the floor. The nurse reaching his side said in a tortured voice, "You suffered a terrible head wound and the training room just kept you alive until I could help. The process unfortunately kept you conscious. There's more to it, but I can't talk about it without losing control. It would've been less painful if your heart stopped, and I resuscitated you. I'm not for this training, for the pain you're going through. If I could think of a logical argument to stop what your trainer is subjecting you to, I would, but I can't. I'm sorry. I'll do the best I can.

A bowl with steam rising from it appeared on the table. Spicy fragrances reached his nose and saliva began to flow. Without thinking, his hand reached for the spoon. Her words had overwhelmed his mind.

In more her normal voice and with an interesting tone Alex couldn't identify, she said, "This will help you to feel better, and I'll feel better too."

The first bite, Alex relished the intense flavors. What did she mean that she'd feel better? "How will you feel better?"

All of the spices in your food are part of a balanced nutrition to help you the best I can, but some of them are also going to give you terrible BO."

BO? "What's BO?"

Tested to Failure

"Body odor. Your instructor hates body odor."

At first Alex didn't understand, but the food seemed to help his clarity. He realized she spoke with some revenge in her voice, leavened with humor. A grin slowly spread across his face, and then laughter bubbled up. Another thought brought words from him. "Thanks for the support, but as much as I hate his training I think he's trying to help me. And more importantly for me," He'd thought of A'idah. "I've got a friend who might be able to come and visit me any day, and I'd rather not stink when she does."

"I doubt if Hheilea would be bothered by a little thing of BO."

Hheilea again. The Tasties had a fixation about her. Alex chose not to clear up the nurse's mistake. "Thanks, but could you remove that spice please?"

"Okay." the nurse waved a hand/paw over the bowl and said, "It's removed."

Before going to sleep, Alex considered messaging A'idah and Hheilea. He needed, wanted to talk to his pod member, but what could he share? Would it be wise to talk about the horrible training? She'd be mad. Still he wanted the comfort of hearing her voice. They could talk about her training.

He decided to first message Hheilea about his other problem. It was only after he started that he remembered their last conversation. |Hello, Hheilea. I mean, hi. What's Hymeron up to these days?|

Annoyance resonated in her response. |I tried to contact him after we got to this city. He's got some explaining to do, but he isn't answering. I've tried some of his contacts I knew he supplied with different things. No one knows where he is, or they're keeping his whereabouts secret.|

Quickly, Alex ended the conversation. |Okay. Thanks. Bye.| He was glad to end the conversation without it getting all awkward.

Hheilea wasn't done. |Alex, I've thought it over, and I think he's upset with you for letting out his secret about the portals. It's pretty obvious that he's the one behind the bounty on you. I think he's actually left this planet. That's good news. I know my brother, and I think he'll try to forget about you and me—| Most of this message came across devoid of emotion, but sadness choked off the end of it.

Again, Alex couldn't believe how emotions and in this case the feeling of sobbing could come across with the message system. He wished he could be with her, comforting her and yet.... Alex didn't want to think about his problems with Hheilea. He couldn't deal with his feelings about her. The intensity of his training had one benefit. It had kept him from dwelling on his problems with her. For a second, he thought of being back in the Weird on another long adventure with just Hheilea. Just the thought of it shook him. He needed to stay away from her. If only he could just forget about the feelings the T'wasn't-to-be-is had created, life would be so much easier.

The idea of Hymeron forgetting about him sounded good, but he's trying to forget about his own sister? That was crazy. Still, hopefully, that would mean the bounty would go away. He gasped at another thought. Was Hymeron being maneuvered by others also?

Maleky chimed in with two thoughts. *Finally, you're starting to understand. Love is too hard to deal with. Good job on putting aside your feelings for Hheilea. That's smart. Also, you've finally started to grasp how these idiots don't care about other's lives or what pain they cause.*

Alex tried to ignore Maleky. He should message something back to Hheilea. Yet, it was easier to push away the feelings.

Maleky discouraged the one good hope. *Ha. Bounties don't go away on their own accord. Hymeron will just let happen what will happen. I understand all too well what's going on. He's upset because of what you did to Hheilea. I think he's the one who tried to kill you. Of course, shooting Hheilea must've been devastating, but for him the best solution is to deny his love for her. It's a logical step. Love just gets in the way. Foolish, romantic people call it hardening your heart, but it's just being smart.*

Alex hated Maleky's thoughts, but this time he realized how the Kimley spoke from relevant experience. The thought of love getting in the way echoed in his mind. His feelings for Twyla had gotten in the way of doing what had to be done. Everyone had almost died as a result. Alex remembered Windelli's warning about hardening his heart. These realizations Hheilea had about her brother were terrible for her. As a friend, he should've comforted her.

Now, he should apologize to Hheilea.

He really should try to help her.

To comfort her.

For a long time, Alex couldn't sleep. He kept picturing Hheilea's distraught face. He knew she was hurting. Yet, he couldn't bring himself to do anything. He thought of messaging A'idah to talk about their plans or really just to get his mind off other things, but every time he started to message her Alex thought of Hheilea again. Was it Maleky's encouragement or his own fear of... of... Hheilea? Being forced to love her? If only he could move on, and not have the struggles with his emotions about her. Why couldn't they just be friends?

The next morning, Alex picked at his breakfast. Emotions, way too many emotions roiled his stomach. He remembered the words about today going to be tougher. How could it be worse? Yesterday had been brutal. He sensed even worse emotional distress lay ahead of him. When his instructor arrived, Alex continued to dawdle over his food.

Finally, the big Tasty said, "We need to get going. We have someone meeting us today."

Who? Alex wished, but didn't think it would be A'idah. He shied away from his sense of the future. His incessant training had made that ability very sensitive. What lay in store for him felt like a mass of black, towering storm clouds. Coming around a corner in the tunnel revealed the threatening door to his training room. His Instructor stopped walking. Alex turned to enter the room, but to his surprise the door didn't open.

The big Tasty said, "You'll be happy to know the rocks won't break up into sharp shards, but you'll be bare foot again. Today, when we are ready to start I've—

A very familiar voice cut through rest of what he started to say. "I'm sorry to be so late."

The instructor said, "Hheilea, thank you for your sacrifice.

At his words, Alex instinctively reacted. Sacrifice? What's going on? He had to know. Even as Alex asked a question, his sense of the future hammered home the idea of great emotional distress ahead of him. "What purpose does Hheilea being here serve?"

"As I was starting to say, I've got a plan to work on your focus of staying alive. Today will be quite familiar for you. The only difference is Hheilea will be in a different part of the training environment. You've probably noticed how this training environment is the same as the Weird on the Coratory spaceship. Today, your training environment will create a separate room for her. You'll be able to see Hheilea and hear her, but she won't be able to see or hear you."

He knew she would distract him. That would force him to concentrate harder on his sense of the future, which was one explanation for her presence. But his sense of the future told him there was much more to this situation.

"Yesterday, you suffered a fatal injury at the end of your training."

What? Alex remembered the pain which wouldn't stop. He could feel what was coming, and he wouldn't allow it. The lesson would start as soon as he entered the room. He had to delay it and talk to Hheilea.

"Yesterday, you cheated by choosing the end of the training, but as I've said to you the whole point of this training is to keep you alive-in the future. It isn't about you winning each and every time, but staying alive even if it is through what you consider, defeat. I believe you can do it. Hheilea believes you can do it. We're both willing to go to extreme measures to make sure we've done all we can. In this case, it's going to be Hheilea that goes the extra mile."

The door opened and Hheilea slipped in. She hadn't even tried to talk to him.

Alex already knew what the trainer meant even before he spoke the odd sentence. He didn't like this. Complaining wouldn't solve anything. He wanted to complain and even outright refuse, but instead... When a large hand/paw of his instructor shoved him through the door, Alex was already moving with the push. The floor felt cool to his suddenly bare feet.

He spoke quickly. Alex hadn't tried this before, but it worked in the Weird, and his sense of the future told him it would work here and give him a moment to verify what his sense was telling him. "City, give me a glass of water before the training starts."

He had a hand up and took the offered drink, but kept moving. Hheilea was just ahead of him, still moving away. He could see the beginning of the walls changing. "City, I'll give this one to Hheilea. I want another one, please. Hheilea, here's a drink for you."

Everything around him changed. Hheilea stopped and turned back at his voice. "Alex, what are you doing?"

Alex sprinted to her, not caring about the water sloshing out of the glass. He demanded an answer, even though he already suspected from his sense of the future what was going on. "What are you doing in here?"

"I think you know."

With one hand, Alex thrust the glass at her.

She ignored it, looking back into his eyes.

He couldn't see any regret or fear there, just resolution. He dropped the glass and it fell, shattering against the floor. Both of them ignored it. He wrapped both arms around her wanting desperately to keep her safe from what he knew was coming. In a rough, pain filled voice he said, "You and your people have already given enough."

She answered, "Would you rather A'idah did this or Twarbie. I think both of them would do this for you."

He knew he wouldn't like the answer, and he already knew it, but didn't want to accept it. "Why? Why?"

"Oh, Alex. This is what I love about you. You just don't give up. You'll do anything for others, but my people decided long ago to do anything too. I prefer my pain now, regardless of how much, to make the future better. I can't live in a future without you."

She disappeared. His arms closed around just air. Looking around, Alex saw her behind a transparent wall. She turned her back to him.

A stick had appeared and hung in the air. The training exercise had already begun. He needed to give himself time to think. Alex wanted to be wrong. He suspected Hheilea would feel his pain and even die-without-dying instead of him. What could he do?

Alex grabbed the stick and threw himself to the side just avoiding a red ball. Landing on one foot, he twirled about and jabbed at the orange ball even as his eyes traced a small boulder falling from above. He didn't try to spear the ball. Today, his victory would be suffering as little pain as possible.

The training exercise had other ideas. The red, pain inducing ball moved more aggressively than any had ever done. Alex swatted it with his stick and followed through with a lunge at the orange ball. He had to make choices to explore how the future might unfold.

Trying to always avoid the red ball didn't seem to lead to good things. He'd have to let it hit him some of the time. Better the small pains than the big ones.

A particularly big boulder was coming. Alex feinted at the orange ball. He had to keep more balls from appearing. At the same time, he lunged back and then forward shoving against the boulder as it fell. It seemed like a good idea to have it fall as close to the wall as possible.

Alex felt a surprisingly gently sting and saw the red ball hit him. He just happened to be turned the right way to look past his room and see Hheilea. She stumbled, almost falling to the floor. Alex recognized the symptom of feeling agonizing pain. He'd been right to be afraid. She felt the worst of his pain in this exercise not him. His heart ached, and he almost stopped moving. He knew his pain at seeing her hurt would hurt her more than the physical pain. For just a second, madness from being pushed too far wanted to claim him. A demented laugh burst from him. Her pain would make him feel pain. His pain would make her pain worse would make his pain worse. Their pain would be infinite. Another demented laugh escaped. His steps slowed and he almost failed to jab at the orange ball again. His knowledge of what would happen to Hheilea if he failed didn't help. He expected to hear gloating from Maleky over how love again had put him into a terrible spot.

Chapter Twenty-Nine
Trouble with Protecting a Friend

Maleky's thought saved him. *Alex, you can beat this. I couldn't, and it turned me into the monster I am, but you can beat their terrible plan.*

The surprise of Maleky admitting he was terrible freed Alex from the madness. Digging deep, finding a reservoir of determination, he picked up the pace of his dance. He wouldn't let Hheilea suffer the pain of dying and yet not dying. The teenage boy almost laughed at the craziness of his thoughts.

How long could Alex keep up the dance? At least the rocks weren't shattering into sole piercing shards. Thuds testified to new rocks and boulders landing. Even when the stones fell on another one, they didn't break. Alex realized his biggest tool lay in how the rocks and boulders aimed for him.

Little rocks, Alex moved with ease. With his bare foot he'd nudge them working all of them toward one side. All the while, he continued the dance of jabbing at the orange ball, thwacking the red ball as it attacked, dodging the falling rocks. At first, he breathed easily, but eventually with the non-stop effort, he began to gasp for air.

Hopping over a larger boulder, Alex barely avoided the red ball. He couldn't let any more boulders fall into the middle of the room. They would add too much difficulty. It was already getting harder to keep up. Soon he'd fall behind in his jabbing at the orange ball, and more balls joining in the dance wouldn't be good. Alex glanced at Hheilea. She stood, hands on hips shaking her head.

Alex gave a tired grin. He pirouetted on one foot to jab in the right direction. Good, Hheilea was mad. This wasn't her plan. She was fuming at her lack of pain. How long could Alex last? At some point, the trainer would have to give up and call quits to the day's training. Wouldn't he?

Alex's sense of the future warned him just in time of a bigger rock, a small boulder falling soon. He couldn't keep this up forever.

He took a couple of running steps. The red ball arced in on an interception course. It either had gotten even more aggressive or his reactions had gotten slower, probably both. This time, Alex wouldn't be able to hit it out of the way. It would be just one moment of agony for Hheilea, but Alex refused. Her brother had hurt her too much. Alex had hurt her too much.

It would break his rhythm of poking at the orange ball, but Alex ducked under the red one and the oncoming boulder. He had to get it to fall in the right place. He rolled out of the way just in time. With a resounding crash, the third boulder landed in a line with three others against the wall.

Two red balls charged at him in tandem from the side. Alex pushed off the ground and they slammed into the wall behind him.

Tossing his stick, Alex whipped his loose tunic over his head and off. Would the training room follow the rules?

Catching the stick, Alex breathed deep trying to gather the last of his energy. Sweat rolled off of him. Back into his rhythm, he poked at the orange ball to keep more from appearing.

Instead of arching about him and attacking with small changes of direction, the red balls hung back speeding at him with sudden, short, mad rushes. A tired snort escaped him and he thought of how the two balls were acting like bulls. With his sense of the future, he knew the two red balls would come at him from either side. At the last second, he swirled out of their path with one arm out and his tunic hanging from it. Alex laughed at the picture he had in his mind of how he looked. His tunic was his matador cape and the red balls two, not one bull.

The onrushing bearers of pain charged forward. Simultaneously, both slammed into the cape and each other. Before they could recover their momentum, Alex deftly swirled

Trouble with Protecting a Friend

his tunic. The balls tugged against the twisted fabric. With his stick hand, he grabbed the other end of the twisted cloth. Quickly, he transferred that end to the other hand. Spinning about on the ball of one foot he stabbed at the orange ball.

Had he been quick enough? What would the room do? His tunic jerked in his hand at the red's attempts of escape. No other balls appeared.

One thing changed. Above him, rocks fell in groups. Alex gasped for air. If he could just keep ahead of the deadly showers of rocks.... Leaning over, he heaved a particularly large rock off the floor. Burdened, his stick arm couldn't move fast enough. Pushing off with his back leg, he lunged at the orange one. Following through, Alex spun, and with the help of his sense of the future guiding his aim slung the rock into a gap between two boulders and the wall. Bouncing against the wall, it almost rolled over one boulder, but settled back to rest between the wall and the tops of two boulders. It left a large gap under it.

His hand holding the tunic ached from the constant tugs of the captured red balls. Alex readjusted his grip on his tunic.

A rock clipped one shoulder. He winced at the lack of pain, knowing who had suffered from his mistake. Hopping out of the way, Alex decided to get rid of a distraction. The falling stones represented an ever increasing danger, but they were also herding the orange ball. It avoided them too.

Using the falling rocks for help and relying on his sense of where the ball would try to escape, Alex forced it back into a corner and grabbed it with his stick hand. Quickly, he transferred it to his tunic hand. Again he resumed his rhythm. The clutter of rocks on the ground rapidly grew worse. Jab at the ball, dodge the falling rocks and snag the right sized rock to heave onto his growing mound against the wall.

The pile of rocks looked useable. It would have to do. Alex turned his back on it. Carefully, he maneuvered between the scattered rocks. The floor had become a dangerous minefield of rocks, with a few boulders scattered about. Soon, he'd be unable to move across it fast enough. The rocks falling from above would catch and pummel him, but it wouldn't be him pounded into an unmoving pulp. He wouldn't feel much pain. Hheilea would. Alex refused that possible future.

Reaching the far wall, he paused even as he kept a pattern of jabbing at the orange ball. His hand holding it spasmed from the effort of staying clenched. He barely kept it and the tunic in his grip. Above him, Alex knew the rocks fell in a constant stream. He waited, until to wait a fraction of a second longer would result in accepting the pummeling.

Alex sprinted. He raced around the inside of the walls. Ahead of him, he could see the mouth of the tunnel he'd constructed. Had he jabbed enough in this last run? One more jab and he took a running dive, arms out straight in front of him. Now, he was grateful for the sweat running off his body. He hoped it would help him slide into the shelter. Alex hit the floor and slid into the tunnel just like a hand into a big glove. Above him, he heard the crashing sound of rocks hailing down onto his shelter.

Even lying down, the hand holding the stick jabbed at the ball in his other hand. The tunic wriggled from the efforts of the red balls. With his arm, he jammed them over against the wall. The crashing of rocks increased to a roar and then silence.

His tunic stopped vibrating and the rocks all disappeared. The orange ball was gone from his hand. Cautiously, Alex stood and looked around. He still held the stick. Instinctually, he whirled about and swung the stick at a rock speeding at him. With a whack, he knocked it away.

Maleky commented, *I think the city's AI has an attitude and you've upset it.*

The main door opened to reveal the instructor. He spoke grimly, "This day's training was a disaster. Your nurse will be glad to see you failed."

Failed? He'd beaten it. At another, different sound, Alex turned around. The wall between him and Hheilea had disappeared.

Without speaking, the Kimley woman stalked across the room.

Alex could see tears tracing paths down her cheeks.

This wasn't what he'd expected. Alex didn't really know what he'd expected, but not this.

The door opened letting her leave and shut behind her, leaving Alex alone in the quiet room.

Trouble with Protecting a Friend

The door opened back up and his nurse stuck her head into the room. In a very surprised sounding voice, she said, "Hheilea was fine, except for... well.... She didn't seem very happy."

Alex said, "No she wasn't. She and my trainer planned on her being terribly injured, maybe as bad as I was yesterday. I didn't allow it. I finished the training without her getting injured. I just need a shower and something to eat."

"Oh, Okay. I'm glad no one was hurt. I'll have some food ready for you."

"Thanks."

After working so hard to protect Hheilea, the result had been a terrible let down. After eating, Alex didn't quite know what to do. He thought about messaging A'idah, but worried she might sympathize with Hheilea once she understood everything.

His nurse must've noticed something was wrong. Maybe it was his pacing or slugging the wall of the clinic not once, but twice.

She said, "Alex, I've been keeping you going with artificial healing. Real healing needs more sleep. Holo-fields are only so good. I think you should take advantage of finishing early by getting a good night's sleep."

"Okay. I might need some help getting to sleep."

"Got it."

"How about some good dreams?"

"No problem."

"Can you talk with Hheilea for me?"

"That's your problem."

Alex thought she'd say that, but with all of the things the nurse agreed to he thought it was worth a try. He wasn't too disappointed.

Then the nurse added more. "I know enough of the situation to suspect your trainer is just going to redo today's training exercise. Sorry, but I thought you should know the truth."

"Can your holo-field technology knock me out and create amnesia so I don't remember that tomorrow morning? What you just said is probably true, but I don't want to think about it until I have to."

"I'll see what I can do. Good night."

The next day Alex felt great. He woke up feeling well rested for the first time in a long time. Breakfast was incredible. The nurse gave him good news. Gursha planned to come by and check on Alex.

After the previous day, Alex expected a royal chewing out.

His trainer didn't say hello or good morning. Wordlessly, he led him to the training room and gestured for Alex to enter. Finally, he spoke. "Today will start out slowly and incrementally add new elements. I want you to let you mind wander."

In surprise, he just answered with one word. "Okay."

A stick and the orange ball appeared. His sense of the future didn't show any other balls appearing even if he didn't jab at the orange. Starting the exercise, Alex considered finally getting a break from the training. He wanted to set his plans into motion. Alex grinned at the thought of being with A'idah again. That idea felt like a candle banishing the dark thoughts of the night. He was going to get things going with her. Oh yeah, and Zeghes too. The three of them would get him back to climbing the mountain.

Alex thought of the devices he'd been given. The one which canceled out the strong force scared and excited him. He went over the explanation again in his mind making sure he knew how to use it. When pressed against something solid it would cancel the strong force holding atoms and subatomic particles together. The result would be the active plate of the device burrowing into the solid exuding a cloud of fine dust and creating a hole or tunnel. Alex gave up trying to understand how it worked when he started to remember the rest of the explanation about elementary particles; quarks, gluons, and color. It was all too confusing and strange.

One thing stuck in his mind. It was the danger of using the device. If the elements having the strong force canceled had too many neutrons in their atoms, the dampening of the neutron's energies would start to fail. Alex had been told quite firmly that his life would depend on him monitoring the metrics which would display inside his face mask. He would have to evacuate the area if the neutron energies went above a certain level and not keep using the device if it automatically

Trouble with Protecting a Friend

shut off. It puzzled him why it had an override option for that important safety feature. It made no sense to him. Why would anyone want to keep using it at the risk of their life?

Alex already had permission to leave his training, once A'idah and Zeghes had a free day. Again, Alex thought of holding A'idah against his chest that other evening. His heart beat faster. Just for a moment, he accepted how he really cared for her.

Slowly, other elements added to his exercise. Alex worked smoothly with his sense of the future. He jumped to avoid the current addition to his regimen. On the floor, balls and logs about eight inches in diameter, rolled in a chaotic pattern. They would phase through each other, but were very solid and heavy if they hit him. Many painful bruises attested to what would happen if Alex failed in jumping at the right time.

The door of his training room opened. He jabbed at the orange ball again. Out of the corner of his eyes Alex could tell it was just his instructor and someone behind him. The stick Alex used and all the balls dancing in the air disappeared.

From the door way, the big guy said, "Alex, come with me."

Alex turned to obey.

Another voice, Hheilea's, from out in the hall gasped out a warning. "Alex, look out."

"Huh." A log rolling on the floor bashed into the back of his legs. "Ahhh!" Down he crashed. Rolling with the fall and disgusted with getting surprised, Alex found solace in the fact that all of the other balls and logs seemed to have disappeared. He groaned and the log rolled up and stopped, resting against his head.

Light running footsteps and Hheilea reached his side rolling away the log. "Are you okay?"

She knelt as he tried to answer. With one cool hand she wiped the sweat and hair off his forehead.

Looking back up into her violet eyes, Alex wished she wasn't so beautiful and nice. With a rueful grin, he said, "I'm about as good as I can be. If I'd succeeded at today's training, I'd be feeling better."

She smiled and said, "I think you're great. Do you want a hand up?"

Accepting her help, he stood up. Yet, a question nibbled at him. How could she be so friendly? At least, she seemed in a better mood than she had at the end of yesterday. In response to one word, both Alex and Hheilea turned to the doorway.

"Come." The big trainer gestured for them to follow him, and he turned and walked away.

Alex glanced over at Hheilea. She shrugged in answer to his unspoken question. Keeping her hand in his, she headed toward the door. Alex let himself get led out into the tunnel. Ahead of them, the big guy turned around a corner disappearing.

Together, the friends hurried to catch up. Unspoken and unanswered questions bubbled in Alex's mind. Where were they going? How could Hheilea be so friendly after being upset after the training session and their last conversation at the celebration? In his sweaty hand, Hheilea's hand felt cool and .... Alex didn't know. He let her pull him along through many twists and turns of the tunnels. He couldn't stop the question. |Hheilea, I was pretty rude at the celebration. How? Why are you being so friendly?|

|Alex| Just one word and it hung in his mind for what seemed hours before more joined it. The longer her message continued the sadder her message felt. |Before I knew you, I was furious with life. Now, everything's different, and it... might be short. I might not have—|

Even as Hheilea struggled to continue the message, Alex couldn't help but wonder what caused her sadness. What did she mean it might be short? I might not have? Alex remembered first meeting the elven alien. She'd been so nice that first time helping him get to A'idah and to comfort her.

Hheilea continued and seemed to shake off whatever had been causing her sadness, but Alex could still tell something bothered her. |Back then, my only escape was to join in with Hymeron in his pranks. He was always busy, but each day, he'd find time to go with me to tease and prank the people we lived near. It was my rebellion against life. Until, I met you. You were a really strange alien, stupid, clumsy, weak, and yet you cared about others even in the terrible circumstances you found yourself. You laughed at the tricks we played on you. I came to hate what I'd done to you. Hymeron called me a weak

Trouble with Protecting a Friend

fool for wanting to treat you nice. He said I acted like a wimp, because I'm a girl.|

The message paused and yet the words echoed in Alex's mind. She'd thought he was a strange alien. He laughed to himself again at how an alien could think humans were strange. He didn't want to interrupt, afraid he'd say the wrong thing, but one thought he couldn't hold back. |You're not a wimp. You're incredibly brave.|

Laughter filled his mind from the beginning of next message. All too soon her message took on a sadder tone again. |You don't know all of me or my experiences. The T'wasn't-to-be-is frightened me, and I fought against it. Yes, what you've done to our T'wasn't-to-be-is hurt terribly. What you've said about it hurts still, but I've known about it my whole life and expected it. Yet, I was frightened and fought against it. I understand you. We are and always will be friends. For as long as we—|

Hheilea tugged on his hand. They'd fallen behind the trainer. |Come on, I know where he's leading us. You might not like this, but it's a big part of my heritage.|

Listening to Hheilea and caring about how she felt made his own feelings more apparent to him. How could he still feel so strongly about her? What about A'idah and his feelings for her.

Ahead of them, the big guy paused at a nondescript, blank wall. Alex watched as the Tasty placed his two hand/paws against the wall. At his touch, the wall morphed creating an alcove.

He stepped into the opening. "Both of you come up here beside me."

Together, they crowded in with him. He placed both hands against the wall again.

Alex gasped as the opening to the tunnel behind them closed off. The three of them stood, squeezed inside a featureless round space only about seven-feet across.

Alex said, "What's going on?"

In front of them, a shimmer moved out from the wall. It looked opaque, with an oily luster. Colors rippled across its surface. Alex stepped back, bumping into the wall behind him.

In a barely controlled voice, he asked, "What is this?"

The instructor said, "We are shifting sideways into a pocket universe."

"What?"

The shimmering had almost reached Alex's face.

Hheilea answered, "You're familiar with the concept of spacetime fabric?" She didn't wait for an answer, but continued talking. "Imagine if you could gather part of that fabric into a bag. We are moving into a secure bag. It is where The Book of Prophesy is kept."

The shimmer advanced. All Alex could see now was blurry waves of colors moving over his eyeballs.

Quickly, Hheilea said, "This is going to hurt."

Zzzap

Alex screamed, but it came out all garbled.

A door appeared in front of them, and the instructor knocked.

The door opened and Windelli greeted them. "Come in. Come in."

On a large, dark wooden stand in the middle of the round room rested a very big book. In Alex's head, Maleky caught his attention, his thought flavored with awe. *It's the Book of Prophesy.*

The thought chilled Alex. In response, he wanted to knock it off the stand onto the floor.

Chapter Thirty
Futures

Hheilea let go of Alex's hand and slowly approached the book.

Windelli said, "I heard your trainer shared with you the possibility you might get married to Hheilea at some point in the future."

Alex latched onto the *might* even as he quickly glanced at Hheilea. She had looked at him and flushed dropping her gaze to the floor. He knew how much this idea would please her, and she knew his determination not to be forced into anything. Yet, her messaging him had softened his feelings toward her. Even though he felt confused and frustrated, they were still friends. "It's okay Hheilea."

She quietly answered. "Thanks."

Windelli continued. "Also, it was told to me that a youngster asked you about the Book of Prophesy. Well, here is the current one. Hheilea already knows about it, because her people created it many thousands or hundreds of thousands of years ago, or as Kimleys say they are creating it. Long ago, a Kimley brought the first one to my people. They showed us how we fit into prophesies in this book. We have safely guarded it from people like Maleky. What this book contains is why the Kimleys have allowed themselves to be enslaved and killed. We have kept a look out for key events and pivotal persons. You might be a very important person. Maleky knows this from a semi-copy of this book. If you want, come and take a look at it."

Alex paused. Curiosity and disgust at something which felt controlling to him warred. He gave into the mystery of seeing something that old which talked of him. Slowly, Alex walked up to the stand, and his eyes followed Windelli's pointing finger. The lines of print blurred in front of him and then became clear. Alex gasped and pulled his eyes from the words. "It changed when I read it."

Windelli nodded her head. "Yes. Your actions have been changing the book quite a bit. It's one indication of how important you have been. Not to make this more complex than needed or to confuse you more, but to help you understand. There are other universes where you didn't give into your curiosity and read from the book. They are probably just shadow universes. Each one a dream to the others, but it's possible your choosing to read has big consequences. In that case, you just created another branch universe which will develop quite differently from this point on, and it will have its own shadow universes. Have I completely confused you?"

Alex hardly considered the idea of alternate universes. Instead, he focused on the fact he chose what the book had written in it. He wondered if he could find a way to get out of the book, to be free from others expectations of him. Again, he looked at Hheilea and pointed at her. "Does Hheilea change the book too?"

Hheilea shook her head. "Alex, remember what I told you about changing the future possibilities? Most of my choices don't affect the future as strongly as yours, unless I'm doing something that affects your choices. Of course, that could change. If you'd really died back at the battle with the Gragdreath, then I or another would have a bigger more important role in the future."

For a moment, she paused and Alex could see her struggling to maintain her composure. What was going on?

"Remember, I can still see some of the future possibilities and not just sense them. My sharing the possible future results of just one of your choices with you would open up a whole new set of possibilities. Some or all of those might be deadly to you and even everyone else. If you were going to die—"

His dear friend looked pale and choked out the words. "If... you were going to die, I... I... wouldn't be able to warn you... even now. If... you did die..., you wouldn't be in the book any longer. I listen carefully to what my father says I should do to keep the future safer." Then a deep flush rushed across her face, and she mumbled, "Well, most of the time I try to." A tear hung onto the edge of her jaw.

Alex had difficulty with all this talk about the futures especially how distraught Hheilea seemed to be, but he grinned at those last words. The rest of what she'd said didn't stick with him. Alex thought about when they'd almost finished the T'wasn't to-be-is. He hadn't forgotten any details of that event, and part of him wished they hadn't stopped. This flashback came easily. He remembered when she'd encouraged him to go against what her father said.

~**********~

Hheilea slipped her arms around his waist. Alex looked down into her violet eyes. His own feelings of fear ebbed. His gaze slipped down to her soft, moist lips. He wanted to protect her. She lifted her face toward his and gently pulled on his back. Alex yielded to her pressure and his desire. Gently he touched his lips to hers. Their music resounded joyfully, but yet still muted in his mind. Their noses bumped, and he pulled back, unsure of himself.

~**********~

His grin dropped. What would've happened if Alex had given into her and his own desire? In another universe were they happily joined together, or had that choice destroyed everything and everyone they cared for? He gulped at the terrible burden and felt once again the terrible weight on his shoulders of his responsibility to the future.

Hheilea had been scared about the future and wanted to ignore her father's instructions for the safety of finishing the T'wasn't-to-be-is would provide for her and Alex. Also, well, both of them had wanted what the ceremony pushed them toward. He struggled against the memory and the feelings. He forced his thoughts to A'idah, and it wasn't too hard. He wasn't going to be forced to marry Hheilea. One good thing about this

Prophesy book, Alex didn't have to worry about dying. He started to say something about it, but was interrupted.

His instructor said, "Hheilea is still going into the future possibilities with her father. He believes you could do so also and was considering giving you the opportunity. The most important thing is to make sure you humans get all the training you need to deal with Vapuc and the Deems. That is one thing we can share with you from the prophesy. The Earthlings' training is in danger, and it is of the utmost importance. The first thing you need to do is find a way to get a String Sword." training

He paused, wrinkled his nose, and said, "Except right now, I think you should go get a shower. Hheilea isn't bothered by your sweat and odor, but you stink."

Alex shrugged and said, "Okay. Thanks for showing me this book. Knowing I'm so important is kind of nice. I guess I don't have to worry about dying." As Alex turned to leave, he paused at a question from Hheilea.

"Windelli, There's an important point in the possible time lines coming up. Do you know anything?"

Alex glanced at Windelli. She didn't say anything. He couldn't read anything from her expression, but when he looked back at Hheilea. She'd gone pale. He looked back and forth wondering what had happened. Whatever it was must be bad. He wondered who was in danger. He gave her what he hoped was an encouraging grin. "Hey, don't look so worried. I know you. You're incredible. You'll figure out and do what's right. The future will be fine."

Windelli said, "Alex, I think your stink is getting worse. Be nice to us and go get your shower."

He'd gone out in the tunnel and around a corner when he heard Hheilea's voice from behind him.

"Wait."

He turned around. Instead of his confident and cheerful friend, Hheilea looked even more distraught. "What's wrong?"

"Just hold me, please."

Confused and concerned about her, Alex closed the gap and gently took her into his arms. Hheilea started sobbing. He remembered the broken sentences of her messages. "Is something going to happen to you?"

Futures

"No." More sobs. "I might not see... I won't... ...di..." She gave up trying to talk and just clung to him.

Alex didn't know what to do. He had to listen close for her last words. Did she say die? He'd never seen her so distraught. Her small frame shook in his arms from the force of the sobs. "Come with me. We'll find an empty room and—"

The force of her answer shocked him. She thrust herself back. "No! No. No. Alex."

Who would die? Concern flooded him "Are you going to die?"

"No."

"Let me hold you again."

"No. It was a bad idea. I can't. I can't talk to you. I might try to warn— Bye." She turned away from him. Her small shoulders still shook. "You were right. I'm having a hard time just being a friend. I started loving you the first time we met when you wanted to get out of your prison to help A'idah. You've been amazing. I'll never for—"

She started running. Alex ran after her. "Wait."

He should've been frightened of her admission, but the other broken sentences and that one word he'd thought he'd heard *die* shook him much more. Alex sprinted as she disappeared around a corner. He got there, but the tunnel split into two different directions. Which one? To the right his sense of the future didn't say much, but to the left danger and something else. That must be the direction she went, but why the danger and what else? Moving slower Alex continued after her.

His trainer messaged him. |Alex, I need you to meet me in the training room, now. No delays.|

What? He sent me for a shower. What was going on? He had to follow Hheilea.

The tunnel in front of him narrowed and suddenly a new wall stood where Hheilea had gone. Reluctantly, Alex gave up following Hheilea. Instead he tried messaging her.

His AI responded. *I can't connect with her AI.*

What? What was going on? Reaching the training room didn't help.

When the door opened the trainer barked. "Get in here now and give me fifty pushups and make it fast."

Even as Alex obeyed his mind sought for answers. Finally, he decided to try messaging Hheilea after his training ended, but by the end of the day exhaustion kept him from thinking, and he collapsed into bed.

His nurse woke him all too soon. Getting up he took in the familiar surroundings.

Gursha stood beside the Tasty. She didn't look happy. "Hello. I've used the holo-field to give you an exam while you slept. I'm not pleased. The holo-field has been overly used to heal you. I understand they are under a time crunch, but your body is in danger of developing a reaction to holo-field healing. That would be bad. I should've been here to check on you sooner, but other flocks have needed my help. I need to give the rest of your flock a checkup too. Suffice it to say, I've talked to your trainer. He needs to avoid getting you badly injured."

She glared at Alex. "And I want you to promise me to be careful. If you develop a reaction to holo-field healing, it would be disastrous for you. The worst of it is I know you can't be careful."

Gursha swallowed and Alex thought she was swallowing unspoken words. Something was wrong.

She held her arms out. "Give me a hug. I've got to get back to the dorms."

Alex stepped to Gursha and held her bulky form. He felt her familiar four arms holding him. "Gursha, what's wrong? I mean other than the normal things."

"I've been having some bad days. I lost an Earthling patient. The training should be safer and other things better with the improved funding, but events have been spiraling out of control. Please take care of yourself. Of all the Earthlings you've been the one most liable to get killed. As a nurse, I should be used to people dying. It happens, but all of your Earthlings have gotten into my heart. Even the most inept of you do things with so much feeling." She pushed him away and with one hand smoothed his hair across his forehead. "I've got to go. Bye."

Slowly he processed what she'd said. His training would have to change? Wouldn't it? Or this could mean he'd be doing more training where he didn't get hurt even physically, but Hheilea would take the injuries. Alex wouldn't accept it.

One thing that helped was the feeling that something very humorous was going to happen.

All too soon the door opened and his trainer said, "Come."

Regretfully, Alex left the remains of his breakfast. Again, he followed the big Tasty through a crowded tunnel. A feeling of humor mixed with dismay made him curious. What would he find funny and yet be disturbed by?

The large Tasty stopped at a door and gestured for Alex to enter.

Alex recognized the training room he'd been using, but there was one new item. On the floor lay a pair of unusual looking high heel shoes. They weren't just high heel shoes. They were stilettos with the longest thinnest heels he'd ever seen. Who was going to wear them? His sense of a humorous situation increased and also a very disturbing feeling of trepidation mixed with awe about the future. The confusing sense of what would happen didn't help Alex at all. Something about those ridiculous looking shoes bothered him and had a humorous feeling to it.

He wondered about his trainer, but no.... The idea of his trainer using them was ridiculous. Most of the time the Tasties moved about on all fours, squatted on their hind legs, or if they carried something, they could walk more like a bipedal creature. Alex's trainer entered the room.

Maleky's thoughts about this new addition followed Alex's own ideas. *What crazy looking shoes. The good thing is these would never fit you. It would be terrible to try and train while wearing them. You'd be fighting to keep from falling down even without doing anything else.*

The big Tasty picked up the strange shoes and standing on one foot proceeded to put one on.

In Alex's mind the Kimley laughed. *Now I've seen everything. Can you believe he can actually stand on one foot? He's not even swaying or fighting to keep standing still.*

Alex's eyes grew wide and his mouth dropped open in amazement when the Tasty next stood on the extremely thin and tall stiletto to put the other crazy shoe on. How could he keep his balance?

Maleky's laughter echoed in the boy's mind, and a snort escaped him. He didn't really think laughing out-loud at his instructor would be a good idea. With an effort, Alex restrained his own laughter.

The big Tasty eyed him and said, "You think this looks funny?" There was a pause of quiet and he continued. You've thought the training I've been giving you is frustrating and hard? If I could've figured out how, I would've made it harder. You've got an amazing ability to sense the future, but you're not using it to its full potential. I don't know how to get you to where I know you need to get with this ability. Tasties don't have a similar trait of being able to sense the future, but I've been to pushing you as hard as I can."

"If you die, it won't be because I didn't help you the best I could. Watch what I can do without your sense of the future."

The next maneuver by the Tasty shocked Alex. Alex gave up trying to keep from laughing. *Ha, ha, ha, ha.* The laughter rolled out of him as the big, burly Tasty in ridiculous stilettos did a cartwheel picking up the stick in the process.

His instructor paused. He looked at Alex, and in that look, the boy knew he was in trouble, but still the laughter bellowed out of him, and tears of mirth dripped down his cheeks. "If you can, control yourself enough to look, watch, and learn what can be done without your sense of the future."

The implied warning shook Alex, but he couldn't control his reaction. What he was seeing looked too funny.

The Tasty shifted to an en guarde position. In front of him an orange ball appeared, but the Tasty just stood waiting. A growing sense of trepidation drained the humor out of Alex.

A black ball appeared and started circling the stick. One red ball circled the orange. Two white ones started a complicated dance in front of his instructor's eyes. A blue one appeared and started pummeling the Tasty. Finally, the instructor started to move. He jabbed and danced about the orange ball. Slowly his jabs grew faster.

Maleky's comment caught Alex's attention and made him watch more carefully. *He's forcing the balls back into a corner to limit their movement. Similar to what you did using the falling rocks for help, but he's doing it with those ridiculous stilettos. I think he could beat me in a fight.*

Now the balls bounced off the two walls. The big Tasty crowded in and easily speared the orange ball. All of the balls disappeared. "It looks easy doesn't it?"

He had made it look easy and Alex unwisely answered, "Yes." He started to add you made it look easy, but the Tasty didn't give him a chance.

"This is where you have to get with this training."

Another orange ball, black balls, white balls, red balls, and blue ones appeared. Alex couldn't tell how many because they kept moving.

The Tasty began his attack and attack it was. He didn't just jab at the orange ball, but he started to grab others out of the air. Again, Alex recognized his own idea of limiting the interference by capturing balls, but his instructor took it much farther. The Tasty speared a red ball and calmly kept jabbing. He speared another, another, and another red one.

Alex knew one red on his stick would hurt, but four? How could he stand the pain? Alex knew how painful the red balls were to touch from the one he'd put into his pocket. With fewer balls in the air Alex could count four blue ones pummeling the Tasty.

His instructor swatted some other balls out of the air with his free hand and jabbed it out next to the orange ball. One of the remaining red balls came around next to the orange ball, and with one smooth lunge the Tasty speared both the orange and red balls.

The Tasty turned to Alex and stood with five pain inducing red balls speared on the stick along with the orange ball. "That's how it's done. You will need to work through each level of difficulty and remember pain is temporary, but death is forever." He held the stick toward Alex. Keep this red ball. Remember how for a while pain helps you to focus and remember the lesson.

Maleky had fallen silent at this demonstration. Neither of them thought about the ridiculous stilettos. Alex took the offered red ball, shuddering at the pain and dropped it into a pocket. At least it didn't hurt quite as bad in the pocket.

"And don't forget to wear your new shoes."

The stick the Tasty had been holding disappeared. Another appeared in the air, and Alex grabbed it as it fell. The instructor left without any more words.

Chapter Thirty-One
Humiliation

For the first lesson only four balls had appeared. He started to jab at the orange one, but all four shot up to the ceiling. Alex couldn't reach them. What? What was he supposed to do? Looking up as he considered, he walked around below them and stumbled on something.

Stopping his consideration of the balls he looked down. Oh no. The Tasty's last words came back to him. "Don't forget to wear your new shoes."

A pair of high heels lay on the floor. They weren't as bad as the ridiculous stilettos the Tasty had worn, but Alex didn't want to accept this reality. What did Maleky think of this?

Alex remembered the Kimley couldn't deal with pain. He was probably curled up in some part of Alex's head moaning. Shuddering at the pain himself, he took the red ball back out of his pocket and looked at it. It would be good to hear Maleky's perspective. Whatever the evil man's reason for being in Alex's head he did have helpful training suggestions. Alex tossed the ball to the ground and sat by the shoes.

As he picked one up, Alex considered the shoe. How he'd hate to have anyone seeing him in these. Then he remembered the Tasty's words. Do as many lessons as you can. Slowly, Alex grasped the idea he might be running out of time for his training. What was coming up? Quickly, he slipped on the shoe and fumbling with the strap got it tightened. Working on the second shoe he heard from Maleky.

Thanks for putting the red ball down. The first thought from Maleky was slow, faint, and Alex could hear the pain in the thought. The next was much faster and urgent. *You need to get going on this lesson. You're in danger, and that means we're in danger.*

Alex jumped up. The balls had dropped back down and he stabbed at the orange one, but he hadn't thought about the shoes. He wobbled, tipped, and his leg buckled as his ankle started to twist. Rolling with the fall he kept stabbing toward the orange to keep from getting more balls.

You forgot the shoes. Stand on the balls of your feet.

He had forgotten them, but… stand on the balls of his feet?

You need to keep your weight on the toes or balls of your feet not the heels.

Surprised, Alex finished the roll back to his feet, but now he balanced on his toes. *How do you know how to use high heels?*

I wear a pair when I meet with certain species. Remember Kimleys are short and some species value height. So I cheat with high heels to get some extra inches. That's it you're doing better.

Once again the Kimley had surprised Alex. He still had a hard time understanding what the Kimley got out of helping him, but Alex was happy for any help, even if the help was from the Galaxy's most evil person.

Maleky responded to Alex's thoughts. *You still don't get it. This idea of me being evil is wrong. I've just got a different paradigm than you. I see life clearly. Everything is about being prey or being the predator. I prefer being the predator. It doesn't mean I always take. Helping others builds opportunities. It doesn't mean I've turned all soft and silly.*

Alex tried to fight back against the barrage of ideas as he continued stabbing at the orange ball. *Others first and then self is the right way to be all the time.*

Maleky laughed. *It's so easy to poke holes in your statement. How are you going to help others if you are weak from giving someone else food you both needed? Taking care of yourself first keeps you strong, and then you'll be able to be noble and help others.*

Alex didn't know what to say. Maleky made his perspective sound so reasonable. He knew he shouldn't be listening to him. *You're distracting me from getting this lesson done.*

Humiliation

Again, Maleky laughed. *You know I'm right, but you're right about this lesson.*

Alex knew one way of shutting Maleky up, and he was supposed to be holding the red ball anyway. The boy reached for the ball and at the same time heard Maleky's complaint.

Oh, no. Ahhh.

For a second, Alex paused in the act of picking up the pain inducing ball. At the same time, he still stabbed.

Maleky messaged him. *Go ahead. I think the Tasty is right. The pain will help you even as much as I hate it.*

Alex picked up the red ball fighting back his reaction to the pain. He shoved it pack into his pocket. Alex shifted his position trying to limit the movement options of the orange ball. The red one hit his stick, but he hardly noticed the additional pain. A white one danced in front of his eyes, but with a quick sweep of his free hand he grabbed it. With quick jabs, he blocked the orange ball from escaping his corralling of it.

A red ball tried to hit his stick, but Alex ignored it and its pain. He thrust out both his free hand and the stick. With his hand he knocked away the red ball. The stick he lined up for a winning thrust. Immediately after he speared the orange ball, all of the balls disappeared except for the red one in his pocket.

He beat the second level without too much trouble, but the third took much longer. The high heels had gotten taller and thinner with each succeeding lesson. They became more like stilettos instead of just high heels, adding to the difficulty. By the fourth lesson, Alex struggled to succeed. He'd caught two of the black balls in his free hand and that helped. He wished Maleky wasn't dealing with pain. Alex wanted to grumble to him about the training methods of the Tasty. Taking the red ball out of his pocket he tossed it away.

Alex side stepped to the left and felt his ankle twisting as the stiletto heel slipped out from under him. Alex went with the fall and tumbled, bouncing back up to stab again. He was too late. A ball, another aggressive black one, appeared. It started bouncing off the knuckles of the hand holding the stick. Alex wobbled on his high heels trying to weave his attacking hand around the black ball to stab at the orange. He hated wearing the high heels. Alex couldn't understand how high heels were a benefit. He wouldn't be wearing them when he fought. At least it couldn't get much worse. If only his trainer would put in an appearance, Alex would love to see how he reacted to getting jabbed with the stick.

Maleky had recovered from the pain, and he grumbled too. *The guy would probably just dodge without seeming to try. He has the best balance of any person I've ever seen. When he showed us how to do it wearing those ridiculous looking stilettos, I mean stilettos on a Tasty? I don't blame you for laughing. I did too, but he didn't even have to work hard, and yet he defeated about two dozen balls at once to stab the orange. Now, you have to succeed at this lesson ten times. You've done two, but the heels he gives you keep getting taller and thinner. Next time, don't laugh at him.*

Alex continued to stab trying to get to get into a rhythm with his sense of the future while avoiding getting more balls to deal with. For a fraction of a second, he stood still wobbling on the heels. At least things couldn't get much worse.

Maleky snorted. *Yeah. Just imagine if your flock showed up and saw you.*

Alex responded. *Shut up. You're too prescient. Remember the last time you said something about the future. It happened.* Desperately, he tried not to think just to feel the right movements.

Back when he'd fought the assassin in the dark, Alex had been able to use his sense of the future to barely defeat the one foe, but now he had to learn how to deal with multiple issues while still focusing on the future results. Frustration weakened his effort. Instead of feeling the right movements, he noticed something else about the future. Something terribly embarrassing was about to happen. Furiously, he narrowed his eyes swaying on the edge of losing his balance. There, he almost had it. A ball hit his knuckles interfering with his defensive pattern of jabs.

The door opened. Voices of his flock members carried in from the tunnel outside. Alex squinted, almost shutting his eyes. He relied more on his sense of the future than his sight of the now. A twist and a dodge— Voices threatened his concentration.

Humiliation

A'idah said, "Alex, what are you..." Her sentence ended with a snort of repressed laughter.

Ekbal said, with humor bubbling up as he spoke until at the last he ended with laughter. "You... you... you've got high heels on."

A staccato laughter which evolved into a rolling bellowing laughter had to be from Osamu. Alex had never heard him laughing and wished he hadn't at this time either. He continued his pattern of defensive jabbing forcing himself to focus on the future possibilities.

Alex started humming, and with eyes now shut in desperation he finally got in sync with the multitudes of future possibilities the dancing balls represented. He stepped back, pulling his attacking hand holding the stick all the way back by his side. He thrust the other hand forward letting the black ball hit it. Quickly, Alex pulled that hand back thrusting the other forward. He lunged simultaneously twisting the stick in a circular motion mid-lunge around another black ball before straightening out the attack and with a forward spring off his toes pierced the orange.

Alex tossed the sick aside, sat down with a thump, and ripped the high heels off his feet.

His flock and trainer had all entered the room. His trainer spoke first. "Well done, Alex. Next time, maybe we should have your flock watch again. Their laughter seemed to sharpen your focus."

Springing to his feet, Alex didn't speak. He did not want to say something he might later regret.

Osamu filled the silence. "Sorry for laughing at you. Those high heels took me by surprise. I can see how they would make this exercise much more difficult. Your ankles must be very strong, and what an amazing display of swordsmanship."

Alex nodded his head. "Thanks."

The Tasty squatted on his hindquarters. "He has to get better. Someone else with a sense of the future and better at using it would defeat him easily."

Those words got through Alex's anger and embarrassment. Who with a sense of the future would he fight? It would have to be a Kimley. The list of possibilities ran through his mind. It wouldn't be Hheilea's parents or her, but that left just

Hymeron and Maleky. When Alex held a String Sword, Maleky would appear with his own sword in Alex's sight. Others, looking on, would see Alex appearing to fight something no one could see. What would happen if Maleky beat him in a sword fight? The last time, Alex had beaten him easily.

A message from A'idah took him away from his own thoughts. |I'm sorry, I didn't warn you we were coming. I've been pestering Ytell to let Zeghes and I have some free time. He kept saying we needed more training. I told him we would be checking out what's going on with the earthworm tunnels and would get plenty of practice.

Yesterday afternoon, he suddenly changed our plans for this week. Today, he had us out in the wild dealing with different creatures and plants. The next thing I knew, we were in the fields. Ytell told us we could have a break from our training just so long as we find something useful to do, or he would assign individual training exercises. He said let's go surprise Alex with a visit, and that you needed to spend some time with us. I was so excited I didn't think of letting you know. I'm sorry.|

While she sent him the long message, Alex quickly said to everyone else, "Give me a moment to get a shower." And moving toward the shower room after she finished the message he responded. |It's okay. I think the embarrassment did force me to sharpen my focus. Not that I want the flock to watch me using high heels ever again. Do you have any idea how hard it is to fight wearing those things? Give me a minute. I'll be right out. One thing for sure, he needed to get better at sensing the future.

The evening went by quickly. Osamu told them, he was going to learn about some of the technology the Tasties thought would be best for helping Earth. Skyler had contacted Windelli about how she flew through the air and planned to work with her to try and teach Sabu how to fly during the morning.

Ekbal had some training setup. He explained his practicing force. "Remember all of the sabotage. Whoever did it is still out there. We still might have to prove how good we are with force to convince the aliens to keep training us."

Humiliation

Alex remembered the warning about Hymeron. "Yeah, I agree with you. Whoever it was is still going to cause trouble for our training. Look, Ekbal, we three are going to do some investigating of the tunnels you mapped. Afterword, I'll take care of something else important, but don't tell anyone else. When I'm done, we'll setup a trap for the saboteur and catch him... or her."

Ekbal said, "I just hope we catch them before they do something to put the training of all the Earthlings back in jeopardy."

"Me too," Alex said. "Good luck with your training. We're headed out early tomorrow. So, I'm going to head to bed."

After a pause, Ekbal asked, "What about the assassins? Are you sure it's safe?"

"Look, none of us are safe. We can't keep from working on things just because of danger. The lessons I've been working on are to sharpen the use of my sense of the future. That's my defense against the assassins."

"I guess you're right." And then Ekbal laughed. "Are you going to take high heels to wear when you fight them?"

Alex shut his eyes in disgust. "Look, those were just for training."

Ekbal, still laughing, said, "I know. It's just that.... You looked so funny in them. It makes for a good joke. Plus you could defeat your opponents more easily while they laugh."

Alex didn't answer, but he thought to himself that while the others had enjoyed the joke he still didn't appreciate it.

He stopped worrying about the high heels and thought about the sabotage. They still would need to find Hymeron. What was he up to? That question bothered Alex late into the night, but it was better than his thoughts about Hheilea. In desperation, he turned his thoughts toward A'idah. She needed his help. She had that mess with the Muslims worrying her, and he thought she might already be thirteen. She'd be twenty or twenty-one by the time we return to Earth. If A'idah was married by then, that would change everything for her. He could protect her. With a smile on his face Alex finally fell asleep. Pleasant thoughts of A'idah filled his dreams.

Chapter Thirty-Two
First Kiss?

    In the morning, A'idah's early morning malaise felt worse than normal. She forced herself to hurry down the path into a chilly breeze blowing tendrils and banks of fog across the fields, obscuring and revealing different areas. She looked up at Alex and wished it was just her and him going on this adventure. That thought made her gasp and brought back the memories of daydreams about being alone with Alex.
    She stumbled and almost fell. Embarrassed, A'idah said the first thing that came to mind, "I'm glad we don't have to worry about anything hiding out in the fog. The Tasties fields with their barrier should be one of the safest places on this planet."
    Alex said, "Wait." |Stop, both of you. Take a moment to look around, and get used to the fog. Communicate only with your AI. Something's bothering me, but I'm not sure what. It's as if the possibilities keep shifting. I think it's something I've heard about concerning my sense of the future. Someone is going to try and do something.|
    Adrenalin pumped A'idah out of her early morning malaise. She ignored the remaining feverish feeling and stopped to glare at the fields around her. |How do we fight them? I don't think we should just wait.|
    Alex responded. |We need to take quick and decisive action. That will change their plan and make them be more decisive too, which will clear up my sense of the future. Zeghes, give A'idah a ride toward the border. Move fast. I'll run to the Tasties bubble generator. I'll meet you at the border.|

A'idah could see Zeghes taking off at high speed toward her. |But, Alex, you'll be alone for a while.|

|I can't sense any immediate danger. Just go. Speed is our best weapon.|

She jumped onto Zeghes' back as he came to a brief stop. She grabbed his dorsal fin and wrapped her legs around his body. Momentarily, he dropped toward the ground before his suit adjusted to the additional weight. Instantly, Zeghes accelerated. A'idah flattened herself against him feeling the wind rushing by. She thrust one hand forward and yelled, "Faster."

"Okay."

With a jerk he accelerated again. A'idah had to squint against the increased wind. She grinned. Even with her concern for Alex, this was fun.

Zeghes warned her. "Hang on."

Ahead, she made out the fast approaching edge of the wild lands. Zeghes slowed dramatically, and she found herself going from getting pulled backward by the acceleration to sliding forward and starting to twist off him to one side. In response, Zeghes slew to the side and ended up twisting around until he came to a stop with his head aimed back the way they'd come. Just for a moment, A'idah thought she saw something moving quickly through a field to the left, and then it was gone. She relaxed her grip and lifted one arm considering using a lightning bolt if something threatened them.

Zeghes said, "Somethings out there. I told Alex. He's changing his direction. We'll go meet him. Hang on."

A'idah dropped back flat against Zeghes. Acceleration hit, and they zoomed along the border to the right. In the distance, she spotted a bubble shining in the morning light. It dipped, bobbed, and zoomed through the air. The friends converged.

Alex messaged. |A'idah, lift your hand up and prepare to join me.|

She did as he asked. A hand clasped her arm. She clasped his and immediately with a tremendous jerk A'idah was pulled off Zeghes and through the tingling skin

First Kiss?

of Alex's bubble. Acceleration threw her against the side of the bubble.

A'idah laughed. "Can we go faster?" She started to slide down the wall, but fresh acceleration held her firm to the wall.

Alex said, "Zeghes is going to travel low and down through the wild land. We're going up toward the crater wall. We'll travel through that broken land and use a canyon to go back down to meet up with him." A free, victorious laugh erupted. "My sense of the future's looking great. Whoever that was couldn't deal with our maneuvers. We're losing them. I let the Tasties know of the problem. They're going to do a patrol of their territory."

A'idah slid down the wall to the flat floor of the bubble. Below them, trees and bushes flew past and patches of grass. Her heartbeat quickened, when she looked up to see Alex looking back at her. She started to say something, but uncharacteristically found herself tongue tied. She could only think of the fact they were alone together for a long bubble ride.

For a long time, only silence filled the air. A'idah felt irritation growing. They were alone. This was their time to... Just when she'd finally gotten her nerve up to say something, anything, Alex spoke.

"Hey, quite the trees down there."

She looked below them at the tree tops rushing past, and chuckled at his comment.

He cleared his throat and said, "Okay that was lame."

This time A'idah laughed. Instantly, she regretted laughing at him. In remorse, she looked up at him.

Alex, his face red, looked away.

"I don't think you're lame. You're amazing."

"Me?" Alex suddenly blurted out, "I think you're beautiful."

The terrain had continued to change until only a few trees and bushes could be seen dotting a grassy land. The edge of a canyon flew past, and the bubble zig zagged around some rocky spires. A'idah found herself thrown against Alex. They held each other as they bounced against the firm and yet giving sides of the bubble.

A'idah gasped at the physical contact.

Alex said, "Maybe I should've engaged the anti-inertia setting."

"No, this is fun." Should she have said that?

They curved around a large boulder, and the bubble dropped out from under them. Both of them hit the curved ceiling. Below, A'idah saw the arid, boulder strewn floor of another canyon. They fell in a tangle of arms and legs. She found her face smashed against his. Her breath came hard and fast.

Down the narrow ragged course they flew. Together, they tumbled up against the back wall of the bubble. Dead ahead of them, a vertical wall of rock stood barring the way.

Alex yelled, "Engage the anti-inertia setting!"

Initially, they were slammed down on the floor as the bubble rocketed up and over the cliff. A sudden stopping of acceleration in all directions calmed the movement inside the bubble. A'idah floated. He must've engaged some anti-gravity to. Her arms were wrapped around Alex, and she didn't want to let go. She noticed her skin tingled where it touched his. Alex held her too, and he quietly gazed into her eyes. Briefly, A'idah thought of her grandma and her warnings about guys.

Together, they settled slowly onto the floor. She hardly noticed the dry and barren landscape flying by. A'idah wished the ride would go on for hours, but she knew all too well they soon would meet up with Zeghes. Tearing her eyes away, but still too aware of Alex holding her, she caught glimpses of a different canyon. She didn't want to be wise.

A'idah felt Alex rubbing her back with one hand and, she felt her tension and stress ebbing away. She squeezed him and then pointed at the canyon. "We don't have much longer." The disappointment in her voice surprised her. What did Alex think of her?

Alex squeezed her back and let go. In a moment, the bubble dropped down over its edge and started following its twists and turns. She turned away to try and get herself under control. This time they descended.

First Kiss?

Ruefully, she looked back at Alex. "I thought this transportation system had a safety setting. That was a crazy ride."

"Sorry, it did get a bit rough." With concern evident in his voice, Alex looked at her. "Your arm, what happened to it?"

A'idah held it out and said, "It' just a scratch," she held her belly and added, "but if I didn't have lots of practice riding in bubbles and some pretty wild maneuvers I've done, I think I'd be throwing up. As it is I don't feel any too good." She'd had much worse wounds heal faster than the irritating scratch, and the animal had only barely scratched her. Maybe, she should've gone to their nurse, Gursha, with it, but A'idah still didn't want to go to her for just a scratch. It'd get better.

"That scratch doesn't look good. You should go to Gursha and get it looked at."

"I'll be fine."

Alex shook his head at her response and added, "I should've turned on the anti-inertia setting sooner. I'm sorry about how rough it got with both of us in here."

"That's okay, Alex. It was fun tumbling with you. I..." She paused uncertain of herself. Should she have said that? Should she have held him as she did? What would her grandmother have said? She really had enjoyed it, but would it give Alex the wrong ideas about her? She remembered her grandma's words.

"Teenage boys and young men are just a mess of hormones. You have to be careful how you act around them. The best of them will always try to be what you want and to treat you right, but part of them wants to let go of restraint and have fun in a way which isn't going to be good for you. Even the best can be tempted to behave in the worst way possible by how attractive we are. You need to help them even as they need to respect you."

Alex reached over to twirl one of A'idah's curls on the side of her temple. "I wish we had more time to ourselves before we meet back up with Zeghes."

A'idah captured his hand with hers. "While we're wishing, why don't we wish to be just normal teenagers who like each other?"

Alex smiled back at her, and then his expression changed. "How old are you now?"

"Don't tell anyone, but if I've kept track correctly, I had my birthday while you were off on your quest with Daren. I'm thirteen. Now, my problems with the Muslims are just drawing nearer."

Pensively, she watched the ground go by. "Some of the women of my people the Kalasha get married at fourteen."

Alex looked at her, surprise evident on his face. "Really?" He looked away and added, "What would happen if you were married, before you returned to Earth?"

A'idah gasped at his words. Through the bubble, she spotted the familiar form of Zeghes jetting toward them. Pulling her hand free, she pointed the dolphin out. "Here comes Zeghes. We must be close to where you wanted to start exploring. Where are you going to land?"

In a disappointed voice, Alex said, "I wish he hadn't been so fast. I like being alone with you."

He pointed down, but A'idah didn't pay any attention. She was thinking of his words.

He continued speaking, "Right down here. Ekbal told me he found this cave-in because he was looking for a certain cave. Years ago, a young Earthling girl found it. She was with a strange alien that no one knew anything about. It's a story with lots of mystery and just the kind of thing to catch Ekbal's attention. Anyway, he didn't find the cave but found evidence of more cave-ins just like the one you fell into. When he looked at them on a map they all formed a line right to here. Right over there's the last subsidence visible from above."

Tearing her eyes away from Alex, to look where he pointed, A'idah saw where the ground had caved in. A shiver ran down her back at the view. She remembered the ground falling away below her and being drawn into a burrow left by a giant earthworm. She'd almost died.

First Kiss?

A'idah felt nauseous at the idea of Alex pretending to die in this location. "Alex, maybe we should wait before we go into the burrow. We could land at the top edge and check to make sure we can still message others. Remember, the last time you couldn't call for help from the bottom of the hole."

"I've got that covered. In my bag is a device which will boost the signals our AIs use to send and receive messages."

"Good, but I still think we should land above first and check it out before we go into the hole."

The bubble slowed, and Alex turned to look at her before he responded. He stepped closer and put an arm around her."

"Hey, I understand. The first time I went into a dark tunnel after almost dying in that worm burrow fear almost froze me."

A'idah shoved his arm away. "I'm not frightened." Grudgingly she added, "Well, maybe a little, but I'm not worried about the tunnel. I'm worried about you. The idea of pretending you're dead frightens me. Doing it here just makes it worse." A'idah looked at him in concern. She knew he wouldn't give up because of her fear for him. She shivered at a sudden chill. She wasn't feeling good. He might postpone this if she told him she needed to see Gursha.

Alex grinned at her. "I'll be okay. The Tasties helped by giving me all kinds of gadgets."

"Yeah, uhm, I'm not feeling very good. It's been days since I got this scratch. You were there. Remember, when Ytell showed us that rabies infection event. It should've healed long ago. Maybe I should go see Gursha now, and we could do this later."

At first, Alex looked at her in concern, but after a moment he grinned. "You just said you'll be fine. Come on. Nothing's going to happen to me. This plan will work. Everyone will think I've died."

She looked at him remembering how many times he'd almost died, and now they were going to pretend it finally happened. "I... I... I don't want to lose you. I..."

Alex drew her into a hug with both arms. This time she didn't push him away but hugged him tight.

Alex whispered into her hair. "It's going to be okay. I... I care for you too. You know that, but we can't be cautious just because of our fear of losing each other." He shifted to gently hold her chin with one hand.

His face and lips were so close to her. Was he going to kiss her? She didn't want to think of her grandma's words or of the alien girl. A'idah didn't want to be cautious.

Softly he spoke. "I've never seen you be cautious before. I guess you must really... care for me."

His lips drew nearer, and then he paused. She could see the questioning look in his eyes. He wanted her to speak up if he shouldn't kiss her.

A'idah wanted him to. How would it feel? Would it be awkward, embarrassing, or wrong? Deep down, A'idah knew it would be wonderful. She answered by— The bubble joggled.

She heard Zeghes say, "Hey, I'm here. Should I leave you two alone?"

Alex and A'idah both hurriedly stepped out of the embrace.

A'idah looked at her dolphin friend in panic. Was he going to embarrass her with what he said?

"Was A'idah finally letting you do the kissing thing? How does it feel, Alex? You are both pink so it must have been a good thing. I've watched the two of you for a long time, and you've turned pink many times. I'm pretty sure pink for dolphins means the same thing. I—"

Alex interrupted him. "Zeghes, let's get on down to the bottom and start exploring. Keep a watch out for the footprint things in the dirt. You do remember what footprints are?"

"Yes."

"Good. I'm contacting Skyler. I let him know Windelli has the location of where we are. If he doesn't hear back from us before the morning is over, he'll gather the rest of the flock, contact Ytell, and come help us."

First Kiss?

The bubble descended toward the bottom of the pit, and A'idah saw Zeghes maneuver next to the bubble and one of his eyes looked at her.

Zeghes messaged her. |A'idah, you're leaking water. You have those tear things on your face. Are you okay? If Alex isn't behaving right, I'll swat him with my tail. He told me that night in our dorm he needed to just be a friend for you, and that you are too young. I promised to swat him with my tail if he didn't behave right. Are your tears because you're too young for what he did or how you're feeling?|

A'idah hadn't realized she had tears running down her face. |Oh, Zeghes. No, I'm old enough now. My tears are because I don't know what to do.| She would never be old enough for how she was feeling. |I shouldn't have almost kissed him.|

Zeghes messaged her. |I don't think I'm the right one to talk to about knowing what to do. I'd probably embarrass you. Maybe, Gursha could help you.|

|Thanks, Zeghes. That's a good idea.|

Through blurry eyes she looked down at the rapidly approaching floor of the hole. A beaten down trail led from one forbidding dark hole and around a heap of boulders to a second gloomy opening at the base of the opposite wall.

Reaching the bottom, the bubble dissipated, and Alex took off at a run. "I don't sense any immediate danger, but there's a lot of activity going on here." He ducked behind one of the boulders and said, "I'm going to get some stuff out of my pack. You two, keep a lookout for anyone coming out of either hole."

Grateful for the activity, A'idah began climbing to a good niche in the boulders to watch from.

Zeghes resumed their conversation. |Are... are your tears because of the married thing I heard of while spying on Alex and Hheilea? I don't really understand, but it seems similar to the buddy thing we dolphins have. Two become one, and we help each other throughout our lives.|

|Pay attention to watching!| She'd appreciated his earlier words, but not these. A'idah hoped an enemy would come. She wanted a fight, anything to distract her from the

pain. At the same time, she couldn't help but be impressed by how Zeghes caught on to new concepts.

A stubborn Zeghes messaged again. |I'm sorry you're hurt, but listen. If I understand, this might help.|

A'idah held her breath and hoped. Nothing moved in the bottom of the pit. With the silence it too seemed to be listening and hoping with her.

|Alex obviously cares for you, but he's being forced to marry. Hheilea is in danger and needs to be married. You've promised to save her, but if we could find another way to save her, Hheilea and Alex wouldn't have to marry. Do I have it right?|

A'idah pumped her fist into the air and whispered an adamant, "Yes." |Thanks, Zeghes.|

Alex said, "Okay, I'm ready. Let's go find out what those Winkles are up to."

In response, A'idah vaulted down from her perch. "I'm ready." She stumbled, and her surroundings spun. She leaned over and breathed deep until the feeling of vertigo passed. She was okay. Everything was going to work out fine. She and Zeghes would make their plan work. They just had to finish finding out what the Winkles were up to. Help Alex fake his death. Afterwards, Zeghes would help her keep Hheilea safe without her getting married. Then Alex could...

Alex stepped out from behind the boulders. He'd strapped something shaped like a cap with antennas onto his head. Holding up a hand with a small object the same color as his skin, he said, "Zeghes, take this over into the mouth of the other tunnel. If someone comes out of that exit, it will give me an alarm. You'll notice it blends into the surroundings. Also, it's supposed to knock out anyone who sets it off. That will give us time to get back out of this pit before we're trapped."

Gliding down, Zeghes gently took the object in his mouth. It changed color to match his skin. "How careful do I need to be in setting it down?"

A'idah stared at Zeghes in surprise that he could talk while holding the device in his mouth, but she remembered he talked through his blowhole.

First Kiss?

"It's pretty tough. Just drop it. Hurry back and help A'idah keep watch while I use this drone to explore the burrow. I'm anxious to get started. If we don't get done soon enough, there's something in our near future that might be dangerous."

Zeghes took off on his mission. A'idah turned back to Alex to see him toss what looked like a small golden ball with wings into the air. It shot off toward the other burrow.

She asked, "What's—"

Alex waved at her and said, "Come over here. I'll show you. That gadget's a drone. With the headset on, I can control it and see all around it."

Following him back into the boulders, she saw a hologram spring up in front of him. The holographic picture showed the entrance of the other tunnel and then into the darkness of the burrow. After a brief moment the hologram changed, and she could make out the burrow as the drone moved farther. A shiver ran down her back. Once again, she saw the sticky strands along the wall a worm left, but they looked old and dried. In this burrow, there were also some additional reinforcements to the walls and ceiling every now and then. Quickly, the walls flew past.

Alex jumped and let out an "Ahhh!"

Chapter Thirty-Three
Cave-In

"What are you watching?" Zeghes asked.

A'idah jumped at Alex's yell and Zeghes voice.

At the same time as Zeghes' talking and A'idah jumping, Alex grabbed something off his belt. With a clicking sound a shimmering three-foot long blaze of light shot out of the device to crackle in the air. "Oh, it's just you, Zeghes."

With another click the shimmering light disappeared, and Alex returned it to his belt. "That weapon isn't as good as a sword, but it's smaller."

Impressed, A'idah said, "Wow, you've gotten some seriously fast reflexes."

"Thanks, but I should've sensed it was Zeghes. I'm afraid my emotions are messing with my sense of the future. My trainer is right. I've got to get better."

Zeghes turned to look with one eye at the hologram. "What's that?"

At that moment, the hologram darkened. Turning the hologram off, Alex turned and started running after the drone. "Uh, oh. Something's interfering with my connection to the drone. I didn't plan on going into the burrows, but I've got to get closer to it."

A'idah said, "We'll come with you." She ran after him. Maybe she'd meet a new friend. The odd thought didn't bother her at all.

Zeghes rocketed past her, but Alex said, "You two keep watch back here. It's safer for you, and I'll be okay with the drone and my sense of the future."

Cave-In

With a snort, A'idah kept running, and said, "You mean your drone which is having difficulty and your faulty sense of the future? We're coming with you."

Alex looked back. "No, it's going to be too dangerous."

"Then you shouldn't go."

"No, I'll be fine. If you and Zeghes come, both of you'll be in terrible danger."

Zeghes said, "I agree with A'idah. You shouldn't go, and if you insist, we're coming too."

Alex stopped running and turned around. "We don't have time for this. We have a chance to find out what the Winkles have been up to and get me back to climbing."

With an expression of frustration, Alex looked at her and Zeghes.

A'idah put her hands on her hips and stared back. "We better hurry up. It would be so embarrassing for Ytell and the flock to come looking for us." The thought of more friends joining them pleased her.

"Okay, on two conditions. One, Hheile—" Alex clenched his teeth biting off the name and looking even more disgusted. "A'idah, you'll ride on Zeghes, and the two of you will obey me and head right back at the first sign of danger. I'll use one of my gadgets to hide and escape later. I want both of you to promise me."

Zeghes arched through the air back by A'idah. "Hop on." |A'idah, do we have to keep our promise.|

A'idah straddled the dolphin and grasped his dorsal fin. "I promise." |Not if we think our Alex is in danger.|

The dolphin said, "I promise." |Is it honorable to promise knowing we might not keep the promise.|

|Zeghes, in my book anything is honorable when protecting a friend.| She liked friends.

Alex started running, and together the three friends entered the darkness. None of them knew their choices created another, darker universe. They were in the darker one. Somewhere in the dimensions of time, Kimleys anxiously tried to find a path past death to a better future.

Zeghes responded to her. |Okay. I can work with that. By the way, I enjoy having you for my friend. Despite your weird human stuff, I like how you swim.|

A'idah considered his words even as she rode on him. She looked at his transparent suit covering him and moving him through the air. Somehow she could feel Zeghes through it. This alien technology and getting to understand a dolphin felt weird and at times like a dream. She grinned to herself. Zeghes liked how she swam. A'idah gasped as Zeghes suit started glowing blue. "What's going on?"

Zeghes said, "My suit's light will help Alex see where he's going. I did this when we rescued you from the first burrow."

A'idah thought she heard a sound and tried to spot the source. Did she spot some sand and rocks moving? She couldn't tell. Terror from her near death in a place just like this suddenly hit her. A'idah sat up straighter and laughed. It echoed in the narrow confines. It gave her a thought. |Alex, should we try and be quiet? Only communicate by messaging?| She told herself that this burrow had reinforcement and it wouldn't just cave in. She ignored the thought that something loud or an explosion could bring it down.

|Yeah. Although after your laughter it might be too late. I'll message Zeghes.|

|Alex and A'idah, shouldn't we be quieter? I think I can hear some noises from up ahead.|

She grinned at Zeghes getting the same idea, and straining, she tried to hear the noises. A'idah couldn't hear anything, but the darkness ahead didn't seem to be as dark. Maybe some more friends are here. That strange thought puzzled her. What was she thinking? Anyone they found down here would be an enemy. She realized in that moment, she'd had other strange thoughts about friends. What was going on? Maybe, she should mention this to Alex.

In front of them, A'idah saw Alex raise a hand and slow down to a walk just as he reached a bend. Zeghes slowed to a stop. A'idah could feel a cool breeze coming from ahead and a musty, dusty smell. Something came around the corner, and she jerked a hand out, finger pointing, and her hair stood on end. It was just Alex's

Cave-In

drone. Just in time, A'idah stopped her prepared lightning strike. Grateful as she did for the control Ytell had drilled into her. Alex wouldn't have appreciated getting his drone fried, and the boom of thunder down here would possibly knock the ceiling down on them.

|When the connection broke, my drone reversed course to reconnect. We'll wait here, and I'll send it back on ahead.|

While Alex messaged them, A'idah puzzled over why she'd considered zapping someone with lightning. They could be her friends. Again, she puzzled over another strange thought about friends. What was going on with her mind? Something, a memory about danger associated with wanting lots of people around bothered her. At first, she couldn't think of it, until a word popped free in her mind, Rabies. She should talk to Alex about the— Suddenly, she didn't feel concerned. Instead, she considered how to get with more friends.

In front of Alex, the hologram from the drone reformed. Zeghes moved up closer. A'idah eagerly looked for friends. The holo was brighter again. The hologram showed one side of the tunnel ahead had large gaps between strangely shaped boulders. Light from somewhere above glowed through the gaps. Artificial supports held the big rocks back from the tunnel. Alex pointed at it and messaged. |Those are good sized gaps. I think we could escape through there.| He pointed at a faint light farther down the burrow. It grew brighter as the drone moved closer. Excitement came through as he messaged. |Down there, we'll find the answer to what the Winkles have been up to and more. There's something special.|

A'idah no longer worried about Rabies. She even grinned at the mention of the Winkles. Maybe they were still there. She'd love to be friends with them. This time, she didn't notice the strangeness of wanting to be friends with deadly enemies. She'd stopped thinking of the danger and didn't notice the sweat rolling off her forehead.

Alex moved around the corner at a fast walk. Zeghes followed with A'idah. When they went past the boulders, the cold breeze shifted and with it the musty, dusty smell increased. She heard Alex make a muffled gasp. He came to another stop and Zeghes stopped by him. The picture in the hologram brightened.

A'idah barely restrained a gasp of her own. The hologram showed an immense expanse, and in the distance stood strange blocky buildings with a few dark windows.

Alex messaged. |I've got to get closer. The drone's fighting interference of some kind. You two start back. Once I get closer, I'll be able to get a view with the drone above those buildings.|

|Alex, there's no sign of danger.| A'idah sent Zeghes a quick message. |Zeghes, let's go on past Alex| She wanted to look for the Winkles. They'd be her friends.

Zeghes moved on past Alex.

"Wait," Alex said. Frustration and more showed in the blurted word. |Stop. My other device just went off. You two should leave now. You promised. I can escape.|

Zeghes stopped. |A'idah, there is danger.|

A'idah slid off Zeghes and landed on her feet. "There isn't any danger. We can make friends with them. Come with me to look for Winkles." She sprinted down the burrow and into the light spilling out of an opening ahead of her.

She could hear Alex running after her. Good, she liked the idea of having plenty of friends around. The tunnels felt hotter to her and for a moment, she wondered why she felt so much warmer.

"Zeghes, we've got to stop her."

"I agree. She's acting crazy. She should know the Winkles don't want to be friends. They tried to kill all of us back at the battle in the Hall of Flight."

"She's got too big of a lead on me, and she's too fast. Can you catch her?"

A'idah grinned and then squinted in the brighter light. The tunnel around her changed into a smooth hard surface. A vast, vaulted space opened in front of her. They would follow her to the Winkles. Hopefully, there would be lots of them. Too late, she saw Zeghes zip up and turn right in front of her. A'idah slammed into his side and tumbled over him onto a hard smooth floor. The need to be with more people thrust her up onto her hands and knees. Inspiration struck as she crawled. "Help me! The tunnel is collapsing!"

Alex said in quiet intense words, "A'idah, stop. You're acting crazy. Why do you think the Winkles can be your friends?" His voice changed, and he yelled as the knowledge hit him. "The animal scratch, acting crazy friendly, A'idah! You've got rabies!"

The words didn't make any difference. She started to get to her feet, and Alex tackled her. Together they tumbled across the floor.

A'idah struggled, scratching, biting at him, and wrestling to get free. "Let me go."

Zeghes said, "I can see the Winkles from here. There are only a few of them. We could go back to the Tasties city. There are thousands living there, and they're all very friendly."

She shoved at Alex. "Let me go. I've got to go with Zeghes." The words pounded in her mind, more friends, and more friends. Yes.

"Gladly." He released her.

A'idah stood up and hurried to Zeghes. I'll ride you back to the pit."

Alex followed her. "It might not be that simple. I'm sensing trouble coming toward us in the burrow."

Hair standing on end, A'idah said, "I'll just use some lightning to clear the way."

"A'idah, don't use lighting. It's too dangerous. Zeghes, take her to where the boulders are. There's a way out there. Be quick. I'll be following. I'll cause a cave in and disappear."

A'idah jumped up on the waiting dolphin. Her hair stood out from her head. "I can feel all those Tasties calling to me. Let's get going."

Zeghes surged through the air and into the opening of the burrow back where they'd come from.

She wouldn't let anyone stop them from getting to the thousands of Tasties waiting for her. Danger waited in the tunnel? She'd clear the way. She lifted an arm with finger pointing. The bright light of her lightning bolt blinded her, and the rolling, echoing boom of thunder deafened and almost knocked her loose from Zeghes.

A'idah felt sand and small rocks pelting her. She fell against her friend and held him tight. "Zeghes, don't let the rocks get me. I need to get to friends. Please, help me." The combination of fever, rocks hitting her, the pounding need to be with many friends, and plus the terror from her previous near death experience wrenched tears out of her. She begged. "Zeghes, please, please help me."

His response cut through the growing rumble, the response to her lightning bolt. It imparted hope to her. "I've got you. Just hold on. I'm getting you to friends."

"Thank you. Thank you."

A blaster bolt cut through the rumble. Zeghes dropped closer to the floor.

Worry and concern filled A'idah's voice. "Are you hit?"

"No. Hold on tight."

She squeezed him with her arms and wrapped her legs tighter around him. Through her recovering eyesight, A'idah noticed the blue glow of Zeghes suit stopped. She muttered. "Friends, I just need some friends. Why are they shooting at us? They could be friends."

Zeghes swerved back and forth surging faster all the time. |Hold tighter.|

Through the sand and rocks, A'idah could make out a glow of light just ahead of them. Flashes of continuing blaster fire, but they aimed at the ceiling. Zeghes dipped head first at the ground. A'idah felt inertia pulling her off and desperately held on even as she inevitably slipped. Ahead of them, the ceiling gave way. Rocks and boulders as if in slow motion poured down from above.

A'idah felt a jolt go through Zeghes. He must've rammed something on the floor with his beak. The jolt loosened her grip but he and maybe the jolt added a slew to keep A'idah upright. Zeghes ended going backwards at the cave-in. A'idah felt acceleration sliding her back. Only Zeghes' flippers kept her on him.

Cave-In

They slammed against one of the boulders, bounced off, and started to move away. Zeghes bucked throwing her away from the falling rocks. In slow motion, the force of it twisted her off him. One leg came free from over his back. She felt a boulder slam against her dolphin friend. One leg was still under him and rocks pelted down against them. Darkness swallowed her up again.

~*********~

Alex tore his eyes from watching A'idah and Zeghes race back into the tunnel, and turned to retrieving the drone. He didn't want to waste time getting it, but he'd seen something incredible in the hologram relayed from it. Very large objects floated in pink holo-fields. The Winkles were moving some kind of gigantic creatures. His sense of the future warred within him. One thread of the future spoke of the incredible importance of the information the drone contained. The other spoke of the doom A'idah and Zeghes faced. Then, Alex felt the first pull of compulsion from the Winkles. He fought off their control, but knew he couldn't wait any longer, or they would capture him. The drone was close enough.

With the drone speeding behind, Alex ran after his two friends. His sense of the future caused him to shut his eyes just in time. Even then, he could see the bright flash of light through his eyelids. The terrible boom of rolling, echoing thunder struck next. Instinctively, as much as through his sense of the future, Alex ducked his head and protected it with raised and bent arms.

The sand gently caressed his arms and rocks followed beating a staccato of pain against them. Trusting his sense of where the worst rocks would fall, Alex dodged and swerved.

His AI screamed in pain and fear in his mind. Alex wished Maleky could quiet it. At least practice ignoring the evil man helped him ignore the frightened babbling of his AI.

Blaster bolts screamed past, but he'd known of them and fell rolling. His headset informed him of the drone getting battered. Too many futures hammered at him.

Zeghes and A'idah getting buried by a cave-in.

The Winkles capturing him.

The drone's data had to get to Ytell.

There were a number of blank walls, and Alex knew what that meant. Was the drone's information worth all of them dying?

Only one path to life for his friends presented itself, and it had its own uncertain risk for them. His own blank wall didn't matter. With one hand, Alex fished out another device from a pocket and pulling the activating pin tossed it behind him. Another cave-in would stop the Winkles, but the future wasn't clear if it would also finish burying him and his friends. Only his visit to the Book of Prophesy gave him any hope. Alex could change the future by his actions. They don't have to die. He could force the one slim possibility to work. It would take a miracle, but someone had been born with stubbornness almost beyond belief, and he believed in miracles. If Alex could just—

He sprinted after his friends turning on his headset's light. More blaster shots blazed from the turn in the burrow, but these hit the ceiling. The cave-in he'd expected started with a terrible rumbling. He saw Zeghes valiantly trying to protect A'idah as he slammed into a boulder. He knew the dolphin, his friend would die. Then rocks crushed A'idah and Zeghes to the ground. More rocks and boulders continued to fall.

Alex sprinted toward his friends accepting blows from rocks and dodging the more dangerous ones. Dust from the cave-in sandblasted him. Frantically in his mind, he went through the inventory of gadgets from the Tasties he had. Nothing, nothing, nothing could save his friend. Only one possibility presented itself and it led to another blank wall. The certainty of death tore any hope he had to shreds.

The rumbling died away, but the dust filled air, blinded Alex. He stumbled on through the dust, coughing, choking, tripping over rocks, and scraping against boulders. Remembering the mask he carried to use with the strong force canceling device, Alex pulled it out of a pocket and fixed it across his face.

He felt the Winkles trying to control him. Using his emotions of grief and distress over his friends, he shattered their attack. His bomb went off, and the concussion knocked him off his feet. Alex tumbled to the ground at the base of the pile covering Zeghes and A'idah. Immediately, he rolled back to his knees.

Working furiously, he dug down into the rocks. He didn't care about ripping fingernails or the cuts he got from the newly broken rocks. As he worked, he knew his golden drone hovered in the air by him. Using his sense of the future without consciously considering it, Alex followed the guidance to uncover his friends. He found a foot and uncovered a leg, the rest of A'idah, and part of Zeghes. She was breathing. One bloody arm had an extra bend and a splinter of white jaggedly sticking out of the skin, but he couldn't find any more serious injuries. There was another bloody spot on her head. Fortunately, nothing like when she'd almost died in the other cave-in.

Blaster sounds came from the other side of the main rock pile blocking the tunnel. Alex knew assassins were working their way from the other side. They wanted to be sure he was dead.

Working fast, Alex uncovered Zeghes. One big rock took all his strength. His dolphin brother didn't look good, and Alex was surprised his brother still lived. Zeghes' breathing was shallow and fast. He had numerous injuries, and where the big rock had been was a smashed in area and lots of blood. "Zeghes, Zeghes, Zeghes, come on buddy. Hang in there. We need you."

Quickly, Alex went back to A'idah. "Come on, A'idah, you need to wake up. Lots of friends are waiting for you."

Chapter Thirty-Four
A Death

Again, Alex pleaded. "A'idah, wake-up. Lots of friends are waiting for you."

A'idah stirred and muttered. "Friends? I need friends."

"Yes, you need friends. There are lots just waiting for you. Zeghes will take you to them."

The dust had thinned out, and Alex could make out her fluttering eyelids.

Ytell's message blasted him. |Alex, where are you? Are you okay? Skyler just told me Hheilea's concerned about you.|

Hheilea? She must've been looking at his future. Why hadn't she messaged him? |Zeghes is in a very bad way. The Winkles are blocked. There are some assassins, I thought they were Dreads, but they've been using blasters. It must be someone else. For now, they're blocked by the cave-in.|

Continuing blaster sounds and occasional noises of shifting rocks and boulders testified to the efforts of the assassins.

Alex continued the message. |I'm trying to get A'idah to heal Zeghes. She must've gotten infected with rabies. She's been acting very irrational and must be in the friendly stage. We're in the burrow closest to the crater wall. Ekbal will know where. Hurry.|

|We'll be there as quick as we can. Keep them alive.|

Using his AI made him aware again of its pleas and complaints. *I'm hurt. Why have you done this? I hate you. Maleky is right. You're bad.*

A Death

Maleky was right? What was that about? More important things demanded his attention, and Alex ignored the baby AI.

A'idah's eyes popped open. "The friends, where are they?" She must've moved her arm and pain hit. "Ahhh!"

She favored the arm but wriggled struggling to get free. "My leg, I've got to move my leg. So I can get to friends."

Alex couldn't believe she moved after hearing the pain in her scream. It must be the rabies. He spoke, hoping and praying for the right words. "Zeghes is knocked out. He's on your leg. He needs healing. You remember the vapuc healing Gursha taught you. Heal him, and then he can take you to your thousands of friends."

"Thousands of friends? Yes. We were going there when... Zeghes, wake up. We've got to go. I need to get to my friends."

Frustration gnawed at Alex. He knew how poor his chances were of getting past the rabies neurological symptoms which currently controlled her, but he tried again. Placing his hands on Zeghes, he said, "I'm trying to heal Zeghes so he can take you to your friends."

A'idah moved and then let out another groan of agony. She placed a hand on his. She frowned. "You're not healing him at all."

"Help me. Put your hands on him. Healed he can take you to your friends."

Did Alex still hear the faint whistling of Zeghes breath? "Zeghes, buddy, don't die. I need you. We need you. Please, hang in there."

A different look crossed A'idah's face and at it Alex gained some hope.

With gritted teeth, she said, "Friend, he's my friend."

Was he getting through to the real A'idah? With more hope, he said, "Yes, he's your friend and he's dying."

Grim determination beat in every word of A'idah's voice, "I— don't— let— friends— die." And then her expression changed again. "I need friends." Again her face and voice showed determination. "Help— me— get— my— hands— to— his— wounds."

When A'idah spoke in her right mind the words were cut off as if each one was a separate battle.

The cave-in shifted again and now Alex could hear the blaster sounds clearer. The assassins were getting closer.

Alex guided the hand already on his up to the worst injury.

Beads of sweat rolled down A'idah's face and yet she moved the other arm. Pain and raw determination pounded in each word A'idah spoke. "Help— me— get— my— other— hand— there."

Through his swirling emotions, Alex knew both lives of his friends rode on the next few moments.

Alex shifted position and prepared to shove on A'idah's poor battered body even as he would move her injured arm. "This is going to really hurt. You can't pass out. Our time is running short. We'll all die."

"Get— my— other— hand— up— there. I— don't— care— how— you— do— it. Just— leave— it— attached— to— my— body— by— some— skin."

Alex almost laughed at the horrible picture that presented in his mind. "Here we go."

She screamed. It over powered the sounds of the blasters. It went on forever.

Zeghes shifted.

Alex held his breath and blinked away tears. She was doing it. He had no idea how she managed to fight off the pain and rabies. Alex continued shoving on her battered body holding her in place. Somehow, through the pain and rabies, A'idah had found the will power to save her friend. He gasped out. "You're doing it. Don't stop." This was his miracle.

Zeghes moved again. And Alex heard his weak voice. "What happened?" followed by, "Was there a shark attack."

Alex grinned. He had hope, just a little. His friends might live. "Zeghes, does your suit work?"

Flashes of blue light lit about the dolphin's body. "It's damaged."

A'idah interjected into the conversation. "Can you get me to more friends?" Followed by frustration and pain

A Death

expressed. "Argh. Zeghes— you— need— more— help— than— I— can— give."

Her voice changed and the words weren't cutoff, sharp, but slowed down. Healing Zeghes must've been taking an incredible effort. "I... want... you... to... live.... Can... you... get... yourself... out... of... here...?" Her determination to speak truths, and not something just about needing more friends resonated in her words.

Zeghes answered. "I don't know."

The urgency of time running out pounded at Alex. "He can't get out without you. You'll need to ride on Zeghes healing him even as he uses his damaged suit to drag you both up and out through those boulders. We have to hurry. A'idah, brace yourself. You can't faint. Zeghes, lift up off of her leg."

The dolphin shifted, moving up and then back down, but it had been enough. Alex yanked on A'idah moving her leg out and free. She screamed again. He didn't have any mercy, but lifted her up and draped her across Zeghes. "A'idah, you'll have to keep healing him." He replaced her hands over the bleeding wound.

She gasped out her response with three bursts. "I'll... do... it."

The blaster fire had continued with some noises of boulders and rocks moving.

"Zeghes, you've got to go now."

The dolphin lifted off the ground, and in the dim shadowy light, Alex stumbled along with them trying to help lift and guide them. A boulder on their side of the pile shifted and rolled down landing where they'd just been. The whole pile of rocks and boulders groaned.

He focused on his words ignoring his own danger. "Zeghes, you'll have to force your suit to get you both up this slope. The gaps between the boulders are big enough for both of you. A'idah has sharks in her blood. They're killing her. Only you can save her from those sharks. Get both of you out and move away from the boulders."

Zeghes said, "Yes... I can... see the gaps. I'll get... her out..." He moved forward and up the beginning of the long climb. Instead of floating over the first boulder he scrapped over it. " or die trying."

"I... won't... let... him... die.... I need friends. Alex..., what... about... you?"

"Once you two are out, then I'll bring all of these boulders down with an explosion. Using a special gadget I've got I'll be able to get out. Zeghes, remember our plan. Pretend I died." As he spoke those words, Alex knew it would be true. With a free hand he snatched the golden device out of the air and stuffed it in the only place he felt sure it would be safe and get to someone who could use the information.

Zeghes didn't reply but kept slowly moving higher.

Alex watched them go. Considering their chances of survival, he decided to give up on his own plan and go with them and try to help. Maybe, they all could live. He scrambled up and over the first boulder, but the next proved to be more difficult. Already his friends had moved out of sight. Alex couldn't keep up with them. Tears of frustration flowed down his face. This had been his great plan. If they died, it would be his fault. Alex just wanted his friends to live. His heart ached at the idea of A'idah dying.

From his friends above, Alex heard a plea or command.

A'idah said, "Don't... you... dare... die. We... need... our... older... brother. I need friends. You... are... more... than... a... friend... to... me."

Very faintly he heard her last words. "I... love... you."

He loved her too. Alex wanted to yell it out loud for A'idah and the world to hear, but his sense of the future and the sound of falling rocks from the cave-in location stopped him just in time. Immediately, Alex turned off the light on his head gear. Now, he could barely see. Carefully and quietly he moved across the boulders toward the side. A compulsion hit him to go back to the cave-in. Without thinking, Alex started back.

Maleky yelled in his mind and this time Alex listened to him. *The assassins are Winkles. Don't listen to them.*

A Death

Shocked out of his trance-like obedience, Alex stopped.

Maleky continued. *You're finally listening to me. Now that it's too late. As so many of your friends say, you're an idiot. You've got to get us out of here.*

Beginning a long battle, Alex turned his back on the Winkles. Slowly, trying to be quiet and having to fight for each foot gained away from the Winkles, he moved across the boulder field. Noises from the pile of rocks testified to the enemy moving closer. At one point, the battle tugged back and forth with Alex not gaining any ground. Often, he swiped the sweat from his forehead. He even took a step back toward the Winkles.

Again, Maleky intervened. *You're losing the battle. You know they'll kill us if they see you. They hate you.* He tempted Alex. *If you surrender your body to me, I can beat the Winkles.*

Sweat from the battle rolled off his forehead. Alex held onto a boulder to keep himself from going to the Winkles. He looked to his sense of the future for guidance. The path of surrender to Maleky was murky. He couldn't tell what would happen, but it felt terribly wrong. *No, Maleky. Not happening.*

A louder rock fall from the cave-in spurred Alex on. At the same time the compulsion weakened. Someone must've slipped.

Alex took advantage of the moment. He scrambled across the boulders. The rock wall loomed very close. He found a place where one of the bigger boulders was jammed up against solid rock above the burrow.

Alex pulled the most important gadget out of the small pack he'd been carrying. For its size, it was quite heavy. Below, there were occasional sounds of shifting rocks and sand. He didn't need his sense of the future to know the approaching threats.

Temporarily, a boulder below Alex gave him protection and cover, but the Winkles would recognize these boulders as a way out. He had to protect his friend's escape.

Alex unfolded the active end of the device and held it against the unyielding rock above him. His sense of the future held him back from turning it on. His friends would die. Alex didn't know why. Above him, he knew his friends still struggled to live. He waited. If he used the device too late, the assassins coming closer every moment would kill him, but if he used it too soon, his sense of the future said Zeghes and A'idah struggling to live would die.

Concentrating, Alex tried to get past his swirling emotions to clearly sense the future. One trembling finger rested on the power switch. Alex doubted he would live. He would rather wait too long than risk his friends' lives, but then A'idah would be furious with him for dying. That would be bad. Alex almost chuckled at the absurdity of his thoughts, but the seriousness of the situation wouldn't let him. Instead, a snort of danger suppressed laughter escaped. Could he do anything to gain a little precious time? He thought of the gadgets he still had. Something he might use in a way to nudge the future possibilities?

A quiet voice spoke to him out of the dark. In confusion he looked about. Was he imagining things? Again, he heard it, but clearer.

"Alex."

"What?" He wasn't certain if he heard the voice or if it was in his head.

More insistently, it repeated. "Alex, you need to use another bomb, now."

This time he recognized it. "Hheilea? Where are you?"

"I'm in time. I talked my dad into letting me try this. You're going to die. Use the other bomb to cause an explosion. Do it now. Our other friends will be okay."

Alex checked his sense of the future. Hheilea was right, but he needed a bigger explosion. He remembered being told the light sword was unstable in an explosion and would explode with great force itself. "How can I hear you?"

A noise brought his head up, and he looked back down into the boulders. Did he see some movement? Alex pulled back into the alcove out of view from below, but also away from the best point to start a tunnel. Quickly, he removed

A Death

the light sword from his belt shoved it into the pack. His questing hand found the last bomb. He pulled its activating pin and shoved it back into the pack.

As he worked, Hheilea talked. Now her voice had lost the insistence and intensity. She sounded worn-out and sad. "Please hurry. You can hear me, because we're still connected through what the T'wasn't-to-be-is did to us, even though you destroyed it. If you live, you will be able to marry A'idah."

Rock exploded near him with a blast of light and sound of blaster fire. He'd taken too long. Taking a desperate chance he moved back out and threw the pack. With a warning from his sense of the future he twisted out of the way of another blaster bolt. Then he dove back into the alcove. Snatching up the anti-strong device, he flipped on its switch.

"If you don't live, someone else will take your place in the prophecy. I begged dad to let me do this for you. I'll always love you."

Alex moved the device back and forth carving out a tunnel away from the boulders. A cloud of dust billowed out. Blaster fire increased and again the compulsion to surrender to the Winkles grew. Only Hheilea's voice kept him from surrendering to the compulsion.

He said, "Hheilea, I'll always love you, but you're right. I love A'idah too."

"Alex, you were right to stop the T'wasn't-to-be-is. The love you have for me is left over from it. Please, find a way to live. I'm losing sight of you."

Alex crawled forward and leaned into the device trying to hurry it. He thought of something he should share. "Hheilea, I was using a drone. It has some strange information. The Winkles were moving some kind of huge creatures using healing holo-fields. I stuck the drone into A'idah's shirt. Be sure Ytell gets it."

Her voice had been growing distant. One last phrase full of pathos made it to him. "I love you."

Alex knew it was a race between the compulsion, blaster fire, and his need for a safe alcove from the explosion. Eventually, they'd get too close. The boulder wouldn't protect him, or the bomb would go off. For any and all of those, Alex would die. In the masks display area, a warning message blinked. The neutron energies were growing dangerous. He flipped the off switch. This would have to do.

Alex wished he knew how big the explosion would be. How would A'idah and Zeghes do without him? All he could feel of his future was a blank wall. AI, send out a message to all my friends telling them I love them.

~**********~

A'idah clung to the dolphin. She concentrated on healing her friend. She had to keep him alive. The need for friends kept pushing at her, but she fought back. She had to save this friend. He would get her to more friends.

The pain from her injuries, the illness, and the effort she was expending to help Zeghes left her increasingly light headed. A'idah knew it would be just moments before she fell off his back. A headache grew pounding in her head. She didn't notice the increased amount of light or how much slower Zeghes moved. Her limbs started to go limp, but strength she didn't know of thrust her hands back against Zeghes' wound. She had to save Zeghes. A'idah felt like a puppet just along for the ride, while another controlled her body.

Zeghes slumped down onto a boulder.

A'idah begged. "Zeghes... we... can't... give... up." In a daze she looked for the next boulder they'd have to go over. There weren't any. They were out. Friends, she saw more friends. |Ytell, help us... Zeghes... is dying. I need to be with friends.|

Ytell's response eased her concern. |We'll take you to more friends and help Zeghes.|

Someone pulled her off Zeghes and into a bubble. She was letting go, surrendering her fight against the pain.

Zeghes said, "Get A'idah away from here. Alex is setting off an explosion. He's sacrificing his own life to stop the killers from following me and A'idah."

A Death

"No." A'idah struggled against the darkness. She couldn't let that happen. Fighting, she sat up. "I need friends." She thought she screamed, but only heard a whimper. "I don't need more friends. I need to save my Alex." Did anyone hear her? Hands held her down.

A voice she didn't recognize said, "She's getting violent. I'm going to sedate her."

Something pushed against her neck and her limbs relaxed. A'idah tried to fight against it. No! No! She screamed in her mind. I have to save— Darkness.

~**********~

A'idah heard voices. Where was she? What had happened? Bits and pieces started to come back. She'd been somewhere with Zeghes and Alex. Something important she needed to do. She sat bolt upright. Eyes wide open.

Gursha said, "A'idah how did you—, you shouldn't be awake yet. I'm going to adjust your holo-field. You'll feel much better when you wake up."

"No. Don't. I need to go. Where's Zeghes? Where's Alex? What happened? Someone's in danger. I must go." She swung her legs down and the holo-field disappeared. Trembling, she staggered, looking for the door.

Gursha stood with two hands on her hips and another one pointing at her. "Get right back into your holo-field young lady. You're not finished getting healed."

A'idah stumbled on spotting the door, but Gursha blocked her progress. "Either you get back in that holo-field by yourself, or I'll put you there. You've been very ill. I don't know how you got out of the holo-field. It should've kept you unconscious. You're in no condition to leave here."

The distraught, young teenage girl swayed. "No, please. Let me go. Someone, I think it's Alex, is in danger. I've got to go. He can't die. I love him."

Compassion replaced Gursha's stern visage. "Oh, A'idah. I can't let you go. And, well, it's been two days since you were brought to me. Any danger is done and over. You can't help."

A'idah fell to her knees. Sobs burst forth. She forced out between the sobs fierce words of denial. "No— no— no. Zeghes— is— okay—. Alex— is—."

Then the tears and words poured out of her. "Nooo! He has to be okay. He wouldn't leave me all alone. He wouldn't leave me. He wouldn't. Where is he?"

Gursha didn't answer. She just gathered the distraught teenager up in her arms. A blue holo-field with pink around A'idah's head appeared and supported Gursha in a sitting position. It rocked both of them back and forth as Gursha tried to comfort the girl, but the lack of an answer had been an answer. A'idah's grief was inconsolable.

Chapter Thirty-Five
Moving On

A'idah blinked. She didn't want to wake up. They'd all been back on Earth and had beaten the invading hordes of Deems. A'idah and her friends were heroes. She had her father and grandmother with her. They both respected and admired her. She didn't have anything to fear anymore. She'd learned so much. A'idah could save any and all of her friends.

At that thought, a brief cloud of sorrow flittered past. Something was important about it, and she tried to focus on it. The dream pulled against her thoughts, but she struggled not to let it succeed. Another thought pushed its way into the dream. All she needed was to finish her training with the other Earthlings, and they'd make that future happen. She blinked again. It smelled antiseptic and reminded her of healing.

"She's coming around. I've given her good dreams. She'll be able to deal with reality."

A'idah heard a door open, followed by Hheilea saying, "Hi, I'm glad you're here."

A door opened again. Someone asked, "Why are you here?"

Opening her eyes, she recognized a nurse's clinic. From the blue-pink haze coloring the view, A'idah knew she lay in a healing holo-field. Hheilea and Twarbie stood looking down at her. Part of her knew why they were both with her. At that thought, A'idah became aware of a great pain in her chest. Why did she still have an injury? It ached worse than any wound she'd ever had. Why hadn't the holo-field healed her? Gursha stood over by her interior office. Someone cleared their throat, and A'idah looked at the foot of her holo-field bed.

A man with a bald chartreuse head and pencil-shaped, bright red nose stood there uncomfortably shifting from foot to foot. Holographic papers flickered in front of him.

A'idah grinned through her pain at the sight of Stick. He was a very funny looking man, but he was also the glue which kept Amable's academy running. He took care of all the terrible paperwork, accounting, and head of staff duties. What was Stick doing here, and he seemed to be very uncomfortable. "Hi, Stick."

Her two friends waited quietly, and Stick said, "Hello, A'idah. It's good to see you feeling better."

Nodding, A'idah frowned. Stick normally didn't act this informal. "Thanks, but what's wrong?" Why hadn't Gursha healed her worst injury?

Stick looked more uncomfortable. His nose started flashing red. Something she'd never seen it do before. A'idah knew it changed color according to his emotions, but didn't have any clue what this one was.

He nervously shuffled the papers and cleared his throat. The nurse, Gursha walked across the room and put an arm around the poor man. Quietly, she said, "Go ahead. Get it over with."

The troubled man looked into A'idah's eyes and spoke very quickly. "With large assets, I encourage everyone to have a plan in case of... in case of.... The Coratory has returned and everyone is very excited and happy at its repairs and improvements. What this means is that the cruiser, *The Heart Song*, is no longer needed by the Academy. There'll be a ceremony to turn it over to you."

He turned around and almost ran out of the room. She heard him sobbing, but Stick managed to say one more thing with a broken voice. "Alex... He left it to you."

The door shut behind him. A'idah lay still trying to take in what had just happened. Stick didn't behave that way. Her eyes burned from unshed tears. She now had a cruiser. Could it fight? She had to learn how to use it. She would— She would— For some reason, she was having a hard time thinking and breathing.

A'idah felt more than saw Twarbie and Hheilea moving up on either side of her and putting their arms around her.

Moving On

Hheilea said, "What do you remember about exploring the worm tunnel?"

Worm tunnel? For long moment, A'idah thought. "I... I went there with Zeghes and —." Someone else she didn't want to think about. "I don't remember."

Twarbie said, "You were ill with rabies."

A'idah thought she'd say more, but instead the Winkle girl began sobbing. The holo-field morphed. It lifted the other two girls and gathered them into something resembling a cross between a rocking chair and a couch.

Hheilea continued with, "You found a hidden and ancient city, but the three of you were attacked by Winkles. Zeghes almost died. In fact, he should've, but somehow you fought off the rabies neurological symptoms to save him. He forced his damaged suit to get the two of you out. An explosion killed everyone left behind."

With shaking arms, A'idah pulled the other two close to her. They had to continue on. Ignoring her pain, she looked at the others. The Winkle girl continued to sob. The white haired Kimley gazed back at A'idah. She had dark circles under red eyes. A'idah figured they were red from crying, but at least she wasn't now. "How are you dealing with this? You and—" Suddenly, A'idah had a lump in her throat preventing her from talking. She swallowed and tried again forcing out the painful words. "You and Alex were very close."

"I've already cried. It's been two days. Plus, I knew from the Book of Prophesy this could happen, but I couldn't do anything. I wanted to warn Alex, but I couldn't. I hate that part of seeing future possibilities. It was one of those futures I could tell would be worse if I interfered. Still, by traveling in times dimensions I managed to be with him at the end. He told me he loved you. There's still— There's other stuff going on. It's going to get worse."

At those words, A'idah clenched her teeth and then spoke in defiant tones. "Not on my watch. You two were really close to Alex. Together, we three teenage girls will make sure he didn't die for nothing." A'idah turned to the still crying Twarbie. "Get over it. Crying won't bring him back."

Trying to speak and control herself, Twarbie said, "I... I'm sorry. I shouldn't have done this."

An unsympathetic A'idah said, "What?"

Gursha moved closer to the girls. "Twarbie, are you talking about loving Alex?"

In weak tones, "Yes. I shouldn't have."

The nurse snorted. "Humph. I've wondered if you Winkles were spineless. Being scared of a little hurt enabled the bunch of you to become such nasty people."

With much more life Twarbie answered. At first, loving someone did scare me, but Alex taught me something you taught him. He said that if you live life well you're going to lose people you care for, but if you never lived life well then you never had them to lose. It confused me at first, but now I understand. As a Winkle, I didn't live life well, and I didn't have any love. Now, I've loved Alex and lost him. I'm glad I loved him, even though it hurts worse than anything, and I don't know how to deal with it. Still, I'm willing to love again. I want to live life like Alex showed me. What I meant about I shouldn't have is..." She didn't finish.

A'idah jumped in. "Yes. Good. Hheilea, you're going to show me this Book of Prophesy. Twarbie, I've got a new ship, and I don't know how to use it. Check it out. We three teenage girls will make sure Alex didn't die for nothing."

Hheilea nodded. "Yes. Count me in."

Both of them looked at Twarbie.

"I want to help, but I've got something I need to tell you. I shouldn't have let Alex get so involved with me—"

A'idah interrupted. "That doesn't matter."

"Hold on. The reason is also a problem I'm going to have. I'm not a teenager. I'm thirty-three."

"Wha—" A'idah's mouth dropped open in shock.

After a long quiet moment, Gursha said, "Has it started?"

A'idah asked, "What started?"

"I'm going to go a bit crazy, and if I don't return to my people's home planet, I'll die. The male Winkles live there like beasts. After I go there, I'll be pregnant."

For a long moment, A'idah stared at her not understanding, and then she felt her face grow warm. "Oh my. That's terrible."

Moving On

Twarbie nodded her head. "Yeah. After learning what love really is, I think I'd rather die. I guess with how terrible Winkle females are it's the only reason our species hasn't died out."

Hheilea said, "You can't die. How will you get there?"

"I don't know. The evil Winkles control the availability of transportation. I won't be given a ride."

A'idah said, "Learn how to use my cruiser. You can borrow it, and if I can get time from training, I'll go with you."

Gursha said, "I'll do some research. I should be able to give you some hormones to slow it down. After my research, I think we should try the holo-fields too. I'll come up with something."

"Thanks."

"No problem, but right now my patient has been up more than long enough. A'idah needs to eat and rest. She can talk with you in the morning."

A'idah watched them leave. She'd save Twarbie. Another thought crossed her mind. That ship, not only could she use it to save Twarbie, but she could give it to Hheilea. With her own spaceship, the Kimley would be safe. She wouldn't have to marry Alex. Then I could— The reality A'idah had been holding off hit her. Sobs and tears she'd been suppressing ripped her apart.

~**********~

The next day, Hheilea gave up trying to sleep, washed the tears from her face and went looking for breakfast. No food looked good to her, but realizing she needed something Hheilea forced herself to swallow a meal supplement. She knew without having to think about her sense of the future that it wouldn't feel good in her stomach, but still... no real foods appealed to her. Shrugging off her own trouble, Hheilea left her home and hurried toward the meeting with A'idah.

Hheilea hoped getting her friend out of the nurse's office would help A'idah feel better, and then Hheilea grinned. Her friend really didn't need much help. She was handling the loss of Alex better than anyone else. Thinking of A'idah lightened her own feelings and quickened her steps. It would be fun spending most of a day with the Earthling girl. Hheilea had never had a girlfriend before. Just thinking about being with her lightened her spirits and quickened her steps. Were all Earthling girls incredible-like A'idah? What would the she think of the Book of Prophesy?

In no time at all, she'd reached Gursha's clinic. When the door opened, Hheilea heard Ytell.

In strident tones, the giant bird forcefully argued. "Gursha, I need A'idah to resume her training."

A'idah sat in a holo-field chair finishing breakfast. Her head turned back and forth between the two combatants.

Gursha said, "And I told you she isn't ready."

"But, you're allowing her to travel today?"

A'idah spoke up, "You know I'm right here."

Gursha and Ytell ignored her.

"Yes, as her nurse, I'm willing to accept some risk for the benefit getting A'idah out of my office and being with Hheilea will grant her. But what's your hurry? Has something happened?"

"Just some small problems of resources coming up missing and shortages of some equipment for repairs. There's a supply ship coming which will take care of all the problems. We bought it and the supplies it carries with a good share of the money Daren gave us."

While Ytell spoke of the problems, a shudder ran down Hheilea's back. She didn't need to consider the possible futures. She knew trouble, new trouble, came like the blast of a supernova explosion. She wished she could warn them, but it wouldn't help. She also desired to have a break from considering bad news. Today was going to be a girls' day for her and A'idah.

Gursha said, "Well, if it's just small problems, then I don't see an issue here. I will not risk her health by putting her back into training early. I don't know when or if her mind will fully recover from the rabies. I don't know how much stress she'll be able to stand. You know the dangers training presents. Getting her back into it too soon would just increase the chances of another death. Do you want that?"

"Can't you fix her problems with your medical holo-field?"

"I took care of the macro damage to her nervous system, but there are uncountable micro damages. If I had just her to work on for weeks, I could eventually fix all of the damage. I don't have that time." Until she's better, I'd prefer her to just practice the Healing vapuc. The Healing vapuc has a mutualistic effect for the applicant as the receiver is being healed. Eventually, she could heal herself to the point where her danger from other vapucs was negligent."

"A'idah and you don't have time for you to heal her. Maybe we could convince her to increase the amount of time she uses to do healing work."

"I'm still here."

Gursha ignored her and replied to Ytell, "I've talked to A'idah about it, but you know her. She feels it would be abandoning her people and all of Earth. Her mind is made up, and you know how she is."

"I'm not that unreasonable."

"Gursha, I accept your diagnosis of her condition. But tomorrow?"

"Ytell, you're as bad as she is."

"I'm not as bad Ytell."

"She might be."

Gursha continued speaking, "I think so, but no promises. I'd rather have her using vapuc for just healing from now on."

At that, the seven-foot tall, blue raptor turned and noticing Hheilea spoke in a much less aggressive tone, even one with compassion. "Hello, Hheilea. I hope you're having a good day."

"I'm doing fine." But she wished everyone would stop treating her so delicately.

Ytell finally turned his attention to A'idah. "We found a damaged, golden gadget stuffed in your clothes. The Tasties identified it as a reconnaissance device they gave Alex. Do you remember anything about it or what it might've seen?"

At the mention of Alex, A'idah paled. At first, she didn't answer and then she said, "I'm sorry. I want to remember, but I don't know what happened."

Ytell left the clinic with one last comment. "Hheilea, you should get more rest. Your eyes are red."

Rest? Every time she closed her eyes she saw Alex. She hadn't been able to sense him at all. Every day, she looked at future possibilities for Alex hoping to see something different, but all she saw was a blank wall. He's gone. The worst of it was she could've warned him. Hheilea turned to Gursha. "Could you help me with my red eyes? Everyone is commenting on them."

"Are you getting good sleep?"

"No."

"Are you still crying a lot?"

"Some. Enough with the questions, if you're not going to help me, then I'll just go. At least if A'idah's ready to go see the Book of Prophesy."

"Yes, she can go, but I want you to promise me you'll go see your own doctor as soon as you're done with A'idah."

Grudgingly, Hheilea said, "Okay." She started to turn back to the door, but Gursha spoke first interrupting her leaving with A'idah.

"A'idah, I've given you my medical permission to leave for part of a day, but—" Her voice hardened and the motherly nurse waved a finger at her patient. "Don't do any vapuc. Remember my warnings." With a gentler voice Gursha finished with, "Now before you go come here and give me a hug."

After Gursha released A'idah from her four armed hug, Hheilea left the clinic calling over her shoulder, "Come on, A'idah." She thought of Ytell's question about the golden gadget. She needed to pass on Alex's last message about the strange creatures the Winkles were moving. Once the other girl joined her, she said, "Your eyes are looking fine."

Walking with her, A'idah answered, "Yeah. Those holo-fields are great. Except, Gursha told me I'll still have a grieving period. I don't have time for that. Speaking of time, I've been wondering if I should take the time, to try and climb the Gadget Lady's mountain and get the sword Alex worked so hard to get."

"You haven't heard?"

"Heard what?"

"Yesterday, after we talked, there was another death at the Gadget Lady's mountain. I've been told it's crazier than normal and has been placed off limits."

"Well that stinks. I hope that String Sword isn't as important as Alex thought. At least with the new supply ship coming, the Academy and everyone's training will be fine."

Moving On

Hheilea didn't want to say anything about the supply ship. Instead, she said, "Those swords are pretty powerful. Did you see the one he had in the battle against the Gragdreath?"

"Only from a distance, at times he seemed to be fighting something I couldn't see."

Hheilea answered "He used it to fight off vapuc attacks and blaster bolts."

"Wow."

"What's going on about Gursha warning you not to do any vapuc?"

A'idah let out a big sigh and didn't answer for a bit. Finally she said, "Apparently, she's worried about some residual damage from the rabies. It's no big deal. She thinks it could give me some trouble."

"What kind of trouble?"

After another long wait, A'idah answered, "Headaches and..."

"Everyone gets headaches if they do too much vapuc. What else?

"Well, you know our nurse. She's a worrier. Gursha gave me quite the lecture, something about the possibility of hemorrhages."

Both of the girls knew what hemorrhages and overuse of vapuc meant. A'idah was prone to dying if she did too much vapuc.

Chapter Thirty-Six
Awesome Girls

"Oh." For a bit, the two walked quietly together. After stepping up onto a bubble generator, Hheilea asked, "How about I tell you of our adventure with Daren? Alex did some stuff I was pretty furious about, but in the end I had to agree with what he did."

In a subdued tone, A'idah said, "Alex was pretty awesome."

Hheilea wiped at her face. "Yeah, he was."

A'idah nodded. "I would enjoy hearing about your adventure with Alex and Daren. We can travel quietly too, whatever you want."

After a long pause, Hheilea started telling the story. After she finished the part where she'd been climbing after Twarbie, Hheilea paused. "I'm not proud of how I acted. Twarbie dealt with the lack of inhibition much better than I did. This next part, I didn't see. I'd been knocked unconscious by a fall. Daren had been slowly transforming into a monster. It was what The Weird, Twarbie, I, and Alex had been working toward."

"We had gotten all of the ingredients for Daren to make these horrible crystals. As each one grew, the monster he was becoming took them and jammed them into his torso. Each new crystal accelerated the transformation process. All of us were willing for Daren to become a monster, because then Alex would be safe. But Alex, he couldn't accept that result."

A'idah asked, "Why?"

"He explained later how he'd seen Daren, a Deem, had loved life and all kinds of living things as something wonderful. And then, how during the quest and Daren's changes, Daren started hating all other living things as he became more and more the monster Deem. Alex saw how it was wrong to help Daren become a monster. He saw a different path."

A'idah said, "It was one of those things Alex was incredible at. He could see possibilities no one else did, and it didn't matter to him how difficult it was. He would just do the next right thing."

Hheilea nodded her head. "That's exactly what happened. I didn't see much of his fight with Daren, the monster. I, well... I've been told I was still under the influence of the drugs from the planet of the cloud berries. I'm not proud of how I acted, at all. I tried to kill Twarbie."

"What?"

"Yeah. The planet of the cloud berries has many different drugs in its atmosphere. The one that affected me and Twarbie got rid of all of our inhibitions and accented our feelings about Alex. Twarbie dealt with it much better than I did. She was amazing. I almost killed Twarbie."

"What?"

"Yeah. I really snapped after Alex stopped our T'wasn't-to-be-is ceremony." Hheilea blushed in shame at admitting how badly she'd behaved. Swallowing down her anguish at her past actions, she continued the story. She didn't finish, until she saw the fields with Windelli's city. Through the bittersweet feelings from talking about Alex, Hheilea felt something strange about the future, a mystery. She couldn't quite figure it out. Maybe her dad could help her understand what it was.

Hheilea started to message him and then stopped. He probably wouldn't help her with the mystery. He'd been more reticent than normal lately. Instead, she messaged Windelli. |Hello, Windelli. We're at the border in our bubble.|

The response came immediately. |I've been expecting you. You can cross the border.|

The girls moved their shared bubble over the fields. Approaching the city, Hheilea spotted two Tasties standing on the hill waiting for them.

The older Tasty and her granddaughter, Delli, greeted the two teenagers.

Delli gave both of them hugs. "I'm sorry for your pain, but it'll get better. Alex—"

Windelli interrupted her. "Dear, you've gotten to greet them. Now, you should finish your preparations."

"Okay, Grandma." Turning back to the girls, Delli started to say something, but Windelli interrupted her again.

Windelli pointed into the city. "Go now, Delli. No more talking."

The younger Tasty nodded and ran into the city.

The elder turned back to them and said, "Follow me."

Together, they entered the city. After a long, quiet walk down many different tunnels, Windelli stopped at a nondescript, blank wall. Hheilea watched as the Tasty placed her two hand/paws against the wall. At her touch the wall morphed creating an alcove.

Windelli stepped into the opening. "Both of you come up here beside me."

The two girls obeyed and Windelli placed both hands against the wall again. Hheilea had done this before and knew what to expect. She watched A'idah, curious as to how she'd react. The Kalasha girl looked all around and gasped as the opening to the tunnel behind them closed off. The three of them stood crowded, inside a featureless round space only about seven-feet across.

A'idah said, "Wow. Cool."

Hheilea braced herself for the next event. Starting in front of them, a shimmer moved out from the wall. It looked opaque, with an oily sheen. Colors rippled across its surface. She had to stop her instinctive reaction of stepping back from it.

A'idah in a barely controlled voice said, "What is this?"

Windelli and Hheilea both said, "Sorry."

And the Tasty finished with, "We should've told you what to expect. We are shifting sideways into a pocket universe."

"What's that?"

The shimmering had almost reached Hheilea's face.

Windelli answered, "You're familiar with the concept of spacetime fabric?" She didn't wait for an answer, but continued talking. "Imagine if you could gather part of that fabric into a bag. We are moving into a secure bag. It is where The Book of Prophesy is kept."

The shimmer advanced. All Hheilea could see now was blurry waves of colors moving over her eyeballs.

"This is going to hurt."

Zzzap

A'idah screamed, but it came out all garbled.

Hheilea wanted to scream to. She'd never get used to how it hurt, and then they were through.

A door appeared. It opened and Windelli gestured for them to enter. Inside the room, on a large, dark, wooden stand rested the Book of Prophesy. Windelli finally spoke. "There it is. Go ahead, A'idah, and take a look at it."

Hheilea watched her human friend hesitantly step toward the book.

A'idah asked, with a surprising amount of trepidation in her voice. "Can I see the past?"

"Why would you want to see the past? No one ever looks at the book to see the past."

"Oh. I was hoping to see what happened. Why Alex—" The human girl swallowed obviously in distress.

Hheilea stepped over and hugged her, but the human girl pushed her away.

"I'm fine." A'idah looked back at Windelli. "How does the book work? Hheilea told me she knew some of the future because of it. Can I use it to look at the past? I want to know what happened in the worm tunnel. I want to know if I caused Alex to die."

Hheilea gasped in shock at the idea. "No, you shouldn't do that. It wasn't your fault."

"If it wasn't my fault, then it shouldn't be a problem for me to verify what happened."

The older Tasty held a hand up to get their attention. "A'idah, I understand your concern and desire, but you need to consider some other things. First, you are concerned about your part in what happened to Alex. Do you think he would want you to check the past?"

Together, all of them waited in silence for the answer. Hheilea looked in concern at her friend. She started to say something to fill the uncomfortable silence, but caught a signal from Windelli and impatiently held her words back. In the longer, quiet moment, Hheilea began to suspect where the conversation was heading.

A'idah slowly spoke, "He, Alex wouldn't want me to look, but the pain of not knowing and my fear that I caused his death is terrible."

Windelli said, "Do you know why he wouldn't want you to look?"

The Kalasha girl swiped a tear off her cheek. She shook her head.

"Hheilea should know. We all have possible paths to follow. Some have greater possibilities and others lesser possibilities of happening. Right now, you are in pain. I understand and I'm sorry, but I know how tough you are. You can deal with this pain and do what is necessary for the future, but how would you feel if you proved your worst fear?"

Hheilea looked from the Tasty back to the human girl just in time to see A'idah's light complexion turn even paler. She had to lean forward to hear the quiet answer.

"It would crush me."

Windelli nodded her head. "Yes. Would Alex want you to be concerned about the dead or the living?"

A'idah spoke a little stronger. "The living."

"Then do what will help you to live and work to help the others who still live."

A'idah's head came up and she spoke firmly. "You're right. For my friends who still live, it doesn't matter how I've failed in the past. I'll use my feelings to fight harder for those who still live."

Windelli smiled. "That's the wonderful young woman all of us Tasties are amazed by."

A'idah said, "What? No. No. I'm not special."

Hheilea said, "I think you are, and Alex thought so too." She could see her teenage friend fighting for an answer, but then she gave up and instead asked a question.

A'idah asked, "How does the book work?"

Windelli answered, "The book is being created many thousands of years ago by Hheilea's people. Very—"

A'idah interrupted her, "What? Is?" How can it be— I mean it's here now. How can its creation still be happening?

That doesn't make sense. I don't even know how to say it to make any sense."

Windelli said, "The Kimley's are creating it in our future by traveling through time's dimensions. It's very complicated for a non-Kimley to understand. Even I only partially understand. Now, as I was saying before you interrupted. Few outsiders have ever gotten to see it. I am giving you the opportunity to satisfy your curiosity only because of your relationship with Alex. As to how it works, it was created within time with all different futures in superposition. Until those futures are experienced, they are all valid and after they are experienced, some results create new universes with different future possibilities."

The girl stopped walking toward the book and actually stepped back. "What? Now I'm even more confused."

"That's okay. I didn't expect you would understand. The book is open to here and now. Go ahead and look at it."

A'idah's normally strong and confident voice sounded weak and doubting as she said, "I... I wanted to see the past, but I can see how that's a bad idea. I also thought I would get to see the future. So, I could know what to do. I need help. I don't want to make more mistakes."

Hheilea said, "I'm sorry, A'idah. I didn't know your need. I've been taught, and I'm still being taught how to understand the future possibilities. It's very difficult."

Windelli spoke up. "I've spent most of my life studying the book. I've learned to recognize when not to look at a future. For some of us, looking at future possibilities affects those futures and sometimes in disastrous ways."

"Maybe, I shouldn't look then."

Windelli said, "Okay." She turned away from the book back toward the door.

Hheilea agreed. There wasn't much use for her human friend to look. But as she turned to leave, she had another thought. A'idah had come all this way. She should look to satisfy her curiosity, or else later she might think she missed out on something. "Wait, A'idah. I think you should look."

The girl had started to go out the door with Windelli, but at those words she stopped and turned around. "Why?"

"Because we are here, and you thought it would help you. It's better to look, and you'll know it can't help you. There's nothing to be afraid of. Nothing will happen."

A'idah nodded her head and forcefully walked across the floor, stopping at the open book. Quietly, she looked, and her mouth dropped open in surprise. "It's changing as I read it."

"What?" Echoed both Windelli and Hheilea.

The Tasty reached the human girl first. The normally calm Windelli gasped out. "It is."

When Hheilea reached her side all of them gasped. "The book just got bigger."

Indeed it had. The unread future sections of the massive book had gotten thicker. For a moment, both the Tasty and the Kimley were frozen at the thought of something so unusual happening.

A'idah turned some pages and started reading. Immediately, the whole book shifted on its stand.

Windelli grabbed the wooden stand as the whole thing threatened to fall over. "Stop reading! Help me!"

Together, the three of them caught the stand before it fell over. After waiting for a moment to be sure it was stable, they stepped back. Quiet echoed in the room. Hheilea heard her own heart beating wild. She looked at Windelli, but the Tasty just opened and shut her mouth.

A'idah asked in a trembling voice, "What just happened? Did I do something wrong?"

Windelli finally found her voice. "A'idah, you have a great role in deciding the future, and the two of you together have an even greater role. I don't know what this means. Hheilea, when you came up to look at the book with A'idah pages of future possibilities were added, but then when she looked ahead into the future possibilities whole sections of the book were added and others taken away. The shifting weight of the book almost tipped it all over."

Windelli quietly looked at A'idah. "Do you remember anything you read from the future?"

"Not really. The words seemed to be moving and didn't make sense, but I did get feelings. There was something terrible, a big disaster. Something better at the Gadget Lady's mountain, something great, I'll be happy. Can I look at the future again?"

Windelli shook her head. "No. There isn't time to teach you how to avoid looking at possible futures you shouldn't see. I've never done what you just did. If I'd known what would happen, I wouldn't have allowed it. Hheilea, you know what I speak of."

Hheilea looked at her friend. "I already knew you're amazing, but now I..." She shook her head. "Don't tell anyone about this or about what I tell you next. My dad has told me that the near future, the next few months, are terribly important. The events will either save much of the known universe or destroy those living in it."

A'idah's freckles stood out in bold relief on her paler than normal face. "I'm so sorry." She backed up falling down. "I could've just ruined the future."

Windelli spoke firmly. "I don't think so. Hheilea, help her up and take A'idah back to her nurse. Let your father know what happened here. He might have some insight he could share with us. I'm going to try and peek at the future and learn what I can. Please, both of you, be careful, be careful, be careful." With a shaking hand/paw she pointed at the door.

Hheilea led A'idah out, and they returned to Gursha.
The trip back was very quiet. Both girls were busy with their own thoughts.

Chapter Thirty-Seven
What Happened?

A'idah started the next day by going to the Academy Island. She arrived early and having nothing to distract her, thoughts and feelings she didn't want started to well up.

Desperately, A'idah looked around for something to do, to think on, anything. Looking up, her eyes followed one of the three incredible gold, silver, and blue arches of the Academy soaring from the island up high into the sky. The arch reminded her of a bow. Each of the three arches curved in toward each other as if three bows were set to fire arrows at a target in the middle of the three. They just lacked arrows. Resolutely, she committed to being one of the arrows this academy produced. She'd strike true in every situation protecting those she loved. Unbidden and unwanted, the thought of Alex's death rushed back in. He'd been an arrow, but instead of being fired he'd turned to ashes.

Tears flowing down her cheeks, A'idah clenched her teeth and adamantly declared to herself that she and the other students would be the arrows fired to save the people of each of their worlds.

A'idah tipped her head back further to look at the bottom of the sphere shaped Academy up in the clouds, miles above her. She had to blink away the traitorous tears which still rejected her force of will to stop flowing. Through them, she could make out the Academy, the miles wide, pearlescent ball, resting on the arches' three upper curves.

A'idah couldn't wait to rejoin her flock at classes up in the two mile wide sphere. There, she'd learn enough to keep her friends and all of Earth safe. A tear escaped her determination not to think on her heartache and dripped off her jaw.

What Happened?

The view and thoughts of learning couldn't provide her an escape. A'idah thought back to her experience with The Book of Prophesy. What did it mean-she and Hheilea were bound to a common future? Regardless of what it was, she'd find a way to protect the other teenager.

At that thought, A'idah remembered the bigger picture. All life was at risk. Somehow, she had to save the universe. She remembered what Alex had said. A'idah, this is what I love most about you. How you don't care about yourself and are so fierce in defense of everyone else. You're the most wonderful girl I know, but you have to know we can't just float along the river of time letting events happen by time and chance or by other's plans. If we're going to save Earth, we have to learn how to take control of events and make things work out right. We've got to do this.

A tear coursed down her cheek. A'idah ignored the hurt at thinking of Alex, and tried not to think of how their efforts had ended in his death. Even more, she desperately tried to ignore her own questions about his death. The memory of his profession of love warmed her heart and chased away some of the gloom. Trying to take care of problems instead of just letting what would happen, happen, was the right choice. She had to keep moving forward and not drift. That meant making sure the Earthlings got and finished the training they needed to save Earth. At least, the new supply ship would resolve any lingering worries about the Academy being able to give them their training.

At that thought, she realized her own big problem might interfere. She was now thirteen. Some Muslims would insist she choose to live as a Muslim, because her dad had converted to Islam. If she didn't, some, especially those who'd shot her back on Earth would think her father should kill her.

A'idah's hair started to float about her head. She wished someone nearby needed zapping with a lightning bolt. Her face creased with a feral grin at that idea.

If only she could get married, it would possibly solve her problem, but Alex had died. How did it happen? Had she caused it by getting rabies? How could she have been so stupid? Another tear traced a path down her cheek.

A'idah almost shouted aloud her next thought. She was too young to be getting married. Sure, some of her people got married quite young, but she wasn't ready for that step even if Alex still lived. Yet, it was the acts of the creator of Islam who by his actions created her problem. He'd married a girl of only nine-years-old. A'idah scowled and sparks danced on her finger tips. How could someone treat a child that way? The ground shook. Did she hear thunder, and she looked up from her own thoughts to see one of the largest species attending the Academy running away from her.

In concern at the possibility of having accidently zapped him, A'idah breathed deep and slow trying to calm herself. Finally, the sparks stopped dancing, and her hair settled back down.

A voice she recognized and her own name being called caused her to look around. A'idah heard Zeghes. He would know if she.... If she'd caused Alex's.... Quickly, she wiped her face of the tear tracks and any telltale drops.

Zeghes swam toward her. "A'idah! It's good to see you up and around. How are you doing? Are all the sharks in your blood gone?"

Normally, A'idah would've found humor in his *sharks in the blood* question, but she wasn't in a mood for any humor. "I'm fine. Where's everyone else?"

"They're coming. I just hurried ahead."

"Thanks." After taking another calming breath, A'idah asked, "What do you remember about the battle, Alex, our getting out, and getting rescued? I don't remember much of anything. I know I had rabies. It's why I can't remember. I want— I need to know what happened." She anxiously waited for his answer.

Zeghes bumped her with his beak. "You saved my life, even though you had sharks in your blood and controlling your mind. You were amazing. Thanks. Oh look, the rest of the flock is coming. Let's head over to the arrival pads." Not waiting for her reply, Zeghes took off swimming through the air.

For a second, A'idah just stood with mouth open looking after him. He didn't want to talk about it. Breaking into a sprint she hurried after him. "Zeghes, I need to know what happened."

What Happened?

"A'idah, I almost died. I don't remember much."

In the far distance, A'idah spotted the rest of the flock coming. In desperation, she pleaded with her best friend. "Just tell me the last things you know about Alex."

"There isn't time to tell you." As he talked, Zeghes darted over to an arrival pad and shot into the air. "I don't know what I can tell you."

He didn't want to talk to her. With a fist A'idah dashed another tear off her jaw, jumped onto the arrival pad, and shot after him.

Chapter Thirty-Eight
Determinism or Self-Will

Much later in the day, A'idah descended from the Academy. So far, she'd had a horrible day and hadn't been able to concentrate on her lessons. The last class had been a disaster. Spark, the charge class teacher, had scolded her. A'idah had created the chain lightning he'd asked her to, but it had been way too strong. She could've killed someone, but Spark had grounded it out. She cringed at the memory of his words.

"If you don't get yourself under control, you're going to kill someone."

Kill someone echoed in her mind. A'idah remembered her friend who'd died back on Earth and now Alex. She thought, it was too late, she'd already killed someone. That's why Zeghes won't talk to me. Spark's right. She had to control herself.

All day long, Zeghes had refused to talk to A'idah about what happened. Didn't he understand she had to know? Landing on the ground, she stepped off the departure pad and walked after Zeghes no longer trying to hurry for another chance to talk. Hundreds of other students walked past her some arriving and others leaving. Students surrounded her. A'idah let the flow of people change the direction she went. Still, she continued toward the beach.

Didn't anyone see her problems? She needed to know if she'd killed Alex. Her fear of the truth slowed her steps. For the last two days, it had been strangling her. She felt as if she couldn't breathe. A'idah didn't know what to do. Like a mountain, her questions about Alex weighed her down.

Other issues pounded at her. She didn't know about becoming a woman instead of just a little girl. Gursha had

Determinism or Self-Will

helped her with getting pads for her monthly cycle and helped her keep it a secret. Part of A'idah felt the need to follow the practices of her people the Kalasha. If she was back there, she would've been isolating herself from others in the women's Bashali house. It would've been a great time with lots of support from the other women. A'idah appreciated Gursha's help and support, but it just wasn't the same. She missed her people. Old nightmares about the night she'd been shot and her friend dying used to happen often. She'd had one last night. Except instead of her friend, it was Alex, and instead of him getting shot it was A'idah frying him with lightning because he stood in the way of her rabies' needs. People from her past laughed in her mind. She felt impure from her menses. Her people's traditions meant she shouldn't be out and about during menstruation. She shouldn't have been with Alex and Zeghes. She should've made a Bashali and followed her peoples' restrictions.

She wanted to scream or dig a hole in the ground and pull the dirt back over herself.

Osamu sent her an AI message. |I'm not going to the Religion class. I don't see the use. I'll spend the time studying technology.|

A'idah grunted and lifted her eyes from the ground. Her feelings weren't so ambivalent. She hated the Religion classes. Her anger beat back the depression.

The dream homework bothered her, and the classes just gave her more questions. She had to have answers. She felt herded toward a choice between freedom with danger or captivity with safety.

She spat on the ground as memories of different Religion classes intruded. She didn't want to remember the classes with her little friend. It still hurt too much. She choose to remember her last Religion class, two students had argued walking past her. The two human teenagers said the most confusing things to each other. "I told you when I tried to get you to cross, you had already done it and it was safe. You didn't listen to me, but when you tried earlier to convince me to cross, I didn't believe you either."

The other teenager said, "We both should've trusted the other more. What a strange and confusing class."

Behind those teenagers, the open door of the class had quietly beckoned her and unease had gripped her as she followed her flock into the class. It turned out to be a lesson in faith. They had to do various things requiring faith or trust in what couldn't be seen or known. A'idah was encouraged to step down onto a path vaulting a great chasm. The problem was she couldn't see it. She stomped down onto it and attacked all of the examples of faith, except for one. The memory of her little friend snuck up on her.

Its lesson on faith didn't so much sneak up on her. It hit her right between the eyes. The little furry creature with big dark eyes had been in some of her religion class experiences. Those classes took place in the Weird room. The creature had given her food and water, not much, it couldn't carry much, but it loved her and always, always she felt better when it appeared. She would never forget the lesson it taught her, even though the memory hurt. Her feelings were still mixed up about the experience. At the end of one class about faith, the little creature begged her to kill it. It held a small crystalline knife in a paw. Again she heard its voice. "Please kill me."

"What!" A'idah had yelled.

"You have come to love me, if you really love me, trust my request."

A'idah had backed up, hands out in front of her as if to ward off the request. "This is crazy."

"No. Not crazy. It is part of your learning about faith, but it's also about me and how all of my species is. You have shown me that you love me a little, now show you love me a lot by doing this."

A'idah said, "I can't. I can't kill someone I love."

The argument had raged on. A'idah angry, hurt, and confused, but the little creature patient, soft, and very persistent. Somehow the knife ended up in A'idah's fingers and then she had thrust it into the sweet, warm little creature she loved. Blood poured out and its eyes shut. A'idah shut her eyes too. Sobs racked her body. Eventually a mewing, many quiet voices, soft words, A'idah dropped her hands from her burning eyes. On the floor in front of her where her dead friend had been, many, many small furry bodies wriggled. She hated the

Determinism or Self-Will

Weird room experiences. Later she had read about the very strange creature. It needed to be killed, in faith, by someone who loved it and didn't know how new life could come from death. The experience hurt, frightened, and confused her. She never understood if it was just real in the Weird room or real somewhere else in the crazy universe.

Never again would she let herself get forced into killing someone she loved, but it had opened her eyes to a better understanding of faith. She understood. Sometimes faith means you do things you don't want to, you no longer feel will make a difference, or you don't do things you want to all in faith. She understood faith had many, many, many other examples, both good and bad. Still, she hated how she'd gotten those understandings. Never again would she be forced to kill someone she loved. She wouldn't do it ever again.

She hated the classes. "I just want answers!"

Stumbling on a rock, she returned to the present and looked at the beach. When she recognized a two-headed person throwing rocks out into the line of breakers, she stood still in shock at having yelled out loud. Still, she'd never, ever again kill someone she loved.

The bald head turned toward her. "I agree with you. We want answers."

The orange haired head asked, "Where is the rest of your flock?"

Embarrassed, A'idah didn't answer. She recognized the one with a beard as Tease. Just when she remembered the other was called Socra, she heard Zeghes from down by the water.

"Ekbal is almost here. Sabu and Skyler are on their way. I don't know where Osamu is."

A'idah said, "Osamu isn't coming."

Socra said, "Okay. Are you ready for the Religion class to start?"

"I'm ready," Zeghes said.

A'idah looked around. "Where's the teacher?"

"I'm the teacher," Tease said.

Socra poked Tease in the nose. "He doesn't know anything. I'm the teacher."

A'idah ground her teeth. A word came out of her mouth as if she was spitting chewed up gravel. "Teacher?"

Tease stopped pulling Socra's ear. "Why do you ask?"

A'idah screamed the word. "Ask! That's it! All you do is ask questions! I need answers!

Tears began to flow down her cheeks. The angry words killed by the pain in her heart were replaced by quiet pleas. "I might be responsible for my, my best friend's death. Yet, I can't let that stop me from doing what I need to do, but I need to know what happened. Even though, that might interfere with my ability to continue on."

A'idah knew she wasn't being logical. She remembered how the two philosophers had helped her to know her core the last time they'd talked. Hope they could help again bubbled all of her problems up and out. "I want to follow my heart." Speaking those words about her freedom to choose also reminded A'idah of her heart's song for Alex. It felt as if someone had ripped her heart out of her chest. Alex and her love for him had given her hope and a song of joy in her heart, but now he was dead.

She fell to her knees. Still quieter, she said, "He's gone." Stubbornly, she got back to her feet and forced out other true words. "I've felt a response to how others live. I can see opportunities of hope, joy, and of living my life free from fear."

With a fist, she dashed the tears from her face. It felt like a stone sank into her belly. The hardness of her pain swiped the soft words away to be replaced by bitterness and anguish. "Some say I am Muslim. And that I must choose to live as a Muslim."

With eyes full of unshed tears, Socra said, "We knew Alex. We talked to him once. You have our sympathy. Who are those who would force you to live a certain way?"

"They're the Muslims who live around my father. They say because my father converted to Islam, I'm a Muslim. They say if when I'm no longer a child, I don't choose to be a Muslim, I must be killed. What do I do?"

Zeghes said, "That's terrible. Not even our prophet, Heyeze, tried to force other dolphins to believe in him. Why would Muslims do that?"

Skyler must've flown up. He said, "It's—."

Determinism or Self-Will

Another voice interrupted him. "Hello. Our AI just informed us we were supposed to be here for a joint Religion class. Are we late?"

A'idah recognized the speaker as Peter. The rest of his flock hurried after him.

The Palestinian boy, curly black hair bouncing, ran past Peter. "A'idah, peace be upon you. I heard about your brother, Alex, dying. You have my sympathy, but be reassured about our future. I know we will be fine. The Earth is in Allah's hands and will be safe."

Socra asked, "How can you know Earth will be safe?"

The Palestinian boy said, "Because Muhammad peace be upon him said how the world would end. It is not by an invasion of Deems."

Tease stroked his beard. "How do you know what Muhammad said is true?"

The boy said, "There is no god but Allah. Muhammad is the messenger of Allah."

Socra rubbed his fists into his eyes. "How do you know Allah is the one and only god?"

"Because Muhammad said so," The boy said, "and through Muhammad, Allah declared him to be his prophet."

Tease nodded his head and said to the boy, "You and I are caught in two spins."

The boy frowned. "What do you mean a spin?"

Wings flapping, Skyler circled. "I know. I know. A spin is something that will continue as long as you do something."

"I don't understand." The boy said.

Socra said, "You know Muhammad is a prophet. Because you know it, what he said reinforces your belief that he is a prophet. I and Tease do not know something because we don't know it or because, we don't have faith."

Scowling, Peter said, "You're using the old atheist idea that people believe in God because their belief is self-fulfilling."

Tease shook his head. "Do you know what free will is?"

"What does free will have to do with what you said?" Peter asked.

Socra held a hand in front of his eyes. "Can you see where someone is trying to lead you in a forest if you don't look and try to follow?"

317

Peter looked at the two philosophers. After a moment, a rueful smile replaced the scowl. "Okay. I'll try and see where Tease is leading. Free will is the freedom to act according to one's self-determined motives free from determinism."

Tease asked, "Is self-fulfilling a form of determinism?"

Peter answered quickly. "Yes. You're saying that because he believes, then he believes."

Tease held a hand up. "You are missing the free will part. If you are in the spin due to free will then you're still free from determinism. Consider this question. If you never execute free will, do you have free will? If you are in a spin not by your free will, you are not free from determinism."

Peter scratched his head and said. "I...." Then he stopped.

Socra asked, "Does anyone know the spin I'm in concerning God?"

Everyone looked at Peter. Moments passed and he stood with his head down. Slowly he lifted his head. "I remember your pain, from when we were one. You don't know if there's a God and every time something draws you toward the idea of God being real, maybe even an experience that speaks of God reaching out to you, you react by questioning and never accepting. Therefore, you continue to reinforce your lack of faith. You actually fear to take a step in faith and never gain the knowledge faith gives. You trust your knowledge or lack of knowledge. You're stuck in determinism not able to use freewill."

"Yes, but there's more. My people and I, we all love logic. Yet we know it is illogical to not take the best option. When there is a choice between hope and no hope. The logical choice is good hope. We ignore the good logic.

Tears rolled down both of Tease and Socra's faces and he continued. "I can't choose to take a step or not take a step of faith and thus we continue to know we don't know. I'm stuck in my fear of what I don't understand. The worst of it is we do know that sometimes one has to choose to take a step in faith. The Religion class you had where each of you stood on a ledge and had to take a step out into the air to get to safety. Many of you had trouble with that class. We can't take the first step of faith that will give us the knowledge it is safe. We also know you can't rule out the impossible, because you never know

Determinism or Self-Will

when an assumption about what was possible might turn out, in this universe, to be false. Thus even atheists are either stuck in determinism or they too believe by faith. We are your lesson for today. Sometimes, you can't find the answer and have to take a step in faith to proceed."

Socra and Tease walked over to A'idah. "You are close to finding your answers. Go to the Mullahs at the Academy. They answer questions, but remember today's two lessons. The first is important to us of exercising free will or accepting determinism. The second lesson is important for you. Sometimes, you can't find the answer and have to take a step in faith to proceed."

A'idah didn't want to accept the wisdom of his words. "I don't have a problem with taking a step in faith."

Zeghes made a noise, but A'idah didn't get the translation. Had he just laughed at her?

Tease said, "You've been having trouble with one very important lesson about faith. Remember the little creature that begged you to kill it in faith?"

She did. How could she forget the terrible experience? Never again would she allow herself to be put in that situation. Her indignation, hurt, and anger stormed out of her. "I'll never kill someone who asks like that again. I complained about that lesson to Amable. It was wrong. I'll never ever kill someone I care for again."

Zeghes changed the topic by asking, "Socra and Tease, I've been wondering how are two people—"

Socra nodded his head, "One? A valid question."

Tease said, "Our people used to look not unlike the humans of your world, but long ago a conjoined twin was born."

Socra said, "When two babies start forming too close to each other their cells can get mixed together."

Tease added, "How much do you want to know?"

Ekbal walked up. "I've wondered about this too."

Skyler laboriously lifted into the air. "I'm so hungry. We missed lunch and dinner time is coming."

Zeghes said, "Wait. This is interesting."

Socra said, "To know? We can't know everything."

Tease said, "The short of it is, if the cells join at the right time, they will mix and match to make a new whole. It was a miracle. They were just like me, except they had a peace no one had ever known."

Socra said, "From then on, all of us wanted to be just like that miracle. So, we employ some science and make our own miracle babies."

Tease said, "Now, we're all miracles, and still none of us believe in God, but we want to have the peace they did. They left one message that none of us have been able to use. Life has many choices. Each one makes new possibilities."

Zeghes spoke-up, "To bad Osamu missed this class. He would've liked it."

Ekbal said, "What? He doesn't believe in God. Why do you think he would've liked it?"

"Because he believes in finding value anywhere it is. He would be able to see the value in considering how each choice we make now affects choices available to us tomorrow. I've asked him, and he said the nonexistence of God can't be proven. He refuses to deny what he can't prove."

A'idah considered her friend's words. It reminded her of the advice she'd been given about not worrying about the past. If she focused on the past, it could negatively affect her choices for the future. Somehow she had to let go of what had happened. She snorted at herself. She couldn't let go of how her raped friend had died. In sudden realization, A'idah knew what to do. She'd made the earlier death into a driving force to help her do what she could for others. She'd have to do the same with Alex's death. It would be want he wanted. At that, A'idah realized she had to find a way to get a String Sword. Maybe Amable could help her or... Osamu. |Osamu, I need to finish Alex's quest for a String Sword.|

He responded quickly. |What? Yes. Of course. I am working on something related to that very thing. I will talk to you tonight.|

|Great, thanks.|

|You are welcome.|

Socra said, "I'm hungry."

Tease said, "Class is over."

Determinism or Self-Will

A'idah had heard the complaints of her own stomach. "Okay, Skyler. Eating might make us all feel better." She felt not only hungry, but depressed and didn't feel like doing anything. Maybe the food would help with that too.

Other voices chimed in. "Good idea."

"We all need to eat."

Ekbal said, "But I wanted to understand better."

A'idah glanced at the mix of humans and animals. None seemed to be in a hurry. It was as if they were depressed too. She had good cause to be depressed, but what was affecting everyone? |Zeghes, Osamu said he's working on something related to getting a new String Sword. Do you have any idea what he's up to?|

No reply came and she looked around. A'idah spotted her friend heading off toward the mountain.

A reply finally came from Zeghes. |I don't know. I'll see you later. I'm going to check up on Osamu.|

At the message from her dolphin brother, she felt a desire to go with him. He might need help. Before she could find the energy to go, A'idah saw Ekbal looking after the dolphin and then following. With a sigh of relief, she relinquished her thoughts of going and gave in to the general air of malaise.

Skyler called from a rock. "Hurry up. The flock should stay together. I think we all need to eat. None of you have any life."

The idea of eating seemed like a good choice to A'idah.

Chapter Thirty-Nine
Choosing

Later, as they floated in bubbles traveling back to their dorms to eat. A'idah tried to take a nap. Lying on the flat floor of her bubble, all she could do was toss and turn. She tried relaxing by watching the sea passing below her, but a gnawing sense of something disastrous ate at her, ruining the view and her attempt to rest.

A message from Hheilea further interrupted those attempts. |Where are you, A'idah?|

|I'm heading back across the sea to eat. Before long, I'll be arriving at Earth's dorms. What's up?|

|There's a couple of problems I need to talk with you about.|

|Okay, this is a good time for me.|

|No. AI messaging isn't secure enough. Where can I meet you at your dorm?|

|I'll be eating dinner right after I arrive. Afterwards, I'll go to my dorm room.|

|Good. I'll see you soon.|

Arriving at the dorms and getting food didn't help A'idah feel any better. She pushed her food around on her plate. The words of Socra and Tease kept coming back to her. It felt like she was stuck in the determinism situation letting something else chose her future.

A'idah hated that idea. She remembered how Alex said they couldn't just float along the river of time. She glanced toward the entrance hoping to see Hheilea. When A'idah looked, she noticed the others. Skyler stood on a perch ripping out some more feathers. The Palestinian boy cast scowls at his plate of food. Sabu paced ears back against her skull. What was going on with everyone?

A'idah took in the rest of the room. At other tables and perches Earthlings moped. What was causing the mass depression? Frustration bloomed at herself and the others. She'd been letting her thoughts about being responsible for Alex's death torment her. She had to let it go and get on with her training. Everyone had vapuc practice to do. They had to keep believing in their efforts or else— The thought of what would happen if the Earthlings failed at their training was too painful to consider. A'idah wanted to stand up and shout at everyone, but couldn't. She felt trapped in the current of time waiting to see what would happen next.

Life was too important to act this way. Alex would be furious at her. She kept getting more upset with herself, and yet she did nothing. Movement by the entrance caught her eyes. A figure wearing white pantaloons and shirt with a bright green vest stepped into the room and stood looking around. A'idah waved a hand and shouted. "Over here."

Hheilea waved back and forged her way through the despondent groups of Earthlings. A'idah turned to the Palestinian boy and said, "Help me make the table bigger."

Both of them grasped the round table by the edge and pulled. The table responded by stretching to double its original size.

Hheilea closed the space between them. "How's your day going?"

"Great." The gloom surged back. "Okay, not so great. I understand my feelings." The questions of how Alex had died and what she should do weighed on her spirit and hindered her from doing anything. A'idah waved her hand. "But look at everyone else. It's as if we're all waiting for some impending doom to strike."

Hheilea shook her head in agreement as she reached their table. "I know. You Earthlings need to be getting things done, but everyone's moving at half speed and not getting anything done. I'm afraid it's the subconscious result of the feeling vapuc. How about you? Have you made any progress about solving your problem?"

A'idah frowned. The feeling vapuc? That was about sensing the future. That would explain her feeling of impending doom. What was it? "No. Socra and Tease said I should go see the Grand Imam of the Academy. But my trying to make the right decision about my beliefs just seems so hopeless."

Hheilea moved closer and grasped A'idah's hand. "Remember what those two women told us about hope being available for all if we are just willing to accept it. Being stuck in indecision is like standing still in the path of an onrushing Deem. You have to make a decision. Standing still is a certain recipe for disaster."

"I know," A'idah said. She hated the idea of not doing anything. Again, she remembered the terrible idea of determinism. Letting time and events control her life grated against her normal nature. She really did want to take back control of her life. What was it called, *freewill*? That was what Alex had warned her about. They had to take control of events.

"Let's go and see the Imam then. Come on. I'll go with you," Hheilea said.

A'idah angrily jerked herself to her feet knocking over her chair. "You're right. I'm being stupid. Let's go."

The Palestinian boy jumped to his feet. "I'll go with you. I know the quickest way to get to the Imam. I've already talked to him."

A'idah's anger acted as a spark lighting up the Earthlings. They stopped bowing to the depression. Skyler burst into the air, scattering uneaten nuts. "I'm going to go practice moving the square boulders. Come on, Sabu. We can make a game out of training."

The group surged toward the door. A'idah could see other Earthlings looking up as the cluster of friends surged past. Other groups stood up. She pumped her arm into the air and shouted encouraging words to all. "We're Earthlings, and we don't give up!"

Leaving the cafeteria, A'idah thought of Alex. He wouldn't want her to give up. She agreed. Life was too precious. She charged across the grass and onto the bubble platform. Hheilea stopped A'idah from stepping into a yellow circle. "Let's ride in a bubble together. Then we can talk privately."

Choosing

A'idah said, "Great idea." What did Hheilea want to talk about? She remembered her comment about the feeling vapuc. What was going to happen?

The girls followed the Palestinian boy over the sea. A'idah wanted to ask Hheilea about the future, but at the same time she didn't want to know. Hheilea kept quiet, except for answering questions in short sentences. At first, this just puzzled A'idah. She thought Hheilea wanted to talk. Getting annoyed, A'idah stared at Hheilea even though part of her annoyance was at her own fear of the future. Hheilea looked anywhere except at A'idah.

A'idah grasped Hheilea's head and forced her friend to look at her. Tears began to trickle down Hheilea's cheeks. A'idah dropped her hands. "What's wrong? You ask me to ride with you so we can talk. Yet, you don't talk, and now you're crying? Is it about Alex?" A'idah feared it was news of how he'd died. Adamantly, she refused to bow to the fear. Why would Hheilea know about that, and why would she bring it up?

"No. Sorry. Now that we're together, it's still just hard for me to talk about either thing."

A'idah bit off an angry retort and sat waiting with her mouth held firmly shut.

Hheilea took a deep breath and said, "I'll start with the easiest thing. This is going to be terrible news for you, but I've been looking at the future with my dad. He can help me go into time and see possible futures. There is one coming that is very sure to happen. Telling you won't make any difference in the outcome, but as a friend I'm glad I can warn you. It's also probably why all of you Earthlings are feeling so depressed."

"What? What's going to happen?" A'idah didn't need more problems.

"The supply ship isn't going to make it. A pirate fleet is attacking it, and they'll take the ship and all of the supplies. This is going to be a terrible blow to the Academy. Earth's training is going to get canceled."

"No!" The denial burst out of A'idah. "No!" The news again brought back to her Alex's words about how they couldn't just react to problems. If they were going to succeed and survive, they would need to be figuring out stuff and taking action to prevent trouble. Her cruiser.... She should've— "My cruiser. Is there any way I could send it to rescue the supply ship?"

"No, it's too late."

"But—"

"A'idah, do you trust me?"

A'idah started to say of course, but thoughts stopped her. She denied them and said, "Of course I trust you. You have my promise. I'll always trust you."

The alien girl nodded her head. "Good, there was an alternative future where you tried to save it. If I'd told you about the supply ship problem sooner, you would've left to save it. That future path ended in a worse disaster. My dad made sure I wouldn't tell you about using your cruiser. Also, there are many things he's not showing me. At first, I didn't notice, but when I asked if there's anything the Earthlings could do. Dad said there is, but he couldn't show me. Afterwards, I started to realize he's been hiding many things from me. There's an event happening very soon which will have huge repercussions. I asked to look at it, and Dad said no. I asked to look at different possible future paths which cascade in a series after it. He said no. My Dad's keeping at least one huge secret from me. I've got my suspicions, but if the big one I'm hoping and praying for is right, I shouldn't share it with anyone, especially you."

The first part of the answer angered A'idah, but the talk about different futures which cascade in a series left her confused. Out of the confusion, she pounced onto the idea of having something big to hope for. A'idah stared at the older teenager's face trying to read the secret hope. Hheilea's eyes were glistening and her mouth struggled with a tremulous smile. At the sight of a tear escaping from the violet eyes, A'idah gasped. Her own eyes and mouth opened wide. It couldn't be, but, but, but. "Is—"

Hheilea held her hand up. "We can't talk about it. Just hope, and if you believe in a God, pray. The other thing I need... to—"

A'idah stared at her. Emotions swirled. She'd pray. She'd pray. She would pray. The training getting canceled was the worst possible news. It would mean the death of every living thing back on Earth. With her cruiser, she could save her dad, her grandma, and — A'idah fought down her panic from that line of thought, but now Hheilea just looked at her. What other news could be so bad Hheilea couldn't bring herself to talk about it?

They'd already suffered from the loss of Alex, but now new hope made her heart beat with less pain. Yet, that old pain felt altogether too fresh like a partially healed wound ripped back open. A'idah closed her eyes trying to control the pain. She swallowed back the tears. She wouldn't lose control.

Hheilea hesitantly began talking again.

At first, A'idah appreciated the distraction from her own agony.

With a very subdued and hesitant voice, Hheilea said, "Your friend... who died.... You almost died trying to save her."

"I wish I had saved her even if it meant I died doing it." A traitorous tear broke from her eye to course down her cheek. A'idah looked at Hheilea. Her friend's face was flushed, and she dropped her eyes unwilling to meet A'idah's gaze. Tears again dripped off her friend's face.

A'idah remembered the first time she learned of Hheilea's true identity and the danger the Kimley girl lived with. The memory clenched her fists. She'd meant what she'd said. She wouldn't let anyone hurt Hheilea. This time she'd— A suspicion began to grow in her mind. "Are you worried about what I'll do to try and save you?"

Hheilea vigorously nodded her head up and down. Tears flew off her cheeks to land on the wall of the bubble and course down the sides. "My dad said I needed to talk to you. He said...." Tears and a sob interfered with her efforts to talk.

A'idah took Hheilea in her arms and held her close. Fiercely she spoke. "I failed to save my other friend and almost died. If I fail to save you, I don't want to almost give my life in the effort. I will save you."

"Why?"

Knocking a tear off her own cheek with a fist, A'idah answered. "I am free to decide what I do. I chose to save my friend, and now I choose to save you. If I fail again, it will be too much. If you can't succeed, what's the use of being free to choose?" A'idah held the smaller girl, the woman, tight to her. "I'd gladly die to save you."

Hheilea cried harder. Another thought hit A'idah. This one staggered her. She had to get her breathe back before she could talk. "Uhmmm. If your dad can talk to you about the future.... Why can't *he* keep you safe?" Then she wouldn't have to risk dying. She and Zeghes would find a way to save Hheilea, but what if it meant A'idah would die? She had this new hope, this possible chance for happiness. She didn't want to die, especially not now. Losing Alex had been agony, but now there was new hope, and yet she wouldn't be able to have that love. A deeper agony than she'd ever known threatened to rip her apart.

Hheilea struggled for composure. Finally, swallowing and breathing hard, she faced A'idah. "That's the crux of the problem. Dad's been having me do things to help a very difficult future path of time work out and... and... he said you have a huge part. I asked him why and he said it's the difference for life or death all across the universe." Hheilea continued to move her mouth, but no more words came out.

A'idah wanted to scream, say what I have to do. Instead, she fought against her own nature and stared into her friend's face demanding with her silence for Hheilea to speak. But A'idah begged that her friend wouldn't say she had to die. She didn't want to die, especially not now. She wanted to scream. She'd been given me a new hope and now her heart was getting crushed.

More tears ran down Hheilea's face and the words finally escaped. "You might have to die."

A'idah relaxed her hug. She couldn't commit suicide. It went against everything she believed in. Slowly, her arms slipped from around Hheilea. "Well... I... If it's necessary to save all life, I could just jump off some high place. Maybe the top of the Academy." No, no, no.

Hheilea spoke adamantly, "No. Suicide is wrong. I would never ask you to do that."

A'idah said, "Good, I was joking about the jumping thing. I couldn't do that. The gift of life is too precious."

Hheilea continued in softer tones, "My dad said you're going to have a terrible struggle. You'll be doing it because— He said you won't recognize it as death, but gladly charge into it."

Choosing

A'idah grinned and hugged Hheilea again. "I like that, charging into the breach without a worry of death." She had always wanted to have another chance for her old friend on Earth. This felt good, like going back to that old battle, but this time winning. And yet, what about her father, grandma, and this new hope? If Hheilea really didn't have to get married, then he'd be free. She didn't want to die. An ear to ear grin covered A'idah's face. She jumped to her feet and thrust her fist into the air. "Yes! I'm doing it twice. I tried to do it for my friend on Earth, but failed. This time I'm going to succeed." She couldn't just commit suicide. What would she do? She needed to talk to her best friend.

Hheilea sat on the floor staring up at A'idah. "You're amazing. I could never have that kind of spirit."

A'idah sat down beside Hheilea and slugged her on the shoulder. "I don't know, maybe I'll rub off on you. From what I know of you, I think you're as brave as I am." As A'idah said it, she tried to squelch her self-doubts. Who encouraged her? How could she do this? It wasn't soon. Maybe events would change this possible future. Hheilea had said she might have to die, not that she would.

A'idah watched in envy as Hheilea with her difficult message finally delivered sighed and obviously relaxed. The human teenager gazed out the walls of the bubble trying to find some calm. With different thoughts and fears chasing around in her mind, A'idah didn't pay attention to the rest of the journey.

Within the City Under the Sea, the Palestinian boy stopped briefly at a doorway and broke the silence. "This is where the Grand Imam lives."

Passing through the doorway, A'idah stopped. In front of her, a huge double door blocked their way. Her eyes traveled up the wall. Above and to the side minarets pierced a sky. "What's going on?" She asked.

"We're inside a story box scene. Remember the toy which creates virtual stories? This is a representation of a real mosque." The Palestinian boy pointed to a shoe shelf containing two sets of shoes. "We take off our shoes before we enter. Place them in a shelf."

A'idah followed behind Hheilea and the boy as they entered the big double doors. Pillars pulled her eyes up toward the domed ceiling. The Palestinian boy's words drew her gaze back down.

"Allah's peace be upon you," he said to two men one standing and the older sitting in front of them.

The older man, with a trimmed gray beard answered, "And God's peace be upon you. Is this A'idah?"

A'idah pushed past everyone. "I'm A'idah. I grew up as a Kalasha girl. While I was still a girl, my father converted to Islam. What would my status be as a girl who has not had her first menses?

The older man smiled at A'idah. "You have the spirit of Nusayba. May you also defend Muhammad. God's peace and blessings be upon him. Others have already asked about your situation for you. And I say to you what I said to them. It is not your menses alone that shows your maturity for the commitment to observe prayer and fasting as a Muslim. Allah Almighty says to prove orphans till they reach the marriageable age. If you then find them of sound judgment, deliver them over unto their fortune. This is a ruling from An-Nisa. I would not force you to follow your father's beliefs, but encourage you to consider the results of your choices as you learn sound judgment. In this, I am supported by other previous fatwas such as one by Muhammad 'Ali Al-Hanooti back on Earth. May Allah guide us all to the straight path and direct us to that which pleases Him Amen."

The younger man coughed and everyone looked at him. "My esteemed father gives you the best answer he can, but I say you are already over nine lunar years old. Yes?"

A'idah felt a chill run down her spine. "Yes."

The man nodded, his hair fell forward and back. "Then by the example of Muhammad marrying a nine year old woman, God's peace and blessings be upon him, you have reached the age of Taklig and are mature. If you're not living as a Muslim you're an Apostate. Here we don't kill Apostates, but on this last part my father and I agree. When you return to Earth you'll face those who will believe if you are an Apostate you should be punished by death."

Choosing

There it was. Anger at his words rose, pushing bitter thoughts and words to her lips.

Hheilea interrupted the unspoken tirade with a message. |A'idah, I'm uncertain about what to do. From what I understand about humans, this young man is saying terrible things. From what I've learned from you and Alex what this man is saying is wrong. This fool is talking about a man marrying a human girl of only nine. Am I wrong?|

|Hheilea we need to get out of here before I cause trouble. You're right, but violence won't solve this problem. I've made my decision. I won't be forced to be what I don't want.| At the same time, she thought about circumstances and the future conspiring against her. Both were saying she needed to die to save all life in the universe. Part of her rebelled against dying. A'idah wanted to live. At the same time, she knew herself. She truly would die for a friend, so why not all life.

Hheilea responded. |Okay. We better go. I'm also afraid of doing or saying the wrong thing. Will you be okay?|

|I'll be fine, but could you help me with the Palestinian boy. He's brainwashed by his religion, and I don't think a conversation between him and me would be good right now. Can you believe he thinks Muhammad was perfect in everything including this marriage?|

|Okay. Let's get out of here.|

The rest of the visit passed as a blur for A'idah. She remembered saying, "Thank you," but she didn't know how she managed to lie.

On the way up to the surface, Hheilea and A'idah managed to travel alone. Hheilea asked, "Did that help?"

A'idah looked at her. Bitterly, she said, "No." Without thinking she added, "It was bad timing coming after you talked to me." Immediately, she regretted her words. At Hheilea's stricken expression she bit her tongue. She's going to think I'm upset with her. After a long moment of uncomfortable silence, A'idah spoke again. She didn't want Hheilea to think she was unwilling for the cost of saving her and all life. This time, A'idah tried to control her emotions and considered what to say. "I should've said, yes and no. Back on Earth, if I don't continue as a Muslim, it will be horrible for myself and my dad. If I die here saving you, I'll be dying as a martyr. Also, I'll be dying true to the peace and joy I've found. I'll deal with returning to Earth when and if that happens."

Silence stretched out between them. A'idah hoped these words were better.

Finally, Hheilea asked, "What do your people the Kalasha believe in?"

A'idah said, "The religion of my people's very different from Islam. You might think my people are superstitious. The one supreme God they sort of believe in is one they are ignorant of and don't really attempt to worship.

"I think most of us stumble through life not understanding. At the hospital, I used to think the nurses were horrible, but now, I think they didn't know I could hear and didn't understand my loneliness. Once, I had a really nice nurse. She told me about a statue for a Muslim war heroine, and said I was similar to that heroine, having been shot, except I'd survived. She said to be brave like Noor Khan. It was a nice thought, but very frustrating that everyone presumed as a Pakistani I was a Muslim."

An AI message blared at A'idah. |All Earthlings need to come to the Academy Island.|

Chapter Forty
Tested and Tried

A'idah stopped talking. A sense of terrible doom weighed on her mind. She could only think of one thing. The summons, the depression all the Earthlings had been dealing with, and the warning from Hheilea could only have one meaning. They were going to be told bad news.

Angry at the news and her depression, A'idah messaged Twarbie. |Twarbie, do you have my cruiser figured out?| Asking the question about *her* cruiser gave her a thrill. She wasn't going to take this news lying down.

|Hello, A'idah. I've talked to your ship's AI, and it shouldn't be too difficult for you to use it. Most of the ship's systems are automated. There is a crew who live on the ship. They're similar to the Zorms on the Coratory. You'll like this. Your cruiser is a fighting ship. It also has a fleet of AI controlled fighters and a different fleet of UAV fighters. Sorry, I haven't sent you a report sooner. I've been learning how to use the UAVs. I think I could get good at it, but I had to stop because of hallucinations I'm starting to have. I almost killed a sky whale.|

Parts of the message A'idah didn't understand, but the news it shouldn't be too difficult to use made her grin. She didn't have a clue about Zorms, and at the phrase *fighting ship* A'idah pumped a fist into the air. What was a UAV? Hallucinations?

|How are you doing? How long do you have?|

|Gursha's been helping me keep the worst at bay, but— I'll be okay. Do what you need to do.|

At those words, A'idah groaned.

It seemed to take forever to reach the surface. Hheilea finally broke the silence. "The Sea Flowers travel much slower since their poisoning. I'm glad none of them died."

A'idah said, "All Earthlings have received a summons. It must be the bad news you told me about. I don't think I want to go hear the news."

Hheilea responded. "Remember what I told you about possible good news. Don't give up."

The teenage girl looked back at her friend. What? Why was she talking about it? The hope? Wasn't it— A terrible thought, but one A'idah recognized as making sense even as she hated how it made sense. The more important thing to hope for... would be for the Earthlings' training. There must still be some kind of a chance of us. Finally, the Sea Flower bobbed to the surface and opened its petals. Climbing out onto the island, A'idah clenched her jaw and hoped for the better choice even as a tear ran down her cheek.

One of the terrible, little Lepercauls ran past her. What was he in such a hurry for? A'idah wondered if it could be Titan. She couldn't tell them apart. All of them wore the same green clothing and had beards. She needed to respond to the summons, but turned back curious about what the little person's hurry had been. He was going toward Hheilea.

A'idah ran back. She worried about Hheilea's safety. Maybe the little terror— In shock, she saw her Kimley friend wave the Lepercaul over. The two of them ducked behind a rock. What was going on? She hurried closer.

Their voices wafted over the rock and A'idah gasped at what she heard. The shock of the words froze her in place.

The gruff voice of a lepercaul said, "This is the event you warned me about?"

"Yes, Titan. The Winkles, your allies won't help you defeat the humans. It will all be up to you."

"I don't need any help to defeat those wimps. I'll go to the spot I've picked out, and it'll be a piece of cake to beat them."

Confusion, horror, and anger swirled inside A'idah. She'd just heard Hheilea helping Titan, giving him advice to beat the humans. How could she?

It was as if someone had just told her up was down.

Tested and Tried

Zeghes' message cut through her emotions. |A'idah, where are you?|

|I'm...| She couldn't respond anymore.

Zeghes messaged. |I see you. Aren't you coming to the summons?|

|I'm coming.| A'idah had to do the next right thing, regardless of what happened around her. First though, she was going to confront Hheilea. Hurrying around the rock, she said, "What are you—" She stopped speaking. There wasn't anyone there. Where had they gone?

Questions and anger swirled through her. A'idah gave herself a shake. Those would have to wait. She needed to do the next right thing. But when she saw Hheilea next time— A'idah forced herself to walk toward a large group of other Earthlings. She'd better contact Gursha and see what she thought about Twarbie's condition. |Gursha, how's your treatment of Twarbie going?|

|I've held it at bay some, but I was going to contact you after this horrible meeting. Twarbie needs to leave today. She told me she's been having some hallucinations, but she could deal with them. Her mother had a meeting with me today and told me the truth. Even leaving now might be too late. I don't know how fast your cruiser is. I want you to be careful at this meeting. I don't know for sure what's going to happen, but Stick shared an idea with me. Don't overdo your use of vapuc. I'd really rather you don't do any vapuc at all. Your brain isn't healed yet and you're more susceptible to injury or death from overdoing it. Promise me, at the least symptoms of a headache you'll stop using vapuc.|

A'idah tried to respond.

Her AI answered her attempt. *The messaging system is getting overwhelmed. I can't get through.*

Why would she need to use vapuc? What was happening? A group of tall thrips amongst the Earthlings caught her attention. In amongst the other thrips, she spotted the dark-blue feathers of Ytell. Bubbles carried other Earthlings from across the sea. Thousands of aliens of all kinds descended from the Academy swelling the size of the crowd. A'idah wondered how the aliens heard about something happening. Maybe they sensed it like she had.

A message broke into her thoughts. |A'idah, this is Osamu. Where are you?|

|I just arrived. Do you know what's going on?|

Osamu's reply confirmed the terrible news. |Ytell says the flock leaders were trying to hold this off until tomorrow, but Amable has insisted on having an announcement concerning something really bad. Ytell won't tell—| The message broke off.

Again her AI told her that the messaging system was having trouble.

At the news from Osamu, A'idah came to a stop.

Hheilea touched her on the shoulder. "It's the news I told you about. Isn't it?"

A'idah felt light headed. Conflicting desires ripped at her. This so called friend had been conspiring with Titan. The anger bubbled up in her voice. "Yeah. I think so. Aren't they even going to let us try and pass the test?"

Hheilea threw her arms around A'idah. "Be strong. There's a way through all of this trouble. It's a narrow way and very dangerous."

Confused and frustrated, A'idah didn't hug her back. Instead, she pushed her away. She didn't tell me this before. "What do you mean? What else is going to happen?" She wanted to ask her about Titan, but was afraid of the answer.

"Trust me. Just don't give up. Remember to have hope. You need to decide what you believe. It will give you the strength to do what you need to do. Just be yourself."

Trust her!? A'idah tried again to respond to Osamu. This time she succeeded. |I'll be right there.| She turned around to ask Hheilea about Titan, but saw the back of the Kimley as she ran away. What's she doing? A'idah choked back a cry of dismay. She squared her shoulders and went to face the news. She didn't need the support of that lying, scheming, — A'idah painfully remembered her vow. She'd said that she would trust Hheilea through anything. "Arrrg."

Desperately, A'idah looked for Zeghes. She even perilously wished for another, dearer person to be with her. Closing her eyes, she fought against emotions threatening to crash overwhelmingly over her. Someone bumped into her. Opening her eyes, she saw Zeghes staring back at her.

"Are you okay?"

Tested and Tried

Hating her weakness, she felt terribly vulnerable and said, "No. This is going to be terrible. Stay close. I need you." More words she didn't want to say forced their way out of her mouth. "I wish Alex was here." Tears threatened her vision and through the blurriness she saw most of her dolphin brother's skin was white.

Zeghes bumped her again. "A'idah, get out of the shallow water. Alex wouldn't want you to give up. He made me promise. I know he—" The dolphin didn't finish what he was saying.

"What happened to you? Your skin's mostly—" Her arm was wet, something warm and wet. Blood? Her friend's words shocked her out of the spiral of misery and anger she'd been caught in. She didn't follow the thought of blood and didn't finish her own statement. What was he saying? Alex had made us both promise, but he'd really died. She remembered the hope Hheilea encouraged her to have, but wasn't that hope for all of the Earthlings?

Could she trust her?

She'd promised.

Zeghes nodded his head up and down.

A'idah stopped walking. What was he trying to tell her? Her eyes opened wide as she noticed a wound in his side. What? There was too much going on. What had happened to him? She opened her mouth and started to ask about it, but another voice out of the crowd of many voices called to her interrupting her.

"A'idah, Zeghes, over here."

She turned and saw Osamu waving at them. His shirt looked bloody. What was going on? A'idah worked her way through the crowd of Earthlings even as the thread of hope or confusion A'idah wasn't sure which tried to work through her other feelings of dread, hopelessness, anger, and now concern. What had happened?

She passed humans waiting quietly with dismay and concern evident on their faces. Some of the animals complained about the crowding. Shoving past the last person, she reached Osamu and the others of her flock. "What happened to you?"

Osamu gave her a strained smile. "A fight, Zeghes saved my life. We don't look like it, but we won. He and I would've been late, but Hheilea warned us about this meeting. We were on our way when Ytell summoned us." He pointed away from them. "It looks as if we're about to find out what's going on."

Following his gesture, A'idah saw the big raptor looking out over the assembled Earthlings.

Ytell shifted from foot to foot. An excited chatter arose as Amable, the aliens' leader, drew near. Ytell forced his way through Earthlings to Amable.

Impatient to know what was going on, A'idah followed him out of the crowd.

The two friends stopped, facing each other. Frowning, Amable stood hands up in front of his face.

Ytell lowered his beak, "We need to wait. This isn't fair to the Earthlings to give them so little notice."

Amable backed up a step. "You flock leaders can't delay the decision. The loss of our new supply ship and all it carried is too great of a blow."

Ytell took a step forward. A'idah hoped he would back Amable all the way to the Academy. Ytell lowered his beak more, almost touching Amable's head. "The Earthlings have made great progress and they have so much potential. I know you've seen the indications that Earth is special. We need to at least let them face the test we had planned for."

Amable lowered his head and A'idah's heart swelled with hope. He lifted his head and stepped toward Ytell. "You talked me into waiting for two hours hoping that somehow the supply ship had escaped. The training of another planet's people is threatened also. It's possible I might have to cancel the training of another set of people."

Ytell shrank back and shuffled backward. "I know. I know. The other flock leaders are upset."

The two friends gazed at each other for a long moment, and Ytell turned about to walk beside Amable. "Let's get this over with."

Amable raised his arms and bellowed. "Your attention please!"

A tear rolled down Amable's cheek and hung at his chin. The tufts of hair drooped like big commas on either side of his face. "Everyone! I'm sorry to report. We've been fighting a budget war and have lost. Earlier today, we received a mayday message from our new supply ship, and then communications fell silent. It was being attacked by pirate ships. We believe it has been captured. This isn't fair to you, but the cruel nature of facts leaves us no choice. We're going to have to cancel your training."

At those words, the crowd of Earthlings broke their silence with angry yells. The louder voices stood out.

"No. You can't do this."

"What about all the life on Earth?"

"What about the test?"

Others heard that question and soon it grew into a chant.

"Test. Test. Test. Test. Test."

Amable sighed and shuffled his feet. He looked up at his friend who stood beside him. His gaze lowered and swept across all the Earthlings. A'idah saw the skinny, funny looking Stick rushing up in a bubble. Normally he always made her grin and sometimes laugh because of how incredibly funny he looked but not this time.

The bubble dissipated over Amable and the tall thin man with a chartreuse head fell knocking the leader down.

A'idah snorted at the clumsiness of Stick. The action even affected the crowd and the chanting died off. For a long quiet moment no one spoke. A'idah stretched up on her toes trying to see what was going on.

Stick and Amable clambered back to their feet and Stick leaned in close talking into the leader's ear. Amable nodded his head a couple of times and his tufts of hair struggled up and began to wave.

Lifting his hands up, Amable addressed the crowd. "Stick has presented an idea to me. He's convinced me we have to do all we can to try and win even when defeat looks so certain. Stick is setting up video equipment."

Right in time for those words, A'idah saw more bubbles carrying something moving out over everyone.

Amable continued. "There they are. We're going to go ahead and do the test we'd planned for during the earlier budget problems. This time, your success will not mean your training will automatically continue, but there is a chance. We will record your effort and transmit the results on the most active of the websites of the alliance we are part of. The hope is your actions here will reach the hearts of enough people to get more funding."

"Stick, also thinks we should go back to the original agreement."

Amable lifted a ways off the ground and turned about with hands up looking at everyone. Somehow, his voice was being amplified. "Earthlings, to everyone a moment comes that will define that group forever. Such a moment has come upon you."

A determined smile stretched across Amable's face. "As Ytell said you Earthlings have been amazing. Many of you have surprised us with your abilities, how fast you've learned, and most of all with your indomitable spirits. I think especially of one no longer with us, Alex. He never gave up on anyone. He always took risks no matter how dangerous to help others."

Amable cast a fierce look out over the crowd. A'idah felt his eyes meet hers for a moment. "This battle against the Deems is all of ours, but this part of the fight only you can do and it'll define you for the rest of your lives. This is the moment Earth's hope will be kept alive. You alone can and must find the strength within yourselves. Dig deep. This is your moment and your goal line."

Amable lifted a hand and pointed at the distant Arena Island floating in the sky. "Your test is to move the Arena Island close enough for one of us to catch hold of a frond hanging below its underside. The person cannot be up in the air when they grab the frond."

Amable's voice dropped to a whisper and everyone leaned in closer. "You can do it."

With a shout he finished, "Bring it here! Now!"

A'idah stomped on the ground, lifted her gaze to grab onto the island. Lifting one arm and then the other, she pulled with all the force she could muster. They would do this. She could barely see the fronds. During a Force class with Titan, the Lepercaul teacher who looked like a leprechaun and hated the Earthlings, A'idah had worked with three flocks. They had moved the island. It hadn't been much, but now with all Earthlings working together, they would do this. Dimly, she heard the voices of Osamu, Peter, the Palestinian boy, and other leaders encouraging the Earthlings. The island fell from the sky, drawing nearer. Above her, A'idah could see Zeghes helping. They were doing it. Get it here now. Words, phrases, and sentences nibbled at her concentration and boosted her efforts.

"... now!"

"Move..."

"...before we tire."

"Think of your family's back on Earth."

"We can do this."

Above, the mouth-like openings on the island stretched wide. Wind blew down at them. A'idah's dress beat against her legs. The island couldn't be more than a few hundred feet away. A savage gust of wind knocked her to the side. She stumbled almost falling. A pounding in her temple attested to a headache. She thrust a hand against a jagged rock and wrenched her head up to glare at the island. It was moving away.

She added her voice to the other yells and shouts. "No! Come here!"

The island hovered and then dropped to less than a hundred feet. The fronds twisted about in the storm. Zeghes had moved looking at the bottom of the island. What was he looking at? Her breathing slowed with the drain of energy. Her head pounded. Out of the corner of her eyes, she saw aliens struggling to help.

Tall thin aliens fought against the winds while reaching for the nearby fronds. The Dwarf people climbed onto each other to build a pyramid. Haal, the first of the Dwarves she'd ever met, climbed to the top of the pyramid, he reached for a frond just above his head and fell.

A'idah snarled at the island. She fought the rising fatigue, and the raging, pounding headache. Staggering from pain, she braced her feet and raised the second hand back up. The fronds tempted, rising and falling, just out of reach.

A huge person with wiry, gold hair thundered by her and snatched Haal off the ground. Spinning, Sparks, the teacher, heaved him back up to the top of the pyramid. Haal would reach the fronds.

A'idah grinned, a fierce feral grin. Nothing would stop them now. She poured her efforts into the joint battle of holding the island close enough. She squinted against the pain. Again, she staggered almost losing her balance.

A'idah noticed Zeghes shifting his body to look at something. Peering intently, she spotted in surprise, intermittently through the fronds, a figure standing, hidden in a crack of the island, Titan, the force teacher. He smiled. One arm held up. Fronds covered and then revealed him. Laughing he raised two arms and the island pulled away. This was what he'd been talking with Hheilea about.

NO! She ineffectually pulled at the island. Again another person controlled her life and threatened those she loved.

The fog of pain she fought on the inside evaporated before her righteous fury. A'idah wasn't going to let pain stop her.

She was free to choose. She'd give everything she had to protect Earth. She wouldn't be controlled by the Muslims or by a two foot tall terror. She wasn't that good at the use of force, but there was another vapuc, and she was powerful with it.

Anger gave her new strength. Through the vapuc, she reached out to the electromagnetic force and instantaneously built a tremendous electrostatic charge in the atmosphere above her. With righteous vengeance, the knowledge this might be Earth's only chance, and desperation helping, she aimed at the terrible man who'd tried to kill Alex and cheered when news of his death spread.

A brilliant, blinding strobe of light first testified to the lightning. The Island lurching down into the top of the dwarf pyramid and the acclamation of a deafening rolling thunder further testified to her successful attack. They'd done it.

She heard Osamu calling out for help for those who had pushed themselves too hard. A'idah hoped they'd be okay, but she willing accepted the cost. She stopped her own fight to remain standing and let herself fall toward the ground. Silence and darkness claimed her senses.

Chapter Forty-One
Osamu

The Japanese man, Osamu sat on the sloping surface of the Academy's sphere thinking of what had happened to Alex four days ago. He should have been at the tunnel with them. If only Osamu had realized how dangerous Alex's plan was, he could have kept them from the situation. His death had potentially given Osamu another problem. It all depended on honor, specifically, the honor of the Dreads. If it came up, he would deal with it then.

Three days ago, the searchers had given up looking for Alex. At least Zeghes was better. From what he had heard, A'idah was not doing well.

She would have to be careful with her use of vapuc for the time being. Knowing the girl's fiery spirit, her life would be in danger. Osamu decided to talk to Gursha about the problem. They could not afford to lose another flock member.

With those terrible thoughts in his head, the incredible view of the heavens above, the beautiful blues and greens of the nebulae, the blazing nearby stars, and the dazzling night sky reflecting off the sea surrounding the island all held no interest to Osamu. Was Alex really dead? Could A'idah recover from her loss of the boy? She needed to get back to training. That too presented a problem. With the strength of her emotions, how could they keep her from overexerting herself and dying?

Osamu grimaced. He did not know how to deal with the problem of her emotions. The emotions of others had always been a problem for him to understand. He too would miss Alex. He would have to do a better job of protecting the others, but how to deal with their feelings? Osamu considered Mel. At the thought of the beautiful and fiery Illusions teacher, he shook his head. An observer watching carefully would have seen a temporary twitch of the mouth. He had almost grinned. The romance with her had been a huge shock, but very pleasant. She would help him with this problem.

Mel would also be happy to hear about his latest victory against his decades old nemesis. Osamu felt sure there would be a reprieve from any new dastardly plans, at least for a little while. Once again, he had foiled the plans of the alien. If only, he could defeat him once and for all. Of course, that might involve killing him, and Osamu refused to do that. The other man had reasons for his actions, and they were valid to him. Once again, the horrors of how easily past lives had been taken in the thousands and millions reinforced Osamu's vow to never willingly take any lives. He would continue to stand as a bulwark against the alien man's evil plans. Maybe someday, Osamu would find a way to change what was going on between them.

Putting aside that problem too, Osamu considered the future. He remembered the wise words of his Sensei. Always be considering the next right move. Never let victory or failure stop you from doing the next right thing.

In this case, the next right thing involved what Alex had been trying to do. The Earthlings needed someone to get a String Sword. Osamu remembered seeing Alex fight with one. It was an incredible weapon.

Getting that tool would be important to save Earth from the approaching threat of the Deems. Too bad what Alex did with Daren could not be done with the other Deems. Even then, there were terrible monsters like the Gragdreath. Also, with a String Sword, maybe Osamu could convince his nemesis it was time to talk instead of fighting.

He looked over at the Gadget Lady's mountain. He did not have time to go there now. Tomorrow, he would investigate. Osamu knew from others in the flock that a path led up the mountain following Alex's progress. With the boy dead, would the path still be there? The Gadget Lady's strange science kept him from being able to see the top of the mountain clearly, but that did not surprise him. What did was his feeling of weariness. For decades, he had not felt so utterly worn out. Tired, yes, but since the old alien had gifted him so long ago he had never felt the need for sleep.

All things wear out. Maybe the gift was wearing out. A nap would feel good, but this was not a good time for it. There were too many things to be done. Earth faced many threats.

Slowly, Osamu pushed himself up. He took one more glance up at the nebulae above him, marveling in its structure. It seemed to move and change as he looked at it. Osamu knew a jet from a black hole caused the glow of the nebulae, but he could not imagine how the jet's energy fluctuated fast enough to make the nebulae appear to move. Osamu shivered at the idea of a black hole jet passing so close to them. How far would the jet have to move before it would hit the ice planet of the Academy, killing all life?

Surely the aliens had considered that danger and ran the calculations to verify the safety of the Academy's location. Looking at the night sky made him think of something else. He could not quite remember what. It was something associated with... a strong emotion. Fear, but fear of what? Osamu could not figure it out. From his guts came a certainty it was important to remember.

At first, he walked up the curved surface, but incrementally, he picked up his pace until at last he ran back up to the entrance at the top of the dome. He could not afford to give in to this weariness. It would not take long for him to reach Mel's quarters. Along the way, a memory came to him. It was a strange memory of two moons, Janus and Epimetheus. As they traveled around their orbits the two moons regularly traded energy and as a result orbits. One moon picked up energy and moved farther out from its planet and the other moon lost energy moving in. What significance did that have?

Frustrated by letting all the different fears trouble him, he frowned. This was not like him. Maybe his slight vapuc feeling ability was trying to warn him of something, but what? Still wondering about it he arrived.

The fiery, red headed Mel greeted him by throwing herself into his arms. "Where were you?"

Osamu said, "I foiled my nemesis again."

She squeezed him tight. "Great, but did it take you all night?"

Without thinking he said, "No, I sat out on the dome considering the next right steps."

Normally, Mel had a pale complexion, but at the mention of where he'd been in the late hours of the night, her face blanched matching the ivory color of her two nascent horns in her forehead.

Osamu felt her arms slipping from around him. That was it, Mel's fear of the clear night sky. He tightened his own hug to hold her up and remembering how she wanted him to apologize, tried not to be his normal, formal self. "Mel, my dear sweet Mel, I... I'm sorry." Her body shuddered against his. He shouldn't've, but he had again forgotten her casasdastraphobia. For her people, it wasn't truly a fear of 'falling toward the stars.' But seeing or even hearing of someone else being under the stars triggered it. Again, he apologized, carefully speaking informally. "I'm sorry, my dear."

It always took him by surprise when her casasdastraphobia came out, but it made sense when he thought of why she and all of her people had the fear. Their home world was a moon with its livable side always facing toward its solar system's star. Other stars were only visible when it orbited back behind the much bigger planet and darkness fell. That planet co-orbited with another planet in very similar orbits. Because of an orbital synchronization the year when their home world moved behind the bigger planet always included a momentum exchange between the two planets causing the planet with their moon transferring to the outer orbit. This caused their weather to rapidly cool. This was a periodic disaster heralded by stars becoming visible in the darkened sky.

Osamu

Mel had explained the terror many times, but for some reason Osamu still had trouble remembering. What made his memory lapse worse was the fact Osamu understood this complex planetary motion because he knew of the two moons of Saturn, Janus and Epimetheus, which did the same thing.

Finally Mel's shuddering subsided. "When are you going to remember how much that terrifies me?"

"I'm sorry. That fear just contradicts everything else I know of you. I think of you as fearless."

In response, Mel grinned up at him. "Most of the time, I am fearless." She frowned and continued. "That fear is annoying. I've tried to conquer it, but it's so frustratingly unreasonable."

"That's the definition of that kind of fear. After generations of having to deal with it, I suspect for your people it might now be a genetic fear."

"Put me down, Osamu. I should get some breakfast. My first class is early."

Letting her stand on her own, he said, "Yes, I should too. Would you check on A'idah for me? I am worried about how she is going to react to Alex's death."

Words filled with sorrow burst from Mel. "Another death for you Earthlings and he had so much potential. I'm worried for your people."

"The Death of Alex has made me think of my own mortality. I too could die. I am thinking of telling them of my secrets. For a long time, it has bothered me to keep them from everyone else. At first, I did not think they needed the additional worry. I also considered the possibility they would not believe me, but now, my other Earthlings should know of my nemesis."

Mel said, "No, they have enough to deal with. We all have our tests. I know of him and his planet. I have safe guarded the information even if both you and I die. Others will learn of the threat. Do not add to their worries. The troubles they have today are enough for them to deal with."

He nodded and said, "We will find a way forward. I have decided to go after the String Sword. We will prevail."

Grabbing the back of his head with both of her hands she smashed her lips against his. Osamu felt a fire burning in response to her vigorous kiss. All too soon, she let go and turned away. Her voice trailed back to him as she departed. "I hope to see you this evening."

Osamu watched her depart. Once again, her passion had shocked him. How had he deserved her?

Late that evening, Osamu walked toward the Gadget Lady's mountain. He walked with more spring in his step. The nebulae above seemed to be brighter. The mountain peak ahead of him and even the stars above made him think of Mel.

At first, he had struggled with spending so much time with her. Now, the thought of being away from her felt like going without water. How had he survived for so many decades without her in his life? He saw Alex's path ahead of him.

Pushing away the thoughts of his lover, Osamu focused on the task at hand. He did not know why Alex's path remained, but he hoped it would allow him to walk up to where the boy had last climbed. Then what? Osamu had a long list of skills and accomplishments, but he knew very little about mountain climbing. He had decided the first step would be to examine the problem. For today, that problem turned out to be a very small problem.

Ahead of him, a figure stepped out from behind a rock at the base of the mountain. Avoiding this encounter was not an option. The stranger folded his arms over his chest. Osamu thought it was a man, a very big man, but he was not sure. The person stood relaxed waiting for him to approach. For the person he faced, this was a matter of honor. With Alex dead, Osamu had hoped this problem had solved itself, but one look at the dreadlocks hanging from the waiting man's head said otherwise.

"Hello, Osamu. Your freeing of our operative from the Tasties surprised us. It has raised questions about you, but that aside we have a problem."

Osamu gave a short nod of his head in greeting. "Yes."

"Your proposal for settling our honorable need to kill Alex met with doubt amongst us. However, we considered

Osamu

it and ultimately found your suggestion appealing. We chose the pair to do the assassination, but now the problem. Alex has had the bad form to die before we could kill him. This is unacceptable."

Osamu had kept walking, but now he paused about four feet from the Dread. The other man stood a good foot taller than the Japanese man. Osamu's hands were open and his arms held out from his body. He radiated a calm readiness. "We found his death to be... disappointing."

"We accepted your proposal, but now the object of the proposal is dead. There must be a replacement. As the originator of this agreement, you are the obvious choice, but I must verify your qualifications. If you die today, our honor is impugned. In response, we will wipe out this planet. " The Dread snapped a shin kick at Osamu. If he had connected, his shin would've hit Osamu's thigh causing pain and maybe costing the Japanese man the use of that leg.

Osamu had been watching and shifted to the side avoiding the probing attack. He continued carefully observing his opponent. Telltale bulges hinted at many weapons waiting to be used if Osamu stymied the physical assaults.

"If you live, I'll consider you adequate for redeeming our honor." The Dread jabbed at Osamu.

Knocking the blow aside with his open hand and redirecting the opponent's arm across in front of them to block any follow up attack, Osamu considered trying to grab the wrist and go for a throw. Instead, he asked, "And if you die?"

A short bark of laughter followed by, "I highly doubt you're capable of my demise. You Earthlings have proven to be surprising, but I'm much more experienced than the fool your dead Alex defeated." He unleashed a flurry of jabs and snapped off another shin kick, advancing all the time.

The shorter, smaller Japanese man blocked the shin kick with his own shin, and knocked aside most of the jabs. One got through and the sting of the blow confirmed the danger of his foe. Osamu kept sliding back. His motions were smooth, and he held his hands open. "I will grant you know how to make threats. Yet, you have only barely hit me once. When does the fight start? I will try not to kill you, but accidents happen."

The Dread stopped his advance for a moment and stared down in shock at the little man in front of him. "You're just an ordinary Earthling. Alex had the ability to see future possibilities, but you don't. According to our reports, you do have some general vapuc abilities, but nothing terribly strong. Eventually, you'll get tired of running, and then the fight as you say will begin. I could've done it with a lightning bolt already or a crude attack with my blaster, but both of them would've diminished my own honor. You'll meet your demise at my two hands." Again, he went on the attack moving faster.

Osamu recognized the circling maneuver as an effort to box him in against a wall of tall boulders. Thoughts of the situation flashed through his mind along with a surprised thought of how he felt. How to get out of this corner? Lightning? Tired? As the fight progressed he'd have to make sure he stayed close, too close for the assassin to use a strong lightning bolt. Right now, Osamu needed more room, and he did feel surprisingly tired. He shouldn't be feeling tired so soon. First, there was his feeling of needing more sleep and now this. Maybe the gift from the watcher was finally wearing out, not the best of timing. Even as he thought, Osamu had reacted. He needed some time. The ground between him and the boulders was covered in loose gravel and small rocks. There were a few more stable looking small boulders scattered amongst the debris. It would be hard to stop or maneuver quickly. The idea of having his AI use an artificial gravity generator tempted him, but he didn't want to use technology against the assassin. That might trigger him to use weapons. Instead, Osamu used the force vapuc to pull some dirt and rocks to fling at the man's face. "You are right. I have no big ability with vapuc, but you confuse me with the grasshopper. Small things used appropriately are very effective."

Osamu

The Assassin backed away using an arm to block the rocks and dirt from his eyes. "The bites of the blood sucking Yadze are barely noticed by the bull."

Meanwhile, Osamu turned and ran farther into the corner toward the tall boulders. Nimbly, he danced over the tops of the small boulders. How much vapuc could he use before the assassin's honor would let him use the lightning strike? Osamu could feel the rocks and gravel giving beneath his feet. Trying to stop quickly would be difficult. Behind him, he heard the assassin chasing. That encouraged and fell into his plan. "Your words are true, but a little mosquito, another blood sucker is hard to catch, and the ant, though small, prepares for the future."

He passed a boulder off to the side. It wasn't as tall as the others, and its shape gave the appearance of a nice place to land on. Again, Osamu used force, but this time to create small bursts of kinetic energy acting as steps in the air. Knowing just how from his hours of practice, he carefully measured his strides to run up into the air.

Twisting the last small burst of force, Osamu went with the resulting momentum, pushing violently off from the kinetic step and flipped back over the head of his opponent even as the other man tried to stop. With an open hand Osamu dealt a ringing slap against an ear of the assassin. The force of the blow twisted Osamu's body and legs through the air. Finishing the rotation, he landed on the boulder and crouched absorbing the last of the twisting momentum. It was time to attack, but each step had to be executed precisely and quickly.

Down below, the other man had stumbled to a halt. He moved a hand with a finger outstretched. "I am losing my patience with you."

It made the Japanese man think of how A'idah used lighting. Immediately, he leapt. Time seemed to move slower as if from a time vapuc. In rapid fire, Osamu acted. Falling not feet first, but head first with a clawed hand extended, he focused an energy vapuc to chill the air directly in front of his opponent's eyes. This vapuc had frightened him when he had first been introduced to it. He had been grateful to learn no vapucs affected living flesh directly, but used appropriately they could hinder and kill others. The suddenly cold air condensed its water into a very small cloud. For just a moment, it blocked the assassin's view.

The memory of how all greater vapuc uses took more time than the smaller inspired him. Osamu's hair rising on his scalp served as testimony to correctness of his earlier guess. At the same time, he too used the electromagnetic vapuc. He needed the assassin to raise his other arm up. From the small cloud danced sparks down at the assassin's face.

A bellow of pain, but mostly annoyance followed. Light flashed and thunder boomed. Thankfully, it had missed. The assassin's hands were both up.

All of this had not taken much time. In fact, Osamu still fell from his jump. He did not worry about how he would land, but focused on the precise and quick movements to end the fight as soon as possible. With one outstretched hand Osamu captured the wrist of one of the raised hands. His momentum easily helped him twist the arm back. With his other hand he captured the elbow. Now, all of his weight and forward and downward momentum went into twisting the assassin's shoulder. The resulting pop and scream happened inevitably.

Both combatants fell to the ground. Knowing just how this would happen, Osamu let go of the arm. In a moment, he shifted his grip to a dreadlock. "Do you surrender, or do I have to remove some of your dreadlocks first?"

Curses filled the air.

Osamu pulled on the hair ignoring the wasted words and considered removing one lock from the scalp.

Despite the anger and pain controlling the assassin useful words finally gasped out, "No, no. Don't remove any of my dreadlocks. Please. I surrender." After those humbling words he managed to again find the ability to throw threats. "You may have defeated me, but your little tricks will not avail you against my assassination team. You have earned the honor of facing them, but there will be three. They will slowly and painfully defeat you here on this cursed mountain."

Osamu

Osamu pulled harder on the dreadlock. "That attempt by" And here he allowed sarcasm to color the next word. "three... will finish this?"

"Yes, it has been decided by the council that this will be settled, one way or the other, by them."

"Good." Osamu released the dreadlock and stood. An ankle hurt to stand on. Ignoring the pain, as he turned his back on the assassin and walked away, Osamu made sure to walk normally.

Osamu frowned. He did not like his options. He needed to check out the mountain some more. Now, with the assassin's threat hanging over him, he had to rethink the situation. There was also the very real possibility the assassins would succeed in killing him. He had better inform Mell of the situation.

If he didn't and the assassins killed him, she'd never forgive him. Maybe he should talk to Zeghes. The wisdom of the dolphin had surprised him and thinking about it made the Japanese man once more regret ever having eaten dolphin meat.

Chapter Forty-Two
Zeghes' Secret

With his last gasp, Zeghes said, "Get A'idah away from here. Alex is setting off an explosion. He's sacrificing his own life to stop the killers from following me and A'idah."

Ytell yelled, "We've got to get them away from here before we start first aid."

Hands pulled A'idah away from the dolphin. Other voices spoke, but Zeghes had a hard time understanding.

Pain lanced through the numbness A'idah's healing had gifted him as some force lifted Zeghes up into the air.

Skyler said, "Careful, I don't think he's breathing anymore. Someone help him. Someone help."

Zeghes gave up. Everything around him started to fade. Something jabbed him, and he heard another voice. Gursha told me these are emergency nanomedibots. I hope they keep him alive."

The pain started to ebb for the dolphin. Zeghes let one half of his brain slip unconscious. He felt another jab. An involuntary gasp of air filled his lungs. The jab brought with it a burning feeling and breathing.

A voice, he wasn't sure who, said, "Hang in there, Zeghes. The flock needs you. The flock needs you."

The dolphin would've chuckled if he had the strength. It had to be Skyler talking. They moved him, but was it far enough to be safe if the explosion happened now?

Skyler said, "Another bubble. Another bubble's coming."

"It's going faster than I've ever seen a bubble move."

Ytell said, "It's Gursha. Keep moving them. We don't know how big of an explosion this will be."

Zeghes winced at new pain from a jolt.

Zeghes' Secret

Ytell's firm voice said, "Careful. We can't drop Zeghes. Even with the nanomedibots it might be too much for him."

Zeghes gazed back at the boulders, worried about Alex. At that moment, boulders shot up into the air. The ground rose in a wave rushing at him. Chaos and pain ensued.

A tremendous, thundering blast overwhelmed the yells around him. A shock wave slammed Zeghes' body. New pain lanced through his head and he couldn't hear. Zeghes tried to get his damaged suit to help hold him up. Another jolt and he tumbled through the air. Again the world around him grew dark. Briefly, he felt more pain all too well until even that pain was gone.

~**********~

Zeghes' eyes popped open. He'd survived and was in one of the clinics. Survived what though? He felt stiff on one side. What had happened? A'idah floated in a holo-field.

Gursha moved into his left field of view. "Welcome back to the world of the living."

"What happened to me?"

"You were with Alex and A'idah. What do you remember?"

Yes, he'd been going exploring with them. They were going to find out what the Winkles were up to, and they were going to fake Alex's death. "Alex died."

Gursha raised one eyebrow even as sadness crossed over her face. "How do you know that? You were almost dead yourself and unconscious for a good part of this day."

What to say? "What's wrong with my body and head?"

"During the holo-field healing, your body grew new skin. At the worst injury, you actually shed a fair amount of damaged flesh. That area is now scarred by a large depression where your injury was. You must've gotten hit pretty hard. Your headache is from the concussion caused by an explosion. By the condition of both you and A'idah, I'm guessing you got caught in a cave-in. Do you remember it?"

Zeghes didn't, but he had an idea of how to keep true to Alex's plan. "Alex was going to set off an explosion. He was sacrificing his life to save A'idah and me from the killers."

Zeghes waited nervously for what Gursha would say. He worried that Gursha would see through his story.

"That's the same thing you said when your flock rescued you and A'idah. Tasties from the nearest farming zone have arrived and taken over the rescue operation."

Experimentally, Zeghes tried to use his suit to move out of the holo-field. As it moved him toward the door, he said, "I'll go help look for Alex."

"No, you get right back into your holo-field. You've healed amazingly fast, but I don't want to let you go until I get that depression in your side repaired."

Zeghes nodded his head and slid back into the holo-field. One thing bothered him. The strength of the explosion hadn't been part of their plan. Had Alex faked his own death as planned, or had he— "How's A'idah doing?"

"She wasn't injured as badly as you, but she had the misfortune of coming down with rabies. A'idah's brain is the worst of her problems. The rabies was moving into the terminal stage. Repairing her brain will take me a while."

At the talk of Rabies, Zeghes remembered some bits and pieces of A'idah's strange behavior.

"I'm going to put you back to sleep."

Zeghes started to reply, but didn't get the chance.

~**********~

Zeghes really didn't think he felt that bad. "Gursha, I don't think I need to sleep anymore."

Ytell stood at the foot of his holo-field bed. Where had he come from?

Gursha said, "I agree. Your body's amazing. What with the help of the holo-field and that last two hours of sleep, your wound healed. Try moving."

What? Sleep? Zeghes used his repaired suit to move out of the holo-field. The stiff uncomfortable feeling had disappeared. "I'm fine."

"Good. You can leave with Ytell. Tomorrow, I might be releasing A'idah. Remember, treat her carefully. If you notice her getting into too shallow of water as you would put it, make her come back to me. Also, I want you to come back this evening. I'm worried about how you're dealing with everything."

Why would A'idah go into shallow water? Things were moving too quickly for Zeghes.

"Come along," Ytell said. "Go get a bubble to the Academy Island, and join your flock for the day's classes. Windelli asked about you and wants to talk with you. They had bad news from their search. Alex is dead. If this news makes it too hard for you to attend classes, let me know right now." The big raptor stared at Zeghes.

Zeghes stopped swimming through the air and just drifted toward the door. What? Alex was dead? How did they know? He was just pretending. The pronouncement crushed the young dolphin. That's why the worry about A'idah and shallow water. What about him? Alex was his brother. Could they be wrong? It didn't feel wrong, but what would Zeghes and A'idah do without Alex? Numbness having nothing to do with his recent injuries gripped Zeghes. "My pod, I mean flock needs me. I'll go." He looked back at A'idah one last time before leaving the clinic. He needed her more than ever.

The flock leader walked out the door with him. "Zeghes, Windelli is going to meet you. She'll be watching for you."

"Okay." Zeghes didn't think about what he did as he traveled in a bubble from the dorm area. He wished there was a pufferfish available to kill the pain. He should've stayed with Alex, except, he had to save A'idah. Out in the middle of the sea passage, Zeghes let his bubble drift down to the sea's surface. Down there he could escape from everything, but he'd still remember. He couldn't do that to A'idah, and he needed to be with her too. Maybe, he should talk to Gursha about the stress and his depression. Zeghes looked up from the inviting water and noticed another bubble zooming down toward his. It soon became evident it carried a Tasty.

Rushing up to his, the bubble slowed to a stop. "Zeghes, Windelli sent me. I'm Delli, Windelli's granddaughter. I have a very cryptic message for you. Disregard the bad news and deliver the supplies secretly at night. Don't tell anyone about this."

Zeghes considered the message for only a few moments, and he rocketed his bubble up through a series of wild celebrity maneuvers. "Thank you."

"You're welcome. I'm glad it means something to you."

That night, back at the dorms, Zeghes left his room through a window carrying a bag in his beak. Soon, he sped low across the sea in a bubble.

Sighting the prominent Academy high against the stars and then the Gadget Lady's mountain, Zeghes dropped closer to the waves. He maneuvered to approach the island from the mountain's side.

Crossing over the beach, he started to circle the mountain staying low and moving slow. Coming around a hill, he saw what he looked for. A sloping path led up the mountain. It would go up as far as Alex had climbed during his last effort. Zeghes wasn't sure why it let friends of Alex use it, but tonight it would be very helpful. Zeghes paused overcome by his emotions. Drifting through the air, the young dolphin considered this evidence of his brother's efforts to get the String Sword. How close to the summit did the path go?

Shaking himself free from the flood of emotions, Zeghes followed the path winding up the mountain. Nebula light illuminated the face of a cliff at the end of the path. When Zeghes tried to go farther, wind started to blow, buffeting his bubble. The harder he pushed, the stronger the wind blew. It held him back. This was it.

The dolphin backed up and began searching back and forth around the path. Eventually, exhaustion slowed his efforts. Zeghes paused closing his open eye to let that side of his mind get some sleep. He opened the other eye and resumed the search. Throwing caution to the winds he started calling out. "Alex! Alex! Alex!"

After many fruitless hours, he paused again considering what to do. Using force, he gathered boulders at the top of the path and dropped the bag in the middle of them. Speaking again, he said, "I'll come back again tomorrow night with more food and supplies."

That day was a long one for the dolphin. Zeghes knew or he thought he knew what the Tasty referred to in the cryptic message. That night, he again wriggled out his open window.

Zeghes' Secret

A voice startled him, as he approached the yellow circles set on the bubble platform. "Zeghes."

The dolphin spun about firing off intense pulses of his sonar. It didn't work the same as in the water, but in the dark it made all the difference. There, in the darkness he spotted a large form motioning to him. At first, Zeghes moved slowly and cautiously. Upon recognizing the shape of a Tasty, he asked, "What do you want?"

The Tasty stepped closer to him, and Zeghes recognized Windelli.

"Hello, Zeghes. Sorry I couldn't meet with you yesterday. Something came up. In this bag is a portable holo-field sprayer for you to take. You don't have to carry it. The bag will float right beside you."

"Thanks. Is... he injured?"

"Yes."

"Why didn't you talk to Hheilea or A'idah?"

"You're keeping the secret?"

"Yes, but those girls have to be devastated. I was. Can't I tell them? " After he found out for sure.

"Zeghes, you know when secrets get told to more people the opportunity for mistakes grow?"

The dolphin remembered inadvertently sharing the secret about Hheilea pretending to be a boy. "Yeah. We have to protect him from the sharks, but why involve me instead of just doing it yourself?"

"A couple of reasons, you were very close to giving up. That would've been a disaster. Your friends need you. Also, you're the best one to do this."

"Yeah, it's easy to be selfish."

"Selfish?"

"Caught up in how I feel and not worried about others. I was close to giving up."

"Wow, you are quite wise. I've heard stories about what you have said. Still, it's quite hard to use wisdom on ourselves isn't it?"

"Yeah. Shallow water has a deceptive allure to it."

"Tell him hi for me."

"I hope I can. I couldn't find him last night."

"Zeghes, you must find him. He needs this holo-field sprayer. He could still die. Bye, celebrate life." She stepped out of his view.

Zeghes dashed over a yellow circle and impatiently hovered while a bubble formed around him. Once it finished, he sped off. Continually, he asked for more speed and more speed. He followed the same careful measures in approaching the mountain and rocketed up the path. At the sight of yesterday's supply sack, now empty, Zeghes nodded his head up and down in joy. Impatient, and needing to see his brother in the flesh, Zeghes called out. "Alex! Alex! Alex!"

From a crevice over his head a tired voice said, "Hi, Zeghes. Is A'idah okay?"

The dolphin zoomed over to Alex. He poked his head out of the bubble and bumped it gently against his brother. "Today, A'idah left the clinic for the first time. She's just about back to normal, but I can tell she's devastated. I was too. Everyone thinks you died. Well, everyone except Delli and Windelli. They encouraged me to bring you supplies. Tonight, Windelli sent you a portable holo-field sprayer."

With a groan, Alex pushed his friend back and jumped down. "Great. I almost didn't have to pretend to die."

Taking the device, Alex moved out of the path. Zeghes watched as he sprayed himself and a blue and pink holo-field lifted him into a prone position. Around the boy's head and upper chest it turned pink.

Zeghes asked, "What happened?"

With a groan of relief, Alex said, "Ah, better already. Finally, I can breathe easier. I'll tell you what happened. He didn't need a flashback to remember it clearly.

~**********~

He'd just turned off the device that neutralized one of the important forces of physics, the strong force. For just a millisecond, all of the atoms, their protons, and neutrons broke apart into quarks. These recombined into the dust billowing out from the device. He'd been told that the original devices were quite dangerous to use because of the free neutrons. The free neutron energy levels had gotten too high.

Zeghes' Secret

These thoughts distracted Alex from the coming blast, and at that moment the blast shock wave slammed into his body. Everything hurt, and the walls of his tunnel flexed. He couldn't hear anything, but felt the ground shaking.

For an eternity, Alex huddled in his small tunnel. The pain subsided except for his ears and an ache in his chest. The need to escape motivated him to move. He wiped blood from his upper lip. Sliding backward, Alex found the little alcove behind him blocked. Lucky for him, the explosion hadn't been great enough to form a crater. Instead, it had just broken the boulders up and repacked them tighter. His headlamp showed the resulting walls of his prison.

One other thing he couldn't miss. The metrics from the strong device blinked in his facemask. The neutron energy levels were still too higher. Alex remembered the warnings. This rock must have some heavy elements. The heavier elements had more neutrons in their nucleus. With this dangerous radiation level, he should evacuate the area. At that thought, a half crazy laugh escaped from his lips. If it got worse he'd have to stop, or suffer from deadly radiation poisoning. I'll just have to stay here forever or die from the poisoning. Another crazed laugh escaped.

Alex returned to drilling his tunnel up bracing himself against the walls to push the device against the ceiling. Action helped to keep the terror of the enclosed space at arm's length.

Working in the narrow tube with the dust all around him, Alex couldn't see except for the blinking metrics. The neutron energy level continued to climb. Stopping, he waited for the dust to settle. What would kill him first, the radiation poisoning or the lack of oxygen? With a shock, Alex realized he didn't know what direction he was headed. That and he couldn't get his breath. Pulling the mask aside, he coughed. Every attempt to breathe hurt. Using his sense of the future, Alex considered which way to aim. A cold chill crept down his back at a realization. He'd been aiming the wrong direction. This time, fatigue hindered his ability to deal with his emotions and his sense of the future. Terrible death in a self-built tomb felt sure every direction but one. Terror crept up on his mind at the realization even that choice wasn't sure. He coughed and spat. It left a nasty metallic taste in his mouth. In the light of his headlamp he saw blood. That explained the difficulty breathing.

Pressing on, Alex became aware of the tunnel filling up behind him with the dust. The metrics screamed at him to stop using the device and evacuate. Yeah evacuate. He wished he could. Alex ignored the warnings. It also got harder to hold the device up to the ceiling. A number of times, Alex had to take a break and let his arms relax down at his side. Again and again he would cough trying to ignore the red and the ache of his lungs. Time passed, and his legs were getting encased in the dust. At first, Alex could still move forward without too much effort, but as the dust packed around his legs he had to struggle to move up. The dust continued to fill his prison, and his breathing grew shallower. The awareness of the dust starting to pack around his torso spurred him into a frantic wriggling. The all too real possibility of failure fed a growing terror of being buried alive.

He thought of Earth, Zeghes, Twarbie, Hheilea, A'idah, and his other friends. Gradually, Alex fought off the terror. Thinking of them helped. He couldn't give up. Alex pulled the device down. Taking short gasping breaths, He once again tried to sense the closest air, the path to safety.

It was close. Alex changed the angle of his attack, but the device wouldn't turn on. He looked at the metrics and shuddered at the information. How would death by radiation poisoning feel? With no choice but to continue, Alex flipped the override switch and turned it back on. Almost immediately, the device pushed through and fell out of his hands. A bright flash lit up the dust filled hole followed by a low rumble. Alex rested crying tears of an empty victory.

Eventually, the dust settled. He tossed his mask aside and looked out the hole. From lightning flashes, Alex could see a rocky slope. Reaching his hands out, he fumbled for hand holds on the side of the hole. Setting his hands, he pulled straining and wiggling against the dust packed around his body. Each time, Alex made progress, but each time he found it harder to pull again. Alex told Zeghes, "I was stuck. I couldn't get out."

~**********~

Zeghes had enjoyed being with his brother, but as the story went on he grew agitated and interrupted. "I should've tried to help find you. Why didn't you send a message asking for help? Dying would have made the secrecy about you not dying unnecessary."

Alex told him, "Zeghes, I didn't think you were up to it. You were in pretty bad shape. Truthfully, by that point, I don't think I was thinking very clearly. My breathing had been getting shallower and more difficult. I had a few supplies, but I hadn't planned on the blast hurting me. As a result, I didn't have anything to heal myself with. I had anti-radiation medicine, but in my pain I'd forgotten about it. I think I would've died there in my prison except for Delli."

"What did she do?"

"I'll tell you."

Chapter Forty-Three
Back at It

Alex gasped for air. He started shivering. The reality of his situation caused groans of frustration. Too many people were counting on him. He couldn't die, but Alex just didn't have the ability to try anymore. He felt just like an orphaned, hopeless boy again. He wept.

He heard a voice filled with anxiety call out his name. "Alex?"

"What? Who's there?" Alex croaked out the questions.

"Delli. Just a second, I'll be there."

Trying to talk, Alex could only whisper. "Thanks. I was so stupid. I didn't plan on getting injured."

Relieved laughter greeted his words. "Are all of you humans so funny? I heard what Zeghes said about you sacrificing yourself so they could escape. Real heroes get hurt. I'm going to talk to my grandma about getting you a specially designed medi-kit to always carry. You need it."

Alex heard her leaping from boulder to boulder and with a quiet crunch she landed next to his hole. With her pulling from the outside, Alex finally scraped out of the hole and collapsed on the ground.

The humor in her voice died, and she spoke in concern. "You're choking on your own blood."

Hand/paws turned him onto his side, and he felt painful jabs in his back. She spoke quickly. "I've got a holo-field spray, but you need a better portable holo-field to treat your internal injuries. I'll see what Grandma can find. In the meantime, the nanomedibots I've injected will keep you going."

Back at It

Questions filled Alex's head. He spat to clear a mouth full of blood. Taking a breath to speak, he coughed up more.

Delli kept firing off information. "Don't message me. Remember, the system isn't secure. I told the search party to give up. They'll declare you dead. Grandma yelled at me in a message. She's never done that before."

Alex's chest ached. Why wasn't his friend sending for Gursha or taking him to her? What upset Windelli? At least his pain had subsided. The realization of peril for Delli slammed into Alex. He forced out a warning. "Radiation. What about the—" He coughed and spat again.

"Yes, we should move." Delli had kept working as she spoke. At Alex's last words, she slipped her fore legs/arms under him. Laboriously, she struggled up onto her hind legs. "Okay, calm down. I'll move you before I finish."

Alex leaned his head against her soft fur. Again, her spicy smell surrounded him. This time it comforted him. Delli's words drifted about him as if from a long ways away. She must've relaxed. She didn't speak so staccato. "Grandma ordered me to grab some basic field medical gear and find you fast. Just before I left the supply depot, she ran in and added the radiation medicine. I think she's been glued to the Book of Prophesy. Something, probably you is making it very hard for her to peek into the future. She hates it." She added, "But she doesn't hate you."

Carefully, she lowered him onto the ground and returned to working on him.

"Thanks."

"You're welcome. The Prophesy really doesn't help Grandma much if she can't see very far into the future. She said if I wasn't in time, you would die. I really didn't like an idiot dying out here all alone. So, I hurried as fast as I could."

He almost grinned at another girl calling him an idiot. Taking a deeper breath, Alex tried speaking again. "Thanks, but why—" He coughed and spat again. "Why didn't... Why keep me from using messaging."

"Alex." Delli laughed and shook her head at him. "Remember, you told me about faking your death. The messaging system isn't secure. Remember, you have assassins trying to kill you.

My people have a huge vested interest in the next few years. They're very nervous about your part. You really don't look that capable to my people. I've learned you don't give up and you're surprisingly capable, but my people don't know what to think about you. You should be recovered enough to travel. You need to get out of here. Go to your mountain. I'll get more supplies to you. Be more careful. No one can have you die. Well, some people would be happy, but from the way my grandma is acting the universe would pay."

The words echoed in Alex's mind. The universe would pay.

After a pause, Delli said, "I probably shouldn't have said that. You're just important to me, your friends, of course my grandma, your home world, the Kimleys, and well... all of us Tasties. Okay, I'm going to stop talking."

Maleky must've recovered from the pain. He responded to Delli's words. *And now you're reminded why I'm in here. You're important.*

His Tasty friend unrolled a portable bubble mat. She leaned over and helped Alex to his feet. This will make a special untraceable bubble.

Alex didn't tell the next part to Zeghes. Delli gave him another warm hug. In his weak state, her smell made him dizzy. She touched her wet nose against the side of his face and whispered. "Take care. If you let some predator kill you, I'll be very mad. You don't want me to be mad."

Afraid to try and speak in his dizzy state, Alex just nodded his head. Another girl threatening him. If he died, what would they do? Crazy, they're all crazy.

Delli slipped a small pack on his back, and he stepped onto the bubble generator. The familiar tingling started. She slapped him.

Alex staggered, "What?"

Delli showed him a small needle between two fingers. "I just gave you a rabies booster. It had to be administered after your first shot I gave you in your back." She slapped him again on his other cheek, more gently this time. "And that was your second booster. Now, you can leave."

In a few seconds, he flew through the air in a bubble waving back at Delli.

~**********~

"Thanks, Zeghes, for keeping to our plan."

"It wasn't easy. I thought you'd died, and I was tempted to give up. I don't understand why it's so easy to forget about others' needs and only focus on my own problems. I'm ashamed. I would've left A'idah without either of us."

Alex remembered the depression he had during his illness. "Unfortunately, I understand, Zeghes, from my own experience. Depression and other selfish voices just like Maleky in my head are hard to deal with on our own."

Maleky responded. *Hey, I'm not selfish.*

Alex didn't let him get away with the lie. *Oh, you're in my mind just to help me. Riiight.*

Zeghes asked, "How's the climbing going?"

Alex held up a hand with pink all around it. "Yesterday was a mess. First, I could barely climb with my lungs the way they were, and I got myself into a nasty predicament."

"What happened to your hand?"

"I got stuck."

"I want the long version of the story. It isn't as if we have something else to do."

"You could go back to the dorm and get some sleep."

Zeghes turned to show Alex his shut eye. "I am getting some sleep."

Alex shook his head. "Wow. It never gets old seeing that. I really wish half of my mind could sleep at a time. I can't believe how little I know about life back on Earth. Let alone, all the mysteries the aliens know about."

"I know. It's tough not being a dolphin. Now, how about another story?"

"Okay. You remember the light greker from the technology class? The mountain lets me use one to make a bag for water and a snack. Also, I used it to make a helmet. It's come in handy. I'd been trying to make some progress, and I'd...."

~**********~

Alex tried to climb the first day after getting back to the mountain, but it was useless. His injuries and lungs made it hard to do much. Delli had given him some food, water, and some basic survival gear. Alex ate, drank, and treated his injuries the best he could. That first night, he slept like a rock and never heard Zeghes calling for him. He used a small cave up in a crevice. It seemed a good idea to hide just in case the assassins didn't believe he'd died.

~**********~

"The supplies you brought me really helped. That and more rest enabled me to actually try climbing. I did better the second day until I trashed my hand."

~**********~

Before climbing, Alex stood at the bottom of the cliff and studied it for a route. Way back before the adventure with the Deem named Daren, he'd worked at climbing this mountain and had gotten close to the top. During that time, he'd learned to aim for at least fifty feet of progress for the day. Otherwise, the mountain wouldn't advance the path, and Alex would have to re-climb the day's pitch.

He saw a potential series of hand and foot holds leading to a ledge. Nineteen feet up it, Alex spotted the perfect inch to two inch vertical crack. Twelve feet up, the vertical cliff face reached an overhang, but the crack continued on out to the edge of the overhang and up over its edge. Hopefully, it continued up the cliff. The hand and footholds would be rough. The ledge was narrow, but if he could get on top of the overhang, it looked good for a fifty foot climb or depending on what he found above the overhang he might reach the summit. Alex ignored the danger of the overhang. He would deal with it when he reached it.

Maleky had ribbed him about it. *How do you think you're going to get to the overhang let alone traverse the crack and*

Back at It

pull your weight up and over the edge? Even if you were healed it would be difficult. This is suicide.

Alex didn't tell Maleky's part of the story. The finger and foot holds had been difficult. A number of times, he fell off the cliff face tumbling to the path below. After a break for a snack and a rest he tried again. This time Alex made the ledge. Getting himself up onto the ledge took all the effort he had. For a long time, he stood leaning into the rock, resting, trying to slow his heart rate and catch his pained breath. He just wanted to lie down and sleep, but the ledge was only three inches wide.

Alex talked himself into edging down the ledge to the crack. Looking at the crack, he grinned, a tired grin, but a real one. Alex remembered again the climbing stories of his dad. How he'd told Alex about how to climb. They were going to have a climbing trip, but then both his dad and mom had died. Even though they were gone, Alex felt as if his dad was with him at times like this.

He repeated his dad's instructions, following action to the words as he did. Reach as high as you can, and slide your fingers into the crack. Try to make a fist. Hold the hand muscles tight. Pull on it to be sure it won't slide out. Pull yourself as high as you can. Lift a foot and thrust it sideways into the crack. Straighten the leg locking the foot in place. Jam the next hand in, clench it, and test it. Alternate hand and foot placements and repeat again and again. Alex enjoyed crack climbing even with aching lungs and shortness of breath.

Then his light greker helmet cracked into the overhang. He'd forgotten about it. Alex leaned into the cliff face and one at a time shook his arms out resting them. He reset a handhold in the vertical crack, tested it twice, and leaned out from it under the overhang. Thrusting his other hand up into the horizontal crack, Alex set another hold. This time he tested it three times. He looked down. It would be painful, but he thought he would survive and hopefully without any broken bones. Alex could deal with pain, but not with that kind of injury.

Loosening his other holds, he released them one at a time. Until, he swung out away from the vertical cliff. Quickly, he thrust the free hand into the crack and set a hold. Now Alex hung under the rock swaying back and forth. One hand at a time he moved toward the edge and then disaster struck. One hand got stuck.

Maleky had been keeping quiet most of the time. Pain and emotions had been helping to keep him quiet. He couldn't handle them.

Alex had just moved one hand to a new hold. He'd been excited by the closeness of the lip and had stretched a little farther this time. When he went to move the other hand new pain lanced down his arm. Tentatively, with teeth clenched, Alex tried again. His hand burned in agony and a gasp escaped his mouth.

A feeble thought from Maleky pushed into his awareness. *You should've rested your arms again.*

Alex moved the new hold back near the hurt hand. Wriggly that hand only revealed more pain and that it was stuck. Hanging from burning arms, Alex considered the problem.

Maleky couldn't help himself. *You're crazy. You're actually considering cutting off your hand.*

Alex responded in a thoughtful way as he hung from one hand caught in a crack. *My big problem is I don't think I have anything to cut it off with.*

Maleky's thoughts shook. *You are forgetting about the pain and loss of blood.*

Alex's distracted thought of, no the pain will pass, and I'll deal with the blood didn't help Maleky's response sound any less worried. *You're crazy.*

Alex didn't want to waste time just hanging there until Zeghes came with more supplies, and he wasn't sure how the dolphin could get him down. Maybe the blood from wriggling would help his hand to slip free. Eventually, twisting his hand caused it to rip free.

~**********~

Alex told Zeghes, "Seriously, I got lucky. It ripped free when I swung into the cliff and managed to slow my fall a bit. I didn't get hurt too badly, but if you hadn't brought the portable holo-field sprayer, I couldn't have climbed tomorrow."

Back at It

"Good, but Maleky is right. You need to pay more attention to resting and being careful. If you're badly injured or dead, you're not going to get that sword."

"Yeah. I just don't think we have much time. Something's happening soon. I'm afraid it will interfere with my climbing again or the Earthlings' training. This sword is very important. I've got to get it."

Zeghes said, "Be more careful. I don't want the major event to be some disaster involving you. I already lost you once, and I don't think I can survive losing you again. At the very least, A'idah would kill me for keeping your secret about being alive, and then being involved in helping you kill yourself a second time."

Alex said, "You know, Zeghes, I'm not sure what you just said makes sense, but I know what you mean. I'll try and be careful, you too. I better get some more sleep. You can talk all night, but I can't."

Zeghes nodded his head. "Okay. Bye." He'd keep Alex's secret and keep any danger from his brother.

Chapter Forty-Four
Danger at the Mountain

Zeghes didn't enjoy the next day's classes at all. He usually liked the Religion class, but the two headed philosopher brought up terrible ideas.

Zeghes liked the religion Alex had told him about where everyone had a personal relationship with God and had revelations from him. They also chose on their own to believe in God or not to believe. The two headed philosopher called it exercising free will. Zeghes liked that idea. The other religion sounded like determinism, and the dolphin didn't like the idea of being forced into something.

When A'idah messaged about Osamu working on something related to getting a new String Sword, Zeghes thought of Alex. What would happen if Osamu tried to climb the mountain? Even as he thought about it, he started drifting toward the mountain and slowly picked up speed. He wanted to message the man, but he couldn't think of how to word the question without creating an opportunity for Osamu to learn about Alex. Suddenly, he realized A'idah had also asked a question. What was it? He remembered. Do you have any idea what he's up to?

Quickly, he messaged back. |I don't know. I'll see you later. I'm going to check up on Osamu.| Concern pushed him to go faster.

Ekbal messaged him. |Zeghes, what are you doing? Everyone else is going back to the dorms to eat.|

"Huh." Embarrassed at being surprised, Zeghes answered without first thinking. |I'm going to check on Osamu. He might be at the mountain. I don't want him

Danger at the Mountain

to...| Zeghes cutoff saying what he'd been thinking. How could he almost give away Alex's secret?

Ekbal didn't seem to have noticed the trouble. Instead, he said, "I'll come with you."

Zeghes wanted to refuse, but it hadn't seemed like an offer, more like a statement. The dolphin worried if he refused, Ekbal would get suspicious. Indeed, he wondered why he hadn't already. In an effort to stay in control, Zeghes said, "I'll give you a ride." He circled back around and hovered by the dark skinned boy from India. This way he'd be able to keep Ekbal from getting to close to where Alex climbed. He didn't want others finding out about Alex. Especially, he worried about the assassins.

Heading toward the mountain, Zeghes realized A'idah hadn't said anything about Osamu climbing the mountain. Maybe, he wasn't anywhere near. He'd just take Ekbal on a cruise of the lower part of Alex's path, and afterwards they'd head back to the dorms for a late dinner. He'd just started to relax and even enjoying the quick trip when Ekbal ruined it by asking a question.

"So, Zeghes, where did you go the other night with the bag?"

"What?"

"You left the dorms with a bag."

"A bag?" What could he say? How did he know?

"Yes, a bag."

"Oh, I thought you were asking about fish." Did that sound lame? Ahead, he could see the beginnings of Alex's trail curving up the mountain. How soon before they could head back?

"That's lame. Bag sounds nothing like fish."

In desperation, the dolphin dug deep trying for inspired obfuscation. Maybe if he said there's nothing there and bucked Ekbal off, he could suggest a race back to the dorm. Thinking of that idea, he continued just rattling, saying words without thinking too hard if it made sense. "Well in your language it might not, but I'm hearing you in dolphin, and let me tell you. Bag and fish sound almost the same, very much the same in fact, very—" He'd intended to keep blabbering away, looking for the right moment to buck him off. Then he could suggest the race, but the sight of someone racing through the sky knocked all the words out of his mind. Seeing people flying through the sky wasn't all that unusual, but this one had arched ahead of them and landed somewhere near the base of the mountain. Who was it?

Ekbal said, "Zeghes, did you see that? Who was it?"

He didn't know, and he was beginning to rethink his unhappiness about the boy from India being with him. In the distance, he thought he saw movement on the trail.

Was that more movement? He wasn't supposed to let out the secret. Yet, he had to protect his brother. Maybe... Somehow... the assassins had learned about Alex really being alive, and even now they were headed up the mountain. The view of the mountain ahead suddenly blurred. "What's happening?"

Ekbal said, "Remember our lesson about how gravity warps the space time continuum."

Zeghes did and just the memory made his brain hurt again, but he realized what was happening. "You're using a couple of vapucs to warp a small area in between us and the mountain."

"Yep, I've just about got it. I'm creating a gravitational lensing effect, just without a massive object or strong gravity. We should see what's going on. Look sharp. It won't last for long."

The section of the mountain with movement expanded in front of them. The two flock members gasped at what they saw.

While the brief effect lasted, Zeghes had seen three people with dreadlocks hanging down their backs going up Alex's trail.

Zeghes commanded, "Hang on." Even as he accelerated, pushing his suit to go faster, he used a gravity generator to pull them toward the mountain, and used the Force vapuc to go even faster. The air roared past them. All he could think of was somehow the Assassins had learned about Alex still being alive. They would catch him by surprise. Zeghes didn't want to think of the result.

~*********~

Osamu had tried to cut classes all day. Each time, he'd been caught by Ytell. He should've been able to avoid him, but all day Osamu had moved slower and stumbled twice.

The last time, the flock leader took him to an empty room. "Osamu, would you please tell me what is more important than being trained to save your home world."

"Alex wanted to get another String Sword. I think he was right. Vapuc is important, but I saw him use the other String Sword. It is an amazing weapon. Earth needs that kind of tool in its upcoming fight against the Deems."

The big bird quietly listened and stayed quiet for so long Osamu began to wonder what was wrong.

Snapping his beak a couple of times, Ytell finally answered. "I agree about Earth's need. Unfortunately, you also need more vapuc training, and I'm worried that might be difficult. There has been a problem."

"What is it?"

"I can't say at this time, but there is probably going to be an announcement later today." The big raptor snapped his beak again, obviously annoyed by the subject. "I've noticed you're limping a bit today, and you seem different. I want you to go and see Gursha. She's here at her Academy clinic."

Osamu shook his head and opened his mouth to protest.

Ytell interrupted. "I know you don't go to the nurse. We've known of your secrets, just not all of the details, for a long time. Sometime, if we ever get some free time, I'd love to hear about your experiences, how you got your enhancements, and all about your nemesis. He's a rather stubborn individual. We've had contact with him, but he remains intent on just living on the outskirts of the Academy's society. For now, just go and get Gursha's help. I suspect you need to be at your best for the events of today."

Osamu stood caught by the interruption with his mouth open. The information Ytell shared, dropped the Japanese man's jaw even farther. How long had they known? How much did they know? Straightening up, he ignored a new soreness in his back and said, "Okay. I will go see Gursha. She knows of my enhancements?"

"Yes. She learned about them during your abduction. We've been waiting for you to open up about them on your own, but developments have made it dangerous to keep waiting on your reticence."

"I will go right now. Thank you for your patience. I should have talked about it before." With a nod to his flock leader, Osamu left the room.

On the way to the clinic, the Japanese man stumbled again and had to stop and catch his breath twice. He found himself squinting to see anything far away. What was happening? When Osamu finally reached her door, he uncharacteristically paused for a fraction of a second. He had never talked with anyone about this other than Mel, and she did not know everything. The idea of sharing his history made him feel strange. He did not know what the feeling was called. The door opened, and he walked in.

Gursha stood in the middle of the room looking right at him. "Hello, Osamu."

"Hello, Nurse Gursha. I am here for some help with my ankle. I injured it recently. I also need to talk to you about my enhancements."

She waved at a pattern on the floor. "Come over here and stand above this. Ytell told me to expect you. The door has the privacy setting on. No one will interrupt us. A holo-field will lift you up into the air. First, I will do an examination. What are your enhancements?"

The walk across the floor should've been easy, but Osamu felt tired, so tired. "I do not know what they are."

"Oh."

Osamu felt his body levitating off the floor. His view of the room changed. Everything had a blue tint to it from the holo-field surrounding him.

Another voice spoke. "There are unidentified lifeforms present in the current subject."

The word burst out of him without thought. "What?"

Gursha's calm voice interrupted him trying to get back out of the holo-field. "It's okay, relax. This is what I found in your first examination. The lifeforms referred to are a nano... well, either a type of nano-bot or new nano-organisms. My technology can't identify them. When and how did you receive your enhancements?"

"It was over a century ago."

That comment made her eyebrows shoot up.

"After I received them, I have stopped aging. Back then, I was a spy." Osamu gave a short bark of laughter. My background is complex. I am not really just Japanese. When it happened, I served as a spy for three different countries at the same time. I think some of them suspected, but did not care, because I always succeeded in the tasks I accepted.

In my last mission, I was not succeeding. A rich terrorist group had gotten some nuclear weapons. All three countries asked me to do the same thing. They each promised backup. My job was to find the weapons. I found them, but the promised backup never came. Much later, I learned the reasons why. One country had an election. The new leader naively thought the terrorist wouldn't destroy the whole world. The other country decided it was too risky to send any of their troops. They expected the third country would take care of the problem. When I informed the third country of the location of the weapons, they decided doing nothing would be to their benefit. They didn't care about the millions who would die. They had come to the conclusion that they would profit from the resulting nuclear war."

Osamu continued speaking in his normal voice, but tears quietly started running down his face. "I hate all of the theys who have caused so much death and sorrow. On any mission, I always gave myself options."

On this one, when the help did not show up. I had already been busy setting up my options. I never trusted anyone else. I had not only gained access to the cave where the nukes were. I had also planted explosives to cause a great landslide blocking the cavern.

I set off my explosives. Once entombed with the weapons, I checked on my latest satellite downloads of information. As I read, I began to suspect none of the three countries would send help. I was on my own, and I knew the terrorists.

For me, there was only one option. I had to destroy the weapons. Unfortunately, I knew very little about those weapons. In later years, I rectified that gap in my knowledge.

With the available equipment, I started to deconstruct the weapons, destroying as much as I could. At first, I settled with just destroying outer parts, but then I realized with the terrorists' money those could be fixed. I dug deeper. This all took time, because of my equipment and lack of knowledge. It took too much time. I had run out of food and more importantly water.

I began to grow worried about the terrorists gaining access and destroyed the tunnels into the room I was in. I had already come to terms with this being my last mission. One way or another, I would not survive. This all took days, but I began to suspect all of my efforts had been for nothing. I had started getting nauseous. Exposing nuclear material in the nukes had exposed me to radiation."

At this point, Osamu's normal, formal voice grew emotional. "I felt my approaching death and rapidly grew too weak to finish. I couldn't fail. The fate of the world rested in my hands. I tried to continue dismantling, but the tools refused to stay in my hands. I cried and begged God for help. I wanted to finish saving Earth. Next, I thought I was hallucinating."

"I saw something. It looked like what I now know as a Deem, but different in ways I am uncertain about."

At this, Gursha looked at him more intently and opened her mouth to interrupt, but stopped herself.

"It was all black and had bat-like wings. I will never forget its red eyes looking at me. I have always been surprised at how clear my memories are of this. It must have been because of what happened. The strange creature hopped all around looking at the nukes. It did not seem comfortable with walking. It muttered to itself, but I could hear it quite clearly. This is what I remember.

It said this would be bad. This would destroy what I'm supposed to be watching for. What can I do? I can't destroy these things. I'm just supposed to watch and not interfere, but these would ruin the watching. It came over and sniffed at me. This will be dead. I can change dead things." It laughed to itself and continued speaking. "The dead thing can finish what it's been doing."

Danger at the Mountain

"It then said goodbye. The thing tipped its head and added, you a good thing. I hope I'm a good thing. I am the Watcher, but I no longer know what I am."

"The next thing I knew, I was awake and feeling better than I remembered ever feeling. I finished destroying the nukes, and—"

Gursha interrupted the story. "The thing which gifted you actually ended up here a number of years ago. When we were collecting some of Earth's plants to build Earth's sector here, it had been accidently collected with a human girl. They... well that doesn't matter. How did you escape— No don't waste your time telling me. Now that I know where you got your enhancements I've got an idea. I need to go get a sample of Teddy's nibbles. You know Teddy as the Watcher. Just stay here. The holo-field will force you to sleep, and it will repair your ankle. I'll be right back."

Osamu started to tell her that he did not sleep, but the next thing he knew the door of the clinic opened allowing Gursha to return. Mel followed right behind her.

He asked, "What? What happened? Mel, what are you doing here?"

Gursha carried a small bag in one hand. She asked, "How do you feel?"

Osamu thought about it and said, "Good, I feel rested. Well, not totally. Did I sleep? I think I could use some more sleep." Was it getting harder to breath? "My ankle feels fine. I should go. I have many things to be doing."

Mel shook her head at his words.

He could see a tear on her cheek. What was wrong?

In a quiet voice, full of anguish, she said, "His hair is whiter than it was earlier today."

Osamu touched his hair at her words. "How could my hair turn white so quickly?" As he did so, he noticed the skin on his hand. It looked... It had age spots. Realization hit. "Gursha, I need you to help me. Too much depends on me being able to—"

She nodded her head, and interrupted him. "I want to try something, but I need both you and Mel to be aware I don't know what will happen."

Mel ran over to him and tenderly smoothed the hair back from his forehead. He heard her gasp and saw something drift down in front his face.

She gasped out, "You're going bald." In a desperate voice, she pleaded. "Gursha, you have to do something. He's growing old and dying right in front of our eyes."

In one hand, Gursha held up something flat and black, very, very black, part of it was blurred and Osamu couldn't tell what it was. The blurred part reminded him of something.

She said, "Okay, listen. Teddy, you knew him as the Watcher. When we met Teddy, he was part way through a rejuvenation process. He had to eat his nibbles in order to finish the process. This was his nibbles, his old shed skin. We've analyzed it, and part of it is *dark matter*."

That explained the blurriness.

"The rest is something we don't recognize. While I hurried to get this, I ran a comparison of the analysis of it against an analysis of the unidentified things in you that have given you so many years of life. They match. When Teddy ate his nibbles, he finished his rejuvenation. It also tried to change who he was. I think... that came from the *dark matter*."

Osamu understood. "I do not care what you do. I have to be able to fight with three assassins." He remembered the Dread's last words. The assassin team will be here tomorrow evening, and if you are not here on this mountain to fight them, we will destroy everyone. "It does not matter if I win the fight, but if I am not there, they will kill everyone here." He thought fast and furious. "Somehow, you have to get me or a reasonable doppelganger able to fight them."

Mel gasped out a painful, "No."

Osamu did not want to, but he had to ignore Mel's pain. His heart clinched at her distress. He knew from past experience, Mel had clamped a hand across her mouth to control any more outbursts. She was strong. She would be okay. Right now, she probably nodded her head yes. He kept his eyes on Gursha.

The nurse had gone pale at his words. She reached into her bag and pulled out a very small tube. It had an odd shimmery look to it.

Danger at the Mountain

Osamu could see glimpses of a bright green effervescence coming from the tube. Even in the dire circumstances, he couldn't help but be intrigued and awed by what he saw.

It tried to change who he was? What did that mean? What would it do to him?

Chapter Forty-Five
Fighting Assassins

Looking at it, Gursha said, "This is the last purified sample of the unknown substance. We had two, but, for a very good price, Stick sold one to a research conglomerate. I think it was called... Star— Well, its name doesn't matter." She walked over to the wall, talking all the way. "We could've sold this one too, but Stick and I both had a strong feeling we shouldn't. Its sale would've been a great help with our financial problems. I hope this is why we held onto it."

Osamu could not believe Stick had not sold the substance. He was a numbers man. It would have been foolish to hold onto it for just an unknown possibility, and yet, Stick had. It made no sense to Osamu.

While he pondered the mystery of how other people thought, Gursha removed a stopper from the small vial. The wall in front of her exuded an odd looking appendage. She held the vial out to the shifting material, letting go as the wall grasped the vial. "I'm hoping that adding this to your body will shock your enhancements into a reset or hopefully some similar rejuvenation as Teddy's.

A drawer slid out from the seamless wall and Gursha retrieved a syringe. "Because the holo-field has issues with this substance I have to fall back on an older technology. This will take me only a moment."

Plunging the needle down into the vial, she carefully pulled back on the plunger. From below her primary eyes, two small hidden eyelids opened, and two small eyes on long, flexible stalks stretched out.

Osamu's own eyes opened wider at this new development.

Fighting Assassins

Gursha explained, "My second brain is using micro eyes to get a closer look. I haven't done this in a long time. I don't want to make a mistake. As it is, there is a danger."

Her eyes traveled up and down the syringe. Apparently, what they saw satisfied her. They pulled back into her head, and the two slits of her second eyelids sealed over them. "Now, where should I inject you?" She continued speaking, mulling over the options. "I could do it intravenously, intramuscular, or subcutaneous."

Osamu understood from his own use of old knowledge. It took effort and following where the thoughts led. Still, he wished she would hurry. What was it about needles that sparked irrational feelings? He wanted this over with. Yet, he also felt nervous at her mention of a danger involved in this therapy.

With a note of triumph, Gursha said, "Of course, intravenously. Osamu, please hold still. I've never done this before, but if this works as I think it should, you won't feel a thing, at least from the needle. After that, I have no idea. Teddy had some problems with his nibbles."

Osamu willed himself to relax. He started to turn his field of view away from his nurse. He knew from very old experience that watching an injection would make him more likely to tense up. Before he lost sight of Gursha, he gasped and jerked back. She had thrown the syringe at him.

Terror filled Osamu's voice. "What are you doing?"

Gursha ordered him, "Osamu, calm down. I'm so out of practice using a... I think it's called a syringe. I would have trouble finding a vein to inject. My holo-fields can't directly work with this substance, but they can easily manipulate the syringe. If you can hold still, the holo-field will locate a good vein and inject you with this stuff."

Osamu nodded his head. He tried to slow his racing heart. Relaxing was easy for him. It beat faster. He could retreat to a calm space in his head, from this odd situation of being injected with some unknown stuff, and by a holo-field. A cold sweat broke out. He could ignore the very irrational desire to jump up and run... okay to hobble or walk, out of this clinic. Osamu clenched his teeth to keep in a scream. Why was he feeling so irrational? His chest burned with a sudden pain.

Was he having a heart attack? A different pain, a burning sensation overwhelmed Osamu and he gasped out loud. The burning ripped across his body.

In a panic filled voice, Mel said, "What's happening to him?"

At least the pain in his chest had gone, but his view of the room fluctuated from pinkish to bluish and back, again and again. With it came waves of nausea, pain, chills, and fevers.

Gursha spoke. Her words sounded frantic. She never sounded frantic. That could not bode well for this experiment.

"I don't know what's happening to him. I didn't want to try this, but we had no choice. Osamu, can you stand? My holo-field is going crazy. I can't control it. The device might try doing things which would be very bad."

At those words, Osamu straightened his legs and forced his body up and out of the holo-field. His body responded with new found energy. With a startling clarity, he knew what he had to do. "I must leave. I have to get to the mountain." Any delay would be a disaster for everyone. Turning to go, he saw Mel standing in his way. Her eyes pleaded with him. Osamu wanted to hold her and comfort her, but with his new clarity of the future he knew the cost of allowing his or Mel's emotions to delay him.

Instead of trying to reason with her, holding her, or trying to dodge around her, he jabbed a two finger strike. He hit her nerve which was similar to the vagus nerve in humans. Instantly, she collapsed. Osamu let her fall, with his heart, crashing onto the floor. Running away, he said over his shoulder, "Take care of my wife for me."

This time, no one interfered as he left the Academy. He jumped onto the first available departure pad and soon plummeted down a departure air-path.

Letting a computer control gravity to lower him through the open air had taken a lot of getting used to. The first few times, he had to do this with his eyes shut. Now, Osamu was at ease and looked around during his miles long descent from the sphere. Below, a group of people moved along the shore. Zeghes and someone else headed toward the mountain. Osamu knew beyond a doubt it would be their death if they

Fighting Assassins

beat him to the mountain. Fortunately, He'd practiced with his AI for just this kind of event.

Running the calculations through his head, and speaking to his AI he said, *Follow these instructions carefully. When I tell you go, use a local gravity generator and accelerate us at a constant nine g, for two seconds, heading toward the path on the lower part of the mountain. When I tell you, decrease our speed at a constant nine g.*

Okay, you will handle the landing?

Yes. Go

Instantly, Osamu felt himself yanked out of the air-path. He heard the roar of air whistling past. His speed increased at almost two hundred miles per hour each second until the wind whipped past at almost four hundred miles per hour. With eyes screwed shut, Osamu felt his cheeks flapping in the wind. All the while, he calmly counted off the seconds. *Decrease our speed.*

Osamu opened his eyes and squinted against the decreasing wind. His newly boosted feeling vapuc told him the enemy approached, but he had some time. Osamu wanted to setup some surprises to improve his odds of survival, but how to deal with the real possibility the assassins might have their own sense of the future. How do you surprise someone who has a sense of the future? Overwhelm it?

Of course, use chance. Osamu remembered how Alex's enemies could use randomness in their plans or attacks to confuse his sense of the future. How to do it? Luckily, the Dreads were not as good with their sense of the future as Alex had been.

Osamu was falling to the rugged slopes of the mountain. Judging his speed, the Japanese man used judicious bursts of force to adjust his course and slow his descent. On the way down, he studied the surrounding rocky terrain. He landed hard and fast, sprinting up the soft sandy path until the momentum of his fall dissipated.

One rock on the path caught his attention. Slowing to a walk, Osamu leaned down and quickly picked it up. The flat sedimentary rock had a red layer on top and a much lighter, sandy color on the bottom. It would work perfectly.

At a turn of the path, Osamu stopped to consider a relatively flat area off to the side. Above it the path curved up a steep cliff covered in cracks, crevices, and fissures. Boulders and rocks rested precariously along the steep path and at the top of the cliff. Between him and the small level area a small ravine dug down descending to disappear between two columns of rock. The columns speared up into the sky and Osamu tipped his head back to consider them. Two capstones of harder material balanced precariously on their tops. "Hmmm. How long would it take for those capstones to fall?"

Osamu almost grinned as he considered how boulders and rocks could fall from almost any direction. For someone able to manipulate the laws of physics this place had great potential for chaos, and it would be the perfect place for a battle against overwhelming odds. Here, he would have a chance. If only he didn't overdo his use of vapuc, and render himself unable to defend against attacks.

Taking a deep breath, Osamu set to work. Kneeling, he picked up a handful of sand letting the crystals flow through his fingers. Normally, sand became sandstone by a long process of diagenesis, but by altering laws concerning how it took place....

Along the closest edge of the ravine Osamu shifted boulders and rocks partially filling in the nearest side of the ravine. Placing bigger ones he created a staggered path of stepping stones across the ravine. Standing back, he memorized the pattern.

Now for the harder part, briefly, he reviewed his lessons in making diagenesis take place quickly. Using the force vapuc, he started a sheet of sand flowing over the rubble. Working quickly he used the vapucs to encourage the quartz crystals to grow together. The resulting sheet looked lumpy and had holes where the sand just flowed down into the gaps in the rocks below, but after a number of tries the result looked just like the sandy path with a ravine dropping off on one side.

Concentrating on the right path, Osamu ran across his creation. It held. Turning about, he took in the rocks surrounding the level area. Amidst the potential chaos his eyes caught sight of a refuge from chaos, a rock shelter. Through his enhanced feeling vapuc Osamu knew he would need it soon. It also alerted him to the assassins approach and gave him a warning of what would be the first attack. In the fading minutes available, he worked at altering the potential energy in the scene. First, he used a vapuc that let him measure the stability of the various potential energy systems present. The rocks in the whole area glowed in hues from green to purple. Purple showed which rocks were the closest to shifting to kinetic energy. A quick glance revealed many small spots where a judicious use of a vapuc could set off rock-falls. The shelter would come in handy.

A few rocks had speckles of red showing the presence of radioactive elements. Their potential energy registered as a different type of energy. Osamu remembered a vapuc that would potentially allow him to cause miniature nuclear detonations with those minute amounts of radioactive elements. Unfortunately, he had much learning and practice before he could do that.

In rapid fire, Osamu used some vapucs to encourage delicate erosion. The slithering sound of sand trickling down from the many affected locations etched away the silence. Harder tumbling, thumping, and grinding testified to a few mistakes as the occasional rocks gave way to gravity's pull sooner than Osamu planned. Along one area, he reinforced the stability of the rocks. He expected the assassins to try and use the boulders and rocks to attack him, just as he did to them. Osamu found himself pointing with his finger as he worked just like A'idah did when she worked with lightning. She would have been a great help in this battle. She had a tremendous capacity for using vapuc, but even she did wear out.

Osamu knew his choices already made for the upcoming battle could be a disaster. His vapuc abilities had felt stronger than ever before, but how much endurance did he have left? Was that a headache starting?

His short hair stood on end at the warning from his feeling vapuc. Stopping his efforts, Osamu raced back to the path. He needed to be in the right place when they arrived. Pulling the two toned rock from his pocket, he looked down to see which side was up. Dark, he wouldn't wait for Zeghes and whoever was with him. Now that the rock had provided the random element of chance, he tossed it aside.

From around the corner a small dust devil spun toward him. Behind it, the three assassins walked. "We heard you like to play with sand."

Osamu did not try and block their blowing sand. Instead, he ran from it following carefully the pattern of footsteps in the sand. Behind him came the sounds of the assassins running after him. They would not be able to stop in time. With nudges of erosion he freed the two capstones.

Knowing the assassins would respond in kind to his attack, Osamu sprinted for the rock shelter. The overhang would provide some protection. Osamu setoff other erosion vapucs in rapid fire action. The resulting rumble of rockfalls quickly grew in volume. Hopefully, the odds in the battle were going to improve.

The cracks of boulders and rocks finally gaining the freedom to respond to gravity filled the air. Some were louder than others. Ducking his head down against his chest, Osamu jumped under the overhang. Hitting the ground, he rolled over slamming against the back wall. Again, he checked the structural integrity of the rock over his head. It would not do to kill himself with a rockfall.

No cracks and the crystalline strength he had encouraged was intact. At the warning from his sense of the future, Osamu broke the last of the restraints for a huge sandstone block. A horrible grinding sound overwhelmed all of the other crashes. With a roaring that overwhelmed all the other noises, dust, sand and small rocks pelted him. The ground below him shook, knocking him off his feet. The light was blocked.

Osamu knew he could not wait in his shelter too long. Before the last noisy rumblings died away, he pushed up from the ground. In front of the shelter, a big block of sandstone now blocked the view. Saving his vapuc related endurance for other possibilities, Osamu snagged two rocks from the ground and hurled one at the far end of the overhang. Pushing off from the ground and with a force jolt, he jumped, slid onto, and ended kneeling on the larger sandstone block.

Below him, only one assassin still stood. Another struggled up from the ground. He really did not want to kill them, but it beat them killing him. Raising his voice to be heard, Osamu said, "Have you had enough? Maybe you should have brought six or a dozen to try and kill me."

The only dread standing said, "Enough of your tricks. Come down here and fight. Then we'll see how tough you are."

This presented a problem for Osamu. He did not have anything to prove. He did not have to fight them, hand to hand, but even with his vapuc boost. He knew, he would soon be testing how much vapuc he could do without risking exhaustion, headaches, and possibly worse. If he refused to fight, they would kill him using other means. The odds for a physical fight would not get better. Osamu vaulted down from the rock. "Life must have no joy for you."

"What is joy?" The dread man said. He moved to Osamu's left forcing him to turn to look at him.

Out of the corner of the Japanese man's eye he caught the other dread standing. The sound of rocks moving testified to the third man not being out of the action. What to do? His tricks had just delayed the inevitable.

~**********~

Dust came from the mountainside ahead of Zeghes. Alex! He had to go faster. The roaring of the wind made it hard for Zeghes to hear the desperate message in his head.

|We have to slow down. I can't hold on any more.|

Even as Zeghes finally heard the message, he felt Ekbal get ripped off his back. No! The young dolphin struggled to choose right. He arced back through the air trying to spot the Indian boy. His amazing suit couldn't handle the inertia. For a moment, Zeghes had spotted Ekbal, but in the next moment he tumbled through the air. The sky and mountainside twirled about him. The rocks drew nearer and nearer. The dolphin could maneuver gracefully in the water and with the suit it didn't take him long to recover from tumbling through the air.

Arcing through the air just above the sandstone, Zeghes spun. Carefully, he scanned his surroundings looking for Ekbal. Below him, Alex's empty trail wound up the mountain. Dust rising from between some crags above him caught his attention. A big boom followed by more dust. Alex! He realized there had been thumps and rumbling crashes coming from the dusty area all this time. A landslide? A fight?

Hoping Ekbal had managed to land okay, the dolphin rocketed up the trail. He knew better than zoom straight into an unknown situation. He considered circling around and above to get a safe view or he could slow down and peek around the bulge in the mountain. He should at the least go off the trail and come in from a different direction.

Zeghes rocketed up Alex's trail and around the bulge.

Amidst the rocky terrain, three Dreads circled Osamu. Each held dark blue swords with bright red streaks running the length of the blades. Osamu held a light sword just like the one Alex had at the tunnel. The bright, blue blade of light crackled as the Japanese man swung it to block an attack. It struck with a snapping sound, but the enemy's sword held firm.

One of the other opponents stepped forward and thrust at Osamu's back. The third attacker moved to attack. Fortunately, he had to deal with some boulders piled between him and Osamu.

The Japanese man stepped away from the thrust. He let his blade slide with a ragged crackling sound against the first man's blade until the hilts struck. With his free hand he flicked his fingers in that man's face while blocking a blow from that man's free hand. Some kind of powder poofed at the man's eyes. The man reeled back with a gasp of pain.

Osamu finished the maneuver by rushing on past that opponent and slashing at him with his trailing blade. The Dread crumbled to the ground.

Zeghes nodded his head in approval of the maneuver even as he prepared to enter the struggle. They'd defeat these three quickly. "Zeghes is here." With force, he pushed the pile of boulders from under the third man. That Dread yelled as he fell and the second man grunted as one of the small boulders gaining speed hit him in the side.

At the same time, he heard Osamu yell. It interrupted him from doing a victory spin. The Japanese man must've seen him before he started helping. "Zeghes, lookout."

Fighting Assassins

The young dolphin noticed for the first time blood soaked one of Osamu's shoulders. A message ordered him, |Zeghes, go up.|

Reacting quickly, he rocketed up and did a quick scan of the surroundings. Three more dreads had appeared. Large rocks flew through the area he'd just been in.

One of them spoke admiringly, "You have good reflexes." Then he barked out, "But you should've realized we would be prepared to keep the odds of this battle the same. Many of us are here to witness and provide any assistance honor demands. Our agreement allows three more of us to enter the fight for every ally Osamu gains."

All of this left Zeghes feeling intimidated. To himself, he said, "I am Zeghes. Heroes are not beaten. I will defeat the sharks." He felt the telltale prickling before a lightning strike. Along with it came an unusual feeling, fear. In a battle using vapuc, he could defeat one and maybe two, but three? How could he help Osamu let alone survive? Even as he considered all of this, he plunged down.

Another message commanded, "Zig zag to your left. Attack the Dread closest to the trail with force."

He obeyed even as he wondered who messaged him. Thunder boomed way to close for his senses. The nearest Dread seemed to be having trouble standing. Zeghes took advantage and slammed his head back into a rock wall.

With a screaming intensity a message ordered, |Backup! Get down lower. Try to be closer to a Dread. They're using some nasty vapucs.|

Zeghes found himself fighting against a current of air rushing past him. An explosion rocked him before he finished hearing the message and making the maneuver. Who had messaged him? Dazed and with a pounding head, the young dolphin found himself down by Osamu's attackers.

In his injured state, instinct took over. These were just two sharks and they needed ramming. Picking up speed and not stopping to think, Zeghes charged.

A message warned him. |Change direction.|

He ignored it even as he ignored the strange rippling of the air just in front of him. Intense heat and pain ripped through his skin.

Warning messages of imminent failure came from his alien suit.

Zeghes pleaded. Please, just function a little longer. Let me take out these two sharks. He moved faster, but with jerks prophesizing the impending failure of his suit. The young dolphin ignored his fears of failure and the pain. Just like with the real shark months ago he accessed the part of his brain which had been changed. Again, he used a pulse of force in front of him, but this time he was much stronger.

Before Zeghes got to him, the Dread looked as if a giant invisible bat hit him blasting him off the ground. Unfortunately for the second Dread, the flying Dread didn't gain altitude fast enough. The two collided. The first Dread cartwheeled through the air for thirty feet before slamming into a cliff. The other one flipped over catching himself against a boulder just in time for Zeghes to catch up with the result of his use of force.

The dolphin slammed his hard beak into the belly of the dizzy Dread. He heard the explosion of the man's breath. The enemy shark folded against Zeghes' head, and the dolphin carried him on for a few feet, until the dolphin shook him off.

In the next moment, the very cool alien suit failed, dropping Zeghes down to land very painfully onto the Dread and the rocky ground. One eye could only see the ugly visage of the unconscious alien. The other eye had the unusual view of Osamu doing strange things and throwing something.

A thud, a yell of pain, and then tumbling noises, until all the noises faded away.

In the quiet, another voice spoke. "You and the strange alien fought with courage. If we had to be defeated in this duel, at least it wasn't embarrassing. You Earthlings are a very surprising sort. We'll be doing some investigations. There is a mystery at play here and therefore potential for profit. My people are retrieving our fellow fighters. They all seem to have survived. How embarrassing for them. Goodbye for now."

Zeghes felt himself shifting and the alien being pulled out from under him. Footsteps approached and he heard Osamu speak.

"Hang in there, Zeghes. I'll get some help and get you to Gursha. She'll get you all fixed up."

Wearily, the dolphin tried to nod his head. Now that the action had ended, the pain from his burns ached with an intensity he couldn't bear. He tried to respond, "Tha—"

Chapter Forty-Six
On the Edge of Disaster

Gursha vehemently spoke, "Those aliens had to attack Zeghes with heat. Dolphins are incredibly tough and can heal from all kinds of wounds, but burns are one thing he doesn't heal as well from."

Zeghes could see a pink room, and Osamu stood with one arm around Mel as Gursha talked to them. "I'm doing what I can, but there's going to be extensive scarring."

The dolphin cautiously tried to move. His view of the room rotated. They must've already given him a new suit. Ekbal stood by his other side. He looked okay.

Gursha continued speaking. "There's one nasty wound on his side. It's still bleeding, but it'll heal fine."

Osamu said, "I've got to go. I've just got a message from Hheilea. There's something happening."

Gursha said, "I've heard something from Stick. I think there's some bad news, and it's going to be particularly bad for you Earthlings."

Zeghes pushed his way out of the holo-field. "I'm going too."

Gursha said, "You get back into that holo-field now."

Stubbornly, Zeghes said, "How bad is this news?"

"Bad, very bad."

"I can finish healing later."

Gursha said, "I'll grab some portable holo equipment and come too."

While they left the Academy, most of them stayed quiet. Other aliens and humans filled the air paths heading to the central arrival and departure platform. They must've gotten similar messages about the bad news. Before they traveled too

On the Edge of Disaster

far, Ekbal messaged Zeghes. |Hey, good maneuvering back there.|

|Thanks. Was that you giving me warnings?|

|You're welcome. We probably shouldn't talk about it. Remember? This messaging system isn't secure. We wouldn't want the Dreads to know.|

Zeghes nodded his head in agreement, before he took his turn on a departure pad. That would be bad.

Plummeting down from the sphere, Zeghes watched a steady flow of aliens and humans joining a large crowd of thousands. He spotted A'idah and went to her.

The closer he came the more concerned he grew. She stared back at Zeghes with wide, wide eyes showing white all around her pupils.

"Are you okay?"

Currents of misery, anger, and confusion flowed in her words. "No. This is going to be terrible. Stay close. I need you." After a short pause she added. "I wish Alex was here."

Zeghes bumped her again. "A'idah, get out of the shallow water. Alex wouldn't want you to give up. He made me promise. I know he—" The dolphin cut off the revelation he'd almost let out.

Sounding more her normal self, A'idah said, "What happened to you? Your skin's mostly—"

The conversation would've gone on longer, but Osamu interrupted them.

"A'idah, Zeghes, over here."

Zeghes let A'idah move away from him. He wasn't sure if he could keep the secret from her about Alex. The terrible announcement about the loss of the supply ship changed everything.

The shock left Zeghes drifting in the air. Around him the voices of other Earthlings rang out.

"No. You can't do this."

"What about all the life on Earth?"

"What about the test?"

Others heard that question and soon it grew into a chant.

"Test. Test. Test. Test. Test."

How could the Aliens stop training them? Alex needed to hear about this. Zeghes turned to go to the mountain, but stopped when he heard Amable speak.

"We're going to go ahead and do the test we'd planned for during the earlier budget problems. This time, your success will not mean your training will automatically continue, but there is a chance. We will record your effort and transmit the results on the most active of the websites of the alliance we are part of. The hope is your actions here will reach the hearts of enough people to get sufficient funding.

"Stick, also thinks we should go back to the original agreement."

It seemed they still had a chance to save everything. Zeghes didn't understand websites, but if they could get the funding needed to continue their training, he would do all he could to help.

Zeghes swam back through the air drawing nearer to Amable.

The leader of the Academy continued speaking, "We battle against the Deems together, but this part of the fight only you can do, and it will define you for the rest of your lives. This is the moment Earth's hope will be kept alive. You alone can and must find the strength within yourselves. Dig deep. This is your moment."

Amable lifted a hand and pointed at the distant Arena Island floating in the sky. "Your test is to move the Arena Island close enough for one of us to catch hold of a frond hanging below its underside. The person cannot be up in the air when they grab the frond."

Amable's voice dropped to a whisper and everyone leaned in closer. "You can do it."

With a shout, he finished. "Bring it here, now!"

Zeghes rocketed off to be closer to the island before he started to use the force. He knew getting closer would help. Ahead of him, the island fell from the sky drawing nearer. Zeghes reversed course, keeping pace with the island's descent and using force with all the rest of his concentration. He pictured the island as a shark trying to kill all his friends. Zeghes had to pull it away from them. The fronds hanging from the bottom of the island twisted and waved in the

On the Edge of Disaster

struggle. It descended to a few hundred feet above the ground and started rising again.

Zeghes thought he saw someone behind the vegetation. He shifted position and saw the force teacher, Titan, hiding above the fronds in a crack. What was he doing there? He was a shark. The sight of him distracted Zeghes' concentration. The little guy was laughing. There was nothing funny about this. Zeghes wanted to ram the disgusting little shark. Instead, the dolphin focused all his anger to his use of force, to push it to greater levels than ever before.

For a long time the island fell and rose never coming quite close enough to the aliens who strove to catch a frond. Zeghes focused all he could on pulling it down with force. His breathing slowed. His side at the location of his recent injury began to ache. Still, an instinctual part of him subconsciously continued to watch for the danger of sharks. Zeghes moved not quite realizing why. Until, he found himself looking again at the two-foot-tall shark. The terror was using force to keep the Earthlings from their chance to save Earth. No! In a flash, thoughts coursed through Zeghes. Could he use a vapuc to attack him? Frustration gnawed at him. He wasn't that good at vapucs other than force. He should ram him.

A brilliant, blinding strobe of light testified to someone rescuing the Earthlings, as Zeghes wrestled with the problem. The Island lurched down into the top of the dwarf pyramid and rolling thunder joined with the cheering of thousands.

Released from the struggle, Zeghes went limp. Slowly, he undulated through the air. They'd won. |Ytell, when will our celebration be?|

The Island released from the force vapuc of hundreds of desperate humans lurched back into the sky. One dwarf still held onto a frond, and his scream trailed behind, as the Island lifted him high into the sky.

|Let me get back to you on that. Okay? I've got to talk to Stick about his ideas.|

Zeghes responded. |Okay.|

He didn't have long to think about it. Another message interrupted him. |Zeghes, this is Windelli. What are you going to do now?|

|I don't know. We beat the test. If I remember right, that means Stick's old idea for making money should work.|

|Yes. That's great news, but, Zeghes, don't you think there's someone you should share the news with?|

For a second, Zeghes puzzled over her comment and then he realized who she was talking about. |That's a great idea.|

|Oh, and, Zeghes, I think it's about time you share your secret with two girls who've been hurting.|

Relief flooded the dolphin's mind. He'd been quite stressed by the secret he bore. | Hheilea, where are you?|

| A'idah, where are you?|

Hheilea responded. |I'm behind the mountain.|

Why would she be doing that? The mountain was off limits. |I'll meet you in a little bit between the mountain and the sea.|

Zeghes didn't hear back from A'idah. He started porpoising back through the air toward where he'd last seen her. His concern grew, as he looked back at the crowd of humans where he'd last seen her. Some of the humans and animals were collapsed onto the ground. Zeghes remembered how a person could exhaust themselves or even die from overuse of vapuc. A'idah had been ill. Gursha didn't want her to do much vapuc at all. Fear for his sister gripped his heart. She's sick. I left her alone. At those thoughts he sped faster through the air.

There, Zeghes spotted her identifying red curly hair. As he dropped down toward her his concern grew. Her body lay as limp as her curls. Easing down just above her, he nudged her with his beak. She didn't move.

Zeghes stood on his head. Someone looking on wouldn't have understood unless they knew dolphins. He did this to better use his sonar. Bringing his head down close to her, he started examining her. Carefully, using his sonar he peered beneath her clothing, beneath her skin, beneath her ribs, and down to her heart. It beat. At first that cheered the dolphin, but then he noticed it was slowing. |Gursha! Where are you!|

|What's the problem, Zeghes?|

|A'idah, I think her heart is giving out. I think she put too much effort into the test.|

On the Edge of Disaster

|I see you. Talk to her, a friend's voice helps life hang on. I'll be there soon.|

He moved right next to her. "A'idah, I need you. Don't go. Stay with us. Alex—" With that word, Zeghes paused, had her heart stopped? No, it just seemed to skip a beat. "A'idah, Alex needs you. He's alive. Live for me. Live for him. Stay with us, please."

Was her heart beating faster? Definitely stronger. He heard a yell.

"Zeghes, here I am!"

He looked up to see their heavy set nurse, Gursha, vaulting over someone rising to their knees. She tripped and started to fall. She was going to crash into A'idah.

Zeghes swung over his sister to protect her. Gursha caught her fall by bracing herself on him.

He pleaded. "Help her."

Gursha knelt by the still woman-child. With one hand she felt for a pulse. With another she sprayed a small holo-field over A'idah's chest. Immediately, it showed pink. She next sprayed a holo-field over her head. It too showed pink. With her other two hands she smoothed the red curls off of his friend's forehead and placed something in her mouth. "She's very weak. If I've gotten to her in time, she'll live. I might need the greater power of a clinic's holo-field. I'm afraid she's damaged some of the weakened blood vessels in her brain. There's a danger of a hemorrhage. Then there's her heart. I've done what I can to help. We'll know in the next few minutes."

Zeghes said, "A'idah, I'm right here. I need you to stay with me. All of us need you." He hesitated about using Alex's name. Would it be okay to share his name? She seemed to do better the last time. He threw caution to the wind. "Alex needs you. Please, stay with us."

He caught Gursha looking at him. "Keep talking to her. You're helping almost as much as any medicine."

"A'idah, your friends need you. Don't abandon us."

The girl stirred.

Gursha said, "She's going to be okay. In a few more minutes, you won't recognize her. I still need to get her into a clinic. The pink around her head is bad, but it's looking better than I would've expected. With the effort A'idah put out, she should've died. I think she probably has an aneurysm. The holo-field will try to repair the damage the best it can. She absolutely can't do any vapuc. Just keep her calm for a bit...." She paused and then added. "Do you know something about Alex that I don't?"

Zeghes looked at her and slowly nodded his head up and down.

The gruff, motherly, demanding, always in control nurse suddenly started crying. "Oh, Zeghes, thank you. I better go check on others. Thank you."

The dolphin looked back at his friend on the ground. Her eyes blinked.

He got a message from Hheilea. |Where are you?|

Zeghes answered. |I'm sorry. I was delayed. A'idah almost died. We'll be there soon.|

|She's alive? Wonderful. Don't hurry. Is she going to be okay?|

|Gursha said she'll be fine soon, but not to let her do any vapuc at all. Can you wait for us?|

|Okay, Zeghes, I'll just go up Alex's path.|

He heard a weak voice from down below. "Zeghes, What happened?"

"We beat the test. Everything's going to be fine."

The pink holo-field around A'idah's chest had turned blue and disappeared, but the pink one around her head remained. "Really? I had the best dream. Someone was telling me Alex needed me."

Zeghes glanced at the people moving all around them. "Do you feel up to taking a ride on me?"

"I think so." Even as she stood up, A'idah showed more life and energy. "Definitely so. Where are we going?"

"To meet with Hheilea, but, A'idah, Gursha just finished working on you. She sprayed you with two holo-fields to save your life. She left me with a warning. Whatever happens, remember, don't do anymore vapuc." Even as he passed on the warning, he knew what her response would be.

A'idah snorted, and said, "You know me. I always obey Gursha."

On the Edge of Disaster

She climbed on him, and he slowly started moving. He felt quite worried about her, but had no clue what to say.

Another voice spoke up. "Where are you going? Where are you going?"

Zeghes winced to himself. He was just going to share the secret with the girls. Skyler wouldn't be able to keep the knowledge secret. He'd have to get rid of him, but he didn't start talking in time.

A'idah answered in a surprisingly strong voice. "We're going to meet Hheilea."

"Oh, great. I'll come too."

Zeghes tried to accelerate and get away, but Skyler put on an impressive burst of speed catching up with them. "I'll just ride on A'idah's shoulder."

The poor dolphin didn't know what to think or do, but just continued on out of the crowd. At least it was just the three he'd have to deal with and not the whole flock. Another voice called out and Zeghes groaned to himself.

"Where are you going?"

It was the cloud girl, Alex's friend.

"We're going to get away from the crowd."

"Great, I'll come with you."

In a flash of brilliance, Zeghes had an idea. |A'idah are you feeling okay? Can you hang on if I go very fast?|

|Yes, Zeghes.|

The dolphin said, "Let's race." He'd leave the cloud girl so far behind she'd never find them, and maybe, Skyler wouldn't be able to hold on. "Hang on!" He shouted to his passengers and accelerated.

"Faster," A'idah said.

Gladly, thought Zeghes hoping Skyler would just get blown off by accident. At the same time, he remembered Ekbal getting blown off, and how A'idah had almost died, and she was still ill. |A'idah, warn me if I get going too fast for you.| He called upon his repaired suit for more speed. Soon, they rocketed across the island. He took a roundabout path to be sure and lose the cloud girl. A couple of times, he turned sharper than he needed purposefully trying to loose Skyler. Coming around the mountain, he spotted Hheilea. With a graceful arch through the air he slowed.

"What a ride. What a ride. What a ride. Let's do it again."

Zeghes came to a stop. What would he do about Skyler? Well, at least he'd lost the cloud girl.

A greenish cloud rose up from behind Hheilea. "What took you so long?"

"What? How?"

Hheilea answered. "Zeghes, it's okay. I asked her to join us."

The poor dolphin looked back and forth between them, frustration building. Not thinking if it was wise for A'idah, he bucked her off and swam on up the last of the path.

From behind him, he heard Skyler squawk. "Hey."

A'idah's, "Zeghes!"

Fear for Alex stopped him from responding to them and stole away his anger.

Chapter Forty-Seven
Team Work

Alex looked at the little tube in his hand. The technologies of the aliens continued to amaze, confuse, and puzzle him, but this one which created things from light was special to him. It had saved his life from an attack by one of his teachers. The feeling of running out of time cut his consideration of the tool short. Alex thrust his arm out and thought of what he wanted to create. In response, light flowed like a liquid from the end of the light greker. He weaved it into a bag to hang from his back. Placing some food and water into the bag and slinging it onto his back, he attacked the cliff face again. The first three phases of this route he had down. First, using hand and footholds Alex climbed up to a narrow ledge. He hated to waste the time, but leaned into the cliff and rested before moving along the three inch wide path to the vertical crack. Doom crashed down through his sense of the future and cut the break short. Alex had no choice. He had to get to the top. Something terrible happened to his friends and their efforts for Earth.

Up the crack he flew. Set hold, test it, and move up. Again, his helmet made from the light greker banged into the obstacle of the overhang. Already his forearms burned, but he wouldn't, couldn't, refused to rest them.

Maleky complained. *I don't mind your idiocy and the falls, but the pain you're subjecting me to is terrible. One of these times, you'll either break bones and have to call Gursha for help, probably letting the assassins know you're still alive or you'll just do their work for them by killing yourself.*

The worst of it was Alex knew Maleky was right. Hurrying while climbing didn't just add danger but made disaster probable. Hating the delay, while he knew the logic of it, Alex took a few precious seconds to shake out his arms one at a time.

You didn't rest them for long enough. Maleky complained. *You're going to kill us.*

Resolutely, Alex ignored the threat and swung out under the overhang using the crack running out to the edge of the overhang for holds. An hour later, Alex hung trembling from the overhead slab of granite. He'd tried to pull himself up by one arm to reach up and over the lip of the overhang to get a hand hold above, but he couldn't quite reach far enough. In his time off from climbing and with his injuries, he'd lost too much upper body strength.

Maybe Windelli could provide Zeghes with some kind of medical tool to give Alex a boost to his strength. He decided to try something else even as Maleky disagreed.

You're crazy. This will chew up your hand. You're too worn out. If you slip loose, there are some nasty rocks a long ways below us.

Alex shoved his hand into the crack as close to the lip as he dared. Clenching his hand to set the handhold, he pulled hard to test the hold. Loosening his other hand, Alex pulled it free. Hanging from one arm, he swung out past the edge. Swinging his legs back and forth, Alex successfully built the momentum needed to reach up and over to grab the crack above the overhang. "Yes." Finally, he would overcome this obstacle. Alex ignored the pain in his hand and arm holding all of his weight. The free hand went up and over the lip. He'd done it, but multiple voices yelling broke through his concentration.

Zeghes said, "What are you doing?"

Others said, "Alex! You're alive!"

"Huh." Alex looked down. He recognized the voices and put them to the people below. Oh no. His secret climbing of the mountain was in serious danger. It wouldn't be long and the assassins would be after him again.

"What are you doing?" The cloud girl asked.

"You've been alive all this time, and I've been dying?!" A'idah screamed.

"Zeghes, did you know about this?" Skyler asked.

Hheilea just looked at him with tears on her face. Alex couldn't tell if she looked relieved or mad. He thought continuing the climb would be safer than going back down to them, but they had broken his concentration. His one hand hold relaxed too much and his weight ripped it free. His other hand scrabbled for a hold. There, he almost had it. The swinging out of his body from losing the other hand hold pulled that hand free before he could get a grip. With a scream of pain and fear, he fell. Others yelled too.

"Alex!"

"I'll grab him."

"Save him."

"Gotcha," Zeghes said.

Alex fell through a cushiony material and heard the cloud girl say in her husky voice, "Hello there," as she slowed his fall.

He slammed against Zeghes and automatically wrapped his arms and legs around the dolphin for dear life. His momentum pulled him over his friend's side. He was going to fall off. Instantly, his dolphin brother dropped from the impact of Alex's weight. Wings flapped above him. Something hard momentarily grabbed him around the chest and pulled him back from the near fall.

Skyler said, "Safe now."

Zeghes descended back to the path with him. Alex tried to grasp what had happened. Who all had saved him? He knew his friends could use his path of progress to visit him without having to climb the mountain themselves, but this was different. They had worked together at the top of the path. At that realization an idea started to coalesce in him mind.

Alex slid off and turned to the girls. He started to speak, "I've got a—"

The closer view of the faces of Hheilea and A'idah shocked the words from completing. Alex wished he had stayed above for longer.

A'idah didn't wait for him to finish. Like a storm cloud with an incongruous, clear pink cloud around her head, she marched up and slapped him hard before yelling and crying. "How could you? Congratulations, on fooling everyone. You died. I was dying. I thought..., maybe I'd... killed you while under the influence of the rabies." Her expression changed, and she wheeled on her dolphin brother. "Zeghes, you suggested we come over here after the test. Did you know about Alex all this time? Is that why you wouldn't talk to me about his fake death? You knew how I was feeling. How could you?"

For the first time since Alex had come to know the dolphin, Zeghes yelled. "Yes! He almost did die! Remember how you taught me to keep my promise about Hheilea? I kept my promise for our brother. I didn't want to be the cause of his secret getting out and having him really die from an assassin. Would you have wanted that? You thought he was dead. Now, he's alive. Aren't you glad he's alive?"

A'idah's crying grew worse, and she grabbed Alex burying her face in his chest. He held her feeling terrible for her and worried about the holo-field. What was wrong with her head?

Over A'idah's head, Alex looked at Hheilea. |You saved my life. Thanks.|

|I didn't know. After the effort of reaching you through time's dimensions, I was unconscious for a whole day. When I came to, I thought you were dead. It's been hard. We need to talk, but not now. How's it going with reaching the top of the mountain?|

That's right... the mountain... and getting the sword... Alex looked around at everyone. "I'm sorry for the pain I've caused, but I have to get this sword."

Everyone looked at him. Different emotions roiled around them, but the anger had evaporated. Even as he looked at them, he put together the pieces of the idea. The cloud girl had somehow turned her insubstantial form into a more solid form to slow him. Zeghes had swum up with his suit to catch him. Skyler had flown up and caught him with his vapuc giant beak. Alex didn't know how the mountain reacted to climbing efforts, or if it could hear what was said, or how long it took to react to something new. Even as he worked out the details, he gasped at an epiphany. The Gadget Lady's mountain was another virtual reality room, except not a room but— The enormity of it almost stole away the clarity of the plan he'd worked out.

Alex gestured to his friends. "Come over here." He led them over to a tight gap between two vertical slabs of granite. He whispered. "I've got an idea. In a moment we'll go back out there. Skyler, try to fly up the mountain. It will use wind to blow you back down. Use your vapuc beak to grab a hold of something and keep trying to go up. Hheilea,—"

She whispered as he spoke her name. "I've got a spot to climb picked out."

"Good. A'idah—" He wanted to ask her about the holo-field around her head and considered leaving her out of the plan, but he knew the futility of that idea.

She swiped the remaining tears off her face with a fist. "Show me the best place to climb."

"Zeghes, carry A'idah around to the left to any spot she says will work. Come back. Get me. We'll go to the right." Alex turned to the last one, the cloud girl. He leaned close and spoke with his lips right in the edge of her cloud as quietly as he could. After some more moments of preparation, they left the crowded space between the slabs.

On Alex's back hung a ball of light made from the greker. A'idah rode on Zeghes back. Gusts of wind came at them from different directions. The sound of grinding rocks filled the air. Alex felt the path shaking under his feet. He could tell the mountain knew something different was happening.

Alex said, "One, two, three."

At the count of three, Skyler burst into the air. He angled off to the left aiming for a crack not much wider than his body.

At the same time, Zeghes darted off without his normal undulations.

Skyler reached high on the crack as a gust of wind blew past him. With his powerful beak, he grabbed ahold of the rock and scrabbled with his claws to force his way up the crack.

Zeghes almost reached the lip of the overhang before a gust of wind hit him. A'idah vaulted off onto the rock. Immediately, Zeghes dropped back to Alex.

Hheilea already ran back between the two slabs and used them to climb up.

Running to meet Zeghes, Alex jumped onto his dolphin friend. Around to the other side of the mountain they went. Alex knew A'idah, Hheilea, and Skyler still fought against the mountain. Hopefully, it would be enough.

Gusts of wind struck at Zeghes and Alex from different directions, but Zeghes didn't challenge the mountain, by trying to go higher. A bulge in the mountain's side appeared around the corner. Fifty feet beyond that was the summit, an easy shot.

Zeghes bucked beside the bulge. Alex went with the buck flipping his leg over Zeghes back. He stumbled just a bit on the treacherously uneven surface of the bulge. The stumble didn't slow him down. He ripped the glowing ball off his back and heaved it toward Zeghes. Immediately, Alex turned and ran toward the peak. With a roar the rock surface buckled in front of him. Through the roar he heard a thump. The ball soared above a new cliff forming in front of him.

Zeghes said, "I'm going to get to the top. This wind can't stop me."

Silence fell. The wind stopped. The cliff in front of Alex slumped down. A smooth path ran from him to the peak. The light greker ball split apart revealing the cloud girl. She danced on the peak. "We did it! We did it!"

A quiet satisfaction filled Alex. Victory shed his weariness.

Maleky commented. *I really didn't think your idea of hiding the cloud girl with the light greker would work. Congratulations. You've beaten the odds again. You were right about confusing the mountain with everyone.*

Alex smiled. He could see A'idah, Hheilea, and Skyler coming from the other side.

The cloud girl stopped her bouncing dance. "I've got to go tell everyone. You did it Alex"

He grinned. "No, we did it."

"I don't think I could've done it without you. The mountain just kept getting more difficult the closer I got to the top."

With his fellow Earthlings succeeding with the test and with his beating the Gadget Lady's challenge the future never looked brighter.

A'idah walked up to him. Alex reacted to her approach by taking a step back. He wasn't sure what to expect.

"Alex..." She stepped closer holding her arms out.

He took her into his arms, and she started crying again. "You're alive. You're alive. I'd given up hope. I thought you were dead. Don't do that to me again, or I'll kill you."

Team Work

Alex ran a hand down the back of her head and held her close. "I'm sorry. Everything's going to be okay now. With my sword, I can defeat any assassin. We'll be fine."

"Come on, let's go get my sword."

A'idah pumped her fist into the air. "We're not giving up. We've gotten to the top. Let's go see this mythical Gadget Lady and see what she's got we can use."

They weren't far from the peak. The cloud girl had actually been up there, but she'd come back down to celebrate with the friends. It wouldn't take them long to get back to the top.

Skyler burst into flight. "There's no wind to stop me this time." He slammed into a wall and fell in a heap of blue feathers to the ground.

In an angry voice the cloud girl asked, "What happened?"

A voice spoke. "This group cheated using all of Alex's progress. Only he can come."

A'idah hurried to the blue Hyacinth Macaw and carefully placed her hands on him. "I think he's okay, just stunned. He'll be okay in a minute and using my Healing vapuc is helpful for my own injuries."

Alex said, "I'll go to the Gadget Lady and see what she has to help us. In the meantime, please don't tell anyone I'm alive."

Zeghes said, "Osamu, with my help, has taken care of the assassin problem."

"What?" All of that terrible training he'd done just to be ready for the Dreads had been for nothing.

"Yeah. It was something about, because of your death, they needed to fight one of us to defend their honor. I hope there aren't any sharks at this Gadget Lady's place. Stay safe."

Hheilea said, "I think we should wait for you at the bottom of the mountain.

Nodding his head even as he tried to shake off his reaction, Alex said, "I'll be quick." Waving to them, he turned and walked through the transparent wall. In a few steps, he stood on the very top of the mountain. He punched the air with a fist. "I did it! Yeah!" In the distance, scattered green clouds hung in the sky. Satisfaction and happiness that his friends had been part of the victory filled him. For a second, Alex thought of another friend who'd died. Twyla would've been happy for him too.

The evil alien in Alex's head, Maleky, intruded into his thoughts and interfered with his feeling of success. *Oh, Alex. Where's the Gadget Lady?*

The air around the peak had a strange shimmering to it. Out of the corner of Alex's eye something caught his attention. Hopeful, he turned his gaze, but nothing was there. Slowly he shuffled in a circle. Warily he watched out of the corner of his eye. There! He froze. A yellow brick step shimmered in the air. He stepped to it and stumbled. The step vanished. No, it moved. Again, Alex carefully tried to step onto it. Again he stumbled. He stopped trying and thought about the problem. Carefully, he considered the problem using his sense of the future, the one vapuc he could do. Alex slowly stepped toward the golden-yellow step. He could sense it would disappear. Still, he tried again. The step just wouldn't stay there, and he couldn't sense where it went or how to try differently. Trying desperately to step onto it, he instead stumbled and fell to the ground.

Alex just stayed on the rough stony ground. He ground his teeth in frustration. His sense of the future didn't help at all. In fact, he now had a premonition things were going to get worse.

Maleky whispered in his mind. *I could help you. All you have to do is to surrender to me.*

A'idah messaged him, providing a welcome interruption, and yet he knew it added more danger. |Alex, are you done getting the sword from the Gadget Lady?|

If he hadn't been discouraged before, her message dragged him to a new low. |Not yet.| He didn't want to share his discouraging situation.

|Well, hurry up. We can see some people headed toward the mountain. I don't know what's going on.|

Alex groaned to himself. He didn't have time. In desperation, he turned to the alien in his mind. *Maleky, do you have any brilliant ideas?*

I know how to help you, but you have to surrender your will to me.

Against his better judgement the teenage boy considered the offer. *How do I—*

A sweet familiar voice interrupted. "Alex, do you need help?" Hheilea stood below him at the edge of the transparent wall. She held a small package and looked up at him with a smile.

Alex smiled back glad for the intrusion into his surrendering. He pried himself up off the ground.

Maleky prodded. *Go to her.*

This Alex could happily agree to. "Why are you still up here?"

"I've got—" Instead of finishing the thought she continued with. "I really thought you'd died."

Alex heard the distress in her words. Again, he realized the alien ritual, T'wasn't-to-be-is which had drawn the two of them together, really must be gone. She couldn't sense him as completely as she used to. Yet, she still should've been able to sense his possible futures instead of a blank wall. Hheilea should've known he was alive. It was the one weak link in his plan to pretend his own death.

She held up the package. "I..."

He painfully swallowed. Somehow, the T'wasn't-to-be-is being gone didn't seem so good. It hurt Alex to look at the young woman he'd come to know so well and to know how he'd destroyed her hopes and expectations of marriage through the T'wasn't-to-be-is ceremony. Now, he'd hurt her again.

Maleky suggested. *We should comfort her.*

In agreement, Alex moved faster. "I'm sorry. I didn't want to cause you or others pain, but I needed to convince the assassins I died."

Hheilea said, "My father must've agreed with you. I think he must've been doing something to hide the truth from me, or just the trauma I suffered by forcing myself through the dimensions of time to save your life. I couldn't sense any future for you. As far as I knew, you were dead."

Maleky grumbled in Alex's mind. *Yeah, the Kimley elders can control access to the future. They don't let me see much of the future.*

Alex moved to hug her, but Hheilea held something up between them.

"My dad gave me something today. He said I would recognize when I needed to give it to someone. They're supposed to eat it. I think it's meant for you." In bitter terms, she added. "I can't believe he didn't just tell me you still lived."

Alex didn't know what to say about her dad. Instead, he just said, "What is it?" He tried to understand her dad's motives, but Maleky interfered.

Maleky snorted in Alex's mind and his thoughts growled. *Adult Kimleys worry more about their plans than peoples' feelings. It's disgusting. He should've spared her the pain. She wouldn't have told anyone. They avoid physical contact. My dad never talked to me, except to leave me cryptic messages dripping with sorrow. I'm glad he's gone. It was the best thing I've done.* Bitterness and anguish washed through Alex. *You need to let me control you. I can save her from becoming an adult Kimley.*

Hheilea lifted something in a folded white napkin to him. From within the napkin wafted a pungent, disagreeable smell.

The odor turned Alex's stomach over. "I'm supposed to eat that?" The memory of getting poisoned and almost killed came back to him.

The folds yielded to her fingers exposing a sickly brownish yellow lump. Hheilea didn't touch the lump with her fingers, but held it up to Alex. "Here, eat this. You'll need it."

Bad idea. Maleky insisted.

The memory of a poisoning reflexively moved his body back from the lump.

Tears appeared in her eyes. "Please. Trust me this time. Remember the vial. If you had trusted me and drank it all, you wouldn't have been poisoned. That path would've been easier. I told you then to trust me and drink it all."

Maleky objected and again the memory of getting poisoned came back.

Alex gritted his teeth and stepped forward. "Maleky is trying to control me with his thoughts. I remember the poisoning was his fault." Alex took the lump and trying not to breathe took a bite. It was cold and slimy. He gagged almost spitting it out.

Hheilea ordered. "Swallow it. You need to eat it all."

In counter to her words came Maleky's thoughts. *Spit it out. It's probably poisonous. Don't trust her.*

Team Work

Other thoughts, Alex now recognized as coming from Maleky crowded his mind. They reminded him of his own doubts and fears of the alien's motives and plans.

Alex gazed into Hheilea's impossibly large eyes and swallowed, forcing it down. Not thinking, not listening to thoughts, struggling against complaining taste buds, the sliminess, and a stomach threatening to rid itself of the substance, he ate until the lump was gone. Hheilea, with a joyful expression, gave him a quick hug. "Thanks for trusting me this time."

"I'm sorry, I didn't trust you before. You're dad has to have his reasons. He isn't trying to hurt you, but give you a better future. Sometimes, that takes pain." Agony twisted Alex's gut.

Hheilea took quick steps back from him and pointed up. "Go. Go quickly."

Chapter Forty-Eight
Sword

Fighting back a reflex to throw-up, Alex returned to the summit. He looked up and back down, puzzled. Out of the corner of his eye, a golden step shimmered in the air. He stepped to the side of it. Where he knew it would be. His foot found firm purchase. Another step appeared. Again he stepped not where he saw it in the air, but where he knew it was. Quicker, he stepped again and again. The shimmering grew stronger, his hair stood on end. After the last step, a screeching sound filled the air. The sky and clouds disappeared or had they been there at all.

Angled panes of glass surrounded him. Alex reached out to one pane. The pane shimmered with blues and greens, streaks of yellow, orange, and red raced across the pane. His hand passed right through the pane. It was just air. Alex froze. He could see the muscles, tendons, red and blue blood vessels, and the bones of his hand. The harder he looked the farther into his hand he could see. Tipping his head he stared in fascination at his abdomen. Yellowish-brown stuff sloshed about in his stomach. Farther down his abdomen, coils of translucent tubes flexed, moving a brown substance. Scraping, clicking, and muttering interrupted his self-examination.

He stood on a platform at the edge of a huge cavern filled with numerous racks. Stuff of all shapes and colors filled the shelves of the racks to overflowing. Most of it had a futuristic look to it. Around the end of the nearest rack, orange antennae waved in the air, followed by a large crab-like creature six feet wide. Alex saw the carapace covering the crab's back, below it pink flesh, and past the flesh a bag filled with squirming worms being mashed by the contractions of the organ. Alex's mouth dropped open at the disgusting sight. "Ewww."

In a voice full of clickings and clackings the creature asked, "Are you looking at my insides? Try relaxing your focus. How am I going to get anything done with him talking so much? Oh, you should be getting very sick and will need to leave right now. Turn around and go back. Well? Get going."

Alex closed his eyes tight. Opened them back-up and rolled his eyes about not looking at anything in particular. Now a shell covered the flesh and organs. "I'm not feeling sick. What's going on? Why do I see into things? I'm not leaving until I get what I came for."

The crab scuttled about with scrapping, skittering sounds. "Not leaving? Ugh. You're fascinating. Did you consume wacune? How did you get here? Are you sure you don't want to leave?"

"Wacune? I ate a yellowish-brown lump. Are you the Gadget Lady?"

It came closer looking intently at him. One claw reached up to him, and Alex ducked back.

"I'm not going to hurt you, although that would be a solution to this interruption and stop your incessant talking. Your hair! No wonder you could come in. You have the shimmers of a young adult Kimley, but your hair isn't white. You're very strange."

Alex's eyes went wide. The treatment his nurse, Gursha, did to hide the evidence of his frightening transformation to a human-Kimley hybrid must be wearing off. His hair was starting to shimmer like a butterfly's wings. Shrugging off what he could do nothing about, Alex asked again. "Are you the Gadget Lady?"

His question was spoken to the crab's back. She scuttled away, complaining to herself. "Someone has invaded my solitude. I should've made the mountain more difficult or maybe.... Hmmm, I could change the stairs. If he would just stop talking so much, I could think. Where did he get wacune? I suppose he'll be collecting a few of my precious items. How am I going to think with him talking so much? Too bad he doesn't just...." As she scuttled out of sight her voice faded away.

Alex kept his eyes unfocused. Around him stood metal racks. On a shelf right below his head rested a short rod. He picked it up. A blaze of light shot out of it and sliced through one of the rack's support poles.

"Uh-oh," Alex said, dropping the rod. The light immediately extinguished.

"Hello, sir. Out of my way, please," a tall, golden, and very thin humanoid robot said. "Oh my, that rack is going to fall."

Reaching up with long, thin arms, the robot grabbed the support pole with two hands. Pulling the cut pieces back together the robot said, "Hit the cut with your number-two laser."

Startled, Alex gazed into the robot. A blaze of light burned within it. The brightness of the light hurt. He ducked his head and threw up an arm. Calming himself, Alex blinked and glanced around. Who was the robot talking to?

A thin beam of red light issued forth from a squat, cylindrical robot floating in the air. The light shined onto the cut.

The gangly robot said. "Thank you. And now, if you would, please, use your number-three laser,"

The other robot responded with a chirping. "You're welcome."

A bright yellow light bathed the cut. "Perfect," the tall robot said, letting go of the repaired pole. Looking at Alex, the robot said, "Thank you for the work." Turning, he walked off into the maze of aisles with the other bobbing along behind.

Alex didn't watch the two depart. He had to find a String Sword., He gazed about the aisles. Choosing one, he started walking. Not noticing, Alex began walking faster. At an intersection, he thought the Gadget Lady would be to the right and decided to go and ask her about the String Sword. Instead of going to the right, he went to the left. Something drew his attention to a shelf, and he moved a large object with strange nobs, dials, and switches over to the side. That revealed a small flat object. Alex picked it up.

Not knowing why, he hurried about collecting other odd objects. They all felt right to him, but Alex had no idea what they were. An empty spot on a shelf drew him. Alex jumped over a couple of items on the floor, caught his foot on a third,

Sword

and tumbled to the floor. All of the strange devices he'd been collecting fell out of his hands and scattered across the floor.

A laugh made Alex blush. What was he doing? There wasn't anything on the shelf. What was his hurry?

He heard the voice of the skinny robot. "Relax and take your time. Let yourself be guided, and you'll find the items you need."

Slowly, fighting the need to hurry, Alex collected the spilled items and stood to his feet. He tried to use his sense of the future. Something was on the shelf. He needed it. Eagerly, he picked up an invisible soft, cloth like object off the empty shelf. Walking farther, the enthrallment directed him to reach for a bag of crystalline spheres. Along the way, Maleky tried to make suggestions about picking up interesting devices, but Alex ignored him. He passed by an entire rack of different types of guns.

The barrel of one the size of a small cannon loomed over the aisle. Another, slender almost knife-like, but with a gun's grip caught his attention. It felt deadly as he slipped it into a pocket. Next, he came to a stop beside a stack of miscellaneous gadgets. He looked down into the pile. Under everything, a folded garment of many colors caught his eyes. Alex carefully set aside the items he carried and began to move the stack.

From below and behind the stack, the brightly colored garment appeared. Finally, there it was before him, a multicolored, full body suit. Alex picked it up and shook the suit out. Without thinking about it, he stepped into the legs of the suit. Then, he wriggled his arms into the sleeves. As soon as both arms were in place, the front of the suit sealed by itself.

It covered him from wrist to ankle. Assorted pockets covered the garment. Most looked normal, but something blurred the appearance of other pockets. When he focused on those, trying to see them better, a headache quickly began pounding in his skull. Why did he put it on?

Holding one of the strange pockets open, he one at a time put all the things he had collected into it. A bulge started forming as he kept adding gadgets. Alex paused with a large crystal ball, in his hand. It would obviously not fit. How did everything he already put in fit?

Maleky answered. *You obviously lack the knowledge to understand.*

Alex held the sphere up to the pocket. Now what? How would he put it in any of his pockets? The pocket's opening swelled, and the sphere slipped in without a problem. More than a little puzzled, Alex walked on. He turned a corner and came to the Gadget Lady standing at some long benches strewn with odd items.

She held a tiny hammer in one claw and with it banged on a tall blue box shaped like a telephone booth, but with the words *police box* near the top. "There you are. Still filling the air with words and confounding my ability to think and work. I don't understand why other people feel the need to rattle on and on filling the air with extra and totally unnecessary words of various lengths and meanings. There is a value to quiet, but most people just don't understand. Humph. I expect you've raided my shelves of items you need." The crab said, turning some of her eyes to look at him.

"What?" Alex blinked. What had he done? What should he say to her?

"This suit—"

"It's yours," the Gadget Lady said, continuing to bang and pound with the tiny tool on the tall box object.

Maleky tried to get Alex's attention.

Alex said, "I just started gathering gadgets—"

"They're yours, also."

"But why did I collect all of—"

"It's what I do because of *dark matter* and why I have to find a place like this to live and work. When someone comes to see me, they eventually start looking at my gadgets. They go into a trance like state and are drawn to what will be of use to them," the Gadget Lady said. "I'm sure you can see my difficulty. If I'm easy to find, I would soon have nothing for anyone. Plus, all of their talking would keep me from getting anything made. Now, let's see what you have." She continued banging.

Alex probed his pocket and found nothing. "I know I put them into this pocket."

"They'll be in the alternate pocket," she said.

"Alternate pocket? What's...?"

Sword

"Your suit has normal pockets and alternate pockets. Remove your hand from the pocket it's so uselessly poking around in and put it back." Part of the box she pounded on cracked.

Following the crab's directions, Alex found his hand in a pocket full of stuff.

Maleky tried again to get Alex's attention.

"How...?" Alex began to ask.

"Oh you visitors are all the same, always asking questions. If you'll be quiet for a moment, I'll explain. This suit you found was created by a master gadgeteer. It's been collecting dust on shelves for centuries. It has some pockets that exist in two realities at the same time. I really can't say how she created it, but I can explain how it works. When you check the pocket by placing your hand in it, you collapse the wave function and find one of the two possible pockets. A pocket of the other reality exists just not here at the same time. Yet, they both do exist at the same time."

While the crab rattled on about the logic of two realities existing at the same time until a deterministic action causes the wavefunction to collapse, resulting in one of the pockets to exist in this reality, while the other still exists, but not in this reality. Alex found himself drowning in her explanation.

"...in denial of superposition..."

In desperation, before the confusion led to him falling unconscious, Alex said, "Great. Thanks. I understand."

"You really don't have a clue. Oh, well let me explain the other items you found." She continued to bang with the tiny hammer, and a loud series of cracks reverberated in the cavern.

In moments, Alex felt overwhelmed with the different gadgets he'd picked up. A few stuck in his mind, such as the visor that would let him see hidden creatures and one that would let him walk through walls. He started to place an apparatus in its own pocket and stopped.

His free hand pointed behind the Gadget Lady. On the wall, behind her work area, hung a scabbard with a sword. The hilt and the guard were a non-reflective black. Mounted on the pommel, a deep purple crystal glowed. On the scabbard grey and black spirals, cruciform curves, spiric sections, and many other patterns covered its surface and its belt in a complex combination of light and dark.

The Gadget lady retrieved the scabbard and sword. "This is my favorite weapon. I loathe parting with it. Use it well." With this said, she handed the weapon to Alex.

Fumbling for words of thanks, Alex struggled to get the scabbard's belt buckled in place. In front of him, the crab tapped on the floor with a massive claw. A feeling pushed against his awareness. "Thanks. I really needed this."

Another object, a black bag drew his attention. Alex pointed at it.

The Gadget Lady retrieved it and gave it to Alex. "You must be involved in something very dangerous and important. You are taking many of my best treasures. Only a great need can help others find and ask for my gadgets." She bashed harder on the box with the little hammer.

A growing sense of urgency drove him to quickly gather the last items and store them in an alternate pocket. Just as he puzzled over a long slender object, a thingamajig, the spell like state he had been in wore off. Emotions from his feelings of the future engulfed Alex as a tidal wave engulfs a beach. He had to get out of here. Danger, death, and even worse a terrible and unendurable pain loomed. Alex dropped the thingamajig. He gasped words. "There's a disaster. I have to get back."

"If there's been a disaster, there's nothing you can do. You should just stay with me. I guess I can put up with your constant chatter." She added, "This little hammer is useless for these delicate adjustments." That said she tossed the hammer aside.

Alex ducked just in time to avoid the missile. He ignored it, but couldn't dodge the future agony. Knowing he would face it anyway terrified him. Ignoring his feelings, he straightened up and pointed a finger at the Gadget Lady. "You're terrible. Because there's a disaster, I need to go and try to help. You're supposed to be a help with your gadgets, but you've set this place up so I'm the only one who—"

The Gadget Lady tried to interrupt. "I—"

Alex raised his voice to a shout. "could get to you! We are fighting for worlds of living creatures. And you hide in here!"

Sword

"My people are solitary. I'm the only one who doesn't live on an isolated and barren world. I wouldn't be here except for Amable forcing me. I am who I am. I can't be different. You don't understand. This is painful to me." Reaching under the bench she said, "I need a bigger hammer to make these delicate adjustments." At the same time, she continued looking at Alex.

Alex snatched the strange spear like thingamajig off the ground and turned away from the Gadget Lady. Quickly, he jammed it hand over hand into a pocket.

He spoke and the words came out choked by the ache they released and the pain he would soon be facing. "You don't know what pain is. I've lost my dad, mom, and now my whole home world is in danger. Not that long ago, a new friend of mine died. If anyone wants to bad enough, they can be different. You're already different just by being here. How do I get out of here?"

"Go ahead, get out of here. Continue straight through the aisle in front of you." With a mighty swing of the truly huge, sledge hammer she gently tapped the box. "That should fix it. If only, I could fix people this way."

His heart pounded, fear of the looming agony threatened to paralyze him. Alex sprinted down the aisle. He stared ahead of him, but everything blurred. He blinked away unshed tears of torment, and as he focused, colored panes hung in the air at many different angles. He slashed through them and took the first golden stair at a run. Alex would do what he could regardless of the pain. His sense of the future made one thing crystal clear. Suffering awaited him.

Chapter Forty-Nine
Her

Alex jumped off the last golden step. A screeching sound filled the air. The sky and clouds reappeared, and Alex stumbled on the top of the path to land sprawled on the ground. Pain from a knee tried to get to his brain. Concern over the disaster drove him to his feet.

He turned and ran down the sandy path. Behind him, he heard a roar. Alex glanced back over his shoulder and almost tripped and fell again. The mountain peak behind him thrust up into the sky. It grew steeper in just that fraction of a second glance. The path behind him disappeared. Stumbling in mid stride, Alex slowed down. Around him, the edges of the path disintegrated.

Go faster. Maleky's thought screamed at him. *You made the Gadget Lady upset with your fancy speech. Why do you have to be so self-righteous?*

Alex sprinted past a boulder the size of a house rolling down onto the path. Ahead of him, holes opened up in the path and more boulders thundered down around him. He vaulted smaller boulders and slapped his feet down on the few remaining level spots. *I wasn't being self-righteous. I just told her the truth.* Alex leaned into a turn of what was left of the path. Using his momentum to keep from falling, he ran across the tipped surface of a rapidly growing cliff. Pushing off the nearly vertical rock wall, Alex landed back onto a section of smooth slopped path. With its sandy surface, he had no chance to slow down. In front of him, the terrain continued to change.

You're so sanctimonious. Telling her your truth was being self-righteous.

Her

Alex responded. *You can see my memories. You know I don't trust my own self. It's you who is self-righteous. You think you're way is the best, and it's all about focusing on you. Now shut up and stop distracting me.* From Alex's sense of the future came more distraction. Pain and confusion waited.

With a few more words, Maleky grudgingly let it go. *I'll stop, only because otherwise you'd kill us. I could prove I'm right. You're still just a kid and don't know anything. Be careful!* The last thought was screamed.

The path ahead had been narrowing, but suddenly jagged rocks spurted out of the ground. Time seemed to slow down. Alex used his sense of the future to help him pick his course through the jagged teeth waiting to rip him to shreds. One rock moved when he hit it with the sole of his shoe. Not getting the boost to the height he needed, Alex tucked his feet up barely clearing one of the sharp edged rocks. With his arms out for balance he slapped his feet down in a shifting dance.

Hheilea messaged him. |Alex, where are you?|

|Almost down the mountain.| Alex relied on his sense of the future even more trying to find the easiest path down the shifting terrain, but his sense of the future screamed of danger and suffering.

|Good. There's a problem. You're in danger. Amable will be calling you. I got a bubble, and I'm coming back. Where should I meet you?|

Alex already knew about the danger. A rumble from higher on the mountain ripped Alex's attention from her warning. A massive rock slide roared down a brand new gorge aimed at and ahead of Alex. He didn't think he could out run it, especially with the distraction of Hheilea talking to him.

|Alex, did you get my question? Where should I meet you?|

|At the bottom, under a pile of rocks or kissing the ground and praying.|

|What?!|

|Can't talk more. Bye. Love you.| Alex didn't think about what he'd said to her. He just tried to move faster. Far ahead of him, a new cliff rose beside the last stretch of path before the level ground began. With one hand, he dug in his pockets looking for the light greker. Maybe he could build a shield for

protection. In one pocket, he found the light greker tube. Ahead of him, a sight froze his blood.

The cliff he raced towards started to crumble. Massive boulders slowly fell down toward the path. If he kept going, he would be racing into that rock fall. A quick glance back told him he had no other options. The first rock slide would be upon him soon.

He'd climbed the Gadget Lady's mountain, but now it would kill him. Screaming, he jumped off the path to the right leaping through chaotic terrain. The landslide behind him shook the ground. A blast of dust swept over Alex, leaving him choking and half blind. He missed a target landing off balance. Relaxing, Alex tried to go with his fall to another safer—

A glance to the side told him there was no time. He hadn't out run the rock fall. Alex swung the greker up, bitter tears burned in his dust filled eyes. He couldn't die. He'd make a shield with the greker. He'd dig his way out from under the tons of rocks. His friends and Earth needed him. He screamed as truly huge boulders bounced off him. It took him a second to realize he hadn't died. The rock fall wasn't real.

He didn't try to dodge a smaller rock, and it hit his midsection, forcing a gasp of pain from his lips. A smaller rock tapped him on the head. Someone messaged him. |Duck.|

Instinctively, Alex obeyed. Something scraped over him and slammed down in front of Alex. The ground shuddered and bucked. Another rock slammed down and skidded to a halt, leaving just enough room for him in-between the two massive rocks.

Alex pointed the greker up and created a shield over the top of the gap. Rocks and gravel bounced off the light greker protection. Alex yelled aloud not knowing if he prayed or asked for time and chance to give him a break to continue on with his efforts. The noise of the avalanche overwhelmed his puny petitions. The shuddering of the ground and the noise seemed to go on forever.

He crouched holding up the greker shield waiting.

The young sixteen year old boy huddled in the crack. Alex suddenly realized nothing hit the shield anymore. Slowly, he lifted it up. Gravel fell off to the side. He stood up and climbed out of the gap. Dust still swirled about, but everything else was still. Boulders, some rocks and gravel stretched out around him. The mountain was gone, destroyed. There was a different noise. Alex didn't recognize it. He shut his mouth, and the wild, crazy laughter stopped.

Alex clambered over rocks he couldn't easily go around. He tried to sort out what had happened. The Gadget Lady had tried to kill him, but something… was it her who had given him a chance? Why had the boulders just bounced off him? It didn't make sense to him.

He moved easily. Somehow, he'd managed not to get injured. After the terrible noise, a strange stillness filled the air.

Caught up in his thoughts and looking down to watch where he jumped and stepped, Alex made his way across the rocks to the edge of what had been the mountain. Only when he saw clear level ground in his peripheral vision did he look up. Alex gasped.

At that moment, he received a message from Hheilea. |Alex, danger.|

The words felt cut off as if she wanted to say more, but had been unable.

In front of him, his friends who'd just helped him get the String Sword stood or in Zeghes case floated. They didn't move and no one spoke.

A bubble floated up. In it, Hheilea stood frozen too. Farther out on the level ground, stood a large group of Winkles. They too stood still. They must've been using the Animal Control vapuc to hold his friends captive.

His eyes refused to look at the nearer figure. Instead, he noticed some odd and very big, white mounds behind the Winkles. His sense of the future labeled them as dangerous. It also spoke of terrible pain and confusion. He couldn't waste time thinking about what trouble they represented.

Alex looked at the nearest person. In-between the Winkles and his friends, a figure stood all by herself. The brown cloaked girl waited. He recognized her figure, but it couldn't be. At the same time, his sense of the future screamed at him.

Danger.
Pain.
Confusion.

The agony he had sensed and now part of him recognized tore at him. Alex tried to get past his emotions, but his sense of the future only spoke of pain, disaster, and confusion. His nose wrinkled at a faint and yet very disgusting smell.

With a sense of inevitability, Alex stepped forward. Remembering to breath, he gasped. This couldn't be her. The smell grew stronger.

All of the last months of training had been preparing him for this. Was he ready?

A sweet voice he knew said his name, "Alex." In the one word, he heard warning, danger, pain, suffering, and love.

Instinctually, he drew his String Sword. Again, just like every time he'd drawn that blade, Maleky stood in front of him holding an identical blade. The Kimley man didn't say anything. He just sheathed his sword and disappeared.

Also, just like every time he'd held a String Sword, Alex remembered his cousin and the time before his abduction. This time, it didn't shock him. The barriers to those memories had already been worn thin, and it was more just an acknowledgment of what he truly knew.

The Winkle facing him lifted an arm. A horrid purple ran from her chest down her arm, and a dark purple blade sprouted from her hand to point in his direction. The oily appearance of the weapon brought back memories of a terrible battle. The memory of that time threatened to engulf his awareness.

Alex almost choked on the feeling of evil. The stench of sewage, dead decaying things, and undefined smells grew worse. He stepped closer. His sense of the future insured that the other Winkles wouldn't take part in this battle between him and the Gragdreath. He wasn't so sure about the white mounds. His feelings about the battle to come left him trembling. A horrible feeling of doom assailed him.

Alex tried to shake off his feeling of defeat. He had a String Sword. Holding it he could see the yellow waves of light, the winkle attacks, freezing his friends. He lifted the blade into the engarde position. The girl lifted her purple one in response.

Alex waited unsure of how to proceed. If this was who he thought of, what should he do? What could he do? Once again, he didn't want to— Alex opened his mouth to ask a question.

The Winkle lunged at him. A voice stinking of evil spoke. "Are you ready?"

Alex responded, moving his sword to block the attack. Something wasn't right. Blocking wasn't the right choice, but how, why? At the same moment, he stepped back. The voice didn't fit the person.

From behind Alex came a guttural sound. "Ahhh"

The two swords came together, and Alex almost lost his balance when the purple sword phased through his without any resistance.

Unblocked, the purple sword slashed at him. "Surprise."

Instead of following through with her attack, she pulled back from the lunge and just brushed his knuckles with her blade. His fingers felt a deadly chill, and Alex found himself struggling to hold onto his weapon. Did his hand have a purple hue or was it just the reflection of purple light from the Gragdreath's weapon?

Alex staggered backward. She had him beat. Why had she held back?

Again a guttural sound came from behind him. "Aaa."

This time, he recognized the voice. A'idah, with her indomitable spirit, fought to break free from the Winkle's control.

The Winkle stepped back. She didn't take advantage of his weakness. The evil voice mocked him. "Are you confused?"

Desperately, Alex tried to understand his sense of the future and what had just happened. Did he hear A'idah trying to speak? At the thought of her, one thing became clear in his sense of the future. This evil monster threatened his dear A'idah.

Grasping his sword with new strength, Alex knew he had to change his strategy. What would work if he couldn't block his enemy's sword? Still, confusion interfered with his efforts. With a quick lunge, he slashed at her legs. He hadn't closed the distance enough and missed by a wide margin.

The monster masquerading as a young Winkle responded with her own lunge.

Only a quick jump back prevented contact. She was playing with him, but why? Looking for confirmation of his suspicion, he asked, "Why didn't you finish me off when you had the opportunity." Even as he spoke, Alex shifted position warily watching his opponent.

"You need to be tortured. This is going to be fun."

It wasn't just him. She was going after A'idah. He knew this girl, but it couldn't be. As he thought, he asked, "Why? Who are you?"

The Winkle pulled the brown cowl of her robe back off her head.

His heart had been right. How? "Gursha and Twarbie said you died."

"She did. I didn't. My other Winkles came and collected her body. They knew I lived."

He'd heard the real Twyla's voice. He had to know the truth. "I heard her say my name." Even as Alex thought of the gentle, sweet Winkle girl he'd come to know, he also knew beyond the shadow of a doubt the Gragdreath monster threatened A'idah. He would do anything to protect her, but what could he do?

"Yes. She's here and watching. I let her speak your name. It was fun to see your response. We revived her to get our revenge. Once I've satisfied the need to torture you and her, I'll kill you and kill her again."

She lived. How could he save her? Multiple thoughts ripped through his mind. Alex realized that although he couldn't block her sword, the monster couldn't block his. Would that be enough?

The Winkle, Alex knew as Twyla, stepped toward him and threatened him with her sword.

At the same time the real Twyla said, "She's in my heart. Finish her off."

The evil voice said, "Isn't it just wonderful. I'm in her heart."

Alex remembered the purple, oily tentacles of the Gragdreath monster and how Twyla had started to turn purple. That must've been when it entered her body. From the one touch of the monster's weapon, he knew it must be similar to the tentacles in danger. He couldn't allow it to hit his unprotected flesh, or he'd soon be unable to fight. It would enter him too.

His hand felt better. The purple hue he'd seen must've been just a reflection. Alex shifted back and forth using a combination of jabs, feints, and lunges. He had to keep the monster from A'idah. He knew his sword could interfere with the Winkle's control of his friends. He just had to get into the right position and...

All of his sword training had involved swords hitting each other in defense and some offensive techniques. None of that training helped him. Multiple times, he just avoided the Gragdreath's attacks.

The evil voice said, "You forget. I know what's in her mind. I know your weakness. You value foolish, silly, and treacherous love. It will be so easy to torture you. In the end, love will torture you. Love will be your downfall."

Alex backed up again. Out of the corner of his eye, he saw the still figure of A'idah.

"Who of your friends should I kill first? Maybe this one, A'idah?"

The hot blade of purpose, the need to save those Alex loved, burned away his confusion. Finally, his sense of the future cleared. Love wasn't a weakness. It gave him purpose. Love fueled him. It set him free, and it helped him to be who he could be, would be. Love was his banner.

With his clearer sense of the future, Alex saw many ways his friends would be killed one at a time. With every retreat, Alex knew the monster advanced toward A'idah.

"Maybe I should save her for last and let you suffer longer knowing the inevitability of her death. Maybe the mysterious, Hheilea should be first."

Out of the corner of his eyes, Alex saw her bubble drifting down closer to them. No, not her, his first alien friend and the one he'd loved and still did love. No, he couldn't stand the thought of her being consumed by the Gragdreath. He could see her terrified expression.

Hheilea said one terrified word, "Alex."

"See how nice my servants are. They let her say your name before I kill her. Twyla is so very helpful. She knows you loved Hheilea and probably love her sill. Then, there is this Earthling behind you. She's your rock. You call her A'idah. Your faith in her and dependence on her is an easy failing to take advantage of. I'll kill her slowly, painfully and revel in your pain."

The Gragdreath slashed at him.

Alex leaned back letting her blade just swish past his chest. Immediately, he rolled back and thrust out his own blade. "I won't let you."

The Gragdreath didn't try to avoid his attack. Instead, it seemed she purposely let her back arm move into harm's way. "You poor little boy, you have no choice,"

His burning blade slashed into the soft, white arm.

A scream burst from the Winkle girl. It wasn't evil. It sounded like...

The evil voice said, "I just love the sound of pain. Don't you?"

Alex's heart burned in him at Twyla's pain. The agony tore at him. Even to him his own refusal had sounded childish. Part of him wanted others, adults to carry the burden of the battle for him. At that moment, he remembered Amable knowing the strength and possibilities of teenagers. He also thought of having defeated the monster once before. "I do love the sound of your pain. I've beaten you before, and I'll beat you this time and save my friends."

With an evil laugh that went on and on, the monster changed strategies. The Winkle held the purple sword pointed straight at Alex and slowly advanced toward him and A'idah. "You're demented. I think your own pain has broken your ability to think clearly. I'll help you. Behind you is A'idah. How will her screams sound?"

From his sense of the future, Alex knew if he shifted to the side the Gragdreath would follow. Another step back and he'd be next to A'idah. He shifted.

Each step took the danger away from A'idah. The Gragdreath followed. Too late, Alex realized what would happen next. The monster slashed her sword not at him, but past him, up, and to the side. He heard the bubble pop and Hheilea tumbled to the ground.

The evil voice said, "I could've done more than just pop her bubble."

Desperate to save her, Alex sidestepped, lunged at the monster, and leapt back just in time to avoid her riposte. Now, he moved back toward A'idah, and the monster followed.

"You aren't keeping your friends safe. I can start killing either one of them all too easily. This is boring. I thought you'd be more of a challenge. Which one do you want to hear scream first, Hheilea or A'idah?"

Forced to retreat, Alex struggled against the fear of that pain, struggled to keep his focus on saving those he cared for. His love burned hotter in him, and desperately sought a solution. Should he sacrifice one of his friends to gain the time to save the others? But— He couldn't— not this one— He couldn't sacrifice A'idah. Anyone else, but not her. "I'll save them."

"You sad little boy, you can't."

His feelings about the situation overwhelmed him. His sense of the future showed all too clearly how this would play out. The Gragdreath had him bouncing back and forth between Hheilea and A'idah. A misstep on his part and the monster would hit one of the girls. He had to keep retreating or get hit again himself, and then he'd be even less able to save his friends.

Desperately, Alex searched for options, something-anything to change the future possibilities. His new gadgets, one of them in particular came to his mind's eye of the future, the thingamajig. It wasn't a set object, but responded to his thoughts to become the tool he needed in the moment.

He would need time to get it out and activate it.

How?

The Gragdreath lunged at his sword arm.

Desperately, Alex leaned away. The enemy's weapon sliced at his arm, but the purple sword bounced off the sleeve of his suit.

If the crab had been available, Alex would've kissed her at that moment.

Surprise colored the evil voice for just a moment and then she cackled. "Oh, what is that suit made of? It doesn't matter. I've tagged you. Your doom is getting closer little boy."

A terrible coldness radiated out from the point of contact. Alex gasped as he struggled to hold onto his weapon. Again, he thought his hand had a purple hue to it.

AI, use a local gravity generator to throw small rocks at this Winkle.

It answered. *Big ones. Kill her.*

He staggered back to bump into A'idah. No, he hadn't paid enough attention. He was supposed to shift back toward Hheilea. Not her. Desperately he commanded his AI. *No, small ones.*

The Gragdreath paused and said in a gloating voice, "How does it feel to have your treacherous love turning like a knife to dig into your own hearts, Twyla and Alex?"

The monster pulled back her purple sword. Alex could tell from his own training, that the Gragdreath gathered herself for a lunge. The attack would reach A'idah's defenseless body.

Alex tried to forestall the thrust. "If you kill her, I'll kill you too. It won't matter to me if I die in the attack."

The Gragdreath held off. "You lack understanding. If I die as you die, I'll live on in you. I'm not just an individual. All of us sisters scattered across the universe are connected. We are one."

Even as she spoke, Alex pleaded with his AI. *You feel my pain. Think of the pain I'll feel if you kill Twyla with a rock.* At the same time, he knew that he'd known this possibility. Killing Twyla and the Gragdreath would save everyone else. What else could he do? The monsters next attack would either kill him or A'idah when he moved out of the way. Again, he felt that he'd waited too long to make the hard choice.

Okay, but get out of the way. I've already sent a big one. I can't—

Alex stopped listening to his AI's thoughts. A moving shadow spoke of the reality of the danger. Why? Oh why did his AI have to be a baby? Why did Alex encourage it to use gravity generators to throw rocks and boulders? Who, in their right mind would encourage a baby to throw rocks and boulders? Alex could jump out of the way, but A'idah stood, frozen in place, right behind him.

Chapter Fifty
She Died

Alex shoved back against A'idah, knocking her over, and falling with her. The large boulder passing above caused Alex to cringe against her soft and unresponsive form.

The Winkle, Twyla-the Gragdreath, dove out of the way of the rock.

Alex felt the boulder pass just over his head. *You almost killed us.*

The baby AI responded. *It's your fault. Your pleading distracted me.*

The boulder smashed down and bounded off.

Alex jumped back to his feet. With a fumbling hand, he found the thingamajig's pocket. Thrusting the hand in, Alex felt the end of the long, spear shaped gadget and began laboriously pulling it out. A quick glance at the monster and he dropped his sword to use both hands to pull the four-foot long weapon out as fast as he could. Again, he thought he noticed a purple hue to the one hand.

The Winkle had jumped to her feet and backed up. She dodged rocks all the time laughing the same evil laugh. A dark purple cloud began to grow about her chest. Tentacles sprouted out of Twyla's flesh. "Thank you. This was going all too easy. I want you to suffer longer."

The purple tentacles swatted at the rocks.

Again, the memory of that battle, when he couldn't choose killing Twyla to kill the monster, threatened his concentration. No! Alex screamed inside. He wouldn't let the past interfere with the present. He had to get past thinking of what had happened. Alex had to do the next right thing, even if... With the thingamajig in hand, he concentrated on needing a gadget to help fight the monster.

Using his sense of the future to guide him, Alex threw the gadget like a javelin. It flew into the air and sprouted white wings.

A flash of purple light followed by a loud boom threatened Alex's vision. What had happened? A question lurked in his mind, and he didn't want the answer. Had the Gragdreath killed A'idah with a lightning bolt? Had she used A'idah's favorite vapuc against her? In terror, he cried out. "What have you done?"

Condescendingly she answered, "What's wrong?"

His sense of the future pounded answers remorselessly at him. Tears threatened what vision Alex had. An emotional storm whirled inside. It threatened his understanding of future possibilities. He couldn't allow his fears to control him. Instead, Alex used his love to fuel his purpose to save the friends he could. Alex snatched his String Sword back up.

He advanced. Small rocks whizzed bye. Slower moving waves of yellow light flowed past. Just like the other times he'd held a String Sword, he could see the vapuc attacks. Waves of yellow light traveled from the Winkles toward his friends.

For the first time, the Gragdreath used a vapuc attack against him. The purple wave of light, its attack, traveled from the monster at him. Moving quickly, Alex blocked it and grinned at the scream of anger from the possessed Winkle.

Tentacles reached to embrace him. Alex jabbed at them. He hit one, and the monster screamed again. The others jerked back.

A rock painfully clipped Alex on the head.

His AI complained. *Oww. You're getting me hurt again.*

It was your fault. Stop playing with the rocks. Pull on her tentacles. Keep them away from me and A'idah. Alex realized his AI should've been doing it earlier.

Dodging an attack, Alex blocked one of the yellow waves of light.

"Alex." One cutoff exclamation came from behind him. A'idah almost had her freedom. More importantly, she still lived.

She Died

The evil voice spoke again. "You can't win. I have too many servants and their allies."

A moaning, groaning sound came from the huge white mounds.

Alex stabbed at a tentacle, and blocked another yellow wave of light. When he moved back, a sight caught his breath and sent a shudder of fear through him. His hand definitely had a purple hue to it, and it felt like a worm wriggled in the hand.

A very angry A'idah said, "Get away from the Gragdreath. I'm going to fry it."

"No. Attack the other Winkles." Alex saw the thingamajig flying about. By the smoke rising from it, Alex figured it had been hit by the lightning. The gadget fired small white things at the monster. They looked like spitballs, but the Gragdreath jerked back from them in obvious pain. At A'idah's freedom and the effectiveness of the other attacks, Alex took a breath, feeling hope for the first time in the battle. He had an idea or at least a hope. There was a way if he could figure it out.

He laughed at how the tentacles were waving ineffectively up in the air. "I'm winning. My friends are getting loose, and if you haven't noticed, your tentacles are useless for you."

The Gragdreath laughed. "Such wonderful jokes you make. Thanks for the lift." Going with the pull on her tentacles, the monster jumped up into the air. Her purple sword slashed down at his head.

Alex ducked.

It almost hit me. It almost hit me.

Pull on its tentacles harder and keep it away from us and A'idah.

All of the tentacles jerked back, but the monster went with the pull, flipping up higher and backward through the air. Behind it lay the prone figure of Hheilea.

Alex screamed when he saw what was happening. Time slowed down. He heard a strange drawn out nnnnnoooooo. Someone dashed past him, moving incredibly fast. *AI, use a gravity generator to pull Hheilea out of danger.*

The person moving as a blur across the field of battle continued even as Alex gave his AI the new order. Up above the Gragdreath continued its revolution, tentacles whirling through the air as the monster descended toward the young, teenage girl. The purple sword stretched out at the undefended body, but the blur interposed itself. Alex recognized the color of the hair even though the figure moved too fast for him to recognize the form. She must've been using a time vapuc.

He remembered the pink cloud around A'idah's head. Would this vapuc use be too much for her?

A bright purple flash, some kind of vapuc attack, followed by a high pitched scream, and the two girls tumbled away from the monster.

A loud angry yell filled the air. Alex found himself at the back of the monster. He hadn't thought of running at it. He'd just done it. With clenched teeth, he cut off his yell of defiance and anger. He slashed at it, and the monster fell back.

He wanted to go to the girls and... and... He tried to seal off his fears for them. He had to focus.

With his sense of the future, amongst all the possibilities of pain and death, Alex felt something he hoped was positive. It only had one drawback. Someone might have to kill him. In that future, the purple in his hand flowed up into his arm. His hand would drop his sword. Alex knew what would happen next. The terror of it shook him to the core. He needed to move faster.

Alex ordered his AI. *Don't just pull on her tentacles. Pull her toward where the mountain was.*

Of all the vapuc attacks Alex saw as waves of light, one wasn't a wave of light. A pulsing purple light had appeared around the monster.

The white mounds stood. He recognized them as the gigantic creatures the Winkles had found in the cavern.

Alex circled the Gragdreath, slashing at more of the yellow waves of light and freeing his other friends.

The monster jabbed at him, but missed. Yet, the purple light pulsed stronger and stronger. The hue of his hand grew darker. Alex fought to hold onto his sword.

His sense of the future couldn't reveal the Gragdreath's plan. Something clouded it. Alex suspected the monster played with chance to prevent him from knowing what came or maybe what infected his hand affected his abilities.

She Died

A lightning bolt crashed down at one of the gigantic creatures, but it just splayed out in multiple forks in the shape of a sphere around the creature not making contact with it.

Different voices of his friends raised in anger, spoke of them entering the conflict.

To his AI, Alex said again. *Pull the Gragdreath toward where the mountain stood.*

Alex charged at the Gragdreath, still wary of its purple sword, but using the danger of his own sword to push it toward the mountain.

From that direction came a familiar scraping and clicking. A voice full of clicking and clacking sounds said, "All of this noise and talking. Why did I come here? Let's finish this battle quickly. I want peace and quiet."

The monster's purple sword grew in length, and it stabbed at Alex. "Enough. You have troubled me too much. It is time for you to die."

Alex backed away from the lengthening sword in dismay. What could he do?

Boom!

A shock wave washed past him. His sword blocked some of it.

Agony throbbed in his purple hand. It pulsed and drove a shaft of ice down his spine. A wave of weakness followed.

The Gragdreath and Alex stood alone inside a shimmering sphere of purple.

He heard multiple voices crying his name in alarm. "Alex."

Lightning flashed bright white, blinding him and the boom of the thunder rocked him. Someone had tried to hit the Gragdreath, but the sphere blocked it.

Blinded by the lightning, Alex used his sense of the future to hold his sword out, and pointed at the Gragdreath in defense.

He shut his eyes. The one future would have to do. He moved to the guidance of his sense of the future. Alex only had a little time left before he'd no longer be able to hold his sword. Left arm out and behind for balance, Alex thrust his String Sword straight at the purple sword. They overlapped.

At first, he had to jerk his own weapon up, down, back, and forth. They had to stay aligned. His sense of the future gave him just the help he needed.

The Gragdreath asked, surprise colored her evil voice again, "What are you doing?"

Her surprise fed his hope and effort. Alex felt her tug, trying to free her sword from his. The weapons were aligned. Tentacles wreathed about him, wrestling against his AI. Alex fought off the feeling of weakness. He had to maintain his grip. "I'm going to defeat you. This time, I'll make sure you're gone."

He poured what little strength he had left into holding onto his sword.

His AI pleaded. *Don't let her hit me with those terrible tentacles.*

Alex growled back. With the demands of his effort with the sword, he could only manage one word at a time. *Don't. Let. Her. Keep. Pulling. Them. Back.*

Alex shoved forward.

Slowly, the purple sword shrank.

His AI pleaded. *I can't. I'm getting too tired.*

Have? You? A? Desire? To? Die?

Alex continued the forced thoughts. This time he lied. *We. Have. To. Make. Our. Future. Don't. Let. Us. Die.*

With what felt like the last of his strength, Alex shoved. His sword point reached Twyla's hand.

The Gragdreath's weapon pushed back.

He couldn't find the energy to resist. His sword point moved back away from her hand

The tentacles lashed closer. They threatened a horrible death.

His hand pulsed with purple. Its agony promised a terrible ending. Death would be better. Soon he'd drop his String Sword.

His AI cried out. *I can't control them. One's going to hit us.*

A tentacle lashed at his head moving faster.

Digging deep for more strength, Alex shoved again. This time he pushed off with his trailing foot, and a horrible scream rewarded his efforts.

His blade pierced into Twyla's hand. She screamed.

She Died

The purple sword, and the purple in her arm disappeared, and smoky, purple oil and blood dripped from the sword.

Twyla, freed by the action for a second, pounded out a message even through her pain. |Now, pierce my heart. Kill it. Please. Free me.|

Alex could see the purple in his hand moving down into his wrist. Hearing her words, he ignored the worm's movement into his arm. Desperately, he struggled to hold onto the weapon for just a few seconds longer.

Death loomed near. Fear tore at him, but he refused to surrender.

Around him, the tentacles had reacted to his stabbing Twyla, by halting their attacks and shuddering.

He had maybe two seconds.

This time, he wouldn't let fear stop him.

He had to save his friends even at the cost of life and the pain he feared.

Alex pulled back and lunged forward.

The tentacles stopped their frenzied shaking and whipped at him. In a fraction of a second, he would feel them finishing his life.

In less than that fraction, the point of his sword hit home piercing the heart of his friend. She screamed. The Gragdreath screamed. Oil and blood burst out of her chest.

Alex heard Twyla's last message. |Thank you.|

She died. He crumpled to his knees. Would this last thing work? He hadn't known and didn't want to try and sense the future.

Alex's limp hand dropped his sword. He felt the worm moving into his shoulder. He didn't have the strength to pick his sword back up with either hand.

For the first time since he'd drawn the sword, Alex heard Maleky. *I can feel it. The new Gragdreath is reaching into your mind.*

The last part of Maleky's thought was a scream. *It's going to kill us.*

Alex pleaded to the Gadget lady. |Your mountain was a weird room. Can it make a holo-field?|

|Yes.|

|Then, please heal Twyla, the one I just killed.|

A'idah fell to her knees beside him. Her hands reached for him. "You killed it, but what's wrong with you?"

Desperately, he pleaded, "Don't touch me."

Even as he spoke, Alex knew she would save him or kill him. With the hand that was still his, Alex pointed to his left shoulder. "It's here. Stab it with my sword."

At his words, A'idah's face paled.

Alex felt the Gragdreath reaching into his mind. Maleky screamed.

Alex begged. "A'idah, you have to kill it."

He gasped at a pain in his chest and blurted one word. "Quickly."

Her eyes grew impossibly big. In a wild voice, A'idah pleaded. "No, no, no. I can't kill someone I love."

Alex tried to sense the future. Could he do anything? The future was just a blank wall.

Drawing a ragged breath, Alex forced out words. "The Gragdreath won't just possess me. It will kill me and become a new monster. Please, I love you. If you love me, stab me in the heart."

"I love you too, but I can't do this."

Alex understood A'idah's problem all too well. He remembered the battle back on the Coratory. He'd needed to kill Twyla in order to kill the Gragdreath monster. Because of his hesitation, a friend died. This time it would be worse.

They had run out of time. Alex caught A'idah's frantic eyes with his own gaze. He had to convince her. "You're not hearing me. The monster that's in me is killing me. It will then kill you and all of the others."

She didn't respond.

Maleky's screams stopped.

Darkness rushed in. Alex couldn't see A'idah anymore. He didn't know if she could hear him. Was he speaking or just thinking his last desperate thoughts. "When you don't like the choices you have, you don't want to just stand waiting for the inevitable. You have to choose. Have faith in the best choice. Please, kill me. Save everyone."

With a determined voice, A'idah said, "I won't let it take you."

She Died

She took up his sword and jumped to her feet. Her teeth glinted between lips pulled tight against them. With both hands she held his sword. She thrust the black-blade edged with burning white light at him.

A sizzling sound filled the air. Alex felt the tip burning against his chest. In the pain, an irrational thought cried out in his mind. She was ruining his coat of many colors.

Tears streaming down her face, A'idah held the sword in place.

Alex couldn't draw any breathe to speak with. He could barely even think. He demanded his AI message her. |A'idah, stab me now before it's too late.|

She had waited too long.

A'idah screamed. "No!"

The blade bit into his body.

Everything went dark.

~**********~

Light greeted his weary eyes. Vague, blurred shapes moved in front of the light. Warm hands rested on his bare chest.

"He's coming too."

Alex blinked and the shapes became his friends. A'idah knelt beside him with her hands on his bare chest.

"What happened?"

Zeghes said, "Your other friend, Twyla, is alive. The Winkles threatened to kill us all. They said, once their ally, Titan, got here with the other Lepercauls, they'd finish us off easily. I told them he's dead. That changed their tune."

Hheilea said, "They threatened us all with some legal mumbo jumbo."

The cloud girl said, "I just had a class covering the same topic. I informed them how that by the actions they took here they have nullified the religious protections they have in the contract with Amable's team."

Skyler said, "They were mad, but they left. The flock is safe, and A'idah saved you. After, she killed you."

Alex looked up into the eyes of the girl he loved. "Thanks for saving me, but why are you healing me instead of using the Gadget Lady's holo-field?"

The Gadget Lady answered. "I tried to use a holo-field on you, but it started having trouble. I don't understand. It couldn't do it. The Winkle girl got healed. I would've tried again, but my mountain weird room stopped working. I suspect it's because…" At that point she stopped talking to add after a pause. "I think this one who cried as she saved you wants to talk. You know, I have to admit. I talk too much. I get tired of my own voice, but other than my robot friends— Okay, I'll be quiet now."

A'idah blushed and looked down at her hands on his chest. "You love me?"

This really wasn't the time or place Alex wanted to have this conversation.

Maleky spoke against it too. *Telling her is stupid. It will give her power over you.*

His enemy's thoughts settled the matter. Alex tried to move his hands and found some of his strength had come back. He moved his hands to hold hers. "A'idah?"

"Yes."

His wonderful, confident friend didn't sound as confident as usual.

Alex grinned and finished. "I love you, and I want to marry you."

She laughed a joyous sound and said, "Oh, Alex. I love you too. It would be wonderful to marry you, but not for many years."

Alex agreed. "Yes, only when we're both older and ready."

A'idah said, "I agree."

He started to say something, but she interrupted by leaning over and kissing him.

Author's Note

Hello, everyone. I'm TLW Savage, otherwise known as Tim. My real name is Tim Walker. I borrowed the last name Savage from an ancestor of mine. It gives me a much more unique pen name and will make it easier for you to find my other books.

There will be one more book in this series, *'Alex and the Crystal of* Jedh,' and I'm looking forward to sharing it with you. Some of you fans will be in this book.

Thank you for reading *'Alex String Sword.'* I hope you had as much fun reading it as I did writing it, and please let me know what you thought of the story and the different characters. Below are two different ways of contacting me. I'm still answering all of my mail. Also, for any of my fans with ideas they'd love to see in future books please share your thoughts. If I use your ideas, I'll give you credit for the joke, character, or whatever the idea was.

You're all amazing, and it was my privilege to share my story with you. Take care. I love you.

TLWalker@TLWalkerAuthor.com

Find me on Facebook: TLW Savage. Be sure to message me. I use to work in Cyber Security and I am careful about accepting new friends. Make sure I know you're a fan, and then I'll accept you as a friend.

Made in the USA
Middletown, DE
04 February 2025